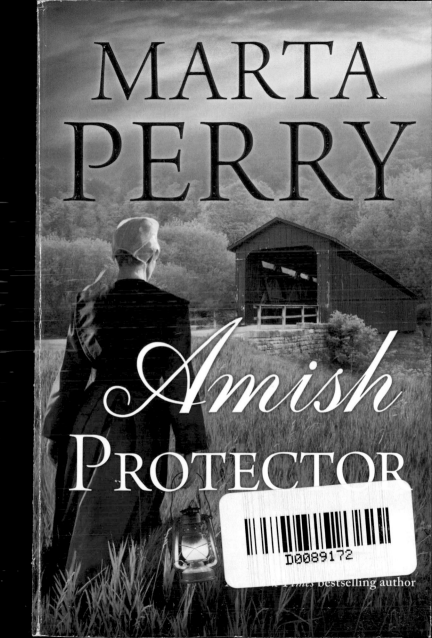

MARTA PERRY

Amish
PROTECTOR

ISBN-13: 978-1-335-04517-1

9 781335 045171

50799

EAN

Praise for Marta Perry

"Abundant details turn this Amish romantic thriller series launch into a work of art."

—Publishers Weekly on *Where Secrets Sleep*
(starred review)

"Crisp writing and distinctive characters make up Perry's latest novel. *Where Secrets Sleep* is a truly entertaining read."

—RT Book Reviews

"Perry's story hooks you immediately. Her uncanny ability to seamlessly blend the mystery element with contemporary themes makes this one intriguing read."

—RT Book Reviews on *Home by Dark*

"Perry skillfully continues her chilling, deceptively charming romantic suspense series with a dark, puzzling mystery that features a sweet romance and a nice sprinkling of Amish culture."

—Library Journal on *Vanish in Plain Sight*

"*Leah's Choice*, by Marta Perry, is a knowing and careful look into Amish culture and faith. A truly enjoyable reading experience."

—Angela Hunt, *New York Times* bestselling author of *Let Darkness Come*

"*Leah's Choice* is a story of grace and servitude as well as a story of difficult choices and heartbreaking realities. It touched my heart. I think the world of Amish fiction has found a new champion."

—Lenora Worth, *New York Times* bestselling author of *Code of Honor*

MARTA PERRY

Amish
PROTECTOR

HQN

ISBN-13: 978-1-335-04517-1

Amish Protector

This edition published by arrangement with Harlequin Books S.A.

For questions and comments about the quality of this book,
please contact us at CustomerService@Harlequin.com.

HQN
22 Adelaide St. West, 40th Floor
Toronto, Ontario M5H 4E3, Canada
www.Harlequin.com

Printed in U.S.A.

This story is dedicated to the love of my life, my husband, Brian, with my love.

Amish
PROTECTOR

CHAPTER ONE

HOME AGAIN. JOANNA KOHLER moved to the door as the small bus that connected the isolated Pennsylvania valley towns drew up to the stop at River Haven.

"Denke, Harry." She lifted a hand in a wave as she stepped down. The driver was Englisch, but he'd been around the Amish long enough to know a few words.

The elderly driver nodded, obviously ready for her to get off so he could finish his last trip of the day. Joanna stepped clear as he closed the door and pulled out.

Glad to be home, Joanna adjusted her packages and started down River Haven's Main Street. Everything was closed, of course. It was after seven, and the days grew shorter with what seemed increasing speed in October. She drew her sweater closed against the nip in the air and thought with pleasure of a bowl of hot chicken soup for supper.

Another few steps brought her to the quilt shop, where she paused, gazing with satisfaction at the window display she'd put up over the weekend. Quilts in autumn colors spilled across an old wooden wheelbarrow, and the pumpkins and autumn leaves she'd added drew the eye. At least, she hoped so. Smiling at her own enthusiasm for the shop she and her aunt ran, she rounded the corner and headed back down the alley toward the enclosed stairway that led to their apartment above the shop.

A whicker from the small stable in the backyard informed her that Princess would not let her go inside without some attention. After setting her packages on the stoop, she followed the noise into the stable, switching on her penlight as she stepped inside. Princess's head poked over the stall bar as she whinnied, the white blaze shining in the light.

"Get on with you," Joanna scolded. "I know perfectly well that Jonas fed and watered you." She patted the soft nose and reached for a carrot from the can that hung beside the door.

But the can wasn't there. Frowning, Joanna moved the thin beam of light. It picked up the can that had tumbled on the floor, carrots spilling out of it. Odd. For sure her younger brother wouldn't have been so careless. The carrots would attract mice, if not something worse.

It took a moment to clean up and give Princess her treat. Joanna double-checked to be sure the nail holding the can was firm and stepped outside. She'd tease Jonas about this one, that was certain sure.

A glow of lamplight from the back of the hardware store next door allowed her to cross to the yard to her door without her flashlight. Noah Troyer, her neighbor, must be working late. Her side of the building was in darkness, since Aunt Jessie was away.

Joanna fit her key into the lock, and the door

swung open almost before she'd turned it. Collecting her packages, she started up the steps, not bothering to switch on her penlight. The stairway was familiar enough, and she didn't need—

Her foot hit something. Joanna stumbled forward, grabbing at the railing to keep herself from falling. The packages tumbled down the steps. What in the world…? Reaching out, her hand touched something soft, warm, something that felt like human flesh. She gasped, pulling back.

Clutching her self-control with all her might, Joanna grasped the penlight, aimed it and switched it on.

A woman lay sprawled on the stairs. The beam illuminated high-heeled boots, jeans, a suede jacket. Stiffening her courage, she aimed the light higher. The woman was young, Englisch, with brown hair that hung to her shoulders. It might have been soft and shining if not for the bright blood that matted it.

Panic sent Joanna's pulses racing, and she uttered a silent prayer, reaching tentatively to touch the face. Warm… Thank the gut Lord. She—whoever she was—was breathing. Now Joanna must get her the help she needed.

She glanced up the steps, but that wouldn't help. Even if she could have gotten over the woman without hurting her, the only phone was downstairs, in the shop. Her aunt was away overnight, so she couldn't help.

Hurrying, fighting for control, Joanna scrambled back down the steps. No use trying the downstairs door into the shop as she'd left it bolted. She burst out into the quiet yard. Even as she stepped outside, she realized it would be faster to go to Noah's back door than around the building.

Running now, she reached the door in less than a minute and pounded on it, calling his name. "Noah!"

After a moment that felt like an hour, light spilled out. Noah Troyer filled the doorway, staring at her, his usually stoic face startled. "Joanna, what's wrong? Are you hurt?"

A shudder went through her. "Not me, no. There's a woman…" She pointed toward her door, explanations deserting her. "Komm, schnell." Grabbing his arm, she tugged him along.

By the time they reached her door, Noah was ahead of her. "We'll need a light."

"Here." She pressed the penlight into his hand, feeling her control seeping back. Knowing she wasn't alone had a steadying effect, and Noah's staid calm was infectious. "I was just coming in. I started up the steps and found her." She couldn't keep her voice from shaking a little.

The penlight's beam picked out the woman's figure. It wasn't just a nightmare, then.

Noah went carefully up the steps, stopping just below the motionless figure. Joanna went behind him, keeping her gaze focused on the woman's pant legs while she waited. Noah had to see for himself, yah, but they had to get help.

Noah bent over the woman, touching her face as

Joanna had done. Then he turned back, his strong body a featureless silhouette.

"Who is she?"

The question startled her. "I don't know. I didn't even think about it—I just wanted to get help. We must call the police and tell them to send paramedics, too."

"Yah." He stepped back down to her. "One of us should stay with her, I think. Do you...?"

He didn't need to finish. "I'll stay with her," she said quickly. "If she comes around, another woman would be more calming, ain't so?"

Not wasting time, Noah was already halfway out. "I'll be back as soon as I've called. Yell if.." He let that trail off, but she understood. He'd be there if she needed him.

But she'd be fine. She was a grown woman, a businesswoman, not a skittish girl. Given all it had taken her to reach this point, she had to act the part.

Joanna settled as close to the woman as she could get on the narrow stairway. After a moment's hesitation, she put her hand gently on the woman's wrist. The pulse beat steadily under her touch, and Joanna's fear subsided slightly. That was a good sign, wasn't it?

But what on earth was a stranger doing on the stairs to her apartment? The poor woman must have come to the wrong door and then fallen on the steps. She couldn't think of another answer. If only they'd found her earlier... It was just chance that this had happened when both she and Aunt Jessie were out.

The suede of the jacket brushed her hand when she moved slightly. It was as soft as butter. Expensive. The thought teased her mind. Not just a stranger—an expensively dressed, strange Englisch woman. Where could she have been going?

She didn't have to think twice to know the woman was a stranger. Anyone who'd lived in River Haven all their life knew everyone, at least by sight.

Her eyes had grown accustomed to the dim light, so she switched off the penlight Noah had left with her. Questions continued to dance through her mind, and she tried to focus on the soft beat of the stranger's pulse. That was a good sign, she reminded herself. The blood was frightening, but head injuries did bleed profusely. Three accident-prone younger brothers had taught her that.

The EMTs would come and whisk her off to the hospital, no doubt for X-rays and stitches and whatever else they thought necessary. By tomorrow she'd be fine, wouldn't she?

The darkness and the silence grew oppressive, and she shivered. If only she had a blanket... She heard the thud of Noah's hurrying footsteps. He stopped at the bottom of the stairs.

"They're on their way. I'd best stay by the door so I can flag them down when they come. How is she?"

"No change." Worry broke through the careful guard she'd been keeping. "What if she's seriously injured? What if I'm to blame? She fell on my steps, after all."

"Ach, Joanna, that's foolishness." Noah's deep

voice sounded firmly from the darkness. "It can't be your fault, and most likely she'll be fine in a day or two. It's not as if she fell all the way down. You don't need to worry."

Noah's calm, steady voice was reassuring, and she didn't need more light to know that his expression was as steady and calm as always.

"Doesn't anything get under your guard?" She was irrationally annoyed that he could take the accident without apparent stress.

"Not if I can help it." There might have been a thread of amusement in his voice. "It's enough to worry about the poor woman's recovery without imagining worse, ain't so?"

"I suppose." She straightened her back against the wall, reminding herself again that she was a grown woman, owner of her own business, able to cope with anything that came along.

But she didn't feel all that confident right now. She felt worried. Whatever Noah might say, her instinct was telling her that this situation meant trouble. How and why she didn't know, but trouble, nonetheless.

NOAH WAS AS concerned for Joanna as he was for the injured woman. Discovering an unconscious body on her own steps had shaken her. The cool, capable woman who took charge at every opportunity was struggling.

At least she wasn't alone. He ought to distract her, maybe keep her talking, but that wasn't so easy. It never had been. The son of a drunken disgrace to the

Amish community didn't have much in common with
the bishop's daughter. In fact, if Bishop Paul were
here right now, he'd not be happy to find Joanna sitting alone in the dark with Noah Troyer.

"How…how do you think she got here?" The sentence started off a little shaky, but Joanna seemed
settled by the sound of her own voice. "I didn't see a
car in the alley."

He glanced toward her, able to make out the pale
oval that was her face. "Gut question. There's nothing
parked out front, either. Seems like a stranger would
have to come by car. She's not someone you've run
across in the course of business? Like a quilt collec-
tor?"

"No. I'd have remembered," she added. "We don't
have that many Englisch customers."

A sound from outside had him getting to his feet.
"There's the ambulance. And sounds like the police
car, as well. No use fretting. They'll figure it out."

Stepping outside, he waved the ambulance up close
to the door, nodding when he saw that Frank Elliott
was one of the EMTs. "Right up the stairs, Frank. It's
going to be tight getting her out."

The older man took one look and whistled softly,
while the woman with him pulled gear from the van.
"Well, we'll manage. Might need a hand." He glanced
at Noah, who nodded.

"I'll be here."

Frank switched on a powerful flashlight. "Who's
that with her? Oh, Joanna. Your shop, isn't it? Come
on down, and I'll trade places with you."

As soon as Joanna reached the bottom, Noah led her clear of the steps. He felt her resistance.

"I need to see that she's all right."

"They'll take gut care. Komm, we have to give them room to work."

Joanna glanced up at him, her normally stubborn jaw getting a bit tighter, and he thought she'd give him an argument. Then the tension went out of her.

"Yah, you're right. Sorry." Her voice trembled slightly.

"You did all you could for her." That would be poor comfort if this didn't end happily, but it was all he could think of to say.

They heard a soft-voiced consultation between the two medics and the young patrolman who'd followed them to the doorway. Then the cop went to set up flares, while the woman pulled a stretcher from the ambulance. She nodded to Noah.

Giving Joanna's arm a pat, he took a step toward the doorway. "I'll have to help with the stretcher. Stay here. Please," he added.

Joanna's nod was reluctant, but he sensed she'd obey.

It seemed to take forever to move the injured woman onto the stretcher. Noah stood a few steps down, realizing all he could do was hold the light still for them. When they finally started down, he helped steady the stretcher for the move from the narrow steps toward the ambulance.

"How is she?" Joanna hovered just out of reach.

"That's for the doctors to say." Frank glanced at

her face and must have read the concern there. "The pulse is strong, so that's good."

The patrolman—who Noah had finally identified as the younger son of Sam Donovan, the pharmacist—looked their way. "Do you know who she is?"

Joanna shook her head. "I've never seen her before."

"You, sir?" His gaze turned to him.

"Afraid not."

They slid the stretcher in place, and the light fell briefly on the woman's face. Noah had his first good look at her. He blinked, trying to focus. He didn't know her, that was certain sure. But something about her seemed oddly familiar.

The feeling was gone as soon as it had come, leaving him faintly unsettled, as if he'd forgotten something important.

"Can't I go with her?" Joanna's sense of responsibility seemed to increase by the moment.

Frank slammed the door, shaking his head. In a moment the ambulance pulled out and was gone.

"I thought you said you didn't know her." The patrolman pulled a notebook from his pocket, dropping his pen in the process. "Why would you want to be with her?"

Joanna stared at him with a touch of surprise. "She's all alone. I thought she might appreciate a friendly face."

It wasn't unexpected for anyone who knew Joanna, but the young patrolman didn't seem to get it. He moved on to writing down names, location of the accident, time, and then circled around to the question of who the woman was.

Noah could feel Joanna's impatience, and he touched her arm lightly. "Neither of us knows her," he repeated. "And we don't know why she was on the back steps of the quilt shop." He considered saying the woman had seemed vaguely familiar but decided that wouldn't be helpful.

"Yeah, right." Young Donovan looked at his notebook again, as if hoping it would tell him what to do next. "Well, guess I'd better check in with the station. We'll be in touch." He tapped his cap in an awkward salute.

"Komm." Noah reached for the back door. "I'll see you upstairs. Unless you want to go somewhere else," he added.

"I'd rather be in my own home."

Joanna shivered a little at her words. Penlight in hand, she preceded him up the stairs, stepping carefully over the spot where blood showed on the wooden stair. "I should…should clean that up."

"Not until the police are done," he said quickly.

Nodding, she fumbled for a moment with her key and then got the door open.

Not sure whether he should follow her inside, Noah stood in the doorway. He'd wait until she had the lamps lit, at least.

In a few moments the rooms were filled with the warm glow of lamplight. Joanna turned back to him with her usual air of calm competence, the woman whose voice had faltered carefully hidden.

"Denke, Noah. I don't know what I'd have done if you hadn't been at home." She brushed a loosened tendril of brown hair back under her kapp. Her eyes, brown with a little hint of gold, darkened.

"Ach, we both know you'd have managed fine," he said lightly. "You always do." But she had shown him her vulnerability, there in the dark stairway, and he wouldn't forget it.

A smile tilted her firm mouth and lit the smooth oval of her face. "I try. But I'm wonderful glad to have help." The smile fled. "That poor woman. I hope she'll be all right."

There seemed little use in repeating his reassurances. "We'll know more in the morning. I'll make sure the bottom door locks behind me when I go out."

Joanna nodded, stepping into the pool of light by the door to see him out. It lit her face from above, much as the light had shown on the injured woman's face, and Noah was jolted by recognition. There was the resemblance he'd sought. The stranger who'd fallen on Joanna's stairs looked like Joanna.

Even as he thought it, his assurance was fading. How could he be sure? It was a chance thing, a trick of the light, maybe.

"Noah? Is something wrong?" Joanna was eyeing him with the same concern she'd shown for the stranger.

"No, no, nothing." The decision was made as quickly as that. Joanna obviously hadn't noticed any similarity, and it made no sense to give her more worries.

"Rest easy, Joanna. I'll check in with you in the morning."

It was probably nothing at all. But it did make him wonder.

DESPITE THINKING SHE'D never be able to sleep, Joanna fell into a deep, dreamless slumber almost as soon as her head hit the pillow. She awoke with the sun, as always, and memory came rushing back, bringing with it renewed concern and a slight feeling of guilt for having been able to forget the injured woman.

Swinging her feet to the floor, she hastened to wash and dress, pulling her hair into the knot that fit under her kapp with the ease of long practice. When would it be appropriate to call the hospital for information? They probably wouldn't tell her much, but it would be a relief just to know her visitor was still alive.

A shudder went through her. Last night she'd managed to avoid thinking of the grim possibilities, but this was morning, and in the light of day she must face facts. She could, she knew, but first she had to find out what they were.

The thought of food caused her throat to close, so she avoided the kitchen and went down the front stairs that led into the shop.

Joanna never came into the quilt shop without a wave of gratitude for the circumstances that had allowed her and Aunt Jessie to become partners. She glanced around at the rolls of quilting fabrics standing on end in long rows according to fabric and colors.

Quilted products of all kinds hung from racks and lay in layers on the display bed, and she felt the familiar pleasure, a bit muted under the circumstances. Somehow, she didn't think she'd be able to focus on work very well today. Something thumped on the wall that separated the quilt shop from Noah's hardware store. It sounded as if he was in early, as well. Noah didn't live above his business, as she and Aunt Jessie did, but traveled back and forth every day from the family farm a few miles out of town. Was he wondering about the woman, also?

Noah had been a rock last night, not that she was surprised by that. The oldest of a large family, as she was, he'd taken on responsibility at an early age. Everyone in the valley knew about Noah's father. An alcoholic, he'd been in and out of trouble with the church for years as they'd tried to help him. Some said that he'd have been put under the bann permanently if he hadn't passed away when he did.

None of that was Noah's fault, of course. But it probably helped to explain his gravity as well as his calm in the face of an emergency. In any event, she had cause to be grateful.

Joanna was just about to pick up the phone when someone rattled the front door. She jerked around, her heart thudding, to see her parents looking at her through the pane in the door, Daad with his hand raised to knock.

She rushed to the door. How had they found out so quickly? She knew all about the Amish grapevine, but surely even the most eager gossips wouldn't have found out about the accident so soon.

No sooner had she unlocked the door than she was enveloped in her mother's arms. "You're all right?" She drew back, cupping Joanna's face between her palms and looking searchingly into her face. "You weren't hurt?"

"Ach, Mamm, of course not. Why would you think that? It was another person who had the accident, not me. I just found her."

"I knew it would come to no good, letting you live here alone like this." Daad shut the door with an emphasis that rattled the glass. "And see what happened. The police called, even."

"I'm not living alone," she said cautiously, reminding herself of all the talking and persuading it had taken to get Daad's blessing on this adventure in independence. "Aunt Jessie—"

"Jessie wasn't here last night, was she? You should have come home until she got back." She could read the worry behind the scolding in her mother's tone and was flooded with regret that she'd been the cause of it.

"I would have, you know that, Mamm. We talked about it." She put her arm around her mother. "But since I was going over to Warren and wouldn't be back until late, I'd have had to take the buggy out in the dark to come home. It seemed simpler and safer just to stay here. I couldn't have known someone would fall on my steps yesterday, could I?"

She kept her voice soft and coaxing as she looked

at her father. Daad was not easily moved by her determination to bend things the way she wanted them.

"I suppose," he grumbled, and she tugged on his arm.

"You probably didn't have breakfast, did you? I'll put coffee on in the back room, and I have some rolls in the tin."

She shepherded them back to the workroom, where they had a tiny kitchen area in a corner. While her parents sat down at the worktable, she put on the coffee, talking to distract them.

"I went to the big fabric store in Warren in the afternoon. Wait until you see the fabric swatches I brought back for dresses for Catherine's wedding, Mamm. Such nice material, and pretty colors, too."

That distracted her mother's attention, as she'd known it would, and they talked about her friend Catherine's wedding, coming up in November. Schoolteacher Catherine, like she, had stayed single for so long no one thought she'd ever marry, until Michael Forster had come back to town.

"Enough about the wedding," Daad said once the coffee was poured. "Sit down and tell us exactly what happened last night."

Knowing she couldn't avoid it, she told them the exact truth. Mammi murmured sorrowfully when she talked about the woman's injury, and an expression she couldn't interpret crossed Daad's face at the mention of Noah. Maybe that was unavoidable. As the bishop, Paul Kohler would have been deeply involved in dealing with Noah's father.

"So they took her off to the hospital, and I don't know anything else. In fact, I was just about to call the hospital and see if I could learn anything," she concluded.

"Ach, yah, that's what you should do," her mother said. "Go ahead, call."

Joanna glanced cautiously at her father, but he nodded, so she picked up the phone. The only one they had, it was normally kept only for work purposes. After a few minutes' delay, caused by the fact that she didn't know who to ask for, she was connected to the nurse on the floor where the woman had been placed.

"I'm calling to inquire about the woman who was brought in last night with a head injury."

"Are you family?" a brisk voice asked.

"No," she admitted.

"I'm afraid…"

Joanna broke in. "Is this Mary Ellen Dover? It's Joanna Kohler, Mary Ellen." She pressed the speaker button so she wouldn't have to repeat everything.

"Oh, Joanna." The voice warmed a number of degrees. "I heard she'd fallen at your store." There was a brief pause. "I'm not supposed to release any information," she said. "But I guess it doesn't matter if you know. She's stable, breathing on her own, but she still hasn't regained consciousness. They're going to run some more tests today."

"It's serious, then." Joanna hadn't realized how much she'd counted on hearing the woman was awake and improving.

"Well, she's not in immediate danger," Mary Ellen

said. "But we've got to find out what causing the problem." Her voice faded on the final word. "Listen, I can't talk now," she said in a hurried whisper and hung up.

"Poor, poor thing," her mother murmured.

"Yah. We must pray," Daad said. He clasped Joanna's hand. "This is not your fault, daughter. You mustn't blame yourself."

"Denke, Daadi." She nodded, hoping she could manage that.

It took her another twenty minutes and a cup of coffee to convince her mother to return home with Daad, but finally they were out the door, their fears allayed for the moment, at least.

No sooner had they gone than Noah came in, the bell on the door jingling. "Noah. You've just missed my mamm and daad."

"Yah, I saw." He walked along the table filled with bolts of fabrics until he reached her. "Have you heard anything?" His dark brows were a straight line across his face, and his mouth looked grim.

She thought, inappropriately, that it would be nice to see him smile.

"I called. Fortunately, I got Mary Ellen Dover, so she was willing to talk. She says the patient is stable, whatever that means, and breathing on her own. But she still hasn't regained consciousness, so we still don't know who she is or why she was at my store."

"Not your store," he corrected. "Your home."

Joanna nodded, thinking that Noah wasn't one to

put a sugar coating on anything. "Why? That's what I don't understand."

Noah's frown had deepened. "Do you happen to have any Englisch relatives? Someone who might be looking for family members or some such thing?"

"No." She was surprised and a little indignant. "Why would you ask that?"

He studied her face for a long moment, his dark green eyes solemn. "I don't know if I should say this or not. And maybe I'm wrong." He seemed to be talking almost to himself. Then he shook his head. "Joanna, did it occur to you that this woman looks something like you?"

Joanna could only stare at him. "No! Why would you think that?"

"I don't want to upset you. But there was something vaguely familiar about her face when I saw her being put into the ambulance. And later, when I saw your face under the light, I knew what it was. She reminded me of you."

Shaken, Joanna turned away from him, not wanting those keen eyes on her face. "I...I didn't see it." She rubbed her forehead, hoping that might help her think more clearly. "I don't know what to say." She straightened, realizing the obvious answer. "I suppose I'd better try to see her for myself."

"Yah, I guess so." He sounded sorry he'd brought it up.

She swung back to him. "We'd best keep quiet about it until we know. But if it turns out we're related in some way… Well, I don't know if that helps the police or not."

"You could tell them," he said. "But you'll have to decide quickly because I see Chief Jamison coming toward the shop right now."

CHAPTER TWO

JOANNA HAD NO time at all to think about it, because Chief Jamison was already coming in the door. With his square, ruddy face, solid build and assured manner, he was exactly Joanna's idea of a policeman. Maybe, she told herself, because he'd been River Haven's chief for as long as she could remember.

She sent a quick glance toward Noah, but his stolid expression didn't give her any help. She'd just have to hear what the chief had to say before making any decision about revealing Noah's idea.

"Good morning, Chief. Wilkom."

"Morning, Joanna. Noah. You decide to open early this morning?"

She shrugged, smiling. "My mamm and daad were here first thing this morning."

"Sure they were." He came toward them, his eyes crinkling. "The Amish grapevine works better than my telecommunications. They were worried about you."

"They were, yah. You'd think I was the one hurt instead of that poor woman."

"No matter how old you get, you're still your parents' baby."

Noah moved slightly away from them. "If you want to speak to Joanna alone…"

Before Joanna could say anything, the chief was shaking his head. "You were in on that business last night, right? You might be of some help."

"That poor woman," Joanna said again, her throat tightening at the memory. "How is she?"

Any hope that the woman had recovered her senses and was well on the way to recovery was blighted by Jamison's solemn expression.

"Not good, I'm afraid. The doc says she hasn't regained consciousness, and the longer that goes on, the more worrisome. They're going to run some more tests this morning." His brows knit. "Don't like it. Bad enough to have a visitor injured, but we don't even know who she is."

"She didn't have any identification at all?" Joanna didn't realize until now how much she'd been counting on some clue to who the woman was, even if it were just an initial on a piece of clothing.

"Not a thing. Young Donovan claims he looked around for a handbag or wallet last night, but I'll have another look myself by daylight."

"I already checked."

Noah's words startled Joanna. "You did?"

"Soon as it was light, I thought I'd have a look around." Noah looked from her to the chief. "I didn't check the steps, because the door was locked, but I went over the rest of the area. Nothing."

"Well, we'll have a look anyway. I already have someone checking the hotel and the bed-and-breakfasts. Somebody must know who she is." Frustration laced his voice.

"When she wakes up…" Joanna began.

It was a sign of how disturbed Jamison was that he interrupted her. "What if she doesn't? What if her brain was damaged? She doesn't look like the kind of person who could drop out of sight and not leave someone worried about her."

"I hadn't thought of that." Joanna winced at the thought of a mother or a husband frantic with worry. "We have to do whatever we can."

"Well, not much we can do but what we already are." The chief sounded as if he meant to be comforting. "Let's just go over what happened and see if we can put any more pieces together. Way I understand it, you'd come back on the late bus from shopping?"

Joanna pushed her thoughts back to the previous evening. "Yah, that's right. It was the last run of the day, so it was a little after seven." She pictured the empty street. "I walked down to the shop and came around to the back like always when we're closed."

"You didn't see anybody around? Or hear anything?" Jamison leaned an elbow against a rack of printed cottons. "Nothing unusual?"

She thought back over it carefully before answering, but the answer was the same. "Nothing."

"So then you started up the steps," he encouraged her.

"Not right away. The buggy horse heard me, so I went in the stable. I gave her a carrot, and then I started up."

"What about the door? Was it locked?"

That gave her pause. "I…I'm not sure. I put my key in, but it did swing open right away—maybe before I turned it. Is it important?"

"The woman had gotten in," Noah reminded her, taking a step closer at the uncertainty in her voice.

"That's right." She frowned, trying to remember. "I just don't know. In my hurry to catch the bus, I might have forgotten." She shivered. "If I left it open and she came in and was hurt…"

"You're not responsible," Noah said.

She met his steady gaze, and she felt sure he was thinking again about that resemblance he'd seen. It wouldn't be right to expect him to keep it quiet from the police.

She nodded. "Noah noticed something he should tell you."

Jamison had remained silent, but that didn't mean he hadn't been wondering. "Tell me what?"

Noah inclined his head. "Yah, all right." He spoke slowly, as if weighing each word. "It was just an impression I had. Seeing the woman's face under the light when we loaded her into the ambulance, and then seeing Joanna's face lit from above, I thought there was a resemblance between them."

It was characteristic of Noah that once he'd decided to speak, he didn't waver or indulge in second thoughts. He went ahead steadily with what he had to do. She wondered briefly whether that was a result of his childhood. It couldn't have been an easy one.

"Hmm." Jamison studied Joanna's face, and she

felt herself blush. "I can't say I see it myself. I mean, the hair's different, and her face had makeup, but I guess there might be some resemblance. You have any relations among the Englisch, Joanna? Someone who jumped the fence and maybe married out there?"

She shook her head. "Not that I know of. I've never heard any talk of it."

"You might not," he observed. "I've known some Amish that didn't like to talk about the ones who left."

"Yah, but…" She hesitated, not sure she wanted to get into the story of her birth. Still, if Jamison was intent on this, he'd easily find out. "My birth mother was actually Mamm's distant cousin out in Ohio. She died in childbirth, and Mamm and Daad adopted me when I was just a few days old."

It was an old story, and one she seldom thought about now. She'd never doubted that Mamm and Daad cherished her as much as if she'd been born to them.

"I don't know a lot about that side of the family, but I think my mamm would have mentioned it," she added.

Or would she? Mamm never talked about Joanna's birth mother. Once Joanna was old enough to understand, she'd realized that it hurt her mother if she showed curiosity about that side of the family, so she didn't. There was too much happening now to dwell in the past anyway.

"I don't think I knew about you being adopted," Jamison said, "but I don't guess it matters. Either way, I think it'd be best if I saw the two of you side by side." The chief gave Joanna a measuring look, as if questioning how much he could ask of her. "How would you feel about going up to the hospital with me?"

"Now?" She was startled by how little she wanted to do that.

"Good as any time. Your aunt's not here?" He glanced around, as if expecting Aunt Jessie to be behind a bolt of fabric. Not, of course, that she'd have refrained from offering her opinion if she were here.

"She'll be back by early afternoon. Maybe I could come then?"

But Chief Jamison seemed eager to move. "You can open a little late." It was a statement, not a question, so she reached for her sweater and picked up her keys.

"I'll come, too." Noah fell into step with her. "It was my thinking that got you into this, yah?"

"I haven't forgotten," she said. "If my parents hear about my riding through town in a police car, you can explain it to them."

"Can't do that," he said with the faintest flicker of a smile. "The bishop might put me under the bann for bearing bad news."

Her heart lightening at his gentle teasing, Joanna locked the shop and slid into the police car.

NOAH HESITATED FOR a moment, looking back at his store. He couldn't afford the luxury of not opening on time, not with the competition from that new hardware chain out near the highway. But young Caleb should be able to manage on his own for a bit, and he also couldn't let Joanna go alone. He'd owe the same support to any member of the Leit.

Joanna was watching him as he got in. "Problem with the store?"

"No, nothing." Any troubles he had he'd keep to himself. "My little bruder came in with me today. He can take care of things until I get back."

"Which one? Caleb or Joshua?"

"Caleb," he said, a little surprised she remembered the younger ones' names. "Aaron claims he's always making excuses to get away from the farm chores."

He and his next brother, Aaron, had split responsibilities for the family between them after Daad's death. Aaron ran the farm with the younger boys to help, and Noah kept the store going. Maybe they'd eventually be able to pay off their father's debts and make things safe for Mamm and the younger ones. He jerked his thoughts back to what Joanna was saying.

"Maybe Caleb isn't a born farmer. My daad says he's fortunate to have at least a couple of my brothers with a feel for the land, because you can't force it."

She looked as if she were talking at random, probably trying to keep her mind off what was coming. It wouldn't be long, though. Already they were headed up the slight hill where the redbrick hospital sat, so far holding off against any plans to merge it with a bigger hospital system.

Chief Jamison pulled up near the entrance and parked the police car. They got out, and Joanna smoothed her hands down her skirt in a nervous gesture. Regretting he'd spoken up would do no good now. And besides, Joanna would be the last person to hold back a word that could help another person.

No one seemed to take a second look when they walked through the hospital lobby. Maybe people in a hospital situation were too intent on their own problems to wonder about others. The elevator whisked them up to the third floor, and he heard Joanna suck in a deep breath as the doors opened.

"She's right down here." Chief Jamison led the way down the hall. "We made sure she's in a private room, just in case."

In case of what? Noah wondered, but they'd already reached the door. Jamison stopped a nurse who was coming out as they went in. "Any change?"

The man shook his head. "Still the same. She'll be having another scan later this morning." He nodded to them and went on his way, apparently not curious as to why his patient was having Amish visitors.

Once they were inside the room, Noah took one look at the still figure surrounded by machines and monitors and had to fight down the urge to flee. The sight seemed to have the opposite effect on Joanna. Her face filled with sympathy, she went directly to the bed and put her hand lightly over the one that lay slack on the white coverlet.

"I'm so sorry," she murmured, though it was obvious the woman didn't respond.

"Do you think she can hear you?" He asked the question carefully, not wanting to upset Joanna, but doubting the unconscious woman, attached as she was to monitors, could respond.

"I've heard that sometimes unconscious people can hear. And even if she can't, perhaps she'll sense that someone is wishing her well." Joanna kept her gaze on the motionless face.

"Maybe." What did he know about it? He hadn't been inside a hospital in years, if ever.

"Go ahead and talk to her, Joanna." Jamison approached the other side of the bed. "It can't hurt. If she could open her eyes and tell us anything, we'd be a lot further on than we are now."

Joanna nodded, seeming unperturbed by the idea. If she'd been reluctant to come, she seemed to be over it now. She spoke softly, intent on the woman, assuring her that she was going to be all right. It was more than he'd be able to do, for sure.

But Jamison frowned at him, seeming annoyed that Noah hung back. "Come over here where you can see both of them. Tell me what you think."

Reluctantly, he came nearer. If he could say he didn't see any resemblance, this might be over. But that wouldn't be true. Since Joanna had started her shop next to his, he'd spent a lot more time than he should noticing her. And like it or not, he saw a resemblance.

Joanna, apparently just realizing that they were both looking from her face to that of the unknown woman, gave her a searching stare and then looked toward them.

"I can't see it. The hair color is completely different." She touched a strand of her light brown hair, pushing it back toward her kapp.

"Yah, but look at the shape of her face." He sketched the line in the air. "Her jaw is just as stubborn as yours is."

"I think he's got you there," Jamison said, suppressing a chuckle. "It isn't proof, but looking at you side by side, I can see some resemblance."

Her expression troubled, Joanna clasped the woman's hand in both of hers. "Who are you? If only we knew, we could have your family here with you." She glanced at Jamison, her brown eyes darkening. "Isn't there anything you can do? If you showed her picture around, someone might know her."

"We've done that already at the likely places where she might have stopped for gas or to get something to eat. No one has seen her. The next step is looking for a car and checking out the bus service." Frustration gave an edge to his voice. "Did either of you notice a car you didn't recognize parked near the store?"

Joanna shook her head. "I wasn't noticing when I walked back from the bus. I don't really know much about cars, so even if I had, it wouldn't be much help."

Jamison's gaze flicked to Noah. "You see anything?"

Again, the answer was negative. "I didn't go out front, but I glanced around. For sure there wasn't any vehicle parked in the alley or in the back."

"Well, she had to get to River Haven somehow. A private car seems more likely than the bus for someone who dresses so expensively. Leaving aside any resemblance between you, are you sure there's no reason why she'd come to your door?" Jamison's tone had become brusque, maybe with frustration.

Noah moved a little closer to Joanna, but she seemed to take Jamison's sharp tone in stride, maybe realizing that his annoyance was directed at his lack of success rather than anything she had done.

"Nothing, I'm sorry. I wish I could say otherwise, but I'm fairly sure I'd remember her if she'd ever been in the shop." She nodded toward the bronze hair that lay against the pillow. "You don't often see someone with hair like that, and it would have stuck in my mind."

"Nobody has contacted the shop, maybe looking for something—like a particular kind of quilt or whatever?" He grimaced at his own question, as if wondering whether it made sense. "Well, I don't know anything about quilts, but I guess it could happen."

Joanna's lips twitched, but she managed to hold back a smile. "It does happen sometimes, that someone will call. But there hasn't been anything recently."

"You'd think if she'd wanted to see you in the evening like that, she'd have set it up ahead of time," Noah pointed out. "And that wouldn't account for the resemblance anyway."

"Resemblance or not, I need something more solid in order to identify the woman. Maybe she'll wake up and remember everything, and maybe she won't." Jamison moved restlessly, as if any activity would be better than doing nothing. "What if the doctors have to make some decisions about her care?"

"I hadn't thought of that." Joanna's ready sympathy had turned toward Jamison. "I wish I could be more help."

He shrugged. "If you've no idea why she was at your door, well, you don't."

Joanna, seeming to take that for dismissal, stood. "If there's nothing else I can do..."

"Hold on a minute. We haven't even talked about the possibility that she's some relative of yours. You sure there's not somebody who jumped the fence? Maybe a brother or sister of your mamm's or daad's? Or of that cousin you were born to?"

"They've never talked about it, but I suppose I can ask, if you want."

Joanna didn't look particularly eager, probably because she knew her father wouldn't want his daughter involved with the police. Noah felt sympathy for the bishop for a moment. He didn't like the idea, either, even though he was at least partly responsible for it.

"You do that," Jamison said. "With all this talk recently about DNA testing and tracing your ancestors, it's at least possible that's what brought her to your door."

JOANNA BROODED ON the chief's words as they drove back to the store. Like many Amish, her mother kept a meticulous family tree that showed every detail of the family, but the tree was of Daad's family, not hers. Mamm's distant cousin wouldn't appear on it.

Still, she'd think that between Mamm and Aunt Jessie, her mother's older sister, she'd have heard something about her birth mother's kin. The idea of a distant relationship between her and the injured woman seemed unlikely to her, but she couldn't quite dismiss it from her mind, either.

Chief Jamison had made the drive without talking, occupied with his own thoughts. When he pulled up at the shop, he roused himself.

"Thanks, both of you. I'll let you know when we get some answers."

Joanna slid out of the car, relieved the trip to the hospital was over, but knowing she couldn't forget about it. The woman would continue to haunt her until there were answers.

She glanced at Noah. Did he feel the same? But Noah seemed far more occupied with his hardware store than anything else. He was already turning in that direction.

"Denke, Noah. It was gut of you to go along." She spoke quickly, aware of his impatience.

He paused, clearly eager to get back to work. "I was the one who insisted on a resemblance, ain't so? It was my responsibility."

No, it was hers. After all, she was the one who'd gone running to him. If she were a properly independent woman, she'd have dealt with finding an unconscious woman on her doorstep on her own. She could have, she supposed, but she was glad she didn't have to.

Noah had already pulled open the door to his store, obviously forgetting her problems in an instant. Reminding herself that she could handle this on her own,

Joanna marched into her own shop. Without glancing toward the street, she turned her mind to getting ready to open.

She started by uncovering the handmade quilts she displayed on a mock bed in the center front of the store. Working with the fabrics and stroking the intricate hand stitching always brought her comfort. Slowly, she relaxed, focusing on business instead of all the trouble the woman had brought to her door. She tried to believe the woman would wake up soon, and then all their questions would be answered.

Joanna hadn't even begun to expect Aunt Jessie when the bell on the door jangled and she appeared, dropping her small bag as soon as she was in the door. "Glad that's over," Aunt Jessie said, frowning in a way that didn't bode well for her relationship with her other sister, the oldest of the family.

Joanna had to suppress a smile. Visits between the sisters always followed the same pattern—the eagerness to get together, the laughter and the chatting, the flare of argument and the quick return home of whichever was visiting.

They must, she'd always thought, have been too close to each other in age. Neither of them quarreled at all with Joanna's mother, who was much younger than both of them.

"Did you have a nice visit?" she asked, ignoring the storm signals.

"Nice?" Her aunt's voice rose slightly, and then she made a visible effort to control herself. "Nice enough,

I guess. It would be even better if Norah would keep her opinions to herself."

"What is it now?"

"If I were to tell you how foolish she is…" Aunt Jessie set her thin lips firmly. With her narrow face and bony figure, she was the exact opposite of Joanna's mother, and she had a steely eye that never failed to intimidate a child entering the store from putting a finger on a bolt of fabric.

"Never mind that," she said emphatically. "What's this I hear about you having the police around here?"

It had come even quicker than she'd anticipated. "How did you hear about that?"

"I heard a garbled account from the bus driver, but I can see for myself that you're all right, so I suppose it was all a fairy tale, as usual."

Any other time she'd laugh at her aunt's characteristic dismissal of gossip, but not this time.

"Not a story, I'm afraid," she said, and went on to tell her aunt everything that had happened the previous night. She felt as if she'd repeated it so often it could tell itself.

"So anyway, the poor woman is still unconscious this morning. I feel terrible about it, and it's even worse that she was hurt right at our back door."

Aunt Jessie gave her usual sharp nod. "Bad business, but it's not your fault," she said, tersely dismissing any notion that they were responsible. "If I'd been here… But I wasn't, and there's no use crying over spilt milk, either. So Noah Troyer came and helped, did he?"

Hoping the question wasn't critical, she nodded. "I was glad to have him. He called for the ambulance and helped them get the stretcher out of the stairway. And today—"

"Today what?" Jessie eyed her keenly.

"Well, Chief Jamison wanted us to go to the hospital. They—he and Noah—both thought the woman looked a bit like me."

She stopped when Aunt Jessie abruptly swung around, seeming to stare out the window. Her back was even more rigid than usual.

"Go on," her aunt said without turning around. "Why did you stop?"

"No reason. I just wondered…is it even possible the woman is related to us? I mean, if some relative jumped the fence and had a family, I suppose there might be a daughter about my age who had a family resemblance."

"Sounds like a pack of nonsense to me." Her aunt's common sense came through strongly. "I'd forget the whole thing, except to pray for the woman. We'll all do that."

"I guess it's unlikely." But she couldn't quite dismiss the possibility. "Chief Jamison thought maybe it was someone trying to trace their family tree. You know how people will have a DNA test and then go looking for relatives."

She might not follow what was going on in the Englisch world, but everyone had heard of that, hadn't they?

"I still say it's nonsense…"

It was a characteristic response from her aunt, who tended to dismiss anything outside her own world as nonsense. Joanna would generally tease her until they both dissolved in laughter. For all her tart manner, Aunt Jessie had a lively imagination hidden behind a dour exterior, and she saw humor in all kinds of things that other Amish might not talk about.

But this reaction seemed different in some way. It was almost as if Aunt Jessie was trying to respond in her usual manner while thinking about something else underneath the whole time.

"Is it bothering you?" she asked.

"Why would you say that?" The question really was tart this time.

"I don't know. I just thought you seemed sort of upset. I think it's unlikely, too, but Chief Jamison is serious about it. He doesn't have any way of tracing the woman's family, so he's clutching at anything that might be a clue."

"I won't be upset unless Jamison makes a nuisance of himself with this business," her aunt snapped, making her relieved that Aunt Jessie hadn't been here this morning.

Joanna hesitated, but it had to be said, and the sooner, the better. "I'm afraid he's not giving up. He wants me to talk to Mamm and Daad about this idea of a relative, so I guess I'll have to."

Aunt Jessie stiffened, and she was already as tight as a drum at this departure from the ordinary. "If he wants to know, he'd best ask his own questions and not expect you to do it." She swung around and headed for the back room. "I could use some coffee to get me going."

Joanna watched her march off. She tried to dismiss the thought that grew in her, but she couldn't. Aunt Jessie looked and sounded like she was trying to hide something.

That couldn't be, she told herself. Aunt Jessie was the most outspoken, forthright person she knew. But still, the concern lingered.

CHAPTER THREE

JOANNA CLICKED TO the mare, and Princess obediently picked up the pace. No matter how you looked at it, you really couldn't make up lost time with a horse and buggy, and she'd gotten a late start. They'd been busy in the shop during the afternoon, with a couple of customers picking fabric for new quilts and pulling out every bolt as they tried to decide. And the quilting class Aunt Jessie taught seemed to run later each week.

All of that had left her with no time to think about Aunt Jessie's reaction to her questions about possible Englisch relatives.

Now that she came back to it, she wondered if she had been imagining things. Her aunt would be upset at the idea that Joanna had gone through such a crisis alone, that was all. And she was probably even more upset by the fact that she hadn't been there for all the excitement.

Smiling at the thought of Aunt Jessie's probable response to the young patrolman and his questions, Joanna turned into the lane at the Brandt farm. Cathy Brandt and Rachel Hurst would be waiting for her, not willing to start on the friendship quilt they were making for Cathy's wedding without her. The three of them were the only unmarried women from their rumspringa group, besides being friends since childhood. That had created a link that even Cathy's upcoming marriage couldn't break.

Cathy greeted her at the door with a hug, and Rachel was right behind her. "At last, you're here. Rachel and I thought you'd gotten lost."

"Not I. Princess would always bring me home if I did." She shed her sweater and bonnet. "Did you start without me?"

"Only if you call admiring each other's patches starting," Rachel said. Her gentle face was flushed and pretty, probably at her pleasure in getting out for an evening. Her father didn't encourage her to have a life of her own.

"I haven't made much progress this week." Joanna set her sewing basket on the kitchen table, wishing as always that there were a few more hours in the day.

"No wonder, with all you've had going on yesterday and today," Cathy said. She took her seat at the table, and the other two joined her. "Have you heard anything new about the woman who was hurt?"

"She's still not awake." While she could confide anything in the two of them, Joanna felt she'd been over the same few facts too many times, and at the moment she'd like to forget.

"That's a pretty one." Joanna reached out to touch the finished square Rachel had put on the table. "That's a piece of the dress you wore for the first singing we went to, ain't so?"

Rachel, always shy when the attention turned to her, nodded. She traced the star she'd created with a combination of solid colors. "Remember how nervous we were?"

Singings for Amish teenagers started off the process of sizing up the opposite sex, and every girl remembered her first one.

"We held on to each other for dear life," Cathy said, laughing softly. "I don't know what we were so afraid of. They were boys we saw most every day."

"We thought nobody would want to talk to us," Joanna said. "I didn't dream of anyone taking me home, but I did want one of the boys to speak to me, at least." She looked pityingly back at her younger self. "Who would have thought we'd all still be single so many years later?"

"Not for long." Rachel clasped Cathy's hand for a moment. "Soon it will just be the two of us. I don't suppose I'll ever get married," she added. "I don't meet anyone."

Rachel so seldom complained about her life that they were both silenced for a moment. Joanna exchanged looks with Cathy. They'd both tried to get Rachel out from under her father's iron rule, but they hadn't succeeded. As far as he was concerned, Rachel's job was to take care of him and to mother her younger siblings since her mamm's death.

Selfish. Cathy mouthed the word, and Joanna nodded.

"You can't tell what will happen in the future," Cathy said. "I thought I'd be spending the rest of my life teaching other folks' kinder, but soon I'll be a wife and mother." Her face was transformed by the love that shone when she spoke of Michael and his little girl, Allie.

"Yah, we all know how your life has changed," Joanna teased. "Once you're a married woman you won't have time for us two maidals."

Cathy's eyes filled with tears. "Ach, no. Never think that. You will always be my dearest friends." She caught their hands in hers.

"We know," Rachel said quickly. "Joanna was just teasing."

Joanna nodded, not having expected such a reaction to her words. "Friends always," she said. "I'm going to be the single aunt who spoils my brothers' kinder, once they get around to having any. Like my aunt Jessie."

"You'll never be like your aunt." Rachel had always been thoroughly intimidated by Jessie. "Besides, at least you can talk to people, being right in town. There are still a few unmarried men, ain't so?"

"What about Noah?" Cathy said. "After all, he's right next door."

"I'm not interested," Joanna said firmly, dismissing a slight twinge. "Hard as it was to gain my independence, I'm not giving it up for anyone. Komm, now. Let's lay out the squares we have so far. Aunt Jessie says she could have made two or three quilts in the time we're spending on one."

"She doesn't count the time we spend talking.

That's part of making a friendship quilt, ain't so?" Cathy said.

"Yah, it is. I just wish I could see you more often." Rachel's expression was wistful, and Joanna thought again that someone had to do something about Rachel. Or more specifically, about her selfish father. If only Rachel would rebel and insist on having some time of her own—but they all knew she wouldn't do that.

Cathy started spreading out patches on the table. "And speaking of talking, what are the police saying and doing about the woman who had the accident?"

"Trying to identify her so they can find her family." Joanna hesitated, still unsure she wanted to speak about the situation. But she could trust Cathy and Rachel, and if they heard about it elsewhere, they'd be hurt. "Chief Jamison had Noah and me see her at the hospital. They… He has the idea that she resembles me. He said maybe she was a distant relative who was looking for family."

Rachel looked doubtful, but Cathy nodded. "It could be, I guess. We have some Englisch relations from my grandfather's brother, but we've never seen them. Grossmammi used to write to them. What do your mamm and daad say?"

"I haven't asked them yet, but Aunt Jessie didn't seem to think it was possible." That was not exactly what Aunt Jessie had said, and the uncertainty coiled through her again.

"She should know," Rachel said. She smoothed out the small pieces that would create her next square. "The police could do a DNA test. Or take her fingerprints." Cathy's forehead wrinkled as soon as she'd said the words. "But I guess that wouldn't really help identify her unless she had a police record."

Joanna couldn't help smiling at the thought. "She doesn't look like a criminal. Besides, what would bring her to my door?" Again, uneasiness pricked her, as if clamoring for attention.

"I think you'd better see her again." Cathy surprised both of them by the determination in her voice.

"Do you really think she should?" Rachel's eyes darkened with alarm. "I couldn't."

"Of course you could. When someone's hurt you have to try and help her." Cathy, always caring for those who were small and helpless, didn't leave any room to wiggle. "Maybe if you talk to her, she'll wake up."

The certainty in Cathy's voice made Joanna feel ashamed. She'd always been the leader in their small group, the one who took on new challenges. But in this case, Cathy was the brave one.

If she went back to see the stranger, her parents wouldn't like it. She knew that without having to ask. And Chief Jamison might not approve of her interference.

But the conviction that grew in her was too strong for argument. If the woman had been coming to see her, perhaps Joanna's voice could wake her. She had to try.

NOAH LOCKED THE back door and started toward the stable. Caleb had hitched a ride back to the farm earlier, so he'd felt free to stay after closing and get his records up-to-date. Unfortunately, the books confirmed what he had already feared—his sales had dropped off since the new hardware chain store opened out by the highway last month.

Maybe it was just a temporary thing. He'd like to believe that his regular customers would be faithful, even if they might want to try the new store, just to see what it was like. But it was hard to stay optimistic when he could see his income dropping.

He stopped at the stable door, surprised. Joanna's mare wasn't in her stall. Wherever Joanna had gone this evening, she wasn't back yet.

Not that it was any of his business, but when he saw how the darkness was drawing in, he hated to head out until he knew she was safely back. The lights were on in the upstairs apartment, meaning her aunt hadn't gone with Joanna.

He leaned against the stable door, surveying the area between the stable and the building. Too little light, he decided, and too many dark shadows where trouble might hide.

Now, what had put that in his mind? Just because someone had fallen on Joanna's stairs, that was no reason to imagine danger around every corner. Still, he ought to see about putting some sort of light back here. The building belonged to Joanna's father, but he probably wouldn't object.

A whicker called him back to the stall where his buggy horse was stabled. Blackie obviously wondered why they weren't on their way home. He patted the horse's arched neck. "Soon, old boy."

Just then he heard the creaking of buggy wheels that meant Joanna was home. He might as well help her unharness the mare before he left.

He stepped outside, reaching for the mare's headstall, and Joanna gasped. "Who is it?"

"It's just me. Noah. Sorry, I didn't mean to startle you." He'd almost said *frighten* but changed it at the last minute. Joanna wouldn't admit to being frightened.

"Ach, Noah, don't jump out at me like that." Relief flooded her voice. "What are you still doing here?"

"Just getting my books up-to-date. I heard you coming and thought I'd give you a hand before I harness Blackie."

"You don't need to take time to help." She slid down from the seat. "But it's gut to have some company." Her glance at the door to the stairs seemed apprehensive. "I know it's silly, but I'm nervous about being out here after dark after what happened."

"Yah. I've been imagining trouble in every shadow." He started on the harness buckle. "We'd best have a light put in back here. Even so, it'll take time to stop picturing that woman lying on the stairs."

"It will." She shivered, and he reached across the mare's back to touch her hand lightly in reassurance.

"I was out at Cathy's house to work on a quilt for her wedding. I forgot about how dark it would be to come home."

"I thought you might have gone to your parents'

house." He pushed the buggy to its usual place near the wall.

Joanna switched on the stable's battery lantern, its yellow light showing him the frown on her face. "I probably should have. They've been fretting too much."

"It's natural, I'd say. You're their little girl." He stopped, wishing he hadn't used those words. "I mean..."

"I know. And I am their little girl in every way that matters." Her brown eyes darkened in the lantern glow. "That's what makes it so hard to do as Chief Jamison wants."

He nodded, wishing he could wipe the worry from her eyes. "Because of you being adopted. I understand. It will remind them." He hesitated, not sure whether he should go on with what he'd started. "Have they kept that a secret at all? I had forgotten until you mentioned it."

"A secret? Not exactly. I've known since I was old enough to understand. But Mamm... Well, I suppose she doesn't like to be reminded that I was born to someone else." She paused, her hand resting on the mare's back. "Once, when she did talk about it, Mamm said that God had put them in the right place at the right time to find their precious little girl to love."

Her voice, always so assured, trembled on the words, and he was filled with a longing to shield her from the things that were causing her pain.

"Maybe it would be better to let Chief Jamison ask

them about it himself," he suggested. "There's no reason for you to do his work for him."

Joanna gave a soft laugh as she guided Princess into her stall and turned to scoop oats from the metal bin. "That's what Aunt Jessie said, only with more emphasis."

Her laugh seemed to touch his heart. "Here's a better idea. Turn Aunt Jessie loose on Jamison. I'm scared to death of her, and he's probably no better."

"That's not a bad idea." Her voice was still filled with amusement, making him doubly glad he'd lingered.

He reached out to close the stall door, but she grasped it first, and his hand landed on hers, the touch tingling. He had to stop this. Joanna clearly felt nothing but friendship for him, and anything else was unthinkable. No conscientious Amish parents would want him for their daughter, even if he was so careless as to take that chance. He removed his hand, stepping back.

"I…I'll walk you to the door before I hitch up Blackie."

"Denke." Joanna spoke softly, her voice sounding a bit shaky. "I'm not afraid," she added after a moment.

"I know. No reason to be." But he fell into step with her as they started toward the house.

They moved beyond the range of lantern light, and the darkness closed around them. "I wonder…" Joanna's voice came out of the dark. "I wonder what brought her here."

He shook his head and then realized she couldn't

see him. "We may never know. I don't mean that I think she's going to die," he added hastily. "Jamison is counting so much on her waking up, but I've heard sometimes people don't remember after a blow to the head."

"I thought of that, too." They reached the stoop, and Joanna fumbled with her penlight and switched it on. By its glow, she looked pale and worried. "You know, I keep thinking about how hard she must have fallen to give her head such a crack. I've tripped on the steps several times, and never had more than a bump on my knee."

"Best to stop thinking about it, maybe." He couldn't help clasping her hands for a moment.

"Good advice." She smiled up at him. "The problem is to take it." She squeezed his hands lightly in return and then turned and ran quickly up the stairs.

JOANNA WAS AWARE of Noah lingering at the bottom until she reached the apartment. She and Aunt Jessie were fortunate to have such a helpful neighbor. She hadn't known him all that well until they'd opened the store, despite being in the same church district. She hadn't thought of it before, but now it seemed odd. He'd always held back from the normal closeness of the community, doing all and more that was expected of him, yet somehow never being part of the laughter and teasing that went on among Amish men with their peers.

Aunt Jessie appeared in the doorway to her bedroom. "You're out late, ain't so?"

"Not very." She managed a smile. Aunt Jessie seemed to consider it her duty to act as mother, whether it was necessary or not. Still, it could be worse. "We had a lot to talk about with Cathy's wedding coming up soon."

She'd hoped that would placate her aunt, and it seemed to. Or at least, she didn't follow up with any other pointed questions. She just gave an obvious look at the clock before closing her bedroom door.

Shrugging, Joanna headed for her own room. She'd best talk to her parents again tomorrow, or Mamm's worrying might hit a new level.

A good night's sleep helped Joanna focus, but it didn't bring any enlightenment. The problem of the unknown woman who resembled her was just as serious as it had been. As soon as breakfast was over, she headed for the shop phone and called the phone shanty at the farm to say she'd be coming to supper.

It was obvious that Aunt Jessie had heard her calling, and she nodded approvingly. "Gut. It's time you talked with your folks again," she said shortly.

To Joanna's relief, Aunt Jessie didn't suggest going with her. That would allow her to depart a little earlier than needed and head for the hospital. She wasn't lying about it, she told herself. She just didn't mention it.

The day at the shop seemed longer than ever. Finally, it was time to close. Joanna collected her bonnet and sweater. Telling Aunt Jessie she'd be back by dark, she headed out, going straight to the hospital.

Joanna had no sooner stepped off the elevator than she spotted Mary Ellen Dover. She quickened her step. Knowing Mary Ellen, she might get some real answers to her questions about the patient.

"Joanna." Mary Ellen swerved and came to greet her. "I thought you'd be up to see your patient again."

"My patient?" She lifted her eyebrows, smiling at Mary Ellen's capacity for involvement in anything that was going on. "Not unless we've changed places."

"You know what I mean." Mary Ellen took a quick look around before jerking her head toward the patient's room. "Our mystery patient is still a mystery."

"There's been no improvement at all?" Disappointment dragged at her. "That's discouraging, isn't it?"

"Depends on how you look at it. It may be that her brain just needs time to heal. And from what I've seen, I'd say her coma is a bit lighter today." She looked around again. "But don't quote me."

"I promise," she said, her heart lifting at the news. "Is it okay if I go in?"

"Sure thing. Nobody's told me to restrict visitors anyway. Just sit and talk to her. It might help and it certainly can't do any harm."

Joanna hesitated as they reached the door. "Talk about what? Should I mention the accident?"

"Just as long as you sound reassuring it won't hurt. They say people in comas do respond to things like music or someone talking. We can hope anyway." She leaned closer. "Did you know that Chief Jamison has been pestering the attending physician to do a DNA test?"

"No." Joanna's stomach lurched, remembering

Cathy's comment the night before. "Are they going to do it?"

"Dr. Parkinson says not without a court order. Loudly." She grinned. "I just happened to be outside the lounge when they were talking." She spotted some-one approaching the nurses' station. "I've got to go. Go on, talk to her."

Joanna pushed open the door, thinking about what Mary Ellen had revealed. She had no idea whether the police would be able to get a court order or not, but it certainly sounded as if the chief was getting more impatient by the day.

Her first look at the woman in the bed lifted her spirits. A faint tinge of color had replaced the pallor she'd seen before, and it seemed to her that the woman moved a little in reaction to her entrance.

Her doubts about coming here ebbed away, and she moved to the chair she'd had before, drawing it closer to the bed.

"I've come back to see you again." She put her hand lightly over the unresponsive one that lay on the sheet. "Do you remember me? My name is Joanna."

Nothing, but she'd go on with it. Just sound encour-aging, Mary Ellen had said. She'd try.

"I run a quilt shop. Did you know that? Your ac-cident happened when you were coming up the stairs to my apartment."

Wait, that might not be considered encouraging. She tried again.

"You're doing much better today. If you could look out the window, you'd see that the trees on the mountain are starting to turn color. Soon, they'll all be gold and orange. I think fall is my favorite time of year in Pennsylvania."

She didn't respond, but it seemed to Joanna that she was listening. Maybe that was wishful thinking, but encouraging, even so.

"Mary Ellen, your nurse, is a friend of mine. She'll take good care of you. We'd all like it if you'd open your eyes and talk to us." *Encouraging, remember?* "I'm sure you will soon. Then we'll be able to talk."

"Sounds to me as if you're already talking." Noah had entered without her hearing him, and spoke Dutch.

"Speak Englisch," she said, smiling. "She might be able to hear you, and I'd guess she doesn't speak Pennsylvania Dutch."

"Good guess," he said, in English this time.

"What are you doing here?"

"I could ask you the same thing." He came a little closer, but she noticed he still averted his eyes from the woman in the bed.

"I'm checking on our...visitor? Would that be the right word? I hate to keep calling her a stranger."

"It'll do," he said. "She did seem to be coming to your door." He shrugged. "I suppose we both feel some responsibility. Is she doing any better?"

"She has more color in her face." Joanna made an effort to sound optimistic, remembering that the woman might hear her. "And Mary Ellen said she didn't seem so deeply asleep. At least, I think that's what she meant." She hesitated, but probably

Noah would want to know. "She also said that Chief Jamison wanted them to do a DNA test, but the doctor wouldn't without a court order."

He said what she had thought. "He must be feeling desperate. I wonder what he hoped that would tell him."

She was about to answer when the door swung open again and Chief Jamison walked in. He frowned at the sight of them.

"What are you two doing here?"

His voice was sharp enough to make Joanna blink. "I wanted to check on her. The nurse suggested I talk to her for a few minutes. That's supposed to be good for her."

"Is there a reason why we shouldn't?" Noah sounded as if he was determined to control himself.

Jamison looked abashed. "Sorry. I didn't mean to bark. It's been a discouraging day. Everything I've tried has turned into a dead end. But somebody has to know who she is. She didn't just drop out of the sky."

In the wake of his remarks, she wasn't sure he'd appreciate something encouraging. Still, in her opinion, things were a bit brighter. "She does seem a little better today. Maybe soon she'll wake up and tell us who she is."

"I'd give a lot to have that happen." He frowned at the serene face. "But maybe she won't."

Joanna considered mentioning the proposed DNA test but didn't want to betray Mary Ellen's eavesdropping. "Isn't there anything else you can try?"

He shrugged. "I thought a DNA test might be useful, but the doctor in charge won't authorize it without a court order. Guess I'll have to see if I can round up a judge to hear it. Meanwhile…" He stopped, then started again. "The fact is I keep wondering how a simple fall forward on a set of wooden stairs could have caused her injury."

Joanna's breath caught. She had idly thought it was odd, given how often she'd tripped going up and down the stairs over the years, but he hadn't mentioned it. It seemed he took the possibility seriously.

"Can't the doctor tell anything from the injury?"

Jamison frowned. "Odd things happen. That's what he said. And that gets us nowhere."

The chief's discouragement must be contagious. Joanna found her earlier optimism draining away. *Stop that*, she demanded.

"I'm sure something will turn up soon." She firmly set her mind on answers to prayers. "At least she's safe and getting good medical care. And folks are praying for her."

Jamison's expression softened when he looked at Joanna. "You're a good person, Joanna. I hope you're right about that."

She nodded, a little embarrassed. "Yah, I hope so. I…" She stopped—startled—and looked down at her hand that still covered the patient's.

"She moved!" Excitement flooded through her. "When I spoke, her fingers twitched. I'm sure. I felt it."

"Let's get that nurse in here." Jamison grabbed the call cord and pressed the button. "You go on. Keep talking to her. You might be just what she needs."

She glanced at Noah and then turned back to the woman. Worrying about anyone's opinion of her was a waste of time. If there was anything she could do to help this woman, she would do it, no matter what.

CHAPTER FOUR

JOANNA WAS STILL having trouble controlling her excitement when she neared the familiar lane at the farm. Princess, spotting a turning she knew, pricked her ears and picked up her pace. Joanna took a deep breath, willing herself to keep as firm a rein on her emotions as she did on the mare.

Should she tell her parents about what had happened at the hospital? She couldn't lie to them, but should she volunteer information? Daad wouldn't approve of her deeper involvement, and she wasn't sure how Mamm would react, but it would doubtless worry her. Maybe she'd just have to see how the talk went and take her lead from it.

Chief Jamison had been about as excited as she was at the woman's response, especially when Mary Ellen confirmed that the patient's pulse and breathing reacted when Joanna spoke to her. Mary Ellen's pleasure at the slight improvement was so obvious that it touched Joanna. Clearly, the staff had grown to care about their anonymous patient.

She'd begun to think she'd never get away, but she'd insisted that she had to leave. Her parents would worry if she didn't show up on time. Finally, when she'd agreed to come back often and speak to the woman, she'd escaped.

Noah had walked down to the buggy with her, releasing the line while she climbed up. He'd stood for a moment with his hand on the buggy, frowning up at her.

She'd reached for the line he held. "I must go. Is something wrong?"

"No." But he'd looked worried. "Take care on the road. Be safe."

Well, she was here, and she'd arrived safely. There must be something about accidents that made people imagine further trouble. But that was no reason for Noah to fret about her. It was bad enough that her family was so concerned.

She hadn't yet reached the hitching post when her youngest brother, Zeb, popped out to take the horse and buggy. At fourteen, he was always outgrowing both his clothes and himself, making him likely to bump his head on things he used to clear and tripping him with great regularity. He always came up laughing, though.

"About time you're getting here." He put up a hand to help her down as if, she thought, she was an old lady.

"Why? Is Mamm worrying?"

He grinned. "When is Mamm not worrying?"

She swatted at him, returning the smile, and went on into the house. A wonderful aroma wafted out from the kitchen, a mixture of pot roast and apple pie.

"Yum, it smells wonderful gut in here. I hope I'm

not too late for supper." She took off her bonnet and put it on her usual hook.

"Here you are." Flushed from the heat of the stove, Mamm hugged her. "Just in time."

"What can I do to help?" she asked, noting that her mother's hug had been extra long.

"Put the milk and water pitchers on the table. I'm ready to dish up. And ring the bell for your daad and your brothers. I don't know why they wander off when supper is about ready."

"I'm here." Daad came in the back door and winked at Joanna, making her laugh. "As soon as I hug my girl, I'll ring the bell."

His arm, still as wiry and strong as that of a younger man, encircled her, and she inhaled the scent of his sun-dried cotton shirt. "Wilkom, daughter."

"Denke, Daadi," she murmured, touched by memories of years of hugs. Funny that her throat went suddenly tight.

Then she forgot it as she was caught up in the hustle of getting the meal on the table and working around the boys as they rushed in. In a few minutes they were all in their familiar seats, bowing their heads for the silent prayer. Joanna's mind promptly started to stray to the stranger, and she hauled it back.

Years of practice allowed Joanna to know just when Daad would look up, ending the prayer. The bowls and platters began circling the table, accompanied by her younger brothers' daily teasing and arguing about who took the biggest serving.

"Stop it, you boys," Daad demanded. "Your sister will think you've turned into heathens since she left."

Joanna looked at them. "I don't know, Daadi. They seem about the same to me. I think I'd miss their squabbling if it stopped."

The boys laughed, and Mamm shook her head with mock severity. "Ach, don't encourage them."

Yah, she was home again. Everything sounded the same. Soon Daadi mentioned something about the silage, and they were off on the familiar subject of the work to be done, the ball bouncing around the table as everyone had an idea what should be done next.

From the vantage point of no longer living at home, she noticed the way Daadi let each one have his say about the work. Maybe that was why they all did their share so willingly. They all felt they were part of the farm. Even young Zeb, who wasn't the born farmer the other two were, was eager to put in his opinion.

Maybe that was a blessing about living away from home—it let her see things a little clearer and appreciate what she wouldn't have noticed as part of it.

Conversation stayed general as they ate their way through tender pot roast, mashed potatoes, baked corn and winter squash, and ended with apple crumb pie. It was as they were getting up from the table that she thought she heard Zeb start to say something about the accident.

With a quick look at Mamm, Jonas interrupted him. Isaac, catching on, challenged him to finish his share of the chores faster than the others, and they were off and running, their footsteps echoing on the porch floor.

Mamm looked a little troubled as she and Joanna started the dishes, but Joanna turned the subject to the challenge of getting the new dresses made for Cathy's wedding. Delighted to focus on someone marrying, even if it wasn't her daughter, Mamm plunged into details of fabric and stitching. The dresses were the same as every other dress they owned, of course, but it was still exciting, and they required extra care.

How could she bring up the subject of whether they might have any relatives who had turned Englisch? Somehow, the more she saw of Mamm, the less she felt that it was wise to ask her. If she could get Daad alone, that would be best.

The sun was nearing the ridgetop when Daadi interrupted the wedding talk with the suggestion that Joanna leave so she'd get home before dark. Here was the chance she needed, and she'd have to take advantage of it. She certainly didn't want to have the police car pulling up the lane so that the chief could ask the questions himself.

Once the endless goodbyes were said, Daad walked out with her to hitch up the mare instead of letting one of the boys do it. Because he realized she wanted a chance to talk privately? She wasn't sure.

"It's as well to leave now," she said, hoping to find a way into the questions she had to ask. "It really is dark back by the stable these fall days. In fact, Noah said he'd put a light up back there, just to make it a bit safer."

Daad didn't noticeably stiffen at the sound of Noah's name, but she sensed some tension.

"That's kind of him, but not right that he should pay for it. Tell him if he'll put it up, I'll take care of the cost. After all, it's my responsibility. I should have thought of that myself."

True, Daad owned the building, but it was unusual to hear him admit that he'd failed to do something.

"That's a gut idea." She started to step up to the buggy seat, but Daad put out a hand to stop her. "I didn't want to ask in front of your mamm, but is the woman any better?"

"As a matter of fact…" She gave him a quick account of how the stranger had reacted to her voice. "So the doctor wants me to stop and talk to her whenever I can. And Chief Jamison seems to think that makes it more likely that she was coming to see me." She hesitated, but it had to be said. "I realized that I hadn't thought of being adopted when he asked about any relatives who might have left the Amish and be searching for family. I don't like to ask Mamm, but…"

"No, don't ask your mother." He spoke almost on top of her words. "I'll look into it. You know how flustered she gets by…anything out of the ordinary."

"By anything about my being adopted, you mean." She paused. "Does she think it makes her less my mother? She *is* my mother, in every way that counts. Nothing changes that."

Daad didn't speak for a long moment, and she thought he struggled against emotion. Finally, he nodded. "I know. But that's how she feels. We can't change other people, Joanna. Not even if it would be better for them."

She wanted to argue, but she knew in her heart he was right. Mamm was sensitive about the fact that she hadn't given birth to Joanna, and it hurt not to be able to make that better for her, just as Mamm had always made every trouble better for her. "I know. I'll try not to remind her."

"Gut." He helped her up to the buggy seat. "I can't think of anyone from the family who might have gone Englisch, but I'll look into it and let you know soon. All right?"

Joanna nodded, her heart warming at Daad's understanding. If only she could convince her mother of her feelings... But maybe that was something only the gut Lord could do.

THE NEXT AFTERNOON Noah grabbed a few minutes while his part-time help was there to start installing the outdoor lights in the back. He could easily walk away and leave things in Floyd's hands. A retiree, Floyd didn't like anything better than gabbing with customers, but since they seemed to like it just as much, Noah figured that was for the best.

He'd hardly set down his toolbox when Joanna came out her back door and headed toward the stable. Seeing him, she waved.

"I'm putting Princess out in the paddock. Do you want Blackie out, too?"

"As long as Princess doesn't mind him eating her grass. But I'll do it. You don't need to."

Not troubling to answer that, Joanna disappeared into the stable and came out leading a horse with each hand. Used to spending their days together, neither Blackie nor Princess gave her any trouble. Not that she'd allow it, he admitted. Knowing she was capable of far more than just putting them in the adjoining paddock, he concentrated on the brackets that would hold the battery lights in place.

Not as satisfactory in this case as electric would be, but they would do the job. He'd put one by his back door and then one by Joanna's back door. With both of them focused on the area, they would dispel the darkness.

Joanna came back from the paddock and stopped to watch his work. "One by my door, as well?" She'd noticed that he had a second box.

"Yah, that should do pretty much what we need. It will go on if anyone moves out here. If you want to leave it on when you go out in the evening, just press this switch to keep it on." He demonstrated. "Then when you get home and you're ready to go in, shut it off."

"It'll go through a lot of batteries, won't it?"

The sound of her voice so close behind him made him lose his grip for a moment, and the screwdriver slipped out of the screw head.

"Not too bad, since it's only on when something moves. And you're not going to want to stand there in the dark while you pump up a gas lantern, ain't so?"

"You're right, you're right," she teased, and he couldn't help smiling at the laughter in her eyes. "It's much better. By the way, my daad wants to pay for the lights."

"Not necessary," he said shortly. He wasn't so poverty-stricken that he couldn't provide the lights.

She shrugged, stepping back as he turned, the bracket finished. "You'll have to argue it out with him."

"Nobody ever wins an argument with the bishop," he pointed out.

"One person does." Her eyes sparkled with laughter.

"Not you," he retorted, reminded of their school days when she'd been just as sassy.

"No, not me. The bishop's wife."

He couldn't help smiling with her. "Sounds like I should get her on my side, then."

Sliding the light into place in the bracket and securing it, he switched it on and off. "Gut. Now I'll do one by your door." As they walked across the back, he frowned at the stable. "Maybe we should have one by the stable, but I don't want to take another one out of stock right now. I couldn't order many this time."

Joanna's eyebrows lifted in a question. "Is business tight right now?"

He didn't want her pity, but Joanna made it sound so normal that he couldn't take offense.

"A little," he conceded. "That new chain store out on the highway is cutting into my business." He tried for a lighter tone. "Be glad there's not a new quilt store out there."

"I am." She looked up at him, making him realize

that her eyes echoed the warm colors of the autumn leaves that drifted along the lanes at this time of year.

He yanked his attention from a consideration of her eyes and back to the current problem. "I have to tell Floyd that I'm cutting back his hours." The words were bitter, close to an admission of failure. "He's been with me since we opened, and there's nobody better, but sales are down, and I can't..." He let that trail off, convinced he sounded like he was asking for pity. He didn't want Joanna thinking he was sorry for himself, but when she looked at him with interest and caring, he couldn't help but respond.

"Yah, I see what you mean." But Joanna looked as if she considered the problem impartially. "Floyd knows how to fix anything, so I've heard."

Noah nodded, feeling guilt closing in on him. "And he can tell customers just what they need to do the fixing, besides being able to gossip with all the old guys, both Amish and Englisch."

The laughter came back to Joanna's eyes. "That's important in a hardware store, ain't so?"

"If you mean it sounds like he's more important to the store than I am, you're probably right." He grimaced. "And he needs the money—he says his retirement check doesn't go far enough."

An observant person could practically see Joanna's thoughts whirling, and he was always observant when it came to Joanna. "What Floyd needs is some work to fill those hours you have to cut, ain't so? Why not help him set up a side business doing odd jobs for folks? You agree he can fix most anything, and plenty of people need things done. I'd guess a lot of the older widows who come in my shop would jump at the chance to have someone they could call when they need some little thing fixed around the house."

He suspected his brain didn't work as quickly as hers did. "Yah, he could, but how could I help him? He could do that himself, couldn't he?"

"He could, but he isn't." Joanna sounded like she was trying to be patient. "He needs someone to prompt him a little bit."

"Push him, you mean."

"You say push, I say prompt." Her face softened in a smile. "You can vouch for him. You can put up a sign in your shop and mention him to people when they come in. That's all he'll need to start getting jobs. I'll put one up in my shop, too, and talk him up to my customers."

He must have still looked doubtful, because she looked ready to start pushing him, too. "Well?"

"All right, all right." He held up his hands. "I'll suggest it to him. You can stop pushing now."

"Are you hinting that I like to take charge?" Her eyes brimmed with laughter, making him feel as if nothing was all that bad as long as Joanna smiled at him.

"Not hinting," he said, trying to match her light tone. "Coming right out with it."

They were standing there smiling at each other when the back door opened, nearly knocking Joanna off the step. He caught her arm just as Aunt Jessie appeared, looking as if she'd been sucking on a lemon.

IGNORING NOAH, AUNT JESSIE spoke directly to her. "What have you been doing out here so long?"

"I was helping Noah put up the new lights." *Help* was probably too strong a word, but in any event, that was why she was here.

Jessie looked at the fixture and then nodded to Noah. "Denke, Noah. Joanna, you're wanted in the shop."

With a glance at Noah that she hoped conveyed gratitude and apology, Joanna followed her up the steps. "I can't imagine a customer has a problem you can't handle."

"Not a customer. It's Chief Jamison again." Jessie's back was stiff with disapproval. "He shouldn't be coming in here so much. He'll be giving us a bad name."

She managed not to laugh. "It's not as if he's here to arrest us, Aunt Jessie. He's trying to identify the woman who was hurt so he can tell her family. You'd think they must be worried to death."

That seemed to get past her aunt's disapproval of all things related to the police. "Ach, well, I suppose he has to do that." They were heading into the shop by this time. "If you take him in the back room, you'll have some privacy."

"Yah, I will. Denke." And thanks be that Aunt Jessie was over her little spurt of temper. What Mamm called Jessie's snits never lasted long, but they were uncomfortable while they went on.

Chief Jamison looked uneasily aware that several

women were watching him, but his face cleared when he saw Joanna. Before he could speak, she gestured.

"I think what you want is in the back room."

His lips twitched as he followed her, and once she'd closed the door, he shook his head. "I've never known you to tell a fib before, Joanna."

"A fib? If you wanted to talk in front of those women, you surprise me."

He chuckled, the laugh lines deepening around his eyes. "You've got it right, as usual. What's your aunt Jessie so testy for?"

Now it was her turn to laugh. "She thinks we'll get a bad reputation if you hang around here."

He was taken aback for a moment. "Well, nobody ever said that to me before. But maybe I'd better make this fast. Are you coming up to the hospital today?"

She nodded. "After work." Something about his expression alarmed her. "Is she worse?"

"No, not worse. But the fact is she's no better today, either. So, much as I hated to do it, I got Judge Conroy to issue a court order. Today I want to get DNA swabs from both of you, if you agree. At least that will tell us if we're right about why she came here."

"For sure I will." She paused, sensing his reluctance to take this step. "Is there any reason not to do this?"

"No legal reason. But I hate to do it without asking the woman. Still, we can't ask her permission when she's unconscious, and it's not as if she's suspected of a crime."

She'd like to say that she was sure the woman

wouldn't mind, just to soothe his feelings, but re-minded herself that she had no idea. Funny that she could feel so familiar with a person she'd never even heard speak.

"If the test leads us to who she is, it will be worth it, ain't so?"

Jamison nodded, seeming energized by the thought. "Right. I'll set it up for later this afternoon. See you there."

He walked out briskly. Joanna followed, wondering how long it was going to take Aunt Jessie to start scolding again. Or to warn her about Noah.

It turned out to be a warning, and it only took Jessie until the customers had gone.

"Now, then." She swung on Joanna purposefully. "It's all very well to have a business relationship with Noah Troyer, but that doesn't mean you should follow him around."

Joanna's temper didn't often break loose now that she was grown, but she came close to it at that moment. "I am *not* following him around. I thought you knew me better than that."

Aunt Jessie's expression said that she was struggling, too. Finally, she gave a curt nod. "You're right. I'm sorry." Worry clouded her eyes. "I don't doubt that Noah is a gut neighbor to us. But his family background—"

"It's not his fault that his father drank too much. As far as I know, he doesn't touch any of it." She didn't really know, she guessed, but surely the rumors would be rife if he did drink. Nobody could keep that quiet in a close-knit community.

Her aunt's face twitched as if she tried to hold something back. "It was not just the drinking, Joanna. You're too young to know, but his mother... She would come to worship trying to hide bruises. Word was that Noah tried to protect her, poor boy."

Images crowded Joanna's mind, and her throat was so tight she couldn't speak. What must that life have been like for Noah? For all of them.

"Why didn't anyone do anything about it?" Surely, the church...her father, as bishop...should have.

"Ach, Joanna, don't you think they tried? Your daad spent so many hours talking to him, trying to get him help. He refused, even when your daad made the appointment. He was put under the bann more than once, but he'd confess, beg to be forgiven, promise it would never happen again. And then it did."

"I feel so bad for them. And guilty that I didn't know." Her voice was choked with tears.

"If there was one thing Noah's mother wanted, it was that her kinder be spared the shame," Jessie said. "But people knew." She hesitated. "Think about it, Joanna. How could a childhood like that prepare a boy for a normal life? Noah could have problems no one can guess. I would hate to see you care for him and then be hurt."

Joanna couldn't help but be moved by her aunt's obvious emotion, especially coming from someone who seldom, if ever, showed her feelings. Still...

"I understand." She kept the words gentle. "But I

have no intention of being anything but a friend to Noah. I promise. Anyway, I'm not thinking of marriage just now. I have plenty to do with the shop."

Aunt Jessie looked at her for a long moment. Finally, she gave a little shrug. "Nobody ever could stop you when you were determined on something, could they? But your daad will have something to say if he notices."

Taking that to mean Aunt Jessie didn't intend to report on her, she gave her aunt a quick hug. "There won't be anything for him to notice."

"We'll see." Aunt Jessie smoothed her spotless apron. "I doubt we'll have much more business from now until closing. Maybe you'd best go on to the hospital."

"If you're sure, I will." She paused, but it had best be said before her aunt found out some other way. "They're going to test the woman's DNA to see if that helps identify her. And mine, to see if she might be a relation." She waited, not sure how Aunt Jessie would take that news.

Her aunt's face tightened, her lips forming a thin line. Then she gave a short nod. "I see. Will you be home for supper?"

"I'm going on to Cathy's place to work on the dresses for the wedding, so don't expect me."

"Yah, all right." Jessie gave a tiny smile. "If you're not back by dark, I'll turn the new light on."

Eased at what seemed a gesture of goodwill, Joanna went upstairs to collect the sewing she meant to take with her to Cathy's place, and then headed out to the stable to hitch up the mare.

The hospital had started to become very familiar, and she could get around almost as if she belonged there. She'd noticed the same odd thing when her brother Jonas was in the hospital once—what was frightening and strange at first became routine when one was concerned about the person, rather than the place.

Chief Jamison met her in the hallway. "Glad you're here, Joanna." Frustration showed in his voice. "The staff has been trying to talk to her, but—nothing. Now we're starting to get crank calls."

Joanna looked at him blankly. "Crank calls?"

He grunted. "You're lucky you don't know anything about things like that. Crazy people claiming she's their sister who disappeared in 1950 or the reincarnation of a girl who died in the Civil War. Crazies."

Joanna felt a wave of pity. "Poor things. How disturbed they must be to think that."

"Yeah, I guess." But he obviously felt more annoyance than sympathy. "Well, let's get this over with. They're sending a tech up to get the sample. You might as well see if our mystery woman responds to you first."

He ushered her into the room. Any apprehension she felt about the DNA testing disappeared when she saw the woman again. She was doing better, wasn't she? Her skin bore a normal flush, and her eyes seemed to flicker for an instant. She might just as easily be napping as unconscious.

Joanna automatically took the chair next to the bed, putting her hand over the patient's. "It's Joanna. I've come back to see you again. You remember me, don't you?"

She'd hoped for a response, but none came, and she tried to control her disappointment. Was this normal, to rouse a little and slip backward again? She had no idea.

The door swung open again, and Mary Ellen came in, accompanied by a young man holding a plastic caddy with various vials and equipment. She gave Joanna an encouraging smile.

"This is Joe. I know he doesn't look old enough to be out by himself, but he's trained, I promise. He's going to take a sample from each of you for DNA testing."

At her comment, the young man grinned, his freckled face blushing a little. "Hey, I can't help my looks. Maybe I ought to grow a beard. What do you think?" He was asking Joanna, but even as he spoke, he pulled out a vial and removed a long swab from a sealed package.

Joanna eyed the swab doubtfully. "Could you? Grow a beard, I mean."

"Ouch. You must be a friend of Mary Ellen's. I did try once, on summer vacation. I just looked like I'd forgotten to wash my face, according to my girlfriend." He took a step closer. "This is easy. Just open your mouth, and I'll run this along the inside of your cheek. Okay?"

She nodded, obeying, and in an instant, it seemed, he had finished and was dropping the swab into a vial.

Then he held it out so that she could see the label. "You see? That's your name and address, right?"

"Yah." Obviously, he'd have to guarantee that it was hers in order for anyone to rely on the results.

"Now we'll take care of your friend's."

Joanna moved back slightly, not letting go of the woman's hand, and in another moment, it was done. He had Jamison check the label on that one, and before Joanna could ask how long it would take, he'd disappeared.

"Okay?" Jamison asked.

"Fine. How long...?"

"They'll put a rush on it given the circumstances. Wouldn't do us much good if they took weeks to do it, right? I got the okay to send it to the lab at the university instead of the usual procedure. We need answers."

With that sentiment, Joanna could heartily agree. Someone, somewhere, must be worrying and wondering. And she had her own reason to want answers.

"If she is related to me, I'd like to know. And I imagine she would, too."

At her words, the woman's eyelids fluttered, and her hand came alive under Joanna's. She squeezed Joanna's hand firmly, and her eyelids fluttered again. For an instant they opened enough that Joanna could glimpse eyes that were brown with flecks of gold, like hers, and then they closed again.

But she had seen. "It's all right," she said softly. "We'll find out."

CHAPTER FIVE

NOAH STEPPED OUT the front door of the hardware store to attend to the last chore of the day, spray bottle in hand. The door was the first thing a customer saw coming in, and to his way of thinking, it had best be shining. Although, given the small number of customers he'd had that day, he wasn't sure it counted for much.

His eye was caught by the neat white card in the front window, advertising handyman services. Thanks to Joanna's foresight, he'd been able to ease the pain of cutting down Floyd's hours. A glance next door showed him a similar sign in the quilt shop window. He'd be a fool to be annoyed that it was Joanna who'd thought of it, not him. The important thing was to help Floyd, and Joanna, always practical, had seen how to accomplish it.

Noah gave the window a last swish with the paper towel and used it to shine the doorknob. A rattle coming from the shop next door heralded Jessie's arrival. She stepped out onto the sidewalk and stood for a moment, surveying him.

He tensed, half expecting a lecture on the subject of her niece. Whatever it was, he'd listen respectfully and then go his own way, like always. It didn't pay to argue—he'd figured that out a long time ago.

"Noah." She said his name and fell silent, standing there looking at him as if she'd forgotten what she intended to say. She cleared her throat.

He wadded up the paper towel and turned to her, not speaking. She was the one with something to say, wasn't she?

"Denke," Jessie said finally, surprising him. "For putting up the lights. It's a gut idea."

"No trouble." He shrugged. "I should have thought to do it before now."

Jessie stood irresolute for a moment. Then she turned and went back inside, closing and locking the door, then flipping down the closed sign.

That was an unexpected development when he'd been expecting a lecture. It seemed the accident had shattered what was normal in more ways than one. Still, if Jessie intended to be a bit more cordial, he'd take it.

With everything finished at the store, he locked up and headed for home, his thoughts still revolving around the intrusion into their quiet lives caused by the stranger. Jamison had started calling her the mystery woman, and that was about what she was. But the biggest mystery might be what part Joanna played in her story. Jessie was trying to protect her, but from what?

Holding the lines slack, he let the horse choose its own pace going home. Funny that he hadn't known, or at least hadn't remembered if he'd even known, about

Joanna's adoption. How did that play into that odd resemblance between the two women? If they were related, it might be more difficult to find out how, unless Joanna's mother had stayed in touch with that distant cousin who was supposedly Joanna's birth mother.

Supposedly—now why had he thought that? It wasn't unusual for family members to step in when some illness or emergency kept a parent from raising a child. His mamm had a couple of cousins who'd been raised with her after their mother died. For the Amish, it was the normal choice.

Maybe it would answer his questions if he knew more about the circumstances. He could ask Mamm. She'd remember what happened at the time. When it came to babies, Amish women had long memories.

Reaching home, he let that simmer in the back of his mind while he unharnessed and turned the buggy horse into the paddock. There, the sound of arguing voices led him to the barn.

"It's not my turn. It's your turn."

"Is not."

"Is so."

He managed not to shout, much as he wanted to. Caleb and Joshua were still young enough to enjoy a squabble now and then. But he didn't.

"Quit it, both of you." The edge in his voice silenced them.

Joshua, never at a loss for words, recovered first. "It's not my turn to shovel stalls tonight. I took Caleb's turn the day he went to work in the store, so he owes me one."

"I wasn't even here," Caleb burst out. "Seems to me…"

"Enough." He glared at them. "What would Mamm think if she heard you arguing like that? You can do it together tonight and tomorrow night." He held up his hand to stop any disputes. "Look at it this way—if you work together, you'll be done twice as fast. Now, don't come in the house until you can be civil to each other in front of Mamm."

He wouldn't ask for the moon, but he figured they could do that much. And by the time they finished working together, their quarrel would be forgotten anyway. Whether it was or wasn't, he wouldn't let it upset Mamm.

Feeling he'd sufficiently intimidated them, he went on in the house. His mother was in the kitchen, stirring a pot of applesauce on the stove.

"Smells gut." He gave her a gentle hug, thinking as always that she was so thin it seemed her bones might snap at something more.

She had her usual tired smile for him, and she patted his cheek. "Hungry? Supper will be ready in fifteen minutes or so."

"That's fine, but I thought it was Lovina's turn to cook tonight."

"Some of her friends were going shopping this afternoon, so she wanted to go with them. I don't mind," she added quickly.

He did, but he knew better than to say something. Somehow, Aaron and his new bride hadn't really settled into a normal married routine. Mamm had expected to retire to the daadi haus and let Lovina take over running the farmhouse and doing the usual chores of a farmwife. But Lovina seemed to think this was still her running-around time.

If he said anything, he knew Mamm would say something indulgent about how young Lovina and Aaron were. And she'd be upset if he suggested having a talk with them. So he kept his mouth shut for Mamm's sake, but one day he wouldn't, he feared.

"How is that poor woman who was hurt in your building?" she asked, probably to change the subject. Since it was a good lead into what he wanted to know, he went along with it.

"Better, I think, but still not able to say who she is." He paused, trying to find the best way into what he wanted to ask. "She looks a bit like Joanna, and they're wondering if she might be a relative through Joanna's birth mother. Do you remember when she was adopted?"

"Yah, for sure." She put the wooden spoon down and turned toward him. "It was a wonderment to the whole community, coming like it did."

His attention spiked. "Why? What was odd about it?"

"Not odd," she protested. "Just… Well, you see, Ella Kohler had had a babe that was stillborn. So tragic. She was just inconsolable." Her eyes filled with sympathetic tears. "The family feared for her health. So anyway, they decided Paul should take her to visit her sister Jessie, who was out West then. And when they came back a month later, they had a baby girl with them."

He considered that for a moment. "You mean no one knew that they were going out there to adopt a baby?"

"No. Well, I can't say what the family might have known and kept silent, but most folks were surprised. Happy for them, that's certain sure, but surprised. Still, maybe they didn't find out about the boppli needing to be adopted until they got out there."

"I understand that Joanna was born to a distant cousin out there." That was what Joanna had said anyway.

"Yah, that's what we were told." Mamm's lips clamped shut on those words, and he knew that was all she'd say on the subject.

But it wasn't everything he wanted to know. There had to be some logical reason for the resemblance between their mystery woman and Joanna. And it seemed more likely by the moment that it was through Joanna's birth mother, whoever she was.

JOANNA ARRIVED AT Cathy's to find her coming toward the house from the phone shanty, a small white frame building with just enough space for a telephone, an answering machine and a phone book. Once more she was grateful that the quilt shop made it necessary to have a phone.

Not that she would use it for chatting, but it was useful. And it allowed her to be the contact point for any messages that had to be passed on about the school. She still shuddered a little at the thought of the day Cathy had called her, saying there was a stranger on the school grounds who might have a weapon. She'd rather not relive that again.

"Catching up on your messages?" she asked as Cathy reached her.

"I am, and a gut thing I checked it." She made a face indicating disapproval. "Rachel called. Her father isn't feeling well, so she thought she'd best stay home with him."

Maybe if she could say something outrageous it would relieve her feelings. "He's perfectly healthy except when Rachel wants to go out. If she'd just walk out on him once—"

"She won't." Cathy pushed open the back door. "If she could, she wouldn't be our Rachel, ain't so? Komm, I have soup and sandwiches for supper, and then I thought we could get the dresses cut out if we have time."

"Why wouldn't we have time?" Joanna took off her bonnet and smoothed her hair back.

"There was another message," Cathy said. "From your aunt. She's over at your parents' house, and she wants you to stop for her after we're finished."

"Really?" She turned back to Cathy from the coat hooks. "That's funny. She didn't say anything about going out when I left her this afternoon."

"Maybe she didn't know then." Cathy set two steaming bowls of ham-and-bean soup on the table and removed the waxed paper from the plate of sandwiches.

"My folks are out for dinner at Daad's brother's. Lots of visiting going on for a weeknight."

They sat down, and Cathy led the silent prayer that began every meal. Once they both had their sandwiches, Cathy went back to the subject of Rachel. "I just wish we could think of some way to get Rachel out of the house more." She looked speculatively at Joanna. "I don't suppose you need to hire anyone at the shop."

"Afraid not. Between us, Aunt Jessie and I can manage the number of customers we have, and we're not making enough to justify hiring someone. Maybe next summer, if we get a few more tourists in town..."

Cathy nodded, understanding. "A regular job would be a challenge anyway. Her father expects her to be there when he needs her."

"Those two brothers of hers are old enough to do a few things around the house." Joanna's tone was sharp, not that it did any good. They both knew that Rachel's brothers, just like her father, considered anything in the house to be women's work. "I'll tell you one thing... I won't easily give up my independence to be at anyone's beck and call."

"It doesn't have to be like that," Cathy said, and her gentle face glowed with love. "If you love someone..."

"Yes, we know you found the perfect man in Michael. And you love his little girl like your own." She smiled, hoping to eliminate any hint of sarcasm. "You are fortunate. And so is he, for that matter."

"I know." Cathy spoke with such conviction that Joanna's heart felt oddly empty.

It wasn't that she was jealous of Cathy, she hastened to assure herself. And she certain sure wasn't thinking of Noah. But still…

Forget it, she told herself firmly. This was Cathy's special time, and she had to focus on her.

She succeeded so well that they were in a gentle ripple of talk and laughter all the time they were finishing the meal and spreading out fabric. Joanna was enjoying herself so much that she'd forgotten all about the DNA test and the stranger who might be related to her.

Until, that is, she glanced out the window and saw that the sun had not only slipped below the ridge, but that even the orange glow it left in the sky was fading.

"Look outside." She put Cathy's scissors back in the sewing box. "I didn't realize how late it was. If I'm going to go over to Mamm and Daad's place to pick up Aunt Jessie, it's time I was leaving."

"Ach, you're right, Joanna. I'm so sorry. I should have paid attention. Now, don't try to clean up. I'll take care of it. Let's get you on the way."

They went out together. As always, it didn't seem quite so dark once Joanna was away from the light, and she climbed up in the buggy. It would be full dark by the time they reached home, but thanks to Noah, the back lights would make it easy to take care of the mare.

It wasn't far to the family home, and most of the drive was on single-lane roads with no traffic. She pulled to a stop at the porch, ignoring Princess's obvious wish to head for the barn. She'd expected Aunt

Jessie to come rushing out, scolding her for not being here earlier, but it was Daad who came out to meet her.

He took the lead rope and clipped it onto Princess's headstall. "It's gut to see you, daughter. Komm in."

She held back. "Doesn't Aunt Jessie want to get on the road?"

"Not yet. There's something we must talk about." Holding her arm, he hustled her in the back door to the kitchen.

Aunt Jessie was pouring out coffee. Mamm took one look at Joanna and rushed to hug her. She squeezed her back, used to Mamm's frequent hugs. But this was different. When she drew back, Mamm's eyes were filled with tears.

Fear sent Joanna's imagination into high speed. Something was wrong.

"What is it? Are you sick? Is Daad sick? Did something happen to one of the boys?" The words spilled out in a rush.

"No, no." Aunt Jessie set the mugs on the table and pushed her toward a chair. "Nothing like that. Just sit down so your daad can talk to you."

But at the moment Daad was bending over Mamm. "You don't have to stay. Why don't you go and lie down?" His tone was persuasive, but Mamm started shaking her head and just kept on doing it. She sat down with an abrupt movement that was almost falling and wrapped her arms around herself.

Daad exchanged a look with Aunt Jessie. She shook

her head slightly, and he pulled a chair over so that he sat facing Joanna, but within arm's reach of Mamm.

"Stop worrying, Joanna." He clasped her hand briefly and then drew back. "No one is sick."

He was silent for a moment, his face brooding. She had no idea what to say, so she didn't speak.

Daad took a long breath. "Your aunt told us that you were going to have that DNA test today."

"Yah." The change of subject sent her thoughts off in another direction. "It just took a couple of minutes. They took a sample from me and from the woman, but they won't have the results for a few days, at least."

Her father's face grew even more solemn, if possible, and the light finally dawned on her.

"This is about the DNA test, ain't so? You're worried about something it might expose. But I already knew that someone else was my birth mother. It doesn't matter. You are my parents." She glanced from Daad to Mamm, to find that her mother was weeping silently. Tears slipped down her cheeks, one after another as if there was no stopping them.

The tears stabbed at Joanna's heart, and she rushed around the table to her mother's side. "Mammi, it's all right. Don't cry. Everything will be all right."

Those were the words her mother had used for everything from a broken doll to a broken heart, and they covered a fierce longing to do anything that would make the pain stop.

"Nothing can change my love, Mammi. Please." Her voice choked with tears, and she couldn't go on.

Daad reached across Mamm to pat her shoulder.

"Hush, now, Joanna. Just listen, please. It's the best thing you can do." He waited, his solemn gaze compelling her agreement.

She nodded and settled onto the chair, holding her mother's hand. "You know that your mammi and I had a babe that was stillborn, yah?" Daad winced a little as he called up that grief.

She nodded again. Was Mamm weeping over that long-ago child who hadn't had a life?

"Mamm was so grieved." He seemed to look into the past and see pain there. "She couldn't seem to get over it. We were all so worried about her. Finally, your aunt suggested I bring her out to Ohio to visit for a time, thinking a change might be good for her."

She knew all that already, but she didn't speak. Obviously, Daad needed to tell this in his own way.

"We hired a driver to take us there, but it seemed like everything went wrong. The weather turned bad, and the car started to have engine problems. It broke down entirely when we were in western Ohio. It was snowing hard—I couldn't remember a time when it snowed so heavy. Anyway, someone took us to a motel where we could stay the night. It was filled with people stuck because of the storm."

He paused, seeming to see that snowy, stormy night. Joanna could almost see it, too—the lights of the motel nearly obscured by the snow piling up. Mamm would have been so relieved to be inside a building. She didn't like traveling in a car at the best of times.

"So we were safe for the moment, and I was able

to reach your aunt. She arranged to send a driver for us as soon as anyone could travel. So we went to bed, thinking tomorrow would be better." He paused as if gathering his strength. "We were almost asleep when we heard something rattling at the door. At first, I thought it was the wind, but then I heard what sounded like a baby's cry."

Joanna understood then. She almost didn't have to hear the rest of the story, except of course that she did. She had to know all of it.

"Your mamm rushed to the door before I could move. She opened it. There was a basket, like a laundry basket, by the door, with a baby in it." He met her eyes. "With you in it."

She looked from his face to her mother's, hardly able to believe. A baby on the doorstep—it was like a storybook. She sat here in the kitchen that had been the center of family life ever since she could remember, hearing something that knocked her life completely askew.

"We brought you in, out of the cold," Daad said. "That was all I was thinking, to get you inside. But your mamm—she gathered you up in her arms and held you close, and her face was filled with such joy as I had never seen. She held you and she wouldn't let you go."

Mamm stirred slightly. "You were my baby. The answer to my prayers. I knew it." Her eyes glistened with tears, but there was a trace of the joy Daad spoke of in her face.

Joanna found her own eyes filled with tears. "But…

you mean you just kept me? How did you do it? You mean no one found out? How could that be?"

"No one knew. That was the only way it could have happened, you see. We were far from home, and no one knew us there." Daad's face was drawn with fatigue and strain.

Aunt Jessie spoke. "Let me," she said, and Daad nodded.

"There was a note in the basket with you. It said to please take you for their own. That the birth mother couldn't take care of you, but when she saw them, she knew they'd love and care for you." She shook her head slowly. "I can scarcely believe it happened, looking back. But when your Daad and Mamm got to me, they had a baby. Your mamm… I don't think she could have survived if you'd been taken away."

"She picked us," Mamm said. "The baby's mother. She picked us to have her baby to love. And we did." She got up suddenly and went toward the stairs. Joanna started to go after her, but Daad caught her hand and drew her back to her chair.

"I know what she's getting. It's all right."

"We were wrong to make that decision," Aunt Jessie said, with a quick glance to be sure Mamm was out of earshot. "At least where the law was concerned. We struggled with it. But if we tried to take you away, I feared what would happen. Your daad and I decided we would live with it, for your mother's sake." She hesitated, emotion showing in her face. "And yours, too. You were loved with us. We wouldn't send you back to a woman who gave you up, even if the police could have found her. She'd said she couldn't take care of you. And they might have put you in a foster home, or an institution. How could we let that happen?"

Joanna knew she ought to be appalled by what she was hearing, but in her numbed state she could see exactly how it had happened. That poor, desperate young mother, not knowing where to turn, finding the very people who were willing and longing to be her child's parents. She understood. Now what was she to do?

For an instant she wished she could erase the first step that had led to this moment. If the stranger had never come to her door, if Noah hadn't seen a resemblance, if she hadn't gone to the hospital...

Before she could find a word to say, Mamm was back. She held something in her hand, clutched against her breast. When she reached the table, she put it down in front of Joanna.

"There. It was in the basket with you."

The object glistened in the yellow glow of the lamp. It was a fine gold chain, so short it could only have been worn by a child. From it hung a tiny gold heart. She touched it lightly, struggling to understand.

A gift from her birth mother? Her heart winced at the thought.

"I couldn't give it to you," her mother said, "but I couldn't throw it away."

She met her mother's gaze and found it filled with love and a kind of desperate longing.

Joanna couldn't stand it. She leaned close, wrapping her arms around her mother, feeling Mamm's tears soak into the fabric of her dress.

"It's all right, Mammi. Don't cry. I love you."

But the words didn't seem to quiet her. Her body shook with racking sobs that were frightening to hear.

Aunt Jessie was there in an instant. "Ach, now, I feared that would happen." She took her sister from Joanna's helpless grasp, and her eyes met Joanna's. "Don't worry. She just needs to be quiet. You go on home, and I'll take care of her. I'll stay the night. She'll be all right in the morning."

Before Joanna could open her mouth to protest, Jessie had taken her mother toward the stairs. She started to go after them, but Daad caught her, shaking his head. "Jessie's right. She knew your mamm would take it hard, but she understands how to care for her."

"I can't just do nothing." She nearly cried the words. "I should go to her."

"It's better this way. Really, it is." Daad's face looked as if he'd aged ten years in the past hour. "Jessie knows what to do, and if your mamm sees you now, when she's so upset, she'll just keep trying to explain. The best thing is for you to go home now and talk to her tomorrow."

"I can't," she protested. But then she saw that Daad was hanging on to his calmness by a thread.

"Komm, now. You must go before it's any later." She let herself be walked out to the buggy, her thoughts in such turmoil that the chill evening air was like a dash of water in her face. She had to think—had to absorb what she'd heard and try to untangle it all.

Daad stopped in the moment of handing her up into the buggy. "Ach, what am I thinking? You shouldn't be going alone this late. I'll drive you home. One of your brothers can bring your buggy back tomorrow."

"No, don't." She grasped the seat, needing to hold on to something solid. "I'm not afraid to drive home. You…you should go to Mammi. I'll be all right. Honestly. It's not far."

His face tightened, and he kept his hand on the buggy seat. "You are angry. You think we should have told you before."

She started to deny it and then realized that part of what she felt was indeed anger. "No… Well, I guess a little. How could you keep it a secret from me my whole life?" The question came out filled with hurt. How could they? But she grasped at her anger, pushing it down. Daad was hurting, as well. They all were.

"We talked about it, so many times. But your mamm—she couldn't…" His voice roughened. "It was my decision. Blame me if you must blame."

That was Daad. The knowledge pierced the cloud of confusion, doubt and anger. Daad would always take the blame on himself rather than see someone else be hurt.

She should say something, but she didn't know what. There were decisions to be made, she supposed, but nothing should be decided in the heat of the moment. She had to have time to think about all of it. Not just about what Daad and Mammi and the faceless woman who bore her had done, but about what it meant to her. When she'd thought about her birth mother, she'd always had a vague image in her mind of a young Amish girl, someone much like her at eighteen or nineteen. A relative, someone connected by blood, someone part of the spreading tree that was Amish people. Now she had to forget all of that and adjust to being someone else entirely.

She could barely believe that Daad, so righteous and honest, and Aunt Jessie, always clearheaded and practical, had kept the secret all these years. But Mamm—Mamm was easier to understand. Mamm was afraid of losing her.

And she couldn't promise that wouldn't happen. How could she promise anything, when she didn't know who she was?

CHAPTER SIX

THE DRIVE BACK to the shop passed in a blur. It was a good thing Princess knew the way, because Joanna found herself unable to concentrate on anything. Why couldn't she put her practical common sense to work? Problems always had solutions. But she couldn't even focus on any one aspect of what she'd heard tonight. If she'd been picked up by a tornado and set down miles from home, she couldn't be more disoriented.

Thank the good Lord that Aunt Jessie had decided to stay with Mamm tonight. If she'd been sitting next to her in the buggy, she'd have wanted to talk, and Joanna felt as if she'd scream at the prospect.

She'd reached the outskirts of town, passing the greenhouses on her left and heading on down Main Street.

Princess turned automatically into the alley when they reached it. When her family had bought the buggy horse for her, Daad had pointed out that Princess was hardly the right name for an Amish buggy horse. But unlike most horses, who didn't care what they were called as long as they were fed and cared for, this mare had a definite opinion. If called anything else, she turned a deaf ear, so Princess she had stayed.

The new lights came on, showing her the area, and she drove directly to the stable. Princess seemed to share her desire for speed, and in a few minutes, she was in her stall, munching contentedly on her oats. Joanna hung up the harness automatically, switched off the battery light in the stable and started toward the back door.

And stopped. The back door hung open, and she could see the damage to the lock from where she stood. Her heart pounded, her breath caught and for an instant she stood frozen, staring at the door. She had to do something. No lights were on in the hardware store, so Noah wasn't there to rush to for help. She didn't dare try to reach the phone in the shop. The intruder might be in there.

Softly, fearing he might hear the slightest sound, Joanna crept back to the alley, the movement taking her beyond the range of the lights. The alley lay dark between her and the streetlamps out on Main Street, but she'd have to go that way to get to lights and help.

Joanna glanced back toward the stable. It looked like a sanctuary, but it could just as easily be a trap. If the intruder saw her…

He was probably already gone, she assured herself. He'd have heard the horse and buggy arrive and slipped out.

But what if he hadn't? What if he was waiting for her? She seemed to see her visitor being struck down on the stairs. No, she couldn't risk going in.

Steeling herself, she stepped into the alley, moving from the light into the dark. Shadows seemed to lurk in the darkness on either side of her. Someone could be there, hidden where she couldn't see.

She fingered the penlight she clutched. If she switched it on, she could see. But anyone who was watching would be able to see her, too. That was even more frightening. The shadows seemed to grow even denser as she went on. She was torn between running to get there faster and creeping so that she wouldn't give away her presence.

But if someone was still inside, he'd know she was there—he'd surely have seen the lights go on. Stricken with panic at the thought, she spurted toward the street, dashing out of the alley into the light. Streetlights glowed, but Main Street was silent, the businesses closed, except—

The coffee shop—it was open. She darted across the street, racing toward the welcoming lights of Miller's Bakery and Coffee Shop. Etta Miller stayed open later than anyone else in town, pointing out that people wanted coffee and sweet rolls at any hour.

Reaching the shop, Joanna yanked the door open and stumbled inside, welcoming the sound of the bell that announced her. Etta appeared behind the counter, took one look at her and came hurrying to put an arm around her.

"Joanna, whatever is it? Are you sick?" Etta's rosy, round face seemed for a moment to be getting larger and larger.

Joanna shook her head, brushing off the momentary dizziness and grateful that Etta was alone. "I'm all right, but someone has broken into our place. I have to call the police."

"Ach, that's bad." Etta seized the phone, punching in 911. As a Mennonite, she didn't have any compunction over using the phone, unlike Aunt Jessie, who always wanted to be certain sure that any call made on their phone was business.

Etta thrust the phone into her hand, and it took only moments to gasp out the facts—coming home alone, finding the back door broken in. Someone would be right there, the dispatcher said. The command not to go inside until they came was really not necessary. Nothing would induce Joanna to go in until she knew it was safe.

As soon as she hung up, Etta grasped her arm. "It will be all right now. I just hope they didn't cause a lot of damage. You sit and I'll bring you coffee."

She was already shaking her head. "Denke, Etta, but the woman said to wait outside for them."

Etta looked reluctant to let go. "All right, but you stay right there where I can see you. Is there anyone you want me to call? Your mamm and daad?"

She couldn't say no fast enough. "Don't call them, whatever you do. Mamm is sick tonight so Aunt Jessie is staying with her. A call at this hour would make things worse."

That might not have entirely made sense, but Etta seemed to accept it. Eager now to be outside when the police came, Joanna hurried out, crossing the street again to stand right under the streetlamp.

The lights were still off in Noah's store, making her wonder if the thief might have been in there, as well. She looked through the plate-glass window, but it was too dark to see if anything was amiss. Should she check the door?

She hung back, almost afraid to find something else wrong, and the police car pulled up, making the decision for her. The officer who jumped out was the same young man who'd come before, and he strode toward her, switching on a powerful flashlight.

"Now, you stay well away, miss. I'll go around back and check on the break-in site. Chief Jamison is on the way, so don't you come any closer until one of us tells you to."

Not waiting for an answer, he jogged toward the alley as if eager to find trouble. Joanna pulled her sweater more tightly around her and tried to ignore the chilly air. Now that the police were in charge, her fear had gone, but it was almost as bad to stand there and wonder what damage had been done.

Fortunately, before she could picture the apartment trashed, the display quilts slashed to ribbons, and the bolts of material splashed with paint, Etta Miller appeared with a thermos and a bag containing cups, spoons and sugar.

"Now you'll have some coffee to warm you up, and it'll be here for the police, if they want it. And I'll keep you company in the meantime."

She wrapped her fingers gratefully around the cup Etta handed her and accepted sugar. "It's wonderful gut of you, Etta. But you must want to get home to your husband."

"Fred? He's watching from the bedroom window upstairs right now. He'd be upset if I didn't stay here with you. Besides, he'll want to hear all about it."

Joanna had to smile at that. Fred Miller didn't mind everyone knowing that he was a walking encyclopedia of everything that happened in town—better than the newspaper, he claimed.

Etta seemed to echo the thought. "He'll probably be dressed and out in a minute. It's the most exciting thing that's happened all month. I hope it's not vandals. I'd much rather lose money than have my place damaged."

Joanna shivered. "That's just what I was thinking, too. I have no idea. I just saw that the back door was broken and came running to your place."

"Much the best thing you could do, that's certain sure." Etta sipped at her own coffee. "I'm so sorry to hear your mother is sick."

Etta's expression was an invitation for her to confide in her, something she certainly wasn't going to do.

"I wanted to stay, because Daad and the boys are no use when Mamm doesn't feel well, but Aunt Jessie said Mamm would be more likely to stay in bed and listen to her big sister than to her daughter."

Daughter. She repeated the word to herself. She wasn't Mamm's daughter, not really. Still, she'd grown up knowing she was adopted, and she'd…

The knowledge hit her. She couldn't possibly be

adopted, not legally. Mamm and Daad wouldn't have dared to attempt it, because they'd have to present papers they didn't have.

She pressed her fingers to her head, wishing that Etta would stop watching her. If she could talk this all out with someone who wasn't family…but that someone couldn't possibly be Etta, who helped Fred collect and distribute gossip every day along with her crullers and coffee.

Before Etta could embark on another attempt to gather information, Chief Jamison pulled up in his car. The doors opened, and she realized he had Noah with him.

A ridiculous surge of pleasure went through her at the sight, and she scolded herself. There was nothing to smile about at this point, and she should be focused on Chief Jamison, not Noah. But when Noah came quickly to her side, he brought reassurance with him, and when he caught her hand and squeezed it, she felt a rush of gratitude for his friendship.

JOANNA WAS CLEARLY rattled by the break-in, and Noah longed to continue holding her hand, but he saw Etta Miller watching them, and knew he shouldn't. So he let go of her hand, but continued to stand close to her, wishing he could do more.

"Are you all right?" He kept his voice low, not wanting to share their conversation with Etta or the chief.

She nodded, trying to force a smile and not succeeding. "No one was in the hardware store, so I had to go over to Etta's for help."

He felt instantly guilty. "I wish I'd been here. Sorry."

"Ach, don't think that. How did you come to be with Chief Jamison?"

"He came by the house to let me know about the break-in. He figured if your shop had been robbed, most likely mine was, as well."

The chief was having a low-voiced conversation with his officer, watched intently by Etta, and then they both went around to the back. "I wish they'd let us go in to see what damage has been done," Joanna fretted.

"We'll know soon enough," he said, mentally calculating how much money he'd left in the shop.

"They'll be wanting to check for fingerprints and all that." Etta inserted herself into the conversation. "They won't want you in there until they're finished."

"I hope they hurry." Joanna rubbed her arms, probably chilled in the night air. If he'd come in his buggy, he'd have a blanket in the back.

He glanced at Etta. "I think Joanna is cold. Would you have a sweater or a blanket handy?"

"Ach, yah. What am I thinking?" She headed back across the street, moving lightly for someone who weighed what she must. "Be right back."

"I don't need…" Joanna began.

"Yah, you do." His lips quirked. "I don't think your independence is damaged by accepting help when someone wants to offer it. Ain't so?"

Her returning smile was rueful. "I'm not that

prickly, am I? Okay, I am a little chilly. Or maybe just upset."

"Some of each," he said, his attention distracted by the movement of a flashlight inside his store. "Where's your aunt? Wasn't she home tonight?"

Oddly, Joanna actually lost color at the question. "No, she…she's at the farm. I just came from there, but Mamm wasn't feeling well, so Aunt Jessie decided to stay with her."

He studied Joanna's face, wondering what else was behind that statement. It would have been more natural for her to stay with her mamm, surely. Especially when she was so obviously concerned.

But she didn't offer anything more, and he didn't think a question on that subject would be welcome.

Etta bustled up to them and wrapped a heavy sweater around Joanna over the one she had on. Etta's sweater was big enough to fit around Joanna's slim figure at least twice, and Etta laughed, good-natured about her size. "Good thing I'm as big as I am. You need the extra warmth. And don't you think about sleeping in your apartment tonight. There's a bed for you at our place, so you just come over when you're ready."

Joanna managed a smile with some words of thanks, but she was obviously becoming restless, moving from one foot to the other.

"Relax," he murmured. "I think I hear them coming now."

Sure enough, the two officers came around the building. Jamison appeared to be giving instructions

to the younger man, who nodded and hurried off to
the car, reappearing a moment later with a camera.
He went back around the building carrying it, and
Jamison came to them.

"They got into both places, I'm afraid."

Noah nodded. It was what he'd expected. "They?"

"No way to know at this point if it was more than
one, but vandals usually run in packs. Whichever, at
least there wasn't much damage, so you don't need
to worry about that." He turned to Joanna. "Let's go
into your place first while Donovan takes some photos in the hardware store."

Noah decided to interpret that invitation to include
him, and he stayed behind Joanna as she unlocked the
front door of the shop. She hesitated for a moment,
and he moved a little closer. They stepped into the
darkness together.

Jamison flashed his torch around, holding it on the
light fixture while Noah pumped it and turned it on.
Joanna seemed to hold her breath while she looked
around. To his eyes, the shop's contents were disturbed, but not damaged. Various drawers had been
pulled open, and one lay on the floor. Some bolts of
fabric had fallen from the tables, but they didn't even
look dirty, much less ruined by paint.

Joanna surveyed it all and seemed more relieved
than anything. Probably, like him, she'd feared to
find open vandalism. Vandals had hit the Eschs' harness shop two years earlier, leaving machines damaged, leather slashed and hateful messages painted on
the walls. They'd all seen it, and he supposed most

Amish would have trouble getting that vision out of their heads.

Chief Jamison had caught up with the vandals, though—boys in their late teens from a suburban area near the closest large town. As far as he knew, they were in a detention facility now.

Joanna had moved behind the counter. She reached toward the cash box, but Jamison put out a hand to prevent her. "Don't touch it just yet. I'd like a couple of photos as it is. Do you know how much cash was in there?"

"Aunt Jessie left after I did, but she'd have put in what we always do to start the day—about three hundred in different denominations."

"I'll need to talk to her, but tomorrow will do. Any other cash around?"

She nodded. "There's more cash in a locked box in Aunt Jessie's bedroom. Did they get in there?"

"Looks like they just went through the apartment to come down the stairs into the shop." He gestured toward the staircase that led to the second floor. "I had a quick look upstairs, but nothing looked out of place."

Joanna winced, and Noah could feel her concern about her home. Anyone would be upset about the idea of strangers in their home. He thought about the farmhouse that had been home since he was born, and his stomach turned at the idea.

"Maybe Joanna should have a look upstairs, just to be sure."

Jamison studied Joanna's face. It looked as if he thought she might not be up to it. Noah felt sure he was wrong. Joanna was a strong woman. She'd be upset, but she'd do what she had to do.

Still, he sensed something else, something behind the surface anxiety about the shop, and he wondered.

Jamison considered for a moment. "I want Joanna to check the back room first, just to be sure nothing's missing. Why don't you head over to your place and talk to the patrolman about what's missing?"

He'd rather stay here in case Joanna needed him, but that would draw attention to feelings he didn't want to acknowledge. So he gave Joanna a look of silent sympathy and left.

IT SEEMED TO take forever for the police to finish up what they were doing, and Joanna felt herself begin to sag. Not surprising, was it? The past few hours had been the most stressful of her life. First, the knowledge that she wasn't who she'd thought she was, and then the invasion of her home and business—the foundations of her world rocked beneath her.

She was Amish, even if her birth parents hadn't been, even if Mamm and Daadi weren't blood kind. To be Amish meant knowing who you were and what your place was in the world. It meant a life bounded by the church, the home and the family. To have two of the three attacked in one evening was unthinkable, and yet she had to think about it. She had to cope.

With Jamison accompanying her, she'd checked the back room,

Where the situation was the same as the store itself—disturbed but not vandalized. Again, drawers had been pulled out and boxes opened, but nothing seemed to be missing.

A quick look upstairs hadn't revealed any problems, but Jamison hadn't let her check more closely, saying he needed photographs first.

Suggesting she wait down in the back room, the chief directed his patrolman's photography. The room was quiet, but hardly restful. She was torn between exhaustion and a nervous energy that needed an outlet.

Hearing noises on the back stairs, she went to see who was coming now. If it was more police…

But it was Noah, carrying a toolbox and coming toward her. "I thought I'd best board up the doors for the night. The chief says it's all right to do it now. Okay if I do both doors at the back? Then we can go out through the front."

"Yah, that's gut. Denke, Noah. I hadn't even thought about that yet. I don't know where my wits have gone."

"It's been a shock." His voice went deep with sympathy. "I'm feeling a bit ferhoodled myself, and I didn't walk in and find the break-in."

If that was all she had to stress her, she'd consider herself fortunate, but Noah didn't know. She tried to smile with a little success. "Can I help you with the doors?"

"Ya, gut. You can hold the boards in place while I hammer. Let's do the outside door first."

They both knew he'd be able to do it alone. He

probably thought keeping her busy was for the best. Well, he was right. She followed him to the doors.

Noah had left several boards on the bottom steps. He put one in place near the top of the door, and she placed her hands on it to hold it stationary. She and Noah were so close in the confined space that she could hear his breath and almost feel the tightening of his muscles as he lifted the hammer.

The first blow made her wince, and she had to steady herself. She couldn't let what had happened make her jump at every sound.

"Was the cash Jessie had still there?"

His question reminded her that he'd been in the hardware store while she'd accompanied Chief Jamison upstairs.

"Yah. The change that had been out in the open in a jar on the kitchen counter was gone, but they didn't appear to have looked under the bed."

He chuckled. "Jessie will be relieved by that. I'd guess they were intent on the shop receipts and didn't bother much with the apartment."

"Thank the gut Lord for that blessing. I'd hate to think of some stranger going through my clothes."

"I don't suppose Amish clothing would be much use to him."

To Joanna's surprise, she actually smiled at the thought. It seemed Noah had been right. Staying busy was better than sitting and thinking.

With the first board finished, Noah picked up another. "Two should be enough, I think. Doesn't seem likely they'd come back, but you don't want the door

hanging open for anyone to see." He darted a glance
at her, and she could read concern there even in the
dim light that came down the stairs. "You're going to
Etta's for the night, yah? Or if you want to go home,
I expect the chief would take you."

"No, not back to the farm," she said quickly.
"Mamm isn't feeling well, and I don't want to disturb her by coming back. She'd be sure to wake at
someone coming in this late." And she might start
the crying that had ripped at Joanna's heart.

Noah put in a final nail to keep the door closed, and
then he followed her to the top of the stairs. Stepping
into the hallway, he closed the door, taking a closer
look at the broken lock.

Joanna ran her fingers down the scraped wood
frame. "I think we'll be able to smooth this down
and repaint it." It had been easy, she thought. Easy
for someone to open the door and come right into
her home.

"I'd say so." Noah was already fitting a piece of
wood in place. "You can see where he put something
like a pry bar in and just popped it open. You ought
to have a chain or a dead bolt on the doors. I'll take
care of it for you."

"Denke, Noah." That reminded her of Daad's reaction. "Daad wants to pay for the lights, as I told you,
and I'm sure for the extra locks, too. He says since
he's our landlord, you must let him do that."

"He needn't, but I won't say no. Sales are scarce
enough right now."

For just an instant, Joanna caught a despairing look

in his eyes that shook her. Was he really in such a bad place financially? She wanted to express her caring but feared offending him. How complicated it could be to say the right thing.

It struck her that in her concern she was completely distracted from her own problems for a moment. Maybe there were benefits in each direction to sharing one another's burdens.

Those thoughts raced through her mind and she knew she had to respond in some way, even if she risked offending him.

"I'm sorry." Maybe the simplest thing was the best. "I didn't realize the new store was hurting your business so badly."

He nodded, for once letting his face show his feeling. "We've been counting on the store to pay off the loans Daad took on the farm."

Joanna realized he was telling her something that few people in the community knew. She was incredibly touched to know he considered her a friend. And honored that he trusted her enough to tell her. "I didn't realize the farm was so deeply mortgaged," she murmured. "I'm sorry. Your father…"

"My father." He seemed to thrust the words away from him. "When he was drinking, he couldn't think beyond the next bottle."

The suppressed anger in his voice hurt her. However much her own father had let her down by not telling the truth about her parentage, she'd never felt anything like what Noah and his brothers must have experienced.

"I didn't realize." She put her hand lightly on his. "I'm so sorry."

His jaw tightened. "Now you know why every Amish father looks at me with wariness. They don't want to consider linking themselves with such a tainted family." He spit out the words as if they tasted bad.

"You mustn't believe that about yourself." Her fingers tightened on his. "You aren't anything like your father. No one could believe that about you."

His hand turned so that he could clasp hers. He squeezed it for a moment, his fingers lingering against her skin. "Yah, they could. Why not? I do."

The words ripped into her heart, and she couldn't hold back her sympathy. "Noah, you can't think that. You're a fine person—responsible, hardworking and kind. Don't let what your father was make you think so little of yourself."

Noah detached her hand, stepping back as if he needed to create space between them. "You don't understand." He didn't say it resentfully, but as if it was an obvious fact. "You've always been the bishop's daughter. And I've always been the drunkard's son."

She tried to protest, but at his bleak, pained look, the words died in her throat. He was suddenly someone she didn't even know.

"You don't know what I might be capable of." The words seemed forced out of him. "Neither do I. But every day I'm afraid of turning into him. Afraid of being a man who could hurt the ones who love him most."

She was in over her head—lost in a tangle of sympathy and caring and feeling completely unable to do anything to counter the hard truths he threw at her. If there were any right words, she couldn't find them. She stood there mute and angry with herself for her inability to help him. And what was worse, he knew it.

"Go and get what you need for the night." He turned back to the door. "I'll finish this and walk you over to Etta's place."

When she stood paralyzed for a moment, he threw the word over his shoulder at her. "Go."

Joanna fled to her bedroom, standing in her familiar surroundings unable to move except to twist her hands together. She'd thought she was so capable, so mature and able to cope with anything that came her way.

She'd been wrong—hopelessly and childishly wrong. She'd have thrown herself on the bed and let the tears come, but if she did, Noah would come looking for her.

Moving nervously, she grabbed a bag and began tossing into it anything she needed for the night. She wrenched open the top drawer of her dresser and froze, as shocked as if she'd discovered a snake among her clothing.

She took a step back. "Noah?" Her voice shook a little. "Will you come here, please?"

His footsteps sounded on the floorboards, and then she sensed him behind her, in the doorway. "What is it?"

"This drawer. We thought the intruder hadn't

touched anything up here. But he did. He went through the contents of this drawer."

Noah didn't question her statement. He came forward, looking over her shoulder into the drawer.

"Everything is moved around. It's neat enough, but he didn't bother putting them back the way they were." She shivered. "It's as if he wanted me to know he'd been here."

"Check the other drawers in this room," Noah said. "I'll take a closer look into any other drawers or cabinets in the apartment and see if anything seems odd."

By the time she'd checked every drawer and shelf in her room, Joanna's hands had stopped shaking, and her mind had started to work again. Noah came back, shaking his head.

"Nothing obviously wrong, but you'll have to look and see if anything is missing. What could they have been looking for? Money? But they didn't touch the cash box."

"No. Not money." She held out her hand, letting the small gold heart dangle from her fingers. "I'm afraid they were looking for this." She turned and walked abruptly out into the kitchen.

CHAPTER SEVEN

ALL NOAH COULD do was to stare at the tiny gold heart swinging from Joanna's hand. A pretty thing, he guessed, but not something any Amish person would wear.

Maybe he was still reeling from the backlash of blurting out things he never talked about, but his mind couldn't seem to make any connection between the shiny object and the break-in. He looked around the tidy kitchen, trying to ground himself in reality.

"I don't understand. What is that? And why would someone be looking for it here?"

"It's a necklace for a baby or a small child." She measured out the length of the golden links.

He nodded. "Yah, I see that, but whose is it?"

"Apparently, it's mine." Joanna seemed to sway, reaching out to hold on to the back of the kitchen chair.

Her obvious distress broke through his bewilderment, and he hurried to guide her to sit down at the kitchen table. He stood over her, feeling helpless.

"Can I get you something? Some hot tea, maybe?"

She shook her head and then pressed her fingers against her forehead. "I'm all right. Too much has been happening, I fear. I shouldn't burden you with my troubles."

The way I burdened you with mine? Noah pulled a chair over close to her and sat down.

"Both our troubles, ain't so? The intruder broke into my store, too. I should know."

She rubbed her forehead again as if her head pounded with pain. "Tonight…before I came back and found the break-in…I was at the farm. Daad told me the real story about my adoption."

Joanna broke off, but his mind must be working again, because he began to see. "This is because of the DNA testing, yah?"

"Aunt Jessie told Daad what was happening. About the woman in the hospital maybe being related to me, and Daad decided I should be told the full story of where I came from. I wasn't the child of some distant relative. I was an Englisch baby, abandoned at their door."

Noah grappled with that, trying to piece it together. "So the necklace was something that belonged to you?"

"It was in the basket where they found me. Mamm had kept it, thinking one day I might want it."

"So you were Englisch." He tried to wrap his mind around it. "I can't see that it matters. The police must have tried to find out who your birth mother was before they could adopt you."

"They…" She stopped. When she started again, he felt sure she'd changed her mind about what she was going to say. "Yah, I suppose…" She stopped again, not seeming to notice that her hands, clasped on the table, writhed together as if struggling.

"Joanna." Without letting himself take time to think about it, he put his hand over hers, holding them firmly. "Tell me all the things you're leaving out so I can help."

Her hands strained against each other painfully. Then, suddenly, they relaxed under his. She let out a long breath.

"Yah. I've told you too much not to go on. The thing is that the police were never involved. The mother left me with them, leaving a note asking them to take care of me. So that's what they did."

He considered it, frowning. "They didn't tell anyone?"

"Just Jessie. They were on their way to visit her when it happened."

"But even if the mother asked them, surely the authorities had to be involved. You're saying they didn't even try to find her?"

"They didn't." Her face firmed, and she looked at him as if defying him to argue. "They did what the mother said and took care of me. Loved me. There's nothing wrong with that."

"I think the law might see it differently." The bishop, of all people, had been hiding it all these years—not just from the church but even from Joanna herself. How could he reconcile that with his position?

"We'll never know, because it won't come up." She snapped the words, pulling her hands away. "I'm the only one concerned, and I'm not going to make any complaint to the law."

"Joanna, make sense. If someone broke into the building looking for that—" he gestured toward the necklace "—it must have something to do with that woman in the hospital."

She straightened herself, and he thought she was trying to gain control of herself. "You're right. That doesn't make any sense." She pressed her hand against her forehead. "I'm that ferhoodled that I'm not thinking straight. It couldn't have anything to do with what Daad told me tonight. After all, no one else knew about it, and even if they did, why would anyone care?" Her hand closed over the chain. "It must just be a coincidence that the break-in came now, ain't so?"

Noah's head was starting to spin again. They'd been spilling out so many secrets that probably neither of them was thinking logically. "Most likely that's all it is. Stores get broken into. Everyone knows that. You're the one who thought there was something to tie the two things together."

"Yah, but that doesn't make any sense. I was so upset…hearing about how I came into the family, knowing I wasn't related to them, after all…" She struggled for a moment before going on, and his heart twisted in his chest. "The worst of it was seeing Mamm crying, almost hysterical because she was afraid of losing me." She put her hand over her lips as if to hold back the words, and her eyes filled with tears.

"Stop now." He touched her hand again, very lightly, fighting for composure. "We're both too tired to figure anything out tonight. We're arguing both sides at once. Go and get your things, and I'll walk you over to Etta's. There's nothing else you can do now."

Joanna nodded, obviously glad to drop it. "Denke, Noah. I won't be more than a few minutes."

She disappeared into the bedroom. He resolutely shut his mind to everything but what to do next. The back doors were taken care of, and Joanna could lock the front when they went out. He gave one last look around as Joanna came back out of her bedroom, carrying a small bag.

"Komm," he said, taking the bag. "You've done all you can. Tomorrow you can tell Jamison the whole thing and let him figure it out."

Joanna stopped halfway down the stairs, turning to face him. "What are you saying? I'm not going to tell Jamison this story. Do you think I want to get Daad and Mamm in trouble?"

His jaw tightened at this closing of her mind to facts. "Joanna, think about it. You have to tell him. There's that woman in the hospital. This might be what he needs to identify her."

"Nonsense." He could almost see her temper spike. "How could that help him? We already decided it couldn't have anything to do with her. I won't have my parents harassed by the police. What they did was done to protect me, don't you see that?"

She turned and marched down the stairs and across the shop, apparently thinking that settled everything.

Well, it didn't. He caught up with her at the outer door, grasping her arm to keep her from going out.

"You can't ignore it, Joanna. You could be putting yourself in danger. What if the intruder was after that necklace? What if you were here when he came in? Use a little common sense."

She yanked the door open. "Go out," she snapped. "My common sense is telling me that I don't want to hear another word. This is my business, not yours."

He wanted to pull her right back inside and keep her there until he could convince her. But he couldn't. Jamison was sitting in the police car, watching them. And even if he weren't, this wasn't the time or the place. Too many painful secrets had been pulled into the open tonight.

Nodding, he stepped outside and waited while she locked the door. When she'd finished, she snatched her bag away from him and hurried across the street. He saw Etta open the door, and Joanna vanished inside without a backward look.

BEFORE SHE COULD leave behind Etta's abundant hospitality the next morning, Joanna had to fend off multiple attempts to discourage her from going back to the quilt shop alone. Much as she appreciated Etta's helping hand the previous night, she really just wanted to get back to normal.

The bright sunshine seemed to forecast another beautiful fall day, and above the town the ridges were blanketed in gold and orange. After very little sleep, the clear light assaulted her eyes to the extent that she longed to retire to her own bedroom for a nap, but that wasn't going to happen. One way or another, she'd have to cope with the aftermath of too many storms hitting her at once.

Pausing for a moment outside the shop, Joanna glanced at the autumn display in the front window. It was just as appealing as it had been when she arranged it, and beyond the window, the first few rows of quilting fabric were as they should be. From this vantage point, no one would guess that the shop had been broken into.

She should feel relieved, but she couldn't quite manage that. Still, it could be a lot worse. An image of broken windows and paint-splattered quilts crossed her mind, and she chased it away while she inserted her key in the lock. A careful glance at the hardware store told her Noah wasn't in yet.

That was just as well. She hadn't yet decided how she felt about him after the baring of so many emotions. After picking up the newspaper that lay on the stoop, she tucked it under her arm and went inside.

"Aunt Jessie?"

Calling out wasn't really necessary. If Jessie had arrived, she'd make her presence felt. At the first sight of her aunt, she'd have to intercept her, so that she didn't try the blocked door.

The sunlight picked out the few things that were out of place in the shop...an emptied drawer on the floor, a stack of receipts strewn across a display of place mats, the place where the cash box normally sat. She dropped the newspaper on the counter, hung up her sweater and bonnet and set about putting things to rights. If they were going to open today, the faster the shop was returned to normal, the better.

The sound of a buggy drawing up in front proved to be her brother dropping off Aunt Jessie. She reached the door in time to wave to Zeb, her youngest brother, as he grinned and drove off down the street...hoping to see a couple of his friends on this unexpected trip to town, she supposed.

But there was something even more important than the break-in to be addressed first. "How is Mamm?" she asked, holding the door as her aunt came in.

"Better this morning." Aunt Jessie gave her a cursory glance and then a second, more intent look. "What..."

"Someone broke into the shop while we were out in the evening." She said it quickly, wishing she could get it all out on one breath. "But thank the Lord there wasn't much damage—just to the back doors and the cash box."

Jessie walked quickly to the back counter, her gaze swiftly darting from side to side. She reached the checkout counter and ran her hand across it, touching the smeared surface where the police had checked for fingerprints. "They took the cash box?"

"No, the police did that—something about keeping it for evidence. The lock was broken in any event, so we couldn't have used it." Shaken by the gray look on her aunt's face, she grasped her hand. "It's not so bad, really. They only got the money that was in the box."

"Yah. Could have been worse." Jessie pulled her

hand away, always determined not to show emotion. "What about upstairs?"

"Not much." She almost blurted out her conviction that her bedroom had been thoroughly searched, but she managed to hold back. "The box under your bed wasn't touched. They took the cash in the kitchen jar, but that was all I could find missing."

As for telling Jessie anything else…that required some thought. In the clear light of day, she felt sure that the break-in didn't have anything to do with her parentage or with the woman in the hospital bed.

Jessie slapped her hand down on the counter, making Joanna wince. "Ach, the nerve of them!" She stared at Joanna. "And you—you came back and found this all alone. Why didn't you call us?"

"I would have, if I could have been sure Mamm wouldn't hear and be disturbed. I didn't want her any more upset."

"No, I guess not," Jessie said grudgingly. Since the thieves weren't here to vent her wrath on, she'd have to find someone else. "What are the police doing about it? Tell me that."

She had to admit she didn't know. What would they do to find the thief?

"The hardware store was robbed, too. The police brought Noah to see what was missing, and it was just his cash box, as well. He blocked the broken doors for me, so I didn't have to worry about anyone else getting in."

"You didn't sleep here last night!"

"No, no, Etta asked me to stay there. And don't say

I should have come home," she added, trying to fend off an argument. "I'd have woken the whole house coming in at that hour. Anyway, by then I was ready to drop where I stood."

Jessie nodded reluctantly. "Kind of Etta. She's probably telling her morning coffee regulars all about it."

"We couldn't hope to keep it quiet anyway. News travels fast in River Haven." Joanna reverted to the worry that lurked in the back of her mind. "You're sure Mamm doesn't need a doctor?"

Her aunt's face softened. "She will be all right as long as she knows you still love her."

"Of course I do." She blinked back tears. "I just don't understand why they didn't tell me the truth instead of saying my mother was a distant cousin."

"Yah, it's easy to see that now, but then… You were a baby. You wouldn't understand any of it. It was all your daad could do to insist you know you were adopted."

"I grew up," she pointed out. "If I'd known even for the past few years, it wouldn't have been such a shock."

Aunt Jessie seemed to wrestle with the words. "You can't understand what it was like. Your mamm was grieving so much after losing a baby that we feared she'd never recover. That's why she was so convinced that God sent you to her. Whenever your daad suggested you were old enough to know the truth, she got so upset again… You saw her last night. We couldn't do it. And we were afraid you might be taken away if it got around. They might say your parents had no right to you."

Joanna wrestled with that question, her concern deepening. "What if it turns out the woman in the hospital is my birth mother's kin, what then? The police…"

"You can't tell the police." Aunt Jessie was as shaken at the idea as she had been when Noah suggested it. "I know it would be wrong to lie, but you don't have to volunteer any information, do you?"

Joanna had a feeling that there was something wrong with that reasoning, but it gave her a way out of a potentially difficult situation. "I guess not."

Her aunt gave a quick nod. "Gut. Now, let's try to forget it for the moment. We'd best get ready to open." She stopped. "Or can we open today?"

"I meant to call the chief's office and make sure it's okay. I guess I'd better do that." She pulled the phone toward her, flipping open the newspaper as she did. Her hand froze when she saw the photo at the top of the front page. It was a picture of the woman in the hospital bed.

Jessie, sensing something amiss, moved to look over her shoulder. Joanna heard her release her breath in a soft hiss.

"So that is the woman."

"Yah." She scanned the article quickly. It didn't name the quilt shop, though everyone local would know it was hers. "I didn't know the police were going to release a photo to the newspapers. The chief said he didn't want to, but I guess he didn't have a choice."

"Seems like the best way to find out who she is." Jessie's cross response to anything she didn't understand or approve of was normal for her. "Better than fooling around with any blood tests."

"We'd best bring the other cash box down, I suppose. And I should make that call." She picked up the phone, hoping to encourage Aunt Jessie to head upstairs, and was pleased when she did.

In a few minutes she was connected with Chief Jamison.

"Joanna, I should have called you earlier. Is everything all right? No more problems?"

Suppressing her doubts, she tried to reassure him. "Aunt Jessie is here now, if you want to come by and talk to her. And is it all right if we open today?"

"I don't see any reason why not." He chuckled. "You might get some extra customers for curiosity's sake."

"We'll take their money anyway," she said, trying to sound untroubled. "I see that you put a photo in the paper today."

"Yeah, and it's being just as much of a nuisance as I thought it would be. Dozens of calls, none of them much use, but we have to check them out anyway."

"If it leads you to her family, it will be worth it." She wondered again why no one seemed to be looking for the woman. She must have family or friends who were worried about her.

"I hope." He didn't sound confident. "One good thing is that the papers in the bigger towns are picking it up. You'll notice that I didn't mention any connection to the Amish."

"All the Leit will appreciate it. We don't want any publicity."

"You won't get any from us. I have to go now but tell your aunt I'll stop by to see her later today."

"I will. Denke."

She hung up, realizing that Aunt Jessie was coming down the stairs.

"Well? Did you ask him what he's doing about the break-in?"

"He's going to stop by later to talk to you, so I thought you'd like to get the information straight from him. And we can open, so we'd best get moving, ain't so?"

That was the best thing to happen anyway. Aunt Jessie was probably more capable of coping with Jamison than she was, and her thoughts were so entangled right now she didn't know what she might say.

As Jamison had predicted, the shop was busier than it had been in weeks. To give people credit, most of them bought something, although enough of them were just plain nosy to sour Joanna's mood. She had to admit that it hadn't been that cheerful to start with.

By afternoon, needing a break, she slipped out the back, crossing to the small paddock next to the stable. Princess came over to nuzzle her hand, and Noah's buggy horse stuck his head over the fence, too, just in case any treats were being given out. Reminded by their nudging, she went into the stable, reaching automatically for the metal can that held carrots. She had pulled out two carrots when the memory struck her.

That night—the night she'd found the woman on the stairs—she'd found the can on the floor with the lid off, carrots tumbled out of it. She'd intended to tease her brother, but in all the excitement she hadn't thought of it from then until now.

She went back out to the paddock slowly, distracted from what she was doing by the thoughts that tumbled through her mind. Did the placement of the pail mean anything? If someone unexpected had been in the stable that night...

Princess snorted, craning her long neck around the corner post in an attempt to reach what Joanna held forgotten in her hand.

She managed to chuckle. "There now, Princess. You have your mind on your stomach, as usual. All right, I have a treat for each of you." She held out the carrots, one on each palm to avoid a disagreement, and the horses nibbled delicately in a taste test and then downed them in a few bites.

"Greedy creatures." Noah's voice spoke behind her, and he reached around her to push their heads away as they tried to convince her they needed more. "You looked as if you were a thousand miles away just now."

Joanna tried to ignore the awareness that slid through her at his voice. "Maybe I was." She turned toward him, frowning. "The night that the accident happened, before I found the woman, I went in the stable to check on the mare. The can that we keep carrots in was on the floor, open. My brother had stopped by to feed and water. He'd never leave it that way."

Noah seemed to grasp the implication quicker than she had. "You think someone else was in there. The woman?"

"Maybe, but why?" Her head was starting to spin again. "If she was looking for me, what would she be doing in the stable?"

"That's another question you can ask her when she wakes up, ain't so?"

Joanna nodded. Noah clearly didn't suspect the thought that had crept into her mind even while they were talking. What if someone else had been in here—someone watching the woman or following her?

That was a foolish thought, wasn't it? Too foolish to mention even to Noah. There'd never been a hint of anyone else with the woman or of anything suspicious about her fall. She was imagining things, and she knew why. She was trying to connect that with someone breaking into her home and searching through her things the previous night.

"Joanna."

Noah's voice recalled her from her wandering thoughts.

"I was watching for you to come out. I wanted to talk to you about last night."

She met his gaze, and an awkward silence fell between them. His expression said he wanted to speak but couldn't quite manage it.

Apparently, this challenging topic was up to her.

"I am sorry for losing my temper. That should never have happened. Please forgive me."

"No." He held up a hand to stop her. "I'm the one who should apologize. You had just come through one crisis after another, and at a time when I should have been sympathizing and helping you, I put even more pressure on you with my own petty frustrations about my father. I don't know what was wrong with me."

Joanna didn't know whether to laugh or cry. Did he really think she found his troubles petty? She longed to say what she'd felt but was afraid of opening up a painful subject. "Maybe we should say that we were both having a bad night and try to forget about it."

"That's generous of you, Joanna." Noah was frowning, clearly not ready to forgive himself. "I'm afraid that I let my feelings about your father affect what I said."

She blinked, taken by surprise. "I don't understand." He'd talked about the humiliation and embarrassment of having the bishop and the ministers come to his house, but how could he blame them? "He and the others were trying to help your father. What else could they do?"

"I know. I know." He touched her wrist lightly as if in apology. "I tell myself that now, and I know it's true. But sometimes I still feel like that humiliated kid who felt sure everyone was talking about his family."

Joanna closed her hand over his, feeling his pulse thudding against her palm and wondering if he also felt hers. "I'm sorry. I wish I had known, back then, how you felt. But I didn't realize any of what you went through. The grown-ups did, I guess, but they must have kept it from the kinder."

"Yah, I guess." He shook his head as if to clear it and drew his hand away from hers. Her skin felt chilled where his warmth had been. "What's past is gone. I shouldn't let it affect me. If you can forget what I said, I'd be grateful."

He was acting as if he could actually dismiss the past and its pain, but she thought it wouldn't be so easy to do. Any more than she could ignore the questions about who she really was and whether or not the woman in the hospital was related to her.

Noah cleared his throat, and she suspected he was as wary of saying too much as she was. "I saw the photograph in the newspaper today. Let's hope it gets some results."

"It won't unless it gets more widespread coverage than just here in River Haven. If anyone in town knew her, I'm sure we'd have heard about it by now. But the chief said nearby newspapers were showing interest."

He nodded. "It's an unusual story. I'd guess other papers would pick it up just because it's different. Someone is going to identify her. I'm sure of it. Then you can stop worrying so much."

"Somehow, I don't think it will be that easy, but if they do…" She hesitated, not sure it was wise to say what she thought.

"Then the DNA test won't be so important." Noah finished the thought for her. "Ain't so?"

She nodded. "Maybe it's being cowardly, but I'm feeling like you did about your father's troubles. I don't want our family issues to become public property."

"Yah. I never thought of that, but I certain sure should understand if anyone does."

"I wish…" Joanna let that trail off, not sure she wanted to say what she'd been thinking.

"What?" He moved a little closer to her as if ready to hear a secret.

"I would still like to know if she is related to me. But that seems selfish, especially when I think about how upset my mamm has been. It might be easier for her if I never knew either way."

"But would it be easier for you?" His voice was low, and she sensed caring in the gentle question.

Joanna raised her eyes to his, knowing how troubled they must look. "I don't know, Noah. I really don't. But I think I probably won't have a choice about it."

Noah was very still for a moment, looking down at her. Then he took her hand gently in his. "If there is anything I can do. Anywhere, anytime. I'll be here."

He held her hand in his for another moment. Then, before she could guess his intent, he raised it to his lips, pressed a light kiss on it and then let go and walked away.

CHAPTER EIGHT

JOANNA HAD TO force herself not to run back to the shop. Noah's action in kissing her hand had been completely unexpected. She hadn't done anything to give him the impression... No, she couldn't have. Just because he'd been a friend when she needed one, that didn't mean that she expected or wanted anything else.

"Where have you been?" Aunt Jessie's tart voice greeted her as she came into the shop. "Chief Jamison wants to see you, not me."

"Now, Ms. Jessie, I didn't say that." He followed her aunt, looking a little harassed, as people usually did who'd gotten the rough side of her aunt's tongue. "I'd like to talk to you later about the break-in, but right now I need Joanna's help." He glanced meaningfully at the few customers in the shop, all of whom were watching him.

"Why don't we go into the back room to talk?" she suggested, and hurried him out of their sight.

"Whew." He closed the door behind them. "Can't say I enjoy having all those women listening so closely to every word."

"I'm sorry if Aunt Jessie was a little…abrupt. She's been upset."

"It's okay. Anyone would be. The impact of being robbed hits people the same no matter how much was taken. Anyway, that's not what I came about. You remember what I said about getting a lot of crazy calls about the picture in the newspaper?"

She nodded.

"Turns out the Philadelphia paper ran it, and there was a tip that came out that might be serious. Not much, mind you, but a name anyway. Meredith Bristow. Ever heard of her?"

"I don't think so." The name didn't mean anything to her, except that it was obviously Englisch. "Was there anything else?"

"The thing is, we don't have anything but the name. The hospital staff tried mentioning the name to her, but she didn't respond. Mary Ellen suggested that if you asked her about the name, she might respond, seeing that you're the only one to get anything out of her."

Joanna pushed away the thought that at the moment she'd like to be left alone. "Yah, of course. Do you want me to come now?"

"No time like the present." He was already opening the door, so Joanna followed him back into the shop. He went outside rather hurriedly, and she explained the situation to her aunt.

"I guess you have to do it." Her response sounded like grumbling, but Joanna could see past it to the worry that lurked behind the words. Unfortunately, it seemed whatever Joanna did would cause problems for someone.

"He wants me to come now. Will you be all right?"

"Yah. Go." She turned away.

Joanna looked at her helplessly for a moment. Then, with a brief touch of her arm, she hurried out to the waiting car.

They were halfway up the hill to the hospital before she'd managed to focus on what was ahead of her. "So that's all you want from me? Just to see if she'll respond to the name?"

He gave a short nod. "That's all we have now. I put someone onto checking out the name in Philadelphia and the surrounding area, so we might know more soon."

"I hope it works out." She hesitated. "I guess if it does, you won't need the results of the DNA test, because she'll be telling us who she is. Did you hear anything yet?"

"Not this soon. Maybe in a few days, since the laboratory is rushing it. Yeah, I'd like to have this cleared up by then."

Joanna nodded, but she didn't know what to wish for. If only it could be cleared up without involving Mamm and Daad...

By the time they neared the patient's room, Joanna found she was repeating the name over again in her mind. But Meredith Bristow didn't mean anything to her.

Mary Ellen was waiting at the door. "So, Chief, I

see you took my advice. Joanna's the only person our patient has responded to."

"Would you have expected more from her by now?" Joanna paused by the door.

Mary Ellen shrugged. "Seems as if her coma is lighter every day. So much so that we wouldn't be surprised if she'd started talking anytime today."

"Let's hope this makes it happen." Jamison ushered them inside. "Here we are, Joanna. It's all up to you."

Again, Joanna hesitated, not liking the burden they seemed to be putting on her. She turned to Mary Ellen again. "Is it bad that she hasn't wakened by now?"

"I wouldn't say bad." Mary Ellen sounded as if she was being deliberately cautious. "Sometimes people wake up after quite a long time. But yes, it would be more encouraging if she'd done it by now."

"Just give it a try." Jamison, apparently tired of the delay, took Joanna's arm and led her to the chair next to the bed. "Remember, Meredith Bristow."

Pulling her arm away, Joanna sat down. If he thought she was annoyed, well, she was. It wasn't fair to put all the responsibility on her.

Then she looked at the woman's face, and the irritation slipped away. She did look much more normal today. She seemed to be in such a light sleep that Joanna would expect her to open her eyes at the slightest touch.

Joanna touched the slack hand lightly and then covered it with hers. "I told you I'd come back to see you again. You look much better today."

Chief Jamison moved restlessly, clearly wanting a

more direct approach. But when the patient had responded before, it had been to an ordinary conversational tone.

"I hoped maybe you could talk to me today. Or open your eyes. It's such a beautiful fall day here in River Haven. I'm sure you'd love to see it."

The hand under hers twitched—she was sure of it. She glanced at Mary Ellen, who stood at the foot of the bed, watching them intently and saw that she understood. Jamison moved again, looking as if he'd speak, but the frowning look he received from Mary Ellen seemed to silence him.

Joanna focused on the still face. "Do you remember me? I was here to see you yesterday." To her amazement, the woman's face was no longer still. She frowned, forehead crinkling, almost as if she tried to remember.

"That's right. We talked yesterday. You had an accident, and I found you on my stairs. My name is Joanna Kohler."

Her eyelids fluttered slightly. Joanna held her breath. Surely, the frown meant that the woman could hear her.

"Are you Meredith? Meredith Bristow?"

The eyelids fluttered again, faster. Then the woman's eyes opened. She moved her head slightly, and her frown deepened. Joanna felt as if no one breathed, waiting.

The woman focused on Joanna's face, looking at her with golden-brown eyes that grew more focused by the moment. Her lips moved. "Joanna."

Joanna's heart leaped. "Joanna, that's right. I'm Joanna. Are you Meredith?"

"Meredith," she repeated slowly. Her gaze drifted away, seeming to lose focus.

Joanna tightened her grasp, feeling as if she had to keep the woman anchored in the present. "Talk to me. Please," she said softly.

"Joanna. Meredith." It was the softest of murmurs. And then her eyes closed, and she slid away into sleep.

NOAH HAD SEEN Joanna go off with Chief Jamison earlier, and since then he'd been divided between watching for her to come back and wondering what had gone wrong now. Not that it necessarily had to be something bad, but the way things had been going for Joanna recently, it probably was.

She had confided in him, and she'd trusted him with her secret. He'd wanted to do anything he could to help her. And instead, he'd taken a liberty that any unmarried Amish woman would resent if not from someone she was courting.

Why had he kissed her hand that way? He could only tell himself that it had seemed the most natural thing in the world. They had been so close in that moment.

He had tried to express his regret, and she had taken it lightly. Maybe...maybe she was telling herself that their relationship was serious. Maybe she was expecting a proposal.

And that was impossible. He'd told Joanna a little about the pains of growing up with an alcoholic and abusive father, but he hadn't told her the fear. He hadn't told that to anyone—the fear that deep inside, he was like his father.

He looked out the window again, hoping to see the car bringing her back, but he might as well not bother. She'd probably never trust him again, let alone confide in him.

There was a step behind him. "Not so busy now, yah?"

Managing a smile for his younger brother wasn't hard. "No, not busy." And it probably wouldn't get any busier.

"You think I could go out for a couple of minutes?" Caleb's blue eyes looked innocent enough, but Noah suspected he had his fingers crossed behind his back.

"Let me guess. You want to go down to the gas station and get a soda out of the machine. And see who else is hanging around."

Caleb grinned and nodded. "I'd come right back."

"Half an hour, right? Not a minute more."

"Right. Denke, Noah." He was halfway to the door when he turned back toward Noah. "Are you... Are you really worried about the business?"

The question, coming haltingly from the little brother he'd always tried to protect, caught him by surprise. It took a moment to arrange his face in the properly cheerful expression. "Not really, no. People will come back, once they've tried the new place. Most of them anyway." He hoped.

"Gut." Caleb's smile flashed. "Because I want to be in business, too." He sobered. "Aaron keeps saying

I belong on the farm, but he doesn't know what he's talking about. Joshua's the one who's got farming in his blood, not me."

Anyone could see that, except Aaron, it seemed. He imagined an unpleasant talk with Aaron would be coming up—at least assuming the store didn't go under.

"I wouldn't worry about it," he said. "Things will work out."

Reassured, Caleb plunged out the door. He stopped for a moment, looking around probably in search of someone he knew, and then sauntered down the street.

It seemed young Caleb had been thinking of the future. Well, Noah would have to make sure he had his chance. That was why he and Aaron had been working so hard, after all—to give the younger ones a good start and Mamm the security she'd never known.

While Noah was still looking at the street through the front window, he saw the chief's car pull up. Joanna got out, saying something to the chief, and then disappeared into the quilt shop.

That was a relief. He could imagine her father's reaction if he saw his daughter riding through town in the police car. That would not be the bishop's image of his family.

It seemed he was still thinking negatively of Joanna's father. He'd left Joanna with the impression that those feelings had been outgrown, but maybe that wasn't so.

Noah was busying himself by cleaning an already

spotless show cabinet when Joanna came through the door, setting the bell ringing.

She smiled up at it, and then turned the smile on Noah, making him feel as if she'd reached out and squeezed his heart.

Tossing his paper towel in the wastebasket behind the counter, he took a step toward her.

"I didn't expect to see you this afternoon. It looked as if you were tied up with Jamison." He was sorry the moment the words were out. They made it sound as if he expected her to tell him what was going on.

Her face actually lit as she looked at him. "It's gut news. At least, I think it is. The chief had a tip that she might be a woman named Meredith Bristow, from Philadelphia. He wanted me to talk to her again, and she actually woke up, at least for a few minutes," she added cautiously. "She seemed to respond to the name, but then she drifted out again. But it's a wonderful gut sign, ain't so? And the chief will try to get someone who knows Meredith Bristow to identify her."

"That is gut news. I'm happy for her and for you. They won't need the DNA, and you can leave it all behind you."

Joanna nodded, but her expression puzzled him. Was that regret in her eyes? He was tempted to ask but pushed the idea away. Best to leave well enough alone. Probably the woman's family would whisk her away to a Philadelphia hospital, and Joanna could go back to normal.

Joanna shook her head as if shaking off her worries.

"What am I thinking? I am here to get the dead bolts that the chief said I should put on my doors."

"Dead bolts are the thing to do, but I remember saying that I'd be happy to take care of it." He kept his tone teasing, but was this a polite way of saying she could take care of her doors by herself?

But her smile reassured him. "I'm wonderful glad to have you install them, but I don't see any reason why I shouldn't pay for them. Retail price, too."

"I'm not charging you retail price, so don't you even think it. My friends get a discount. You know that."

"You'll never get rich that way," she warned, smiling.

"It's gut I don't want to be rich, then." He brushed aside his worries about the shop so he could keep the conversation light. It seemed clear that Joanna wanted to pretend those moments when he'd kissed her hand hadn't happened, and that was fine with him. "I'll stop over after we close with my tools and the locks. If that's okay with you, that is."

"Yah, sure. But what is the price?" With a show of determination, she reached for her bag.

"I'll have to look up what I paid for it. You can pay me when the job is done."

Before she could continue the argument, Caleb came in, looking uncommonly pleased with himself, and he was saved from more discussion of something he was determined to do.

By CLOSING TIME, Joanna was ready for a long nap, and a glance at her aunt showed her someone who needed it even more. Jessie's face was drawn and her usually brisk movements slowed almost to a stop. Joanna's heart clenched. Most of that was caused, she knew, not by too much work and too little sleep, but by the sheer emotional stress of the past two days.

"I can finish up here," she said impulsively. "Why don't you lie down for a bit?"

"I'm not dead yet." Jessie glared, but then she seemed to try to relax her face. "At least we had plenty of sales today, even if some folks were just nosy."

"I think most of them were trying to help. Once folks know you've had trouble, they rally around."

She couldn't help but think that the hardware store had been empty of customers when she'd been there. And she hadn't seen anyone go in for the rest of the day. He'd been broken into, as well. She'd think his customers would be curious.

Maybe it had to do with the fact that most of her customers were female. Amish women were the primary source of information gathering for the Amish grapevine, after all.

A thump from the rear of the building had them both looking up. "Sounds like Noah is here to do the locks," her aunt said. "You'd best go through and see if he needs anything. I'll take care of finishing the receipts."

The mildness of her tone when she spoke of Noah was a change. Maybe, in view of everything else that had happened, Joanna's friendship with Noah Troyer didn't seem such a problem, after all.

It's not as if there's anything between us, Joanna

reminded herself. *A man and a woman can be friends, can't they?*

"Denke, Aunt Jessie. I guess we'd best make sure the doors are secure." She escaped before Jessie could decide to object.

By the time Joanna got to the back door, Noah had already removed the boards that secured the door and was looking at the doorknob.

"This doesn't seem damaged," he said, moving over to make room for her beside him. "I think you'll still be able to use the lock in the knob if you want. We'll add the dead bolt, and you can lock it that way at night."

Her shoulder pushed his arm as she leaned closer to see. "You're not thinking of putting a chain on?"

"The dead bolt is more secure." He glanced at her. "You're not changing your mind, are you?"

She shook her head, trying to tell herself that she wasn't affected in the least by being so close to him. "I trust your judgment on it. Caleb not here to help you?"

"I set him to work mopping the floor. He had enough of an outing today already."

"He was looking awfully pleased with himself when he came back. Whatever you sent him to do, it must have been pleasant."

He chuckled, and she liked the sound. He'd been too solemn lately, between the break-in and his troubles with the business.

"Caleb's lucky he wasn't supposed to be doing any work for me. If he had been, he couldn't have been chatting with a girl down at the soda machine."

"So that's the attraction. I wondered why he was so devoted to helping lately."

Noah gestured for her to hold the door steady. "It's not just being in town. I don't think so anyway. The boy really does have a mind to be in business, but Aaron thinks he should be helping on the farm."

She could see that it worried him. He'd taken on responsibility for the whole family, she knew, and it must be difficult with the three younger ones and his mother to support. Wishing she had some wisdom to offer, she found some words drifting into her mind.

"My daad always says it's no good setting a boy's hand to the wrong plow. If Caleb isn't a born farmer, Aaron's bound to be disappointed."

Noah stopped what he was doing for a moment to look at her, smiling just a little. "The bishop has it right, as always, I guess."

"Are you being sarcastic?" she asked, remembering the feelings he'd revealed to her only last night.

He shook his head, his eyes crinkling. "No, I'm really not. I hope maybe I've outgrown some of the resentment I used to carry."

"I'm glad," she said simply, letting her hand rest on his arm for a brief touch before drawing it back.

Noah moved away slightly. "It's not going to be much use for Caleb to learn the business if the hardware store fails."

"It can't. Really. I'm sure your customers will come back after the novelty wears off. And anyway, you still have your Amish customers, don't you?"

Now he lifted his eyebrows. "Do I? I haven't seen much of them in the past week, either."

For a moment Joanna was too shocked to speak. "Seriously? I just don't understand that. My Amish customers might go off to a bigger fabric store for dress material. I do myself, since I mostly carry quilting fabrics, but they still come to me otherwise." Her temper was rising as she spoke. "The Leit should support each other."

"Maybe you shouldn't go around telling them so," he suggested, his lips quirking. "They might not like it."

"I don't care about that a bit. I'm ashamed of them."

His face seemed to close up. "There's a difference between supporting the bishop's daughter and the son of the community's drunkard. Face it, Joanna. You had the answer about Floyd, but you can't do anything about this."

"We have to," she said, moved by his pain. "Please, Noah. Let me help." She put her hand on his, and this time she didn't immediately pull it away. And he didn't move.

They were so close she could hear his breath, so close she could see the tiny networks of lines around his eyes. Something seemed to tremble in the air between them. His eyes darkened, and the slightest movement would have made their lips touch.

Then Aunt Jessie called to her from upstairs, and the spell was broken. Noah began putting his tools in the toolbox.

"I'd best get on to doing the front door." He turned away, carefully not meeting her eyes.

It didn't matter whether he looked at her or not. The attraction was there…real and very intense. And this time they both knew it.

CHAPTER NINE

JOANNA FOUND SHE was tensing as she turned the buggy onto the farm lane late that afternoon. She'd rather hoped that Aunt Jessie would join them for supper, thinking she might be a cushion between Joanna and her mother's tearful reactions to the true story being out. But her aunt had insisted that it was best for Joanna to go alone and try to get the situation back to normal.

That was odd, no matter how she looked at it. If things were normal, her mother would be the first person she'd talk to about any problem that came up. All her life, Mamm had been the one she could turn to, and now she was afraid to speak to her.

Maybe it would be better today. After all, Mamm had had time to get used to her knowing the truth of how she'd come into the family. Surely, if she was careful not to let any hint of blame into her voice, she might at least mention it.

Clinging to that hope, Joanna pulled up at the back door, as always. Zeb waved to her from the kitchen garden, where he seemed to be picking the last of the fall crop of lettuce. Tossing a handful into the strainer he carried, he leaped over a row of winter squash and hurried in her direction, thrusting the lettuce into her hands.

"Why didn't you come a little earlier?" His grin emphasized the dimple that, at twelve, he'd give anything to be rid of. He wouldn't believe her when Joanna insisted that one day he'd use it to appeal to the girls. "You could have done this instead of me. It's woman's work."

"Get used to it, little bruder." Her heart warmed at the usual teasing. "You've got a few more years to go before you have a wife to pick the lettuce for you."

"Yuck." He grabbed the lines from her. "I'll take care of Princess. You can help with supper."

"Okay. Just to please you," she said. Reminding herself that she was going to act normal, she went on into the kitchen.

"Mamm, here's the lettuce." She'd barely gotten the words out when her mother turned from the sink, tears brimming over at the sight of her.

"Ach, Mamm, don't." She dropped the strainer into the sink and hurried to embrace her mother, feeling a mixture of guilt, pity and sheer frustration at not being able to make everything better. "It's going to be all right." Those were the words her mother had used each time Joanna's young world crumbled. She could only hope they'd work the other way around.

Mamm clung to her for another moment, and then drew back slowly, wiping away tears. "Ferhoodled, that's what I am." The scolding tone was reassuring. "I was just thinking of you, and then I turned around and here you are."

"Yah, I'm here, just in time to help with supper. Zeb traded me—he'd rather take care of the horse." She picked up the strainer of lettuce and held it under the tap. "I was surprised you still have some lettuce from the fall planting."

"Not much more." Mamm was obviously trying to sound normal. "It's only because the weather has held. So we'll enjoy it while it lasts."

"What can I do to help?" She glanced around, looking for something that needed doing.

"Everything's almost ready," Mamm said. "So set another place at the table while I get the biscuits from the oven."

Relieved to hear her sounding like Mamm again, Joanna threw herself into the last-minute flurry of getting the chicken cut and the potatoes dished up so that everything arrived on the table still hot. Daad and the boys trooped in, and another in the endless line of family meals got underway.

Joanna felt her inward tension easing as she sat in the chair she'd had since she left the high chair. The usual talk bounced around the table—what everyone had done today, what was planned for next week, who needed to make a trip to the lumberyard or the hardware store.

At the mention of the hardware store, she focused on Jonas, the oldest of the boys. "I hope you're going to Noah's hardware store and not that new place out on the highway."

Startled, Jonas glanced at Daad. "Yah, I guess."

"Why would you say that?" Daad leveled a frowning gaze at Joanna. "We always take our trade to him."

She felt almost as if she'd insulted him, but at least it gave her a chance to say what she needed to say. "Noah's business has been off ever since that new chain store opened, and it isn't just the Englisch customers. The Leit has been going there, too."

Joanna sensed that Daad's deepening frown was no longer aimed at her.

"That is not right. Our people support one another."

"Noah has certainly supported me and Aunt Jessie. Today he came over and put new dead bolts on those doors that were broken."

There was a momentary silence—long enough for her to realize that she'd said something wrong.

"What doors?" Mamm looked up, alert. "Why were they broken?"

Joanna glanced at Daad, but he seemed to be leaving explanations to her. It hadn't occurred to her that he'd succeeded in keeping the break-in from Mamm.

"Somebody broke the back doors at our shop and at Noah's." She kept her tone light. "But everything was all right." Seeing the fear in her mother's eyes, she hurried on. "You should have heard Aunt Jessie when she saw it. If she could have gotten hold of whoever it was, they'd have been sorry for the rest of their days. Kids, I guess, looking for mischief."

Jonas, picking up his cue, jumped in. "I wouldn't want to get on the wrong side of Aunt Jessie, that's for sure. But I'd have come and fixed it for you."

"No need," she said easily. "Noah was right there,

and he had to fix his door, too, so it wasn't any trouble. He says the new locks would keep anything out."

"That's wonderful kind of Noah," Mamm said, and everyone breathed a little easier. "Be sure you thank him for us."

"I will, Mamm."

"And pass the biscuits to your bruders," Mamm added. "They are always hungry."

"That's right," Zeb chimed in. "I'm still a growing boy, remember?"

Isaac nudged him. "You'd best do it in a hurry, or you'll never catch up with me."

Zeb elbowed him in return.

Back to normal, thank the gut Lord. Joanna handed the basket to Zeb, who was closest.

Obviously, Daad had decided to keep quiet about the break-in as far as her mother was concerned, but wasn't it better that she knew at least a version of it? She could have heard something from a neighbor that alarmed her.

She glanced at Daad, but she couldn't talk to him about it now.

As always, she helped her mother with the supper cleanup, but it wasn't really the same. Did Mamm realize that? She was talking about the worship services leading up to Fall Communion, saying how busy Daad would be. But was her voice a little too high, her words a bit rushed? She'd like to try to bring Mamm's worries, whatever they were, to the surface, but for the first time in her life she wasn't sure where she was with her own mother.

Was Mamm afraid that their relationship was forever changed? She'd think that the calming influence of the normal family meal would reassure her, as it had Joanna. But Mamm had been worrying about this for a long time, so it must be harder for her.

That was the point, wasn't it? Mamm's worries and fears, whatever they were, went back to that snowy night so long ago. Her knowledge of it had created a chasm between them, whether she wanted it or not.

It wasn't until she was loading a loaf of homemade bread and half an apple pie into the buggy, over Zeb's objections in regard to the pie, that the subject of the woman in the hospital came up. And it came from Mamm, oddly enough.

"That woman who had the accident," she said, "how is she doing? Is she better now?"

"Yah, much better." She glanced at Daad, who nodded. Apparently, this was safe to talk about. "The chief called the store to say that they'd contacted some relatives, and I'm sure someone from her family will be with her soon."

"That is gut news," Mamm said, patting her arm as if she'd been the one injured. "It's a shame not to have family nearby. She'll be going home soon, then, won't she?"

"Most likely," Daad said. "Her people will want to take her back where she belongs, even if she needs to be in a hospital there."

And then we can all forget her. He didn't actually say the words, but Joanna sensed what he was thinking. What they were all thinking, she suspected. This unknown woman had come into their lives and forced change on them. Now she would go away, and everything would go back to normal.

But Joanna wasn't so sure. Would that heal the rift she still felt in her family? Or would it just cover it up with a thin patch that would break at the slightest strain?

One thing she knew, she realized as she climbed into the buggy. She wanted to see Meredith once more before she vanished back into her normal life. It wasn't all that late. She could stop at the hospital on her way home for one last chance to find out what had brought the woman to River Haven and to her door.

NOAH LINGERED AT the hardware store long after he'd closed, finishing an inventory he'd started earlier and then balancing the books. That sad task proved to be a reminder of just how bad the past month had been. How long could he keep going if his customers didn't come back?

Frustrated, he headed out back, making sure the dead bolt was fastened and hoping Jessie and Joanna had done the same. There was no sense in putting in proper locks if you didn't use them.

But when he reached the stable, Noah found that Joanna's mare and her buggy were missing, even though the lights were on upstairs. Had she gone to her parents' place? Relations there were most likely still very touchy, he'd guess. From what Joanna said about her mother, she was taking this hard. Remembering his mother's words about her grief after losing a baby, his heart winced. Maybe they'd been wrong in keeping Joanna without telling anyone, but he could understand how it happened.

He hadn't missed Joanna's reaction when he'd suggested that with the injured woman's family found, she'd soon be leaving. Everyone else involved would breathe a sigh of relief, but not Joanna. Her stubborn need to know the truth was going to be thwarted, it seemed.

Soon on his way, Noah realized it was a little later than he'd thought. All the stores on Main Street were closed, and the empty sidewalks looked lonely. Time he was home, and no doubt he was due for a scolding from Mamm, who would have kept some supper warm for him.

His way led past the hospital, and he glanced at its bland red brick, wondering if the woman's family had arrived yet. He'd think...

He lost that train of thought as he started past the section of the parking area devoted to buggies, empty now except for one very familiar one. It had to be past visiting hours, but it seemed Joanna was still there. Still in search of answers, he supposed. Without even thinking about it, he turned into the parking area.

Given that it was past visiting hours, someone might kick him out, but he walked down the hall to the elevator without a problem. The woman at the reception desk was turned away from the door, talking on the phone. She was still talking when he entered the elevator and the doors slid closed behind him.

If Joanna's buggy was here, she was here, and the

only place she could be was in Meredith's room. He forced himself to stop calling her "the woman." Now that they knew her name, it was disrespectful.

The elevator stopped. He stepped out into the hallway. No one was at the nurses' station at the end of the hall, so he turned toward the room, grown familiar by so many visits. Noah found himself walking quietly in response to the stillness of the area, thinking how oppressive silence could be in a place that was usually bustling.

Joanna was there, on the far side of the bed. Someone in hospital scrubs towered over her. For an instant he didn't know what he was seeing. Then he knew. The man had his hands on Joanna's throat.

Panic and fury surged through Noah, sending him flying toward them. He barreled into the figure, grappling for a hold to rip the man's hands away from Joanna. He yanked one hand free and both of them crashed against the wall, rattling his teeth. The man got a hand free and knocked him back. His head hit the footboard of the bed and he saw stars.

Joanna—he had to get to Joanna. He shook his head, trying to shake away the mist before his eyes. Vaguely aware of the swish of the door, he stumbled toward Joanna, who lay on the floor, gasping for breath.

"Help," she managed to whisper. "The call button…" She gestured toward the cord that dangled from the bed.

He grabbed it, pressed the button and then shouted for help, his voice echoing in the room. Joanna caught his arm, using it to pull herself to a sitting position.

"Wait, take it easy. Lie there until someone comes."

But she was shaking her head before he finished. "Meredith." Her voice rasped. "Pillow. He... I came in... Pillow on her face." She struggled, trying to rise.

"It's okay. You stay quiet."

The pillow wasn't on the bed. It had been tossed or fallen several feet away. He bent over the woman, murmuring a silent prayer. She was breathing. Thank the good Lord, she was breathing.

"I think she's all right." He grasped Joanna's arm. If she was determined to get up, she would, with or without his help. "Really. There's nothing you need to do."

Running footsteps sounded in the hallway, and the door flew open, letting in a nurse and an aide, followed in a few seconds by a security guard.

"Call the police. Someone attacked Joanna and tried to hurt your patient."

The nurse bent over her patient, rapping out quick orders to the aide to check on Joanna. The security guard was inclined to argue about the police, wanting to question Joanna himself, but when Noah reminded him that the chief was responsible for the woman, he scowled and turned to the phone.

Suddenly, there seemed to be nothing he needed to do. Noah leaned against Joanna's chair, longing to put his arm around her. Was it a comfort to her to know that he was there? He felt better at being a touch away.

The aide checked Joanna's neck, murmuring at the vivid red marks of the man's fingers. At an order from the nurse, she rushed out to retrieve an ice pack.

"How is she?" Joanna whispered, nodding toward Meredith.

"She's fine." The nurse came around the bed to bend over Joanna. "Better than you, I'd say. Who did this?"

Joanna tried to shake her head but stopped, hand going to her neck as she winced. "I couldn't tell."

"A man," Noah said. "Wearing hospital scrubs… A mask covered his face. I never got a good look at him."

A couple of minutes later he was repeating the same thing to Chief Jamison, while one patrolman went off with the security guard to find out if anyone had seen the man leave, and the other began a minute search of the room.

"He had one of those white things over his hair. I never got a good look at him."

"You're sure it wasn't anyone you knew? Think. You have to have seen more than hospital clothes and a mask."

Easy enough to understand what had put the sharp edge to Jamison's voice. He'd thought his problem had been resolved with the woman identified and her family ready to take charge of her. Now someone had thrown a monkey wrench into his neat solution, and he was inclined to blame anyone around.

"He was about my height, I think. Sorry, but that's all I can say. It was over almost before it started."

It occurred to him, belatedly, that although he hadn't struck the man, he might well be considered guilty of breaking the church's stand on nonviolence. Since he knew he'd do the same again, he couldn't bring himself to regret it. A glance at Joanna, leaning back in a chair with ice packs around her neck, assured him that saving her was worth any cost.

Seeing Jamison turn to Joanna, Noah wished he had something else to say, just so that he could give her a few minutes' respite. But Joanna made the effort necessary to sit up, and her answers, delivered in a whisper, didn't add much to what he'd said.

After a chat with the aide, she'd come in quietly and seen who she took to be a doctor at Meredith's bedside. She'd almost retreated so as not to disturb him, but when he picked up the extra pillow from the bed and pressed it over Meredith's face, she had rushed to her defense. To the chief's disappointment, she couldn't give any sort of description of the man, either.

"I would if I could. But like Noah said, he was all covered up." Her voice rasped and she put a hand to her throat, wincing.

The need to protect her was stronger than any other consideration. "I think I should take Joanna home," he said, before the chief could plunge into more questions. "She ought to be in her own bed with her aunt taking care of her."

Jamison looked ready to snarl at him, but at that moment the aide pushed the door open. "There's someone downstairs, asking for the patient, Chief Jamison. He says he's her cousin."

"Tell him to wait there. I'll be with him in a few minutes." He turned back to them. "All right, you take Joanna to her aunt. I'll send Donovan along with her buggy. He knows horses. Meanwhile, I'll deal with this cousin. If you think of anything—the slightest hint—that might help identify him, you call me immediately." His scowl would be enough to cow anyone who dared to argue. "I'm putting a guard on this room, and nobody is getting in unless I say so."

There seemed nothing else for them to do. He helped Joanna rise, cherishing the way her hand clung to his arm. Carrying the extra ice bags the nurse forced on her, he led her away.

JOANNA MOVED RESTLESSLY, trying to block out the light that intruded on her sleep, but it was no use. She forced her eyes open, tried to sit up and barely suppressed a groan. A light touch informed her that her neck was even more painful than it had been the night before. Still, she couldn't stay in bed. Too many jobs loomed ahead of her.

Slowly and cautiously, she sat up and swung her feet to the floor, feeling the familiar braided rug under her toes. She was back in her own bed, in her own room. She was safe. She pressed her fingers to her temples, trying to get her thoughts into some sort of order. Noah had brought her home, saying little as if knowing how hard it was for her to speak, and delivered her to Aunt Jessie with one last comforting clasp of her hand.

Jessie had fussed and scolded, of course, but her hands had been gentle as she'd tended to Joanna, comforting her with a cup of tea with honey to soothe her throat and tucking her in bed with the ice packs arranged on her neck. Neither of them had mentioned sending for her parents.

She'd never thought she'd sleep with the memories of hands closing around her neck. But there had been comfort, too, remembering Noah's arm protectively around her when he drove her home. The comfort of his embrace stayed with her after he'd left, and she'd fallen asleep at last.

Forcing herself to her feet, she'd taken one step when the door opened, and Aunt Jessie surged in.

"You're up," she said. "I'd hoped you'd still be sleeping. You need your rest, but that Jamison is downstairs, and he says he has to see you. I told him to come back later, but he wouldn't."

It sounded as if Aunt Jessie was building up a strong resentment against Chief Jamison. Joanna tried to sound better than she felt.

"It's all right. Just tell him I'll come down when I'm dressed." She reached for the dress that hung from a hook on the wall and winced.

"I'll get your clothes ready for you." Aunt Jessie bustled around the room, arranging Joanna's clothes on the bed and keeping up a string of annoyed comments.

"You'd best go back and speak to the chief before he loses patience and comes up here. Then I'm fixing something soft for you to eat. Cream of wheat will slide down easily, so don't bother to argue."

Joanna gently turned her toward the door. "I'm all right. It's just my voice." She could hardly disguise the raspy whisper that was all she could manage.

Aunt Jessie gave her an assessing look and nodded. "Better wear a sweater," she said, and stalked out, clearly disapproving of Chief Jamison and all his doings.

Dressing as quickly as she could, Joanna moved to the mirror to pin up her hair and blinked at the sight. The red marks on her neck had darkened into livid bruises. A plain dress wouldn't hide them. Jessie had been right about the sweater. She pulled it on, arranging the sweater's neck to cover as much as possible, and stood back to look at the result.

Not good, but the best she could do. And now she'd best go and rescue Chief Jamison from Aunt Jessie.

She found them silent but glaring at each other, and she could only be relieved no one was in the shop this early. "I'm sorry to keep you waiting."

"My fault." Jamison met her at the bottom of the stairs. "I'd have waited until later, but Ms. Bristow's cousin was on my doorstep at dawn, insisting on seeing her."

"I thought you wanted him to see her, so he could confirm her identity."

Jamison's face hardened. "After what happened, I'm not letting anyone see her until I'm sure they're okay. That's why I need you. Come on."

"But what—" she began, but Jessie charged into battle.

"Look at her. Poor child hasn't even had her breakfast yet and you want to drag her off. It's ridiculous. What are you thinking?"

"Aunt Jessie, it's all right. But I don't know what you think I can do. I've never met the man."

If possible, Chief Jamison's ruddy face got even darker. "Sorry. I'd just like to get this cleared up. You go ahead and eat something. I'll wait."

Knowing perfectly well she couldn't choke down any food with the chief waiting for her, she shook her head. "I couldn't get anything down now. Later, I'll try." This last was addressed to her aunt, who nodded but sniffed in an unbelieving way.

"Good. I mean, well, this won't take long. I just want you to see the man before I let him in. He could be the man who attacked Ms. Bristow."

She was about to say that she couldn't recognize him, but that would just encourage Aunt Jessie to argue, so she followed Jamison out to the car.

By the time they reached the hospital, Joanna felt as if she'd been up for forty-eight hours, and every separate muscle in her body ached. But she'd agreed to look at the man, and Jamison probably wouldn't allow her to change her mind. He led her directly to a small room off the hospital lobby where he said Landon Bristow was waiting for him.

She went in a little hesitantly, hoping the chief didn't intend to call any attention to her. A man stood by the window, talking on his cell phone. He glanced at them while continuing to talk, giving Joanna time to assess him against her slight memory from the previous night.

Well dressed, that was her first thought. In a country town where men didn't wear a coat and tie except for weddings and funerals, he was overdressed. Not young, somewhere in his fifties, probably, and he had an air of expecting and getting the best of anything.

"All right, just come in the lobby. The first door on the left. I see the police officer has just arrived. Maybe we can finally get something done."

He slid the phone into his pocket as he came toward them. "The family's attorney. He came along to help get things settled."

"Fine." Jamison didn't seem intimidated, if that was intended. "The more, the merrier. I just want to get the patient identified."

"Then you should have shown her to me instead of keeping me waiting here."

Joanna expected him to add that he was a busy man, but he restrained himself. *Shown her to me.* Joanna repeated the words silently, her initial impression of the man worsening. As if Meredith were a lost item. She must have some relatives who actually cared about her.

Whether the chief would have responded she didn't find out, because the door opened to reveal the man he'd said was the family's lawyer. He came in unobtrusively, nodding to them. Assuming that the chief would want her opinion of him, as well, she tried to form one, but found it impossible. Average height, average weight, average face of the sort one would soon forget. He did have a pleasant smile, though, as Chief Jamison introduced himself.

"Tom Watson," he said, shaking hands with him.

"I hope you have good news about Meredith. Everyone has been worried."

There was the concern she expected from Bristow, and she couldn't help smiling as he looked at her.

"This is Joanna Kohler, the one who found Ms. Bristow and called the paramedics." The chief introduced her quickly. "Ms. Bristow seems to respond more to her than anyone else, so I thought it would be useful to have her there when you see her."

The attorney's expression grew warmer. "I'm sure we all owe you a debt of gratitude."

"I was glad to do what I could," she said, feeling her face flush at his words.

"If we can get on with this now," Bristow said. "I'd like to be sure it really is my cousin, so we can make arrangements about having her transferred to a hospital near her home. And then I have to get back to the office before the day is over."

Chief Jamison looked at Joanna, clearly waiting for her opinion. She gave a slight shrug. It was impossible. Her only sense of the man who'd attacked her was of someone overpowering her. It could have been either of them or someone entirely different. The thought sent a shiver of apprehension through her. She was perfectly safe with Jamison there, she reminded herself.

Grasping her meaning, he opened the door. "Let's go up." He led the way to the elevator, the others following.

Joanna began to feel more and more out of place as they approached the room, but the chief didn't give her any opportunity to retire. He ushered her inside. Bristow followed, but Mr. Watson held back.

"I'm sure you don't want a crowd of people in there. I'll wait here unless I'm needed."

Jamison nodded, ushering her over to the bed where Meredith lay, eyes closed. "See if you can get her to wake up, all right?"

"I'll try." She took the chair next to the bed. "Meredith, it's time to wake up. It's Joanna, and I've come to see you."

Her eyelids fluttered.

"That's right. Wake up now." She sensed the men moving closer.

Meredith opened her eyes, seeming to focus on Joanna's face. Her lips curved slightly and then moved. "Joanna," she said softly.

"That's right. Here's someone else to see you." She gestured toward Bristow, but Meredith didn't turn her head.

"If you look over that way…" she began, but Bristow interrupted her.

"Don't bother," he said. "I confirm that this woman is Meredith Bristow. Now, if I can arrange to have her moved, I'll be on my way."

Jamison's expression was often hard to decipher, but at that moment Joanna had no difficulty. He looked as annoyed with the man as Joanna felt.

"I'm afraid that's not possible yet," he said. "The doctors don't want her moved right now, and I can't let her go until the investigation has been wrapped up."

Bristow's face reddened. "Do you expect me to

hang around here for days? Let's see what my attorney thinks about that." He charged out of the room. Jamison shrugged and followed him.

Attorney or not, she didn't think he'd succeed in moving Meredith until Chief Jamison decided he could. There was no reason why that should make Joanna happier, but it did. As long as Meredith was here, there was a chance of finding out why she had come to Joanna and what she might have to do with the secret of her adoption.

CHAPTER TEN

JOANNA HAD STAYED on in the room when Chief
Jamison had taken the other men away. She'd en-
joyed the quiet, and Meredith seemed to like having
her there. Once Meredith had been propped up to sitting position, she'd seemed much more alert. She'd
even tried to brush her long hair until Joanna offered
to do it for her.

Sitting next to her on the bed, Joanna had eased the
hairbrush through the strands of deep coppery hair
that curled around the brush. She'd often thought how
much fun it would have been to have a younger sister
to do just this for. Of course, if she had, the exercise
would have ended in braiding the hair and twisting it
up into a snug knot to fit under a kapp. Not for Meredith, clearly.

When the nurse had chased her away at last, she'd
gotten all the way downstairs when she realized that
she didn't know where she was going. Joanna hesitated in the lobby, wondering if she should ask at the
desk for Chief Jamison. But they probably had no
idea where he was.

She'd been left behind, and it was hardly surprising
that Chief Jamison should forget, given the number

of problems on his mind. It wasn't far, so she could walk back to the shop.

By the time she'd reached the parking lot outside, Joanna knew that wasn't going to work. The fatigue that had receded in the past hour had surged back, stronger than before. She could almost sit down on the pavement and weep.

Like the answer to a prayer, a buggy pulled up in front of her. It was Noah, coming quickly around to help her into the seat.

"Denke." She leaned heavily on his arm as she sank into her place. "How did you know I'd be needing a ride?"

Noah gave an annoyed glance at the car behind, whose driver was honking impatiently. He deliberately, she thought, took an extra moment to disengage the brake and pick up the lines. Once they were clear of the portico by the front doors, he turned to her.

"Jamison called the shop and asked if Jessie could get someone to pick you up as he had to leave. Since she was single-handed, she couldn't get away without closing, so she asked me to pick you up."

"SHE ASKED YOU to pick me up?" That was unusual, to say the least. Aunt Jessie didn't like to ask anyone for help.

"Surprising, isn't it?" His slight smile teased her.

"I didn't mean it that way," she said. "And you know it. She just doesn't like to ask for help. But I'm very glad she did. I couldn't have walked back. But weren't you single-handed?"

"Caleb wanted to come in today," he explained.

"Caleb always wants to come in, doesn't he?" She remembered the teenager's expression when he'd returned from his jaunt down the street.

"Pretty much." He hesitated. "Mamm had a little talk with Aaron. She pointed out what I had, that Caleb's interested in working at the store and Aaron has Joshua to help on the farm. It's the same thing I told him, but he listened when Mamm said it."

Joanna managed a smile. "My bruders are the same. They don't dare accept advice from an older sibling, I guess."

They sat in silence for a few minutes, stopped behind a traffic light on a busy Saturday morning. Once they were moving, Noah shot a glance at her.

"Don't talk unless you feel like it. You look as if you should go back to bed."

"I suspected I looked pretty bad. But go on with what you were saying. It's no trouble to listen."

He gave a soft chuckle. "Not if you go to sleep. But I meant to tell you, speaking of bruders, that yours was in this morning right when we opened."

"Which one?" she asked, surprised she hadn't seen him in town. Still, Aunt Jessie had obviously let her sleep until the chief put an end to it.

"Isaac, the middle one. He had a long list from your father of things he said he needed." He looked at her again. "Did you have anything to do with that?"

She shook her head and regretted it, touching her neck carefully. "I didn't—well, maybe I mentioned something to Daad that you hadn't had many customers from the Leit recently. It upset me."

"Maybe that's it. Sorry. I shouldn't ask you questions when you need to rest."

She did, and the thought of her soft bed called out to her. But...

"I did want to tell you what happened this morning. A cousin of Meredith's came and identified her. A distant cousin, I'd guess," she added, remembering the man's lack of caring.

"You act as if you didn't like him."

"I shouldn't judge him, I know. But all he could think about was getting back to his business, not about her at all. But he didn't get it all his way. Chief Jamison refused to let him take her back to the city."

"I'd think he'd want her safely out of his charge."

"He said the doctors wouldn't okay it, and I suppose that's a good reason." She thought about the chief's attitude. "But he also said she couldn't leave as long as he was still investigating."

"I thought all he was doing was trying to find out who she was." They'd passed the bank, and the quilt shop was in the next block, but there was little traffic and he slowed, probably wanting to hear the answer.

"Yah, that's what I thought. But after the attack on her last night... Well, maybe he's not satisfied." She paused, hoping that investigating he talked of wouldn't lead him anywhere near her parents. "I guess you're disappointed. You wanted her to go, didn't you?"

She felt him glance at her.

"If I did," he said carefully, "it was only because I wanted to spare you all this trouble and let things get back to normal."

Her emotions, still balanced on a thin edge, wobbled dangerously. "*Normal*—I'm starting to hate that word. How can I go back to normal with all the unanswered questions? Surely, any adopted person would want to know something, at least, about her birth parents. Especially for an Amish person, given how important the family tree is to us. It's part of who we are and how we fit into the community."

Noah turned into the alley beside the shop and drew to a halt beside the sidewalk. He reached across the seat to envelop her hand in a warm, supportive grip. Friendly...and something more.

"Then that's what I want for you, as well." But he sounded almost afraid of the answer she might find. "I'll help you down."

He was around the buggy before she could say it wasn't necessary, and when she felt his strong arm supporting her down, she was just as glad to have it to hang on to. Without speaking, he kept his hand under her elbow, helping her to the sidewalk.

"Rest for the remainder of the day if you can," he said again. "Don't forget it's worship tomorrow. The first preparation service for communion."

At the thought of all the next day entailed, Joanna wanted to stay in bed. She could only hope she'd be able to disguise her bruises from curious eyes.

Noah opened the door for her, but before she could turn to thank him, there was a flurry of steps and

then her mother's warm arms wrapped about her. Joanna's tension released. Even if she didn't know who
her birth mother was, when she was with Mamm,
she was home.

"My poor little girl," she murmured, almost sending Joanna into tears again. "Why did you think you
had to go through this alone?"

"She wasn't alone." Aunt Jessie sounded as if this
discussion had been going on for some time. "I took
care of her just fine."

"You're not her mother," Mamm said, unanswer-
ably. "I'm here now, and I'll take care of her."

Patting Joanna as if she were about six and crying
over a scraped knee, her mother led her to the stairs.

"We'll put some ice on that sore neck, and some
herbal tea will soothe your throat. And then it's off
to sleep with you. Don't worry, I'll be here when you
wake up."

Joanna was torn between laughter and tears.
Maybe they'd been wrong to try so hard to protect
Mamm.

One thing was certain for the moment. The chasm
that she'd seen so clearly between them had disappeared, at least for now.

WORSHIP THE NEXT morning was at the King farm,
and Noah was out early with his mother and the two
youngest boys, while Aaron and Lovina followed in
the smaller buggy. They arrived in plenty of time, pulling into the lane in a stream of slowly moving buggies.
As they reached the back door of the farmhouse, boys

came running to take the horses and buggies, leaving them free to find the lineup for worship.

The King family had recently completed refinishing their large basement, so everyone would fit comfortably inside. Just as well, as clouds were gathering in the west, and the wind had begun to whip down the valley.

Folks were gathered at the sheltered side of the house, talking quietly as they separated, women, girls and young children to one side, men and boys to the other. He joined his brothers and tried to pretend that he wasn't scanning the other side for Joanna.

It was natural to want to see how she was this morning. After all, she was a friend as well as a neighbor, and he knew how difficult the past few days had been for her. There was nothing more to it than that.

But he didn't believe his own words. His feelings for Joanna were far more complicated than friendship. Knowing that didn't make it any easier. If only he could get rid of the deep fear of what he might have inherited from his father. Unless he could, it put marriage out of the question for him forever.

Aaron nudged him. "You can't go to sleep out here. At least wait until you're settled on one of the back benches."

"I'm awake."

He smiled back at his brother's good humor. Somehow, since Mamm had talked to him, Aaron had lost some of his prickliness. As Caleb had muttered a few days ago, if marriage made you that cranky, he didn't know why anyone wanted to marry. Maybe that message had gotten through to Aaron.

Despite his efforts, Noah didn't get a good look at Joanna until the moment when the women's line started to move. It looked as if the other women had clustered close around her, maybe to keep others from gawking and wondering.

She looked better, he thought, although the dark bruises against her fair skin had him wanting to smash something. Then they'd gone through the bulkhead doors to the cellar, each one pausing to shake hands with one of the ministers, and she was out of sight.

The worship service moved on its usual way, with a little added gravity as the Leit prepared for October communion. Noah settled himself on the backless bench, knowing it would become harder during the three-hour service. Maybe Joanna should have stayed home rather than attempt the service, but he could imagine her reaction to that suggestion.

Rain began to patter on the cellar doors, its rhythmic sound making it a challenge to those who were fighting sleepiness. Noah frowned toward his two youngest brothers, seated near the front on the men's side with the rest of the boys their age. If their heads started to nod, Mamm would be mortified, but they both looked fairly alert.

Since today was the first of the five Sundays leading up to Fall Communion, everyone knew that the service would be centered on the Nicodemus story of being born again. New Birth Sunday, it was called, and folks took it seriously as part of the preparation for communion.

The bishop began the long sermon predictably, talking about the importance of forgiveness and harmony in the church. The words struck Noah in a way that surprised him. How much was Bishop Paul struggling with that himself just now? He was suddenly ashamed that he hadn't thought more of the pain recent events must be causing Joanna's father. Both as a father and as a bishop, he had to be torn, his heart battered by events he couldn't control.

He didn't recall ever feeling sorry for the man before, but he did now, and it shook him. Maybe he'd become too comfortable with the opinions he'd formed as a boy. He was a man now, and he should be understanding that way.

These thoughts were so intense that he almost didn't notice when the bishop veered into new territory, quoting the injunction to the faithful to do good to all, but especially those of the household of faith.

"We have all been taught to do good to our brothers and sisters in the faith. We know that means supporting them in every way, whether it's taking food when someone is sick or tending their animals or helping to raise a barn. But it also means supporting each other by taking our business to Amish-owned stores and services, for that is doing good to them."

Bishop Paul took a long moment to study the faces of his people as if weighing and measuring their understanding. Suddenly, a quiver of awareness went through Noah. People were sending covert, shamed glances at him—gazes that dropped abruptly when he looked.

The bishop was talking about him. Or if he wasn't, people were taking it that way. He had a sudden desire to slide under the bench, but he knew better. His only choice was to sit here and pretend that he had no idea that the bishop was referring to the way even his Amish customers had stayed away recently.

Had Joanna known that her father was going to do this? He didn't dare look at her in an attempt to read her expression. If she'd known...

His first instinct was to be annoyed, to rebel against the idea that he couldn't make a success of the store on his own. And he knew what the bishop would say to that. The same thing his mother—or any of the older people—would say. That he was prideful. That he thought too much of himself and not enough of others.

Warmth crept up under his skin, and he set his gaze firmly on his feet and kept it there until the end of the service.

A bustle of activity burst forth as the men started turning some of the benches into tables for the traditional lunch. He watched helplessly while Joanna went up to the kitchen to help. Would he never have a chance to speak to her? If she had known what her father intended to do... He wasn't sure how that sentence was supposed to end, but he'd like to believe she'd have warned him.

Finally, the tables and benches were ready. As food started to flow down the steps, Noah ducked his way around the women and went up, trying to look as if he had some purpose. Several women were still in the kitchen, stirring bowls of the sweet peanut butter and marshmallow spread that rewarded the taste buds after three hours of restraint. The oldest King daughter, probably a little shy at being allowed to help, was urging her mother to taste-test the bowl she was mixing.

Joanna wasn't there, and he hadn't seen her go back downstairs. He slipped past the kitchen before he could be asked to taste-test anything, and went down the hall. A pantry opened up on his right, and Joanna stood with her back to him, reaching up to a high shelf.

"Is it this one, Leah?" she asked, not turning around.

"I'm not Leah King, but I'll lift it down for you."

That wasn't what he'd intended to say. He'd meant to ask if she'd put her father up to mentioning his situation, but somehow the sight of her scrambled his intentions.

His tongue, as well as his thoughts, had gotten out of his control. Having that happen once was bad enough, but it was becoming a habit when he was with Joanna.

Joanna swung around, startled by his voice, and the bowl she'd reached for slipped. Noah was just in time to prevent disaster, moving closer to her and catching the bowl in his hands.

"I've got it," he said, suddenly breathless.

Joanna grabbed the bowl, her fingers brushing his, and the touch nearly made him lose his grip.

For a moment the small room was very still. The low murmur of voices from the kitchen formed a background noise, as did the gentle patter of rain against the windowpanes.

Joanna seemed to catch her breath, and he sensed her searching for a response that might sound natural. "You should, since you were the one who made me drop it."

"If that was meant to be scolding, you didn't sound annoyed enough." He looked down into her face, so very close. Whatever his intention had been in seeking her out, it was suspended, lost in the air that seemed to tremble between them.

Think, he ordered himself. *You have to get this clear between you.* He trusted Joanna, and he didn't want to believe she'd pushed her father to defend him. It damaged that trust, and made him feel weak.

"Your father was talking about my business this morning," he said, forcing the words out.

"I…I suppose he was." The velvety brown of her eyes had golden flecks in it when seen this close, distracting him again.

Annoyed at himself, Noah shook his head. He had to ask the question. "Did you put him up to that?"

Neither of them had moved, but the air froze between them, and they were farther apart. Joanna's eyes cooled, her face growing taut.

"I did not. My father doesn't ask me for advice about his sermons. And if he did, it wouldn't be your concern." Beneath the snap in her voice, he thought he heard disappointment. In him.

"I didn't mean…" But he had, so how could he deny it? He was doing this all wrong, and he was angry with himself. He knew, only too well, that his defensiveness had become a pattern. But not with Joanna.

Before he could come up with an apology, voices sounded in the hall.

"Joanna, my mammi says, did you find…" The question died as two young girls stared at them, wide-eyed, clearly aware of having interrupted something. Then, not waiting for an answer, they departed, giggling.

"I have to take this bowl out." Not meeting his eyes, Joanna held the bowl like a shield in front of her and moved around him.

"Wait, Joanna. I didn't mean it that way. I'm sorry." But he found he was talking to the empty air, and he had a strong desire to knock his head against the nearest shelf.

JOANNA WAS BACK at work on Monday, the bruises a little less visible and feeling more like herself. She paused to look out the front window at the street, now shining in the sunlight and looking newly washed after yesterday's rain. She heard movement behind her and hurried to help her aunt with the quilt frame they'd have to set up for her quilting class.

When she grabbed one end of the frame, her aunt gave her a questioning look. "You sure you want to help with this?" Aunt Jessie sounded concerned. "I can manage."

"I'm fine now, Aunt Jessie. You don't have to baby me."

Her aunt nodded, accepting, and together they dragged the heavy frame to the spot under the windows they'd chosen. She grabbed one end of the frame and swung it into place.

"It's a shame we don't have space to leave it up all the time."

But no matter how many ways they figured it, that just couldn't be done. Everything in the shop contributed to their income and was necessary.

"Well, never mind. We'll see how this group takes to quilting. I thought they'd never get the top pieced together, slow as they were."

Aunt Jessie had been less than impressed at this particular class's abilities, and while she had endless patience with them, she always had to let off steam afterward.

"They were beginners," Joanna reminded her. "Some of them hardly knew how to thread a needle when they started and look at them now."

"Yah, look at them." Aunt Jessie gestured as if they were already there, sounding skeptical. "If Jenny Lee Moore doesn't sew her skirt to the quilt backing, I'll be surprised."

Joanna chuckled. Aunt Jessie had a point. The woman did seem to be all thumbs, but she certain sure was enthusiastic. She chattered the whole time she worked, mostly about what seemed an endless number of near catastrophes in her life.

They began to put out the layers that would become

the quilt—the backing, the batting and finally the quilt top that had been so painstakingly pieced over the weeks. They'd planned a joint project for this class, with the quilt to be donated to a nearby nursing home for one of the patients. Hopefully, he or she wouldn't mind a few inconsistencies.

Joanna let her mind drift from the job at hand, so of course it went right back to the previous day and her anger at Noah. Somehow, it wasn't as easy to drum up the anger as it had been then. He shouldn't have blamed her so quickly, but she thought he probably regretted opening up to her as much as he had. She'd known, somehow, that he seldom did that with anyone outside his family, if he even talked about it there.

She smoothed the quilt top flat with her palm, enjoying the blending and contrast of the colors. Aunt Jessie liked to tell beginners that piecing a quilt was like piecing a life together. Life had bright spots and dull ones, times of pain and times of joy, but all the pieces together could form a beautiful quilt. Or a beautiful life.

Did her parents think Joanna's adoption was a bright patch? Certainly, it had brought joy in many ways, but today's confusion and worry were a part of it, as well.

"What are you fretting about?" Aunt Jessie's question was so apt that it startled her.

"Nothing, really." But that wasn't true. On impulse she spoke. "Aunt Jessie, do you think a person…like Noah…ever gets over all the sadness and fear he experienced as a child?"

Her aunt's face showed her concern. "Has he talked to you about his daad?"

"Just a little. He said he still gets the feeling that people, even the Leit, look down on him or feel sorry for him. I wish…"

"I think I can guess what you wish," she said.

"Really? Because I'm not even sure what I wish myself." Joanna saw Noah's face again in her mind.

"This is about what your daad said in the sermon yesterday, ain't so?" Aunt Jessie shook her head. "Noah should realize that meant your daad was calling the whole congregation to repentance. Preparing for communion demands it. No one may come to the table while nursing a grudge against his neighbor. It's not just about Noah. It's about all of us."

"Yah, I know. I just wish I could help him see that."

Aunt Jessie fiddled with the roller handle as if her mind was elsewhere. "It's not easy to help someone, even if you think you know how. So often there are unexpected consequences to even the kindest deed."

Joanna suspected Aunt Jessie was thinking about her adoption, not Noah's troubles. Jessie had done what she thought was best in helping Mamm and Daad cover up the circumstances, but now so many complications had come from that.

Before she could speak, the front door rattled. They both turned to look. Chief Jamison came in with Noah following him and looking as if he'd rather be anywhere else.

"Joanna, I need to talk to you," Jamison said, and added a perfunctory, "Sorry to interrupt."

"I don't think Joanna wants me here." Noah's hand was still on the door as if he'd flee at a moment's notice.

"Don't be ferhoodled," Joanna said. "Komm."

"Go in the back room." Aunt Jessie sounded resigned. "I can take care of things."

No one spoke as the two men followed Joanna into the small room at the back and Jamison closed the door.

"Now we can talk," he said.

Joanna's mind flew to Meredith. "Is Meredith all right?"

"She's fine for now." Jamison's square face tightened. "I want to keep her that way."

"Don't we all?" Noah still looked impatient.

"Not the person who attacked her." Jamison snapped the words.

Apparently trying to control himself, Jamison shook his head. "Look, here's the situation. Right now she's in the hospital and I've got someone keeping an eye on her room, but I can't do that forever. What if that cousin of hers gets the court to send her off to Philadelphia? How can they protect her when they don't know what's going on?"

"It's not as if we know," Joanna pointed out. "I wish we did."

"Here's what I want. I need you to think over everything that's happened again. Since the attack on Saturday, I'm not content with saying Meredith's original fall was an accident."

She had never really thought it was, Joanna realized. Before she could say anything, Jamison went on.

"And what about the break-in here? Was it connected? That's where I need the two of you to think
through the whole week. Was there anything odd,
anything that didn't seem to make sense to you? I'm
grasping at straws, and I don't like it." His ruddy face
had turned the color of a brick.

Noah turned to her, and she knew what was in his
mind. "I think you'd best tell him."

Joanna closed her eyes for a moment, trying to shut
it out, but he was right. She turned to the chief, orga-
nizing her thoughts—what to say, what to leave out.

"After the break-in, when I was getting my things
together to stay overnight, it seemed to me that someone had searched my bedroom." She lifted her palms
in a helpless gesture. "I can't be positive, but I thought
everything was just a little off where it should be."

"Nothing missing?"

She shook her head. "No. I'm sure not. I went over
it again and again. The only thing I wondered about
someone looking for was this." She drew the fine
chain out from the neck of her dress and let the small
gold heart dangle from her fingers. She had to force
herself to go on. "My mother said it was given me by
my birth mother."

Jamison touched it lightly, making it swing. "That's
not the sort of thing an Amish woman would own."

"No," she said, and braced herself for the questions.

Jamison seemed to study her for a long moment.
Then he shook his head. "I don't want to know every

secret good people have. But if your birth mother was English, that goes a long way to explaining this." He pulled some folded papers from his pocket, spreading them out for her to see.

She looked at the printed sheet blankly, not sure what she was seeing.

"The DNA results," Jamison said. "The lab came through with it faster than we thought. This one is yours—" he pointed "—and this one is Ms. Bristow's. According to the analysis, the chances are very good that you're related. Closely related, like cousins or siblings."

CHAPTER ELEVEN

JOANNA STOOD, STUNNED and shocked. Jamison, looking as if he needed to escape, thrust the papers at Joanna and started toward the door.

"I'll give you a little time to get used to it. And think again about everything that happened. There has to be something that will point us to the truth. We'll talk again."

He left, closing the door firmly behind him. Joanna stared at the papers in her hand, trying to focus on the words, but they jumped and danced before her eyes. What was worse, she didn't even know if she wanted to be able to see what was written there.

Aware of Noah standing silent next to her, she held them out to him. "You look. I can't make any sense of it."

"Are you sure you want me to see this?"

She pushed them toward him again. "Why not? You already know everything that I do."

His hand closed over the pages, and Joanna was relieved to let them go. It was too much, happening too fast. Still, she'd known all along it might come to this—known from the moment when Noah had pointed out the resemblance.

It hadn't just been the resemblance, though. When she sat next to Meredith in the hospital room, teasing her gently to respond, she'd known that they were connected. She'd felt it, and that was why she'd been so determined all along to learn the truth. She and Meredith shared a bond even though they'd barely started to know each other.

Joanna leaned against the counter she and her aunt used for cutting quilt squares, needing to feel something solid. Everything else was whirling out of control, especially her thoughts. Even the familiar room with its bolts of fabric and row of quilting books seemed oddly askew.

Next to her, Noah's solid frame was the only still point. He studied the papers, frowning a little as he looked from one to the other, his eyes grave and intent. Finally, he put the report down on the table, centering it before leaning back again, his arm brushing hers.

"I don't understand all the charts, but the conclusion seems clear enough. Like the chief said, it shows that you two are closely related." He turned the frown on her. "Does that sound possible with what your parents told you?"

He was waiting for a response, but she couldn't find one.

Noah nudged her elbow. "Joanna?"

"I suppose. I mean, they obviously didn't know anything about the mother, so anything is possible."

"Yah, well, this is the answer you said you wanted, ain't so? Now you have it."

"I guess I did." She shook her head, then pressed her fingers against her forehead as if that would help settle her thoughts. "Now...now I'm not so sure."

"It's a shock, maybe. But you can handle it." His voice was steady; for an instant she resented it. Easy enough for him to be calm. He hadn't just had his world turned upside down. But that was childish.

"I thought I could, but now I look at myself and I see a little girl, playing at being grown-up. Playing at being independent and handling everything herself."

She seemed to have traveled very far in a short time, making her look back a long distance to the girl she used to be, so foolishly confident. "Now...I have to live up to what I've claimed to be."

"Yah, that's so."

Noah's voice didn't give any clue to his opinion. She wanted to look at him, to see what expression was hidden in his eyes, but she couldn't.

"I guess what I really want is to stay safe in my own little world." Joanna tried to manage a smile at her own foolishness.

"It hasn't been all that safe," he said. He touched the bruises on her neck with his fingertips, very lightly, sending a shimmer of warmth through her. "All right, so now you know. What will you do about it? How is it going to change your life?"

She frowned at him. "That's not being very sympathetic. Do you really think I know the answer to that?"

Noah's lips quirked. "Now you're sounding more like your usual self. As for being sympathetic...well, I can either prod you to face facts or I can sympathize.

And if I try to comfort you… I don't think that's a good idea." His voice was husky with emotion. "It means too much now to touch you. To me, at least, and maybe to you. I can't pretend you're just a friend, Joanna. I care too much for that."

There was no playing games about it. He was right…they were both aware of how strong their attraction was, all the more dangerous because of its strength. Whether it would lead to anything was a complicated question, so they'd best be careful. Their beliefs didn't allow anything else.

Joanna straightened, giving a short nod. "You're right. I have to face it. This is what my parents have feared all along…that I would want to know. And that, in knowing, I would want to leave them for the Englisch world."

"Is that what you want, Joanna?"

Joanna's breath caught in her throat, and she spun around. Aunt Jessie stood in the doorway. Joanna had been so deeply engrossed in what they were saying that she hadn't even heard the door open.

"To leave?" Revulsion at the thought surged through her. "No, I don't want that. At least, I don't think I do." She bit her lip.

"But you can't leave it alone, can you?" It wasn't said in a critical way, but as a simple statement of fact. Jessie knew her too well.

Joanna struggled with the answer and came up with the truth. "No, I can't. Meredith is my kin, even if she doesn't know it. I can't leave her alone when she's in danger." At least that was clear, if nothing else was.

Aunt Jessie nodded as if she hadn't expected anything else. "What are you going to tell your parents?"

"I...I don't know." She felt like a coward. "Maybe they'll never need to know."

Her aunt just looked at her for a long moment. Then she turned and walked away, leaving them alone.

"Jessie makes her feelings known without saying a word, ain't so?" Noah's expression was as disapproving as her aunt's had been.

"Don't." She felt like striking out in her frustration, and Noah was the only one there. "I don't want to hurt them. Is that so wrong?"

"Now it's my turn to say don't. Don't be so foolish. You can't keep something like that from them. They're bound to have questions. Will you lie to them?"

"If I did, would it be so terrible? I'm trying to protect them." How had she become the one doing wrong in their eyes?

"They kept the truth from you," he reminded her. "That didn't help matters in the long run." He paused, and it seemed to her that he was struggling with himself over what he wanted to say. "Listen to me, Joanna. I do know something about lying in families, even for the best of motives. I grew up with it. Mamm and I tried to keep the truth about Daad from the younger ones, and we both tried to pretend it wasn't happening to the rest of the church."

"Anyone would do the same."

"If they did, they'd be wrong." Passion filled his voice. "People know, at some level, that they're being lied to. Even if they don't admit it, they know. The kinder did, and I think it hurt the younger ones even when they tried to hide it." His face tightened, his skin drawing against the bones, making him look years older. "We tried so hard to protect Daad from the church knowing, and we probably kept him from getting the help he needed early enough."

Joanna saw the pain in his face as he admitted it. She wanted to reach out and comfort him, but when she remembered his words, she didn't dare.

"I'm sorry," she whispered.

"Just don't do it to your family," he said, the pain clear in his voice. "The truth is always better."

He went out of the room, leaving her alone. They'd all left her alone, because they knew she was the only one who could deal with this knowledge. And she had begun to fear she couldn't.

NOAH MADE HIS way back to the hardware store, thinking if he had talked to Joanna any longer, she'd probably end up angry with him again. He hadn't missed the fact that the offense she'd taken when he spoke about her father had vanished, rolled up and swept away by more recent developments. Still, he did owe her an apology for blindsiding her about the bishop's sermon.

The news Chief Jamison brought had clearly knocked Joanna off her usual steadiness. She'd thought she'd been prepared to know about her relationship with Meredith, but she wasn't.

That was natural enough. Anyone would feel the same way at finding out they weren't who they thought they were. And Joanna had such a burden to keep from hurting anyone, especially those she loved.

He had longed to help her—he still did—and the desire to put his arms around her and comfort her had almost been too strong to resist. Almost, but not quite.

Talking about his past had made it all worse. He couldn't remember his father without remembering the drinking and the violence. Without making him wonder how much of his father's weakness was in him.

Thank the gut Lord he'd never been attracted by strong drink, but the violence, turned so quickly against loved ones, wrenched his stomach. What man could truly be sure he'd never strike out against anyone, even knowing the church's teaching? His own memories were too vivid to let him risk it.

To Noah's relief, he began to have customers almost as soon as he turned the door sign to Open. Amish customers. It was pretty clear that the bishop's sermon had hit home, and he couldn't help being annoyed that people who should be his brothers in faith had to be lectured about patronizing his store.

All he could do was smile, say thank you and be helpful to everyone who walked in the door. He couldn't let customers get away because of his pride, not when he had a family to support.

Midway through the afternoon, Michael Forster

came in, no doubt prompted by the bishop as the others had been. Michael had come to River Haven back in the spring, after years away from his family and the Amish faith. He'd returned under a cloud, but he'd stayed to become a part of the community again and was soon to marry Joanna's good friend Catherine.

Noah moved forward to greet him. "Michael. Can I help you with something today?"

"Yah, denke." Michael put a list down on the counter. "I'm working on an addition to a house over near Smithton. Ready to start on the finishing, so there's a lot I need."

Noah leaned over to check the first item on the list. "Cabinet knobs and handles. The owner doesn't want to pick those out?"

Michael grimaced. "Husband and wife can't agree, so they left it up to me. Show me what you have, and I'll do my best, but…"

"They probably won't like them." Noah finished for him, leading the way to the appropriate rack. "No problem. You can exchange as many times as you need."

He stood by while Michael browsed through the selection. "I hear you and Cathy are doing up that house on the nursery property."

Michael grinned. "News flies, ain't so? We just made up our minds last week. We'll like being close to family." He took a porcelain knob off the rack. "What do you think of this one?"

"They wear well, but they're not as popular as

they once were." He shrugged. "Sounds silly that I know such a thing, but I have to carry a variety for my Englisch customers—not that I have so many of those now."

"Yah? I guess the chain store's the big novelty now. I'd think they'd come back once they've tried it. You can't match the service you get here with any chain store. But even if they don't, you still have the Leit anyway."

"Thanks to the bishop." He tried to sound grateful, but he couldn't.

Michael looked at him blankly. "The bishop?"

"Yah." He couldn't believe Michael's presence here today was a coincidence. "His sermon practically told people to buy from me."

"I must have missed something." Michael honestly looked blank. "I didn't hear anything about you."

The truth dawned, leaving Noah feeling foolish. Michael hadn't gotten the inference, maybe because he hadn't been back in town all that long.

"Sorry," he muttered. "Business has been off lately. I shouldn't have said anything."

Shrugging, Michael picked up another package of knobs and compared them. "When I came back, nobody wanted to do business with me. I figured everyone in the community was looking down on me. But they got over it. Maybe I did, too."

Michael moved on down the row, comparing various knobs and handles. Noah stood where he was, struck by the words. Michael had experienced the same thing, and it shamed him that he hadn't even realized it at the time. He of all people should have been sensitive to that in others, and it had passed him without notice.

He'd told himself he was past the damage his father had caused, but the least setback brought it surging back again with all the feelings that came with it…anger, pain, grief and, most of all, the sense that he wasn't good enough. That if he had been, none of this would have happened to him.

The truth hit him like a blow, stunning him. It was so visceral he nearly stumbled back a step. How could he have been so blind for so long? His father was dead, but as long as he held on to those feelings, the old man still controlled him.

"There now, you're ready for a trip, aren't you, Princess?" Joanna patted the mare as she led her out of the stall late that afternoon. She wanted to reach the hospital before the supper trays started coming to the rooms.

Maybe Meredith would be well enough this afternoon to talk a little more. Not that she'd be able to discuss the relationship problem, at least not yet. In fact, there was no one she could safely do that with. Aunt Jessie and her parents were too involved, too ready to be hurt by her words. And she couldn't risk upsetting Meredith by bringing up a subject that could sidetrack her recovery.

How would Meredith react to learning that Joanna was a close relative? The most likely possibility was that she'd known something about it before, and she'd come to River Haven looking for Joanna. If not...

But surely that was the answer. She couldn't imagine anything else that would bring someone like Meredith to her door.

Well, if she couldn't talk about it to anyone else, there was always Princess.

"I'll talk to you, right?" She ran the brush down the mare's back. "You won't argue."

The mare also wouldn't have any helpful suggestions, but she couldn't have everything.

"I've never known a horse to argue unless you try to go in a direction they're afraid of."

Noah spoke from behind her. After a momentary jolt to her heart, she glanced back with a smile.

"No, I guess not. Or if they're ready to head back to the barn. We used to have a pony that would charge back into the barn no matter what you did."

"Ponies can be stubborn." Noah leaned against the stall, his steady gaze seeming to assess her. "It wondered me how you were doing after Jamison's surprise visit."

"All right, I guess." Then she stopped and dropped the brush back in the grooming caddy, realizing that this was what she'd wanted—someone to talk to. "Well, not really."

"I thought not." He ran his hand down the mare's neck, his thoughts obviously elsewhere. "It was a shock to see it in black-and-white, even if you'd thought it possible."

She stared down at the caddy, not really seeing it.

"I keep trying to think it through and make sense of it. I can't talk to Aunt Jessie or my folks about it, at least not right now. They'd be too upset."

Noah shrugged. "They might be stronger than you think. They must have understood the possibility all along."

"That's different from having it in front of you to deal with," she pointed out. Easy enough to dismiss it lightly when it wasn't your family.

"Yah, I guess so. You probably never thought much about your birth mother when you thought it was a distant cousin. That kept it in the family, yah? But finding your mother was an Englischer—that's something different."

He'd hit it exactly, and his calm acceptance somehow made it easier to talk about.

"I just can't figure out how it happened. I mean, Meredith is obviously from a well-off family. People like that—they surely just don't lose track of a baby."

"Not unless…" He let that trail off.

She frowned at him. "Not unless what? If you have an idea, I'd like to hear it."

"I was going to say, not unless they wanted to. But I don't see how that could be. Do you know anything about Meredith's family?"

The question startled her. It also made her think. "Not very much. That's odd, isn't it? Since she's been identified, Chief Jamison must have found out something about her life, but he hasn't said much. I wonder why."

Noah shifted his weight from one foot to the other

as if getting ready for something. "Would there be some reason for him to keep quiet?"

"Not that I can think of. He was certainly sure eager for me to have a look at that cousin who came here with the attorney."

"She must have nearer kin than that." Noah's voice expressed disbelief, and she felt it herself. Most Amish had more relatives than they could count.

"I'd think so, too. Where are her parents? Or brothers and sisters?"

Noah's lips twitched. "Most Englisch aren't so well supplied with brothers as we are."

She had to smile in return. Having all those younger brothers made a link between them, she guessed.

"True, but it's still puzzling."

"Since she's doing better, maybe you could ask her." He nodded toward the horse and buggy. "I'm guessing that's where you're headed."

She nodded, reaching for the harness, but he beat her to it. She stood back and let him settle it on the mare's back.

"I've been afraid to ask her anything that might cause a setback. I mean, if she tried to remember and couldn't, would it be bad for her? Still, I guess I might try to bring it up if she seems better today."

Putting that idea away for later, she glanced at him as they put the harness on together, one on each side. She thought he looked as if his worries had been lifted a bit.

"Was business any better today?"

He was focused on the harness buckle, and for a moment he didn't respond.

"Yah, it was," he said finally. "Partly because of your father's teaching, I'm thinking. Joanna, I'm sorry." His voice roughened with emotion, making her own throat tighten. "I overreacted to hearing what he said, and I blurted it out to you. I shouldn't have."

"Which?" She tried to keep her voice light, afraid to give in to the emotion she felt. "Overreact, or blame me?"

"Both," he admitted. He frowned. "Still, it made me think. If I'd really grown out of my shame about my father, I guess I wouldn't be so sure that everyone is looking down on me, ain't so? Maybe we don't know ourselves as well as we think we do."

A few days ago she'd have answered differently than she did today, when she wasn't quite so sure of herself. "I guess it's the same for me, or else why do I dread so much the circumstances of my adoption becoming known? It seems like it puts me apart from the community I love, like a wall between us."

"Yah. I know," he said quietly.

Joanna stood looking at him for another moment, and it seemed that genuine understanding moved between them. Before it could change to something else, she picked up the lines.

"I'd best get moving. I'm going out to the farm to see how Mamm is after I leave the hospital."

Noah gave her a hand to the seat and looked up at her, his face serious. "I don't like the idea of you driving back alone after dark. Can't you postpone going out in the evening until someone can go with you? Or, better yet, hire a driver?"

She'd been thinking that herself, but it made her feel childish to admit it. "I'd feel so silly doing that. Don't worry. I'm used to the drive, and it's not very long." She lifted the lines.

"Be careful." He stepped back. "And if you're not back at a reasonable time, I'll come looking for you."

Smiling at what she was sure was a joke, she waved and set out. That conversation with Noah had been easier than some of their encounters recently. It was good to think they could just talk, without that fierce tug of emotion flaring up between them. Wasn't it? Still, she couldn't deny that it had been there, beneath the surface, threading itself through every word they spoke.

There wasn't much traffic on Main Street, and Joanna arrived at the hospital in a few minutes. Leaving Princess in the buggy parking area, she hurried inside.

When she stepped off the elevator, the first person she saw was Mary Ellen.

"Have you heard the latest?" Mary Ellen fell into step with her. "Our patient is sitting up in a chair and remembering more. The doctor is so pleased."

"Thank the good Lord." Joanna matched the words with a prayer. "I'm wonderful glad to hear it."

"And some other relatives are coming to see her. They're supposed to be here tomorrow morning, and I certainly hope they're better than the last batch."

Joanna had to suppress a laugh at Mary Ellen's

outspokenness. "Only one of those was a relative—a distant cousin. The other was her family's attorney."

"Imagine being rich enough to have a family attorney. We certainly don't have any use for one." Mary Ellen left her at the door to the room. "Have a good visit."

As soon as she stepped inside, she knew that Meredith had improved. She was sitting up in a chair, her long hair pulled back in a hair tie, looking at a flower arrangement on her bedside table.

"Joanna." She smiled. "I do remember your name."

"Wonderful." Joanna skirted the bed and pulled over a chair so that she sat facing her. "You look so much better. You even have color in your cheeks."

Meredith grimaced. "I'd look better with some lipstick. I don't suppose you have… No, I guess you wouldn't."

"I don't have any need for it, but I'll ask Mary Ellen to bring you some. She'll be glad to." It had to be a sign of improvement that Meredith was thinking of her appearance.

"Will you look at the card on the flowers? I can't make it out."

"Of course." Joanna leaned across and pulled out the card, which was hidden behind a large chrysanthemum. "'Best Wishes, Tom Watson.'"

"Tom." She frowned. "It seems familiar. Why can't I remember? It's so stupid." She slapped her hand against her forehead as if that would force her brain to work.

"It's all right." Alarmed, Joanna caught her hand,

wondering. She hadn't thought it odd that Meredith didn't say much when she first woke up, but this made it seem she had problems with her memory. Still, a blow to the head could affect that memory, she'd heard. Surely, the doctors would be aware. The important thing seemed to be to reassure Meredith.

"Don't fret so much. It's coming back to you every day, ain't so? You remember more than yesterday."

"You're right—I do, don't I?" The tension went out of her face, making her look younger.

She was younger, Joanna realized. Meredith was likely in her early twenties. Joanna hadn't even thought of her age before, but realizing it raised again the question of why she seemed so without family.

Meredith was still focusing on the card. "But who is he? Do you know?"

"He came to see you. From Philadelphia." She fed the information in slowly, giving Meredith time to remember what she could. "Tom Watson is a lawyer. He said he worked for your family."

Meredith shrugged as if trying to dismiss it. "The name seems familiar, but that's all."

"I wouldn't worry about it. Just concentrate on getting better. The rest will come." She hoped anyway. What must it be like not to remember whole segments of your life? Her problem was what she hadn't known, not what she hadn't remembered.

Meredith's eyes sparkled suddenly. "Maybe there are some things I don't want to remember. Don't you have anything like that?"

Heartened at the flash of humor, Joanna smiled

back. "Well, maybe. A few embarrassing moments with boys when I was in my teens."

A spark of interest lit Meredith's face. "You're Amish, right? Do you go on dates?"

Not recently, she wanted to say. "You could call it that, but probably not what you're used to. Planning to meet a certain boy at a picnic, or a volleyball game."

Or riding home from a singing with a special boy. She'd done that a few times, but there'd never been anyone she'd liked enough to give up her independence for. "What about you?" She turned the question back to Meredith, again wondering what she remembered of her life.

"Oh, sure. But..." She looked troubled. "I don't think I remember anyone special."

Joanna wanted to soothe away the trouble. "Maybe you haven't met him yet. There's plenty of time, ain't so?"

"I guess." She rubbed her forehead. "I should remember, though. Shouldn't I?"

The lost look in her eyes seemed to grab Joanna's heart and twist it. "You're tired, that's all. You've had quite a week. It will come back soon, I promise."

Could she promise that? She probably shouldn't have said it, but somehow, she had to encourage Meredith.

Mary Ellen swished through the door in time to hear the last few words. "No worrying allowed," she said with a warning look at Joanna. "The doctor is on her way down the hall to check on our patient, and I can hear the supper carts coming up. Joanna will come back."

"For sure I will."

Joanna stood, and after a momentary pause she bent and pressed her cheek against Meredith's. Her cousin, maybe? A relative, at any rate. Close enough to warrant a hug.

"I'll see you tomorrow."

Meredith smiled, but Joanna could see her drooping as if the tiredness had set in. "Tomorrow," she said.

Joanna had almost reached the door when Meredith murmured a few more words. "You look just like I thought you would."

She stopped, shaken, not sure she'd heard correctly. She started to turn back, but the door opened to let in the doctor, and she had to go on out.

But she couldn't rid herself of what she thought she'd heard. Did Meredith mean she'd known something about Joanna before her injury, as they'd speculated? Or just that she unconsciously formed a picture of her from hearing Joanna's voice coaxing her to consciousness? Of course, if she'd come looking for Joanna, that made sense, but they didn't know that for sure. Maybe she should have asked that question, but her instincts said to go slowly.

Nodding to the auxiliary policeman who'd been pressed into duty and sat on a folding chair by the door, Joanna went slowly on her way. If she hadn't promised Mamm she'd come to supper, she'd be tempted to try to talk to Meredith again, tired or not.

Pulling into the lane at the farm, Joanna spotted her youngest brother, Zeb, racing Isaac to reach her first. Zeb grabbed the mare's headstall and elbowed off his brother.

"Get off. I got here first."

"So what. I'm here, too."

"Knock it off, the two of you." She jumped down. "You're not usually so eager to be helpful."

The two of them exchanged looks. "We want to ask you something," Isaac said.

"I got here first, so I get to ask her." Zeb was tenacious, glaring at his brother.

"Okay, so ask." Isaac glared back, and Joanna suppressed a laugh.

"What is it, Zeb?" If she didn't interrupt, they'd be out here all night.

"So we were thinking, if you're adopted, like Daadi says, are you still our sister?"

The smile froze on her face for a split second, and then she reached out and grabbed each of them in a hug. "That's certain sure, and don't you forget it. You can't get rid of a big sister that easily."

"Okay." They had identical smiles. Peace restored, they both led Princess to the hitching rail.

Feeling as if she were shaking internally, Joanna headed inside. Where had that come from? She'd never thought much about being adopted in the past, and as far as she could remember, none of the boys had shown any curiosity about it. Were they overhearing things from Mamm and Daad? Or worse, had rumors started flying around the church? People would know, eventually, but she'd rather not face a lot of curiosity just now. And if it became known that Daad and Mamm had just kept her, what would happen to them? That didn't bear thinking about.

Should she say something to Daad? She rejected the idea after a moment's thought. She'd reassured the boys, and probably they wouldn't mention it again.

It seemed that Mamm and Daad were as eager as she was to keep things normal…or at least, as normal as possible. She got Mamm onto the subject of Cathy's wedding, and that kept Mamm happy throughout the meal. Other than insisting she check Joanna's fading bruises, nothing was said about problems or Meredith or any possible relationship.

It couldn't go on, she guessed, but she'd take the relative peace for as long as possible. Teasing her brothers about volunteering them to help prepare for the wedding, she kept the conversation lively while they ate Mamm's delicious chicken potpie.

Naturally, the moment came when she and Mamm were left alone in the kitchen to do the dishes. For a few minutes Mamm didn't say anything, then she looked at Joanna.

"I heard what you said to the boys outside. I was by the window."

Joanna clasped her hand, her own wet and soapy from the dishwater. "They surprised me. I hope I said the right thing."

Mamm squeezed her hand. "Just right. You did mean it, didn't you?" Her voice turned anxious, and Joanna's heart clenched painfully.

"Of course I did. Nothing can change what I feel for my family."

What else could she say? Mamm probably would only be entirely relieved if she said that Meredith had left, never to be heard of again.

She couldn't do that, so they'd all have to stumble along as best they could. But she knew now that she must not say anything to Mamm about the DNA results. She'd have to keep silent and hope for the best, whatever that might be.

At least her mother seemed content with that answer. They talked easily about the dresses for Cathy's wedding and the new quilting class Aunt Jessie wanted to start until the darkness was drawing in, and she knew she had to leave.

Spotting Daad bringing the horse and buggy to the porch steps, Joanna hugged her mother, pulled on her sweater and hurried outside. She'd thought she might be able to talk to Daad about what the test showed, but she should have gotten going earlier to do that.

"You should have gone earlier." Daad echoed her thoughts as he helped her into the buggy. "I don't like you coming out alone now that it's getting dark so early."

"I'm not used to it yet, or I'd have planned better, but I'll be fine, Daad. It's only three miles, and Princess could do it in her sleep." Everyone seemed to be worrying about her, but she wouldn't let herself start jumping at shadows. "Tell the boys I said good-night."

Daad held her hand for a moment, looking as if he wanted to say something more. But then he stepped back, watching. When she reached the turn onto the main road, she glanced back. Daad still stood there, watching.

By the time she'd gone a mile, Joanna realized Daad had been right. It had begun clouding up while they were eating, and that made visibility worse.

Still, her buggy was well equipped with reflective tape and lights, unlike those of some church districts. But the darkness pressed in, and she could only see as far ahead as Princess's nose.

A car passed her going away from town, slowing as it came closer. Most folks around River Haven were used to buggies on the road, and it had been a couple of years since the last accident. Still, it paid to be cautious.

Glimpsing the reflection of lights coming up behind her, Joanna urged Princess a little to the right. There was plenty of room to pass, that was for sure, but the driver behind her seemed to be moving fast.

There, he slowed down, and she let out the breath she'd been holding without being aware of it. Then, before she had time to think, the car accelerated, coming fast, too fast. Heart pounding, she pulled Princess's head to the right, trying to get off the road. Better to turn over than to be hit, but she couldn't get far enough; it was going to hit her—

With a wordless prayer, she braced herself. The car struck, jolting her so that she clung to the buggy rail. It raked the side of the buggy with a loud shriek. She felt the buggy tip, then lurch and topple over toward the ditch.

CHAPTER TWELVE

STUNNED, JOANNA GROPED her way toward understanding. She heard the car screech off in the distance, but she couldn't see it. Moving her arms cautiously, she found that they were still working. She reached out with her hands and felt soft, damp grass underneath her, while above her the darkness formed itself into the buggy.

That explained it. The buggy had tipped. She'd slid off the seat and the soft earth of the roadside ditch had cushioned her fall. Squirming a little, she found that she'd probably be able to get out with a bit of help, but Princess—

Her heart clutched, and for an instant she couldn't breathe. "Princess."

As if in answer, she heard the horse move. Working her way up on her elbows, she could see the mare's paler color against the darker surroundings. No way of telling if she was injured, but she'd certainly be trapped between the harness and the shafts.

Hearing her scrabble with her legs, Joanna reached out to pat what proved to be the mare's haunch. "It's all right, girl. Just be easy. I'll get you out. Hush now."

The tone of voice, if not the words, seemed to get

through to the mare. Princess stopped thrashing, and in another moment, Joanna heard her champing at the damp grass.

Now to get herself out. Before she could make the attempt, she heard a car approaching, heading for town. Thanking God that the battery lights were still working, she crunched herself as far from the road as she could get.

But she'd obviously been seen. The car slowed, drawing carefully to the side of the road, and warning lights started flashing. Relief flooded through her. She wasn't alone.

Car doors slammed, and footsteps rushed toward her. "Hello? Is anyone there?"

"I'm here," she called. "Under the buggy."

She heard exclamations, and then someone moving toward her. A flashlight shone briefly in her face and then moved away.

"Are you all right?" It was a man's voice, and she could see the shape of him now.

"I don't think I'm hurt." Until she could move entirely, she wouldn't be sure.

Beyond him, illuminated by the battery lamp, a woman leaned in. "We'll get you out." She spoke in much the same comforting tone that Joanna had used to Princess.

"Looks like it's just your foot that's caught under this piece of metal." The man gave an experimental tug. "If I lift it up, can you pull it out?"

"Yah, I'm sure I can. Denke. Thank you," she added, not sure they would understand the word.

"Okay, on the count of three." He didn't waste any time. "One, two, three." He lifted, and she scrambled out, feeling the woman's hands helping her.

Sensing Joanna's movement, the mare made a convulsive attempt to free herself. Joanna spoke quickly in Pennsylvania Dutch, soothing her.

The woman touched her arm. "Are you sure you're not hurt? Maybe we should call 911."

"No, please don't." She probably sounded upset and hoped they couldn't tell how shaken she was. Thinking of all the fuss if the police came made her feel worse. "I'll be a little bruised, but I'm all right." She took a breath, trying to get her mind to work. She had to see if Princess was hurt. Her stomach tightened at the thought. "Can you shine the light over here? I must see if the horse is injured and get her out before she hurts herself."

"I don't know much about horses, but..."

Before he could go on, a voice called out from the farm lane, and Joanna realized that it belonged to an Amish neighbor. Relief flowed through her. Aaron would help her with the horse.

"Aaron?" she called out in Pennsylvania Dutch. "Is that Aaron Esch?"

A figure materialized out of the dark. "Yah, it's me. Joanna, what happened?"

"A car just clipped the buggy and sent us into your ditch." Realizing the Englishers wouldn't understand, she switched to Englisch. "These kind folks helped me get out."

With the added light from the lantern Aaron was

carrying, she could make them out more clearly. Fortyish, a married couple, she'd guess, the woman looking anxious and the man clearly relieved that someone else had come to help.

"I'm Joanna Kohler," she said. "I have the quilt shop in town, if you know it."

"Of course," the woman exclaimed. "I should have recognized you. I'm Patty Moore, and this is my husband, Tim."

Now that the courtesies had been observed, Joanna turned her attention to Princess. Aaron knelt beside the mare as two of his boys hurried up to them with large flashlights.

"Mamm says to say come in the house if you want." The older one, Thomas, smiled shyly at Joanna.

"Denke, Thomas. And tell your Mamm I said thanks, please."

She turned back to the mare, kneeling beside her head. "Is she all right? I haven't had a good look at her yet."

Aaron moved around the mare, studying her by the lantern's light. "No scrapes or cuts. We'll have to get her out to see anything more."

"Thank the gut Lord. We'd best try to get the harness off first, and then I think I can lead her out."

Both the men started talking at once, suggesting the best way of doing that, and Joanna's head started to spin. She couldn't very well shout at them, but she'd like to.

Before she lost control of herself, a buggy was heard coming quickly down the road. The relief she felt when she saw Noah told her too much about her feelings for him, and she struggled to control the tears that rushed to her eyes.

She stood as he ran to her. "I'm not hurt," she said quickly, glad of his stolid calm. "We need to get the mare out."

With a searching glance as if to be sure she was telling the truth about herself, Noah nodded. In a moment he had begun unbuckling the harness. He and Aaron, working together, had it off in minutes and checked to be sure nothing else was entangled in Princess's legs.

"I think she can…" But before Noah could finish the thought, Princess gave a convulsive heave and scrambled to her feet. Shaking a little, she turned to nuzzle Joanna.

"You're all right, girl." She stroked the mare, relieved.

"She can stay in my barn tonight," Aaron offered, running a hand along the mare's legs.

Noah glanced at her. "If she's moving all right, maybe it's best to keep her moving so she doesn't stiffen up, ain't so? I can tie her to the back of my buggy and take both her and Joanna home."

"I think that would be best," Joanna said. "Denke, Aaron."

Her smile included the boys. Thomas, without a word, handed her a lead rope he must have pulled from the buggy.

"That's just what we need. Denke."

She and Thomas led the mare a short distance

along the road, to be sure she was walking all right. It also gave Joanna a chance to assess her own body. There'd be bruises, for sure, but she seemed to have come out of it whole.

Thomas looked at her for approval, and she nodded, smiling inwardly at his shyness. With an air of pleasure at helping, he led the mare to Noah's buggy and tied her to the back.

When Joanna returned to the others, they were already getting into position to lift the buggy onto its wheels. She moved as if to help, and Noah gave her such a frown that she backed off.

"Ready?" he said. "One, two, three." On the count, the buggy lifted, rocked a little and then settled on its wheels.

Aaron played the light around it. "Doesn't look too bad," he said. Relief swept through Joanna. New buggies came expensive.

"That's gut."

"We'll pull it into my lane," he said. "It will be fine there until tomorrow. I'll stop at the farm and let your daad know first thing."

He obviously assumed her father would take charge of repairs, and she didn't feel up to pointing out that it was her buggy. Besides, she had no doubt that Daad would insist on taking over anyway.

"Denke, Aaron." She hesitated. "Try not to let my mamm hear, yah? She worries."

He grinned. "She's your mamm. For sure she worries. I'll catch your daad when he's milking, yah?"

Nodding, she thanked the two boys, and turned

to the Englisch couple. The man looked a little un-comfortable but the woman clasped her hand for a moment.

"You get a good rest tonight. I'll stop by the store tomorrow to see how you are."

They left almost before she could finish thanking them. She was free to go home at last. She raised a hand toward Aaron and his boys, already moving the buggy into their lane. Then she took the few steps to Noah's buggy, feeling as if she were carrying an enormous load on her shoulders. With a quick movement, Noah lifted her up to the buggy seat. He was moving around the buggy to his side before she could react, and she sank back with a sense of relief.

Noah reached behind him, pulled out a buggy blanket and wrapped it around her. She hadn't even realized, until she felt the soft folds settling against her, how chilled she'd been.

"Denke." She hugged it close against her as Noah clicked to the gelding and started the buggy moving down the road, Princess trotting along behind. Joanna leaned back again, feeling safe for the first time since she'd heard that car roaring down at her.

NOAH TOOK A lingering look at Joanna next to him on the buggy seat. The fears that had driven him out here had been realized, but she was all right, no thanks to the driver of the car. The anger that roiled inside him at the thought had to be dealt with, but he wasn't sure he knew how.

She moved a little on the seat, and he reached over to tuck the blanket more closely around her.

"You must be cold, landing in the wet grass that way. You need to get home."

She snuggled into the blanket, moving a little closer as he did so. Well, if his warmth could help her, he'd gladly provide it. And control himself.

"I didn't realize it until I sat down, and then I started shivering."

Her voice was faint, making him long to have her home more quickly. But it wasn't safe to try to speed up on this narrow road.

So instead he patted her arm. "Probably shock, as well as being wet and cold. We'll soon be home, and Aunt Jessie will take care of you." He found he was gritting his teeth. "She should have been with you, and maybe this wouldn't have happened."

She roused. "I don't know why you think that. The car might still have clipped the buggy."

"Maybe. But maybe the driver would have thought the better of it if he saw you weren't alone."

He could almost feel the intensity of her stare. "You think running into me was deliberate?" Her voice rose.

"Don't you?" It had been his first thought when he saw her, as well as being the fear that had driven him along the road to find her.

"You think this has something to do with Meredith. But it might have been a coincidence. Accidents do happen, especially at night."

He shot a glance at her, wondering if she really

believed that. "I don't think I believe in coincidences any longer. Not after everything that has happened. At any rate, Jamison will have to do something about it now."

She stiffened. "I'm sure he is already doing something. He had a guard on Meredith's door, and he's trying to find out who would want to harm her."

"Yah, fine." He fought to control his anger at circumstances that had put her in danger. "He should be putting a guard on you, it seems to me. It's not just Meredith, it's you. You're the one whose home was broken into and searched. The man at the hospital attacked both of you. And now this."

She was silent for a moment. "I suppose so." She sounded reluctant. "If only Meredith could remember more about her life. Even if she didn't remember the accident or the attack against her, she could tell us who would want to harm her."

Her voice shook a little when she spoke of someone harming Meredith. Her kin, in one way or another. Joanna would feel responsible even if it weren't for the relationship. He knew that, because he knew his Joanna.

"It has to have something to do with your relationship. You know that, don't you?" He spoke harshly out of his frustrated need to keep her safe. "That was probably what brought her here. Why else would she come to River Haven?"

"I don't know." He could hear the fatigue in her voice, and he felt instantly guilty. He shouldn't push her when she was shaken and upset. But if not now, when? They had so little chance to talk… Things were happening too fast.

"There's bound to be some way of finding out." He tried to keep his tone gentle. "Whatever reason someone thinks he has for hurting her, it has to go back to her life in Philadelphia. She was only in River Haven long enough to have an accident. If that's what it was."

Joanna moved slightly, and then she reached across the seat to grasp his hand. Hers was cold, and when he wrapped his fingers around it, it felt fragile in his grasp.

"Jamison doesn't seem convinced that she fell, and with the other things that have happened…" She let that trail off, but still she clung to his hand. "Maybe she was attacked *because* she came here."

"You mean somebody didn't want her to talk to you? You know what that means. He can either get rid of her or get rid of you."

His fingers tightened on her hand, and he had the crazy notion that he could take her away and hide her someplace until all the danger was past.

"If he was trying to get rid of me, he didn't pick a very good way." He could sense her rallying, summoning her courage. "The buggy tipped over, but it slid me into a nice soft ditch."

"He may not have realized what the effect would be of hitting the side of the buggy. Just because he's not very good at it doesn't mean he won't try again."

She shivered, withdrawing her hand and wrapping the blanket more securely around her. "Stop it. You're scaring me."

"You *should* be scared." Did she really not see that? "And you shouldn't be running around in the dark by yourself. If your family wants to see you, let them come to you."

"I couldn't tell them that—"

"Yah, you could. And when we get to the shop, you can call Jamison and tell him what happened tonight."

"Not tonight," she said quickly. "Please, Noah, I can't. All I want to do is lie down."

He might have known he'd melt the instant she said his name. How could he insist? She must be exhausted, and the last thing she needed was to be questioned by the police.

"Sorry. I wasn't thinking. But first thing in the morning, then, for sure." He couldn't possibly go off home and leave her and Jessie alone and unprotected. "And in the meantime, I'm putting a cot up against the wall on my side of the building." Not that he intended to sleep. "If I hear a sound, I'll be coming if I have to break in."

"Not just any sound, please. Aunt Jessie snores like a freight train sometimes, although she might not sleep much after she hears about this."

If she was able to make what almost amounted to a joke, that was an encouraging thing, but he needed to be sure she was taking her safety seriously.

"Don't, Joanna. Can you imagine what it was like when it kept getting darker and you didn't come? I could hear Jessie pacing the floor, and I knew just how she felt. When I told her I was coming to look for you, she didn't even argue."

"I'm sorry." She turned toward him impulsively.

"I promise I won't go anywhere alone." She fumbled with something. "Here, take this."

"What is it?" He felt cold metal against his hand.

"It's the extra key to the dead bolt. I think even Aunt Jessie would agree that it's a good idea for you to be able to get in if there's an emergency."

"Denke." *Thank you for trusting me.* He couldn't see her face, but when he reached out, she clasped his hand. This time he wasn't letting go, not until he had her safe at home, if anywhere was safe.

Palm against palm, he felt a connection he couldn't deny. He didn't want to. He loved her. He wanted to marry her. But what if…

He couldn't get away from that what-if. Even if Joanna returned his feelings, how could he risk hurting her? He'd like to tell himself that he wasn't capable of violence, but he remembered how he'd felt when he'd seen the man attacking Joanna. What might he have done if he'd had a weapon in his hand?

He'd been protecting her, but how could he be sure that violence wouldn't turn against someone else. He knew, only too well, how his father had destroyed the feelings of everyone who cared about him, especially Mamm. He couldn't bear to think of his brave, smart Joanna wearing the helpless, defeated look his mother had worn, and knowing he was responsible.

But even believing what he did, he couldn't help holding her hand all the way home.

ENTERTAINING THE POLICE chief first thing in the morning wasn't Joanna's idea of an appropriate start to the day, but there'd been nothing even slightly normal in what had happened in the past week. At least she'd had wits enough to suggest he come the back way to their apartment, rather than driving up to the front door and attracting the attention of everyone on Main Street.

Aunt Jessie didn't even bat an eye when Jamison came up the back stairs, followed by Noah. She set mugs on the table. "Coffee's ready. I'll see to the shop until you're finished."

Jamison barely waited until she'd disappeared downstairs before he started. He pulled out a kitchen chair, sat down solidly and planted his hands on the table.

"All right. Now, tell me all the things you left out when you called me."

Joanna lifted the coffeepot and poured into three mugs, trying to organize her thoughts and feeling as if she needed a few more hours of sleep. Wordlessly, Noah distributed the mugs, adding the cream and sugar she had ready on the counter.

"I think I told you everything on the phone," she said, taking the chair opposite Jamison. "I was driving home from the farm when I heard the car coming behind me. He seemed to slow down, so I was sure he saw the buggy. Then all of a sudden he sped up, coming right at me. I pulled the mare over to the right, hoping to get out of his way, but he clipped the side of the buggy and sent us into the ditch."

She stopped for breath, knowing she'd blurted it all out in a rush, wishing to get rid of it. Reliving it made her shake inside. She sensed Noah moving closer to her.

Jamison frowned. "You should have called me as soon as it happened."

Keeping silent seemed the only possible answer. If he didn't understand why she hadn't, explaining it wouldn't help.

"Never mind," he muttered. "What was the vehicle like?"

She looked at him helplessly. "I don't know. I didn't see it."

"Joanna, you knew it was behind you. It hit you. You had to have seen something." He sounded as if he was trying not to snap, but she knew it was frustration speaking.

"I heard it behind me. I saw the lights. Then I was toppling into the ditch with the buggy on top of me."

Noah moved even closer to her, so that he was standing behind her chair.

"Right. Sorry if I snapped. But I want you to think it over calmly. You might have had a sense of the size and shape, right? Was it a truck? A pickup? A sedan?"

"A car, not a truck." She wasn't sure why she was sure of it. Maybe she'd seen more than she thought.

"Color?"

She shook her head. "I have the impression it was dark, but I can't be sure."

"You know how dark it is along that road," Noah put in. "And there's not much traffic at that time of night."

"No. But what about the other car that came along?

These people who stopped to help you. I'll talk to them, but do you think they could have seen the car?"

"I...I don't really know. It seemed like forever that I was lying there wondering if Princess was hurt and how I was going to get out, but it might not have been more than a few minutes."

The memory flooded back too vividly, and her voice trembled. Noah's hand grasped her shoulder, and she felt warmth and strength flow into her.

She couldn't turn to look up at him, but she put her hand up to touch his, drawing comfort. Jamison looked from one to the other of them, but suddenly she didn't care what he was thinking.

"Okay, just a few more questions," he said as if answering an unspoken complaint. "Where is the buggy now?"

She shook her head. "I'm not sure. It's either still at Aaron's place or Daad may have picked it up."

Jamison gritted his teeth. "How about calling to find out?"

"Yah, of course I will. But he may not be near the phone shanty."

Was he holding back a complaint about people who didn't have a phone in their house? She wouldn't be surprised.

"Never mind. I'll find it. I'm going out there as soon as we finish. I need to see that buggy before anyone starts working on it."

"Is it that important?" She didn't see why, but he was obviously determined.

"Very," he said shortly, and then seemed to feel

he needed to explain. "We may be able to find out what color the car was that way. We can analyze any scrapes of paint from the vehicle." He frowned down at the table. "Joanna, I want you to think back to when you left the farm. Did you see any car pulled over, maybe sitting in one of the farm lanes around there?"

She tried to send her thoughts back to those moments, but she knew it was no good. She'd been so preoccupied with her thoughts about the family that she probably wouldn't have noticed anything that wasn't right in front of her.

"I'm sorry. There was nothing that I could see. But I wasn't looking, except at the road."

"I didn't really expect you had, but just in case." He took a gulp of the coffee before he went on. "What about anything that might have passed you between home and the place where you were hit?"

She brightened at finally having something positive to contribute. "There was another car. It passed me, going away from town, not long before I was hit."

"What did it look like?" He leaned forward, intent.

Joanna shrugged helplessly. "I don't know. I didn't really notice. Dark-colored," she added before he could jump on her with that question.

Jamison seemed resigned to her lack of knowledge about cars this time. He sat quite still, staring down at the tabletop, apparently deep in thought.

"If that's all…" Noah began.

Ignoring him, Jamison shook his head. Finally, he looked up. "I wasn't sure about telling you this, but I've been back and forth with police in Philadelphia."

He studied Joanna's face. "You're sure you and your folks don't know anything about Meredith's family?"

She'd feared, all along, that he'd come back to her family. She had to protect them, but how?

"No. How could we?"

Noah's hand tightened warningly on her shoulder.

"Come on, Joanna. You came from somewhere. Your blood says you're related to Meredith. I don't want to question your parents—"

"Then don't." She rushed into speech. "They can't help you, and if you upset my mother, I don't know what might happen to her."

Jamison's expression softened. "Then you tell me what you know. I'm not looking to cause needless grief. Or to make my neighbors the center of a big newspaper story. But I have to know."

"He's right," Noah said softly. "You'll have to tell him."

"But they don't know anything that will help you. My birth mother left me with them, asking them to take care of me. That's all they know about her."

"Where did this happen? Here?"

"No. They were on their way to visit my aunt. Somewhere in Ohio. That's all I know. I'm not even sure they remember. They were stuck there by a snowstorm, and I was left at the door of their motel room with a note."

"Why theirs? Had they talked to the woman?"

She shook her head. "No, they hadn't, but she must have seen them. Maybe she thought that an Amish family would be a good place for her baby." She hesitated, but the rest should be said. "My mother was just recovering after losing a baby. When she saw me and read the note, she felt as if it was an answer to prayer. That's all they know, so there's no use in asking them."

IF JAMISON WAS DISAPPOINTED, it didn't show. "I won't say anything to them unless I have to, but there has to be some connection between that woman and the Bristow family. If we knew what, it might explain at least some of what's going on."

Relieved that he didn't pursue the question of her parents, she ventured a question. "You said you talked to the police about Meredith…"

"Yeah, right. Maybe it's best if you know. Seems like the Bristow family is well-off."

Without thinking, Joanna nodded, making him zero in on her. "You're not surprised. How did you know?"

"I might not know fashion, but I do understand fabric. Everything she had on was high quality. It had to have been expensive."

Was he looking at her with suspicion? Uneasiness crawled along her nerves.

"Any woman would have noticed it," she added, wondering if she was making it worse.

Jamison gave a short nod before going on. "Apparently, when she turns twenty-one, Meredith comes into a sizable trust fund. That's in another six months."

"You think that has something to do with what's

been happening?" Noah asked the question, and Joanna thought the pressure of his hand was telling her to stay silent.

"I don't know, but most of the time crimes are motivated by greed. If she could remember what happened, she could tell us, assuming it wasn't just an accident."

That brought her to attention in a hurry. "The man in her hospital room wasn't an accident, whether her fall was or not."

Without responding, he shrugged. "Are you going to see her today?"

"I hadn't even thought of it yet. Not right now, that's for sure. Maybe later."

"Those other relatives we located checked in at the motel out on the highway this morning. Maybe she'll remember something when she sees them. When the other cousin was here, she was still so unresponsive that it didn't help. If you can get up there by early afternoon, you can get a sense of how she reacts to them."

"Any of the nurses could do that," Noah put in before she could respond. "Why does Joanna have to be involved?" He was so close behind her that Joanna felt the warmth of his body. She had to stop noticing things like that, but she couldn't.

For a moment she thought Jamison would ignore him, but then he answered. "Joanna is involved," he said mildly. "The Bristow woman will say more to her than to anyone… It's almost like she feels a bond, isn't it?"

Joanna's hands clenched in her lap, but the chief got up as if he was finished.

"I'll talk to you later—" he began, but Noah interrupted him.

"What about Joanna? She needs protection, too."

Jamison reddened. "You think I wouldn't like to have an officer watching her every minute? But she wouldn't want it and, anyway, who would it be? As it is, I've got auxiliary and fire police pulling extra duty, as little good as they are in this situation. Directing traffic, that's what they should be doing."

"It's all right," she broke in. "I don't want anyone. I'll be careful."

"No more jaunts out to the farm by yourself, mind you," Jamison said. "If you have to go somewhere, tell me, and I'll find someone to drive you. Otherwise, stay home. Until we know what's behind all of this, we can't take chances."

"Don't worry, I won't." She shivered, remembering.

"Good girl. I'll send someone to drive you to the hospital at about one. You take care, and, Noah, it wouldn't do any harm if you kept an eye on her, too."

"I intend to." Noah's hands tightened on her shoulders. It felt…and sounded…like a promise.

CHAPTER THIRTEEN

JOANNA FELT HERSELF sag in her chair once Jamison had gone. How much longer would this go on, and what would the end of it be? She couldn't even guess any longer. She had completely lost control of her life, it seemed. Her own kitchen, the room she and Aunt Jessie had painted a sunny yellow and furnished with a table and chairs they'd picked up at an auction, no longer seemed like a safe haven.

Noah dumped her cooling coffee and poured another cupful, setting it in front of her. "Get that down you. It'll make you feel better."

She took a sip. "I don't think coffee will cure what ails me right now." She said aloud what she'd just been thinking. "I thought I knew where my life was going. I didn't."

Noah sat down next to her. "None of us knows that, not for sure. If we think we do, we're just kidding ourselves."

The note of regret in his voice struck her. Was he thinking of his father? Or of the struggle he had just to take care of his mother and the younger boys?

"I suppose you're right." She took another swallow of the coffee, feeling its warmth. Noah had been right—it did help a little. She glanced at him, seeing the frowning gaze that he had fixed on the table. "Denke, Noah."

He darted a questioning look at her.

"For standing by, of course." She answered the unspoken question. "I just wish we… I could do something more. I feel as if there's danger all around Meredith, and Jamison is no closer to knowing where it's coming from."

"Maybe you ought to worry about yourself. Seems to me you're at risk, too. Jamison ought to do more to keep you safe."

"Wouldn't that look nice, an Amish woman being trailed around town by a policeman in uniform?" She couldn't help smiling at the thought.

"Anything would be better than Jamison doing nothing. Next time this man might try something more dangerous than sending your buggy into the ditch."

She shivered at the thought. "Believe me, I haven't forgotten. If only we knew why." That question was never far from her. Why?

"Jamison said she belonged to a wealthy family. Money certainly does make people do awful things."

That was true, but much less so among the Amish. Money couldn't buy family, or faith, or community.

Noah eyed her thoughtfully. "Are you feeling more worried about her because she's probably a close relative?"

She took a moment to consider it, not sure she'd totally accepted the idea that Meredith was her kin. "I hope I would feel that way about anyone who was hurt. But maybe there's some truth to the idea that the relationship makes a difference. I feel..." She let that trail off, not sure she wanted to put her feelings into words.

"What?" Noah seemed intent on getting to the bottom of it. He'd gone from being supportive and protective to questioning like a policeman. "What is it you feel?"

She shrugged, searching for words. "I guess I'm wondering if that's why I haven't been like other Amish girls, wanting marriage and a family of my own instead of the business. Maybe I'm different because I wasn't born Amish."

"Now that's ferhoodled." He was almost sharp with her. "Amish isn't a matter of bloodlines. It's how you're brought up and what you choose. Adopted or not, you're still yourself."

He'd leaned forward as he spoke, intent and impassioned, so that she could feel his determination coming at her like a strong wind.

Then, as if suddenly aware of his passion, he drew back. "Sorry. I don't guess you want my advice. I'd best be going." He stood up abruptly as if eager to get away.

The thought hurt. How could he go from being so caring and supportive at one moment and then talk as if they were mere acquaintances the next?

In any event, she had to hide what she felt and put a good face on it. "No, I'm sorry. I've been keeping you away from the store when you need to be there." She rose as well, feeling as if he'd taken away her source of support. She didn't need support, she reminded herself.

Noah shook his head. "My brother's there again today. Caleb. He's turning into a pretty good salesman." His expression grew lighter at the thought.

"I hope that means that sales are better," she ventured, not sure he wanted to talk about it.

He hesitated, but then gave a nod. "Yah, they were yesterday anyway. If they hold up again today…well, I'll feel pretty sure that my Amish customers are back, for now anyway."

She expected him to say something about her father, either grudging acceptance or edgy annoyance, but he didn't do either.

"We'll do okay, I think, even though the Englisch… Well, seems like they're happier with the chain store. I'm trying to meet their prices, but it's not easy."

She wanted to say something encouraging, but she couldn't find anything. "I guess not. At least you found out what Caleb really wants, thanks to all this."

"Yah." His face lightened. "Funny. Working together in the store, I've gotten to know my little bruder a lot better. I think he's a lot more grown-up than I thought he was. Yesterday he said—"

He stopped. All of a sudden, it was as if a door had slammed in her face. Why? What was suddenly wrong that he couldn't finish what he was saying?

"You can say it, whatever it is. I'm not a blabbermaul."

Noah looked startled, and then his face warmed. "Right. I know." He hesitated, but this time he seemed to look for the right words. "Caleb reminded me of a time when Daad was driving us in the buggy. Daad had been drinking, and he scraped a car, so the police came."

He paused again. Maybe he needed time to bring out words that had to be painful.

"Daad wanted me to say I'd been driving. He said... He said it was my duty as his son." His lips twisted. "I wouldn't."

"You couldn't." The pain she sensed in him seemed to cut into her own heart. To have his father try to put the blame on him—she couldn't begin to imagine how that must have hurt. She wanted so much to touch him, comfort him, but knew he wouldn't welcome it.

"No. I couldn't. I didn't even think Caleb would remember it. Or if he did, he'd blame me. But he said that I taught him something that day." He blinked rapidly as if to deny a tear. "Well, it's foolish, maybe, to make something of it."

"Not foolish." No, it wasn't foolish, because she could see how it still pained him today. Now she did touch his arm, fleetingly, withdrawing her hand before he could pull away. "You taught Caleb to be honest, no matter what. I'd like to think I've had that kind of influence on one of my little bruders. I'm glad he told you."

Noah nodded, not looking at her. "Yah. I am, too." He straightened. "I'd best get back to him before he decides to have a sale or put up a new sign."

"Enthusiastic, is he?" She forced a smile, shoving away the instinct that made her want to weep for Noah's lost childhood.

"He'd be running the store himself if he had his way." Noah said the words lightly as he started toward the stairs. Then he looked at her, frowning a little. "Mind you be careful if you're out."

"I will."

He moved quickly down the stairs.

NOAH STOOD AT the front window, watching the vehicle carrying Joanna to the hospital speed off up the street. All very well for Jamison to tell him to keep an eye on her. He couldn't very well do so when she was off again, trying to help—not Jamison, he supposed, but this unknown relative of hers. She seemed to be slipping into the world that belonged to Meredith Bristow and even further out of his reach.

Did her parents know the results of the DNA test? He could understand her wanting to hide that to protect them, but either way, they'd be hurt.

It was foolish to stand here staring at the street. He had work to do. Just as he thought that, he saw Floyd, toolbox in hand, pulling the door open. The handyman came straight toward him.

"Floyd. It's good to see you. How's the work going?"

"Fine, just fine." He grinned at the sight of Caleb busy with a customer. "I see you've got the boy working. Replacing me with free labor, right?"

"He just costs me a couple of cans of soda a day, but he doesn't know as much as you." He clapped the older man on the back. "You staying busy? Getting enough work?"

"Busy? I'll tell the world I'm busy. I didn't know there were so many people who didn't know one end of a hammer from the other."

"That's good, right? That means they need you."

"Guess I can't complain. As a matter of fact, that's one reason I came in today. I wanted to thank you. Never had so much fun working before you pushed me into giving the handyman business a try."

"You mean you like having all the ladies in town asking for your help." He knew as well as anyone that Floyd's wife, Betsy, was the only woman in the world for him, but he liked being fussed over.

Sure enough, Floyd flushed, a little shamefaced. "I keep telling Betsy she better appreciate me. But what can I do? Nobody makes a mixed berry pie like she does." He sobered. "Anyway, thanks for getting me started. I owe you."

"Not me," Noah said as Joanna's face filled his thoughts. "I told you it was Joanna's idea to start with. And you know Joanna—she's so determined you just might as well do what she wants to begin with."

"That's Joanna, all right." Floyd gave him a side-long glance. "A woman in a million. Just like my Betsy."

He'd best change the subject before he was the one blushing. Floyd had already guessed something was going on, and the last thing he wanted was to fuel any rumors about him and Joanna.

"Consider me thanked anyway. Can I do something for you today?"

"Just you look at this." Floyd reached into his toolbox and pulled out a set of shelf brackets. Broken cabinet latches.

Noah turned them over in his hands, frowning. "You didn't get these from me, did you?"

"I did not. I didn't buy them at all. See, I'm putting up some shelves for a young couple just moved into a house on Elm Street." He indicated the direction with a jerk of his head. "This young guy had these out when I got there—wanted me to use them, saying how he got such a good buy on them. I picked the thing up and it fell apart in my hand. I said to him, 'You put junk like this on those new shelves, you'll find them collapsing on the floor as soon as you put something on them. I can't work with junk.'"

Noah had to smile at Floyd's indignation. "So were you out of a job?"

"Not a chance. He was a nice kid, smart enough to know when he'd made a mistake. Told me to get what I wanted and he'd pay for them. I told him I was going straight to Troyer's Hardware." He nodded his head sharply a couple of times.

"Denke, Floyd." Not that it meant that much business, but he was touched by the older man's loyalty. "I appreciate it." He waved toward the appropriate rack. "Let's go pick some out."

It didn't take long to find what Floyd needed, and after a little more talk and some teasing of Caleb, Floyd was on his way. Noah found himself smiling. Ridiculous to feel so elated about such a little thing, he guessed, but he did.

Maybe Floyd's visit had been a good sign, because

the store stayed busy throughout the afternoon. Even Caleb didn't have time to go for a can of soda.

Eventually, the last customer left, and with a glance at the clock, Caleb flipped the lock and turned the sign to Closed.

"Pretty good day today, ain't so?" Caleb was looking at him for reassurance, and for once he could give it with a clear conscience.

"Sure looks like it." He opened the cash drawer.

"Maybe we've turned the corner." Caleb's tone was optimistic.

Noah reminded himself that Caleb was always optimistic. He seemed to have been born with a smile on his face, and nothing got him down for long.

"Maybe so." He smiled at the boy. "You put in a gut day's work."

Caleb grinned, blue eyes sparkling. "Once I figured out that sometimes what customers need isn't what they think they want, I did a better job."

"Right. Just be sure you know what the answer is to their problem before you recommend something. And don't ever try to sell them more than they need."

"I'm learning, right?" For once Caleb looked uncertain, and again Noah's heart was touched.

"I told you. You're doing fine. Now, why don't you sweep up while I tally the receipts?"

"Right." Caleb went off to the back and returned in a moment with the broom and dustpan. But instead of sweeping, he lingered, looking over Noah's shoulder while he counted bills.

Finally losing count, Noah turned to him in exasperation. "You forget how to use the broom?"

"No." He made a token gesture with the broom, frowning. He looked up as if to speak and then looked down again.

Noah put down the stack of ones. "What's up? You have a problem with a customer?"

"Not, well, not exactly."

"What, exactly?" Usually the boy talked up a storm, but he was tongue-tied right now.

"Well…you know Thomas Booker?"

"Yah, I do. Did he give you grief about something?" Thomas could have a sharp tongue, but he had nothing on his wife, Ella.

"He kept asking me things."

Clearly, whatever it was, the questions had upset Caleb.

"What kind of things?" Was something about Daad coming up after all this time to plague them?

"About Joanna." He looked relieved to have the words out, but relief was the last thing Noah felt.

"What about Joanna?" The words were tart enough to have come from Joanna's aunt Jessie.

"He… Well, he was kind of hinting around. Like did I know why she kept going up to the hospital, and why were the police here so much. And did we know about her being adopted. That kind of thing."

And that kind of thing was probably just what Joanna's parents had been fearing…talk going around the community and questions about the bishop's family. There had been a time when he'd have been glad to learn of the bishop having problems, but that time was long gone.

Noah's fists knotted at the thought of Thomas questioning Caleb that way. He'd been smart enough not to try it on Noah, so he'd figured Caleb would be easier.

"What did you tell him?" He reminded himself to be patient with his young brother. If he'd let something slip...

"I played dumb, that's what I did." Caleb was indignant. "You think I'd go gossiping about Joanna to the likes of him? Anything I said would be around the county in a day with that wife of his—she's the biggest blabbermaul I know."

"Gut." He tried to manage a smile but could only think how hurt Joanna would be if she knew. "You did the right thing. Anybody else asks you questions about Joanna, you send them to me."

Caleb's grin flashed. "Will do."

Noah clapped him on the shoulder. "Gut. Now, get on with the sweeping so I can finish."

But when his brother had moved off, wielding the broom energetically if not accurately, he didn't immediately go back to the till.

That sort of talk was the worst thing for Joanna, as well as for her family. If Thomas had dared to say anything to him...

Noah looked down to see his hands clenched so tightly the fingers were white. He wanted to strike something, even if it was just the countertop.

He didn't, but he felt the anger surging through him

and faced the hard realization. He'd begun, he realized now, to think he might actually be like other normal men instead of like his father. He'd let himself hope that he might love someone and have a happy life.

That was a stupid hope. He couldn't deny what was in his blood, and he had to stop fooling himself about it before he hurt someone. No, not just someone. Joanna.

THE AUXILIARY POLICE officer dropped Joanna at the hospital door that was closest to the elevator. "Now, remember, don't try to go home by yourself. Just call the station when you're ready. Someone will come to get you. Okay?"

Like most of the auxiliary officers, this one was probably in his sixties and looked as soft as a pillow. But he was willing and concerned about her, and she didn't doubt he'd do his best.

"Thank you. I won't forget." She closed the door and walked quickly along the short stretch of sidewalk into the hospital.

The surroundings had grown so familiar that she hardly looked around before stepping into the elevator. She pressed the button, the door started to close and a man she didn't recognize slipped in.

"Thanks." He nodded to her as if she'd been responsible for his making the elevator.

She gave a slight nod, turning back toward the array of buttons. There was no reason to be nervous— he was a perfectly normal young Englischer, nicely dressed, probably going to visit a friend or relative.

But she could feel him studying her, and vague apprehension crept along her skin. She wrapped her arms around herself and stared at the buttons. Obviously, the red one would be the one to push if anything alarmed her.

Her sensible side told her not to be so foolish, but she couldn't help the relief that swept over her when the doors opened. She hurried off, only to find that he'd come off behind her. She could hear his footsteps closing the distance between them.

Joanna was within sight of the door when he caught her arm. She spun, taking a breath to cry out, but in that instant he let go, backing away with his hands in the air.

"Sorry, sorry. I didn't mean to scare you. Honest."

He looked horrified, and she realized in the same moment that he was young, probably not much more than twenty, if that. Before she could say anything, he babbled on, obviously embarrassed.

"I apologize, really. I didn't mean anything. I just…"

"Why are you following me?" She cut across his talk, having been too frightened to bother sounding polite.

"I'm not. I'm going to see my cousin. It's just… seeing you going the same direction, I thought maybe you were the woman who helped my cousin. The one the police chief told us about."

Joanna's alarm fizzled away to nothing, leaving her as embarrassed as he probably was. "Your cousin… Is that Meredith Bristow?"

"Yeah, right." Relief flooded his boyish face, and she saw the resemblance in the shape of his face and the color of his eyes. "You're the one who found her?"

She nodded, ashamed of overreaction. "I'm Joanna Kohler." She looked at him inquiringly.

"I'm Owen Graham. Merry is… Well, my mother is her father's cousin. So I guess that makes us… what? Second cousins? Something like that anyway."

Joanna started walking again, and he joined her.

"My mom's in there with her," he said. "I went out looking for coffee, but I didn't have any luck."

"It's down on the first floor, in the pavilion."

"That's what the nurse said, but I didn't find it." He made a face. "Hospitals give me the creeps. And I hated seeing Merry just lying there."

So her family called her Merry. It was a pretty nickname. Maybe she had lived up to it when things were normal.

Joanna pushed open the door. "She was probably sleeping. She'll seem more natural when she's awake."

A middle-aged woman was sitting where Joanna usually sat, patting Meredith's hand with quick, repeated motions. She looked up, startled, but her face cleared when she saw her son.

"Owen, where have you been? And who's this?"

"Sorry, Mom, but I couldn't find the coffee. This is Joanna Kohler. She's the one the police chief told us about. The one who found Merry and called the ambulance."

The woman bounced off the chair and scurried toward Joanna with her hands extended. "Oh, you sweet person. How can we thank you enough? We've just been so worried about Merry and then to find out she's in the hospital…" Distress made her soft, round face crumple like a fading flower. She looked a bit like a flower, too, with silvery curls, rosy cheeks and a comfortable figure.

Joanna wasn't sure what to address first. "We were so glad to be able to help Meredith." She glanced toward the bed. "Have you tried to wake her?"

The woman—she supposed it would be Mrs. Graham—looked toward the bed, too, and lowered her voice. "I didn't know if I should or if it might be the wrong thing. I wouldn't want to make her worse. They told us she might not remember us."

"She might not, but maybe she will. She seemed to be remembering much more yesterday, but she gets frustrated, too."

"Of course, of course. We have to be careful not to push." Mrs. Graham frowned at her son. "Remember that, Owen."

Owen rolled his eyes, looking like any teenager anywhere whose mother was embarrassing him.

Joanna smiled, looking past them. "I see she's already waking up. I thought she'd hear us talking."

Meredith moved, stretching, and then she opened her eyes. When she focused on Joanna's face, she smiled.

"Joanna. I'm glad to see you." She reached for the bed control and raised herself to a sitting position. Then she saw the other two people in the room. Her forehead wrinkled, and she seemed puzzled. "I don't know…"

"Don't you know us, Merry?" On the other side of the bed Mrs. Graham leaned forward, her face child-like in its disappointment.

"I don't think…" She was still puzzled, but not alarmed, and something that had been alert and pro-tective in Joanna relaxed a bit. "Wait… It's Emily, isn't it? Cousin Emily."

"That's right." Mrs. Graham's blue eyes welled with tears. "You remember. I knew you would." She grabbed her son's arm and tugged him forward, while he gave every sign of wanting to be elsewhere.

Because he didn't like hospitals, as he'd said? Or because he was afraid Meredith would name him as her attacker? He could have been the man in the hos-pital room that night, Joanna realized. That hospital jacket might have made him look bigger.

"You remember your cousin Owen, don't you?"

"Hi, Merry?" He raised his hand in an awkward wave. "Good to see you."

After a moment she shook her head. "I'm sorry. I… Things come in and out." Meredith turned to the older woman with a look of relief, maybe at recog-nizing her. "When I saw you, the name just popped into my mind."

"Never mind," Joanna said quickly. "It'll come if you don't force it. That's what the doctor says."

She addressed that to both of them, hoping they really did understand and would control their eager-ness. If they pushed Meredith, her recovery might be stalled, at least that was how Joanna had interpreted what Mary Ellen had said.

"That's right," Emily added, catching on. "You just relax. Do you want anything? A drink of water? Something to eat? Another pillow? Maybe just a little snack? Or I could brush your hair. Remember when I put your hair in braids when you were a little girl? You looked so sweet."

Joanna had the feeling that if she'd been presented with that many choices, she'd have wanted to pull the blanket over her face. But Meredith seemed fine, maybe because she was used to Emily's mannerisms.

"Give it a break, Mom. You're overwhelming her." Owen glanced at Joanna. "You should hear her fuss if I get a cold. If I sneeze, she's all over me with remedies, everything from cold pills to peppermint tea."

"Basil and ginger tea," his mother corrected. "Peppermint tea for an upset stomach."

"My mother is the same way," Joanna said lightly, wondering how they would react if they knew she was, in a way, a relative. But no one said anything, although she thought Meredith's gaze lingered on her. "She grows her own herbs and has something for every ailment."

"That's right," Emily said. "You can't beat nature for keeping you healthy. Now, if you had a tablespoon of molasses every day like I wanted you to…"

"Mom, please." Owen grimaced, freckles showing up more as he flushed.

Surely, he was what he seemed. Joanna couldn't believe that his reaction wasn't genuine.

Meredith, smiling, touched Emily's hand. "Never mind. Why don't you sit down and talk to me? Maybe I'll remember something more."

For just an instant Joanna felt a tinge of jealousy that Meredith was turning to this newcomer instead of her. Then she chased the thought away. She should be delighted that Meredith was talking so much more easily and knowing her relative. That was a good step toward remembering other things, and if she remembered, she might be safe.

CHAPTER FOURTEEN

SOMETIME LATER JOANNA settled herself in a booth at the hospital cafeteria, accepting the cup of coffee Owen had insisted on getting for her. Meredith had drifted off to sleep again, maybe as a defense against Emily's incessant chatter. If she didn't wake when Emily rearranged her blanket for the third time, Joanna guessed it had been safe to show Owen the way to the cafeteria.

She'd come out of the room thinking she might call for her ride home. Meredith surely was safe with an officer on the door. But then it occurred to her that this was a chance to learn more about Meredith and her family. That was important, both because it might provide an indication of why she'd been attacked, but also for Joanna's sake. Maybe Owen would drop a clue to where she might fit into the Bristow family.

"Are you sure you shouldn't have taken a coffee up to your mother?" she asked, pushing the sugar bowl across the table to Owen. She watched in awe as he put three heaping spoonfuls of sugar into his coffee.

He caught her expression and grinned. "I have a sweet tooth. Not like Merry, who believes in eating healthy. As for Mom, I'll take a cup to her when I go back, but I'm glad to have a break from that hospital room."

"It's hard to see someone you care about in the hospital." And he was young enough that he probably hadn't experienced it often.

"Well, yeah, it is, but we're not really all that close as far as family goes. Merry lives in the city, while we've always been out in the suburbs. So we went to different schools and didn't see a lot of each other."

"Are you in college now?" She really wanted to ask about Meredith, but she'd have to lead into it, or Owen might feel he was being cross-examined. But no one ever objected to talking about himself, it seemed.

Owen nodded. "It's my first year at Penn. That's why Mom didn't come as soon as we heard. She doesn't like to drive this far, so she waited until my break started. That way I could bring her." He made a face. "It isn't that I'm not concerned about Merry, but it's not what I planned for my fall break."

"What about Meredith? Is she in school?"

"Not now. She has a year to go in Wharton, but she surprised everyone by taking a year off. I never did know why."

Was it something to do with whatever had brought Meredith to her door? She couldn't help but wonder.

"That's a business school, isn't it?"

He nodded. "Just as well she's interested in it, because she inherits control of her grandfather's business and the trust she gets when she turns twenty-one."

"Not you?" Was that a possible source of conflict in the family?

"Not a chance. With his own children gone, the old man settled everything on his only granddaughter, as far as I know. Not that I care," he added quickly. "I wouldn't mind coming into the money, but I don't want to be stuck in an office for the rest of my life. Merry can have it."

Owen sounded genuine, but she didn't know enough about his world, and Meredith's, to judge.

"I'm sorry about asking so many questions. It's just that it seemed such a long time that we didn't know who your cousin was. We felt so helpless. So naturally, I was curious."

"Sure, I can see that." He stirred his coffee vigorously. "She's probably curious about you, too. I never knew any Amish people, except for the ones that bring things to the city market, and I doubt she does, either."

"She'd be busy with school, I guess."

"Busy with everything. Mom keeps holding her up as an example to me. Merry volunteers for every charity that comes along, gets A's at school, visits her grandfather's business, you name it. And she's happy doing it."

The surprise in his voice amused her. "Not you?"

"Listen, if I did all that, I'd just be waiting for an excuse to run off. I figured old Gregory Bristow wouldn't have left any part of the business to me anyway. The business was all he ever thought about, and Merry was his little partner."

Did Owen realize he was handing her a reason for the attack on Meredith? Or did he assume everything that happened was an accident? She couldn't tell.

"Just Meredith? Didn't he have any other grand-children?"

"Just Merry. Her father was the first boy, the one who was supposed to inherit everything, but he died in an accident when Merry was small. He had a sister, but she fought all the time with the old man and finally ran off. So it just came down to Merry."

She tried to digest all that information, filing away the runaway sister for future considering. "What about her mother?"

Owen shrugged. "She remarried, moved out to San Francisco with her second husband and left Merry with her grandfather. They get along okay, I guess, but they don't spend much time together."

A wave of pity went over her for the child who seemed to have lost both parents. "That's such a shame."

Owen drained his cup. "I guess. I should get the coffee to take to Mom. Are you coming back up?"

"No, I'll let you visit with your cousin. Will you be going home soon?"

He shrugged. "I don't know. Mom was talking about staying until Merry could go home and taking her with us. I think she wants to talk to the doctor about it first."

"I must go and find a telephone to call for my ride. Perhaps I'll see you again."

"Here, don't bother." He pulled out a cell phone. "Modern convenience, see?"

She smiled as she took the phone, wondering if he

thought she'd never seen one. He waited while she called and then retrieved his phone.

"Denke. Thanks," she added, sure he wouldn't understand the word.

"No problem. See you later." He headed for the coffee, and Joanna started down the hallway toward the entrance where she'd been dropped off. Chief Jamison had said he'd meet her there.

It was sprinkling when she reached the door, so she stood inside to wait. True to his word, Jamison pulled to the curb a few minutes later. Hurrying through the drops, Joanna scurried to the car and got in beside him.

"Good," he said, pulling away. "I'm glad you were sensible enough to stay inside until you saw me. No point in taking any chances."

Since that hadn't even occurred to Joanna, she could hardly accept his praise. Better to remain silent, she decided.

"Well, what did you think of them?"

For an instant she was startled. "I thought you wanted to see what Meredith thought of them."

"Both will do. Start with either one."

"I didn't really have a chance to hear what she thought of them, but she did recognize Emily, and she seemed perfectly friendly to her." She hesitated, not sure she liked the role of informer.

"What about the son?" Jamison was determined.

"She didn't seem to recognize him, but she wasn't at all afraid of him. In fact, she explained that her memory wasn't back entirely, so I guess she knows that and accepts it."

He frowned, seeming to file the information away. "What did you think of them?"

"I couldn't really form an opinion in such a short time," she protested.

"They must have made an impression on you. What was it?"

If Owen had felt like this when she was asking him questions, he probably disliked her.

"I thought Emily was concerned about her. She fussed a lot, and she talked a lot about things that had happened, I guess to see if Meredith remembered them." She frowned, thinking it over. "I couldn't tell if Meredith did or if she was just going along with her. Eventually, she dozed off, and I took Owen down to the lunchroom for coffee. He said he hadn't been able to find it," she explained.

"Hard to believe a city type couldn't find his way around our little hospital," Jamison said. "What did he have to say for himself?"

She shrugged, not sure what he was looking for. "He's a college student, and he brought his mother because she doesn't like to drive. He said... Did you know that Meredith comes into her grandfather's business and money when she turns twenty-one? Yes, I guess you mentioned it. She must be almost that now."

He nodded. "I did find out some information from the Philly police. Most people would call it a fortune. That's enough to make a person think about how to get a piece of it."

Joanna thought of her own family and shuddered. "It's hard to believe any of her relatives would try to kill her, money or not."

He slowed as they approached the corner by the quilt shop. "Listen, Joanna. I've just heard that the other cousin is coming back, lawyer in tow. They're going to push taking her home, and I'm not sure how I can stop it. If you know anything you haven't told me, now's the time."

"If I knew anything that would help, I'd tell you. But I don't. If she goes home…will the police there protect her?"

"I don't know." He looked grim. "What I do know is that both of you are clearly in danger." He reached out and patted her arm. "Be careful. If anything feels wrong, you call for help."

She nodded, but he grasped her arm.

"I mean it. Don't risk your life because you don't want to cause gossip. It's not worth it."

NOAH, LOOKING OUT the window for at least the hundredth time that afternoon, spotted Jamison's car turning into the alley with Joanna seated next to him. That meant he was taking her to the back door.

He was already moving to the back of the store. He told himself that it was his duty to make sure she got in safely…as a neighbor. It was a simple act that didn't mean anything.

And if he could believe that, he could probably believe anything. He went out onto the stoop and headed down the three steps.

The car had pulled to a stop, and he saw Jamison glance at him, smile and say something to Joanna. She turned away and got out, apparently not answering.

They met in the middle. "I just wanted to be sure you got back safely. Are you in for the rest of the day?"

Joanna nodded. "You don't have to stay on watch. I'll stay where no one can bother me." She smiled, but it was a strained gesture.

That obvious effort to smile and the way she'd turned away from the chief troubled him. "What did Jamison say to you?" he asked on impulse. "Just now, I mean, when you were getting out."

She looked startled, and then a pink flush tinged her cheeks. "He…he said I should be nice to you." Before he could react, she hurried on. "He doesn't understand. He thinks just because he's seen us together a lot lately that we're…well, involved."

No wonder she was embarrassed. It was hardly fair to her that the circumstances had thrown them together. Some instinct told him to treat it lightly.

"He's like an Amish grandmother. Always wanting to pair people up. Funny for someone as hard-headed as he seems."

She appeared relieved at his response, but he could see the worry clouding her eyes.

"What's wrong? I mean, besides all the things that were already wrong." He drew her a little closer to the building, where they couldn't be seen easily by someone glancing their way.

"Nothing new, I guess. I was just thinking about the

relatives of Meredith's that I met today. Nice people. I can't believe they'd have anything to do with attacking Meredith."

"That should make you feel better," he pointed out.

Her eyes flashed. "How can it? Someone has done these things. Chief Jamison said he suspects everyone when there's a lot of money involved."

Noah turned that over in his mind. "Do you mean that he suspects you?"

"How could he suspect me? I had no idea Meredith was related to me until after the accident." She hesitated, obviously considering it. "You mean he might not believe that I didn't know. I guess that's possible. He'd just have my word to prove it. But even if I did know, it wouldn't benefit me if anything happened to her, even if I were that wicked."

"No one who knows you could possibly believe that," he assured her. "I'm just trying to figure out how a policeman thinks."

She gave a reluctant nod. "I suppose you're right. But I think mostly Chief Jamison is just worried about Meredith's safety. He told me that other cousin is coming back to town, and he thinks they'll insist on taking her back with them."

He leaned against the wall, looking into her face and trying to read the warring emotions there. "You don't want her to leave, do you?"

Her gaze escaped his. "I don't think she will be safe."

Noah wanted to lift her chin so he could see into her eyes, but it would be too dangerous to touch her.

Even just imagining the silkiness of her skin against his fingers had him longing for what he could never have.

But regardless of his emotions, it was important that Joanna face the truth.

"Komm, Joanna. We both know that's not all. She's a link to the mother you never knew. Isn't that it?"

"I know my mother," she said instantly. And then she paused. "Maybe there's something in what you say. I've learned such a very little about my birth mother. Nothing about my birth father. Isn't it natural that I'd like to know what kind of people I came from?"

He wanted to say that he'd be just as glad not to know everything he did about his parents, but that wouldn't help Joanna. He didn't suppose it would help him, either.

Still, it was hard to get rid of that old anger and frustration and disappointment. He hadn't realized how hard it was until he'd fully accepted it and really wanted to.

"I guess so," he admitted. "But I'd hate for you to get hurt. Or anyone else, either."

"I have to take that chance for myself. I'd rather know the truth, even if it's that my birth parents regretted I'd ever been born. It's the uncertainty that's so hard."

That was his Joanna. Brave and vulnerable at the same time. He just had to remember that she wasn't *his* Joanna.

"I hope you won't be disappointed. But even if

she goes back home soon, she might still remember later why she came here. It might even be easier for her once she's there. And if she did come here to find you, she can still get in touch with you."

"I know that. But only if she's all right. That's what Chief Jamison is worried about. He's afraid the police there aren't taking it seriously, and if she goes back, she won't be protected."

Her fear for Meredith reached out to him, and he tried to resist.

"She'll be around friends when she goes home. There must be people who'll look after her." Noah found himself hoping that might calm her fears, even knowing as he spoke that it wouldn't. It didn't even convince him.

She shivered. "I think… No, I feel…as if it's getting more dangerous every minute. The more Meredith remembers, the more someone wants to silence her."

"And you," he pointed out. "That car sideswiping your buggy was no coincidence."

"I'm really not afraid for myself, not now. As long as I stay here, I'm safe. Nobody would try to take on both me and Aunt Jessie."

She'd obviously intended him to smile, and he did, but he wished he had her confidence. "Yah, your aunt Jessie can be scary, but just in case, I'm still sleeping upstairs at night." He jerked his head toward the second floor above his store.

"Ach, Noah, don't you mean you're staying awake

upstairs? You shouldn't, really. You have too many responsibilities already without taking on me."

He could see the complicated emotions written all over her face. And he knew his must be just as confused. If only he did have the right to take care of her...

They were silent, inches apart, and the longing built up in him. If he leaned forward just a little—

The back door slammed open, revealing Jessie staring out at them. "If you two want to talk, you'd best come inside to do it."

That was sufficiently intimidating to make him back up. "I have to get back to the store."

He strode to his storeroom entrance, covering the ground in a few long strides. But he didn't go in, not until he saw the door close and heard it lock behind Joanna.

JOANNA HURRIED UPSTAIRS while her aunt went on into the shop. She'd have to tidy herself, but more important, she had to make sure she wasn't blushing. Halfway up she came to a halt, clutching her ribs. She'd been too preoccupied to heed it before, but all those bruises she'd acquired last night were making themselves known.

If she told Aunt Jessie, her aunt would insist upon some awful-smelling salve that she declared would heal anything. Maybe, but it could also be smelled a half block away. Deciding she'd take an aspirin and keep quiet, she walked into the kitchen and found her middle brother, Isaac, taking up residence. He was sitting at the table with what looked like half of a shoofly pie and a glass of milk.

She pulled herself together. "What happened to you? Did they run out of food at home?"

Isaac grinned, the dimple in his cheek flashing. "I'm a growing boy. You don't begrudge me a little snack, do you?"

"You call that little?" At his startled reaction, she smiled. "I don't mind as long as you leave some for me," she said. "Just be sure to tell Aunt Jessie how gut it is."

"I know that," he said. "I always say something nice to the cook. That way they'll make it again for me."

"Smart aleck," she said. "You'll be too sure of yourself one of these days. It isn't that I'm not glad to see you, but what are you doing here?"

"Besides eating, you mean? Bringing your buggy back. Aaron stopped by while we were still milking this morning, so when we finished, we went and got it. Daad and I fixed it ourselves once we saw the frame wasn't bent. But you should have heard Daad about your driving."

"I'm just as glad I didn't," she said, knowing that was Isaac's idea of humor. "Did you really help?"

"Sure I did. I held things and carried things and I even got to jack up the buggy."

He looked a little offended that she'd doubted him, and she ruffled his hair affectionately. When he wasn't squabbling with his little brother, he was a good boy.

"That's the way to learn, ain't so? Denke, Isaac. Am I supposed to take you home?"

He shook his head, then swallowed an enormous mouthful. "I brought Mammi in, and Daad's coming back to pick us up later. He said to tell you not to drive at night anymore."

For an instant she felt cold as the memory of her buggy accident swept over her. "No need to worry about that. I won't. I don't want to end up in the ditch again."

"So what happened?" His blue eyes were sharp with curiosity. "You used to be a pretty good driver."

"I still am." She gave a mock slap at his head and he ducked. "It was the driver of the car who wasn't. Road hog."

"So say this saltshaker is the buggy, and this is the ditch." He put his knife alongside it, sprinkling crumbs and molasses over the table. "Where did the car come from?"

"Behind me." Playing along with him, she took the pepper shaker and ran it up behind the salt, giving it a tap. She must have hit it harder than she'd intended, because it skittered across the table, adding salt to the crumbs. "He just clipped me enough to push me into the ditch."

"You get the license plate number?"

Tiring of Isaac playing detective and her head beginning to pound, she put a snap in her voice. "I did not. When you're upside down in a ditch, you don't notice too much."

"I would have," he said smugly.

"Tell me that after it happens to you." She gave him another smack, a bit harder this time, but of course he only grinned.

Making a detour to the kitchen cabinet, she swallowed a couple of aspirin with a glass of water. "I'm going down to the shop," she told him. "Try not to eat us out of house and home while you're here."

Then she headed on downstairs, hearing his laughter behind her. One thing she could say about her pesky little brother. He'd made her completely forget she'd been upset.

She reached the bottom and saw her mother, getting an armload of quilt squares from a drawer. On her face, Joanna read such a mixture of emotions—apprehension, uncertainty, fear—that she didn't know what to say.

She wanted to slap herself for causing her mother so much grief. Instead of doing something so useless, Joanna hurried to embrace her mother.

"I'm wonderful happy to see you, Mammi. I didn't know you were coming today. To help with the quilting class, yah?"

Her mother nodded, releasing her reluctantly. "Your aunt thought I could be of help with the beginner class. Is it all right?"

"All right? It's perfect." She forced a lightness into her voice. "You have much more patience than Aunt Jessie does. She scares some of them half to death."

"They should listen better." Aunt Jessie sniffed. "Nobody pays attention these days. They're too used to televisions and computers and all that stuff."

Joanna exchanged glances with her mother, glad to see that Mamm was amused. She'd always relied on her older sister, but she certain sure knew what Jessie was like.

"I'll help you set up." Joanna grabbed a couple of folding chairs, only to be stopped by her mother.

"You shouldn't be carrying things. Not after having a buggy accident. I'll take them."

Joanna held them firmly out of reach. "I'm fine, Mammi. Honest. All I did was slide off the seat into the nice, soft, wet grass. Is Daad very mad at me?"

Her mother was distracted from the chairs. "Ach, Joanna, you know better than that. He's just upset that he didn't insist you get on the road while it was still light."

"As bad as some of the drivers are, I don't know if it would have made a difference." Joanna carried the chairs over to the folding table they used for class, setting them up a little more slowly than usual.

When Joanna started to go back for more, Mamm put her hand on Joanna's arm to stop her.

"Honestly, Mammi, I'm all right."

"You don't look all right the way you're moving."

"Just a few bruises. Don't tell Aunt Jessie, or you know what she'll want to put on it."

Her mother patted her cheek. "I brought some of my own liniment. I'll put it upstairs before I go. You use it before you go to bed so you won't get stiff."

"I will," she promised. At least Mamm's stuff didn't stink.

Her mother paused, her hand resting on Joanna's

shoulder as if to keep her there. "I wanted to say... wanted to ask, I mean...about her. The woman in the hospital. We heard she was awake."

Joanna had a brief struggle with herself. Daadi wouldn't like her saying anything that would upset Mamm, but she couldn't refuse to answer the question.

"Yah, she's awake. Getting her strength back, I think. She's talking a lot more."

"And remembering?" The anxiety in her mother's voice couldn't be mistaken.

"Some things, not everything. I don't think she knows what brought her to River Haven." She waited, wondering what Mamm hoped to hear. Or what she feared to hear.

"I'm glad she's better," Mamm said. "I'm praying for her." She hesitated, and Joanna felt that other words were hovering on her lips.

"Tell me, Mammi," she said softly. "What is it?"

Mamm met her gaze. "Daad keeps trying to protect me, but I have to know. Is she a relative of yours? I know why Daad is trying to keep things back, but I really do need to know. Wouldn't you?"

It was exactly what she'd been thinking. "Yah, Mammi, I feel the same. The test they did said that we were pretty close relatives, like, maybe cousins. But that's all I know, and she may not know even that much."

"I saw her, you know." She looked past Joanna as if focused on something else.

"Saw who?" Her mind was blank. Was she talking about Meredith?

"The girl. The one we think was your mother—your birth mother."

"Saw her?" Joanna absorbed the shock. "But you never said. Daad didn't, either."

"Daad didn't, but I did. And I never told him. I think it was her anyway."

"When? How?" New information kept coming to light, and each time she had to adjust again. She wouldn't have believed that Mamm would keep anything from Daad.

"Earlier that night. I had pulled the curtain over a little bit to look out at the snow, and I saw someone on the walk. She was young, and she looked...I don't know...kind of worried and upset."

She wasn't sure that added up to the person being her mother. "What did she look like?"

"Young, maybe twenty. She had on one of those big jackets...parkas, I think they call them, so I couldn't see her very well between that and the snow and the dark. But..."

"But what?" She had an urge to shake the words out.

"She looked up for a minute, and the light caught her face. Pale, thin. She looked so worried, like she was at the end of her rope. It made me want to help her. But then she was gone, and after a minute I heard the door close in the room next to us."

"You didn't ever tell Daad?"

Mamm shook her head. "I didn't know it was

important, you see, and by the morning, she was gone." She clasped Joanna's hand. "I wish I could have helped her, whether she was the woman who gave birth to you or not."

Joanna's voice seemed to be caught in her throat. She patted her mother's hand.

"You did, Mammi. You did. If she was the one, she asked you to take care of her baby. And you did that better than anyone else could possibly have done."

CHAPTER FIFTEEN

JOANNA WOKE THE next morning to the sound of pans clattering and the aroma of something baking. Had she overslept? A quick look out the window reassured her. The sun was barely over the ridge. It couldn't be later than six, so what was Aunt Jessie doing in the kitchen?

Yawning, she stumbled out to the kitchen in a nightgown and bare feet to find Aunt Jessie hauling a large pan of gingersnaps out of the oven to join the ones already on the cooling racks.

"Aunt Jessie? What's going on?" She headed for the coffeepot as she spoke. She definitely needed something to get her going this morning.

Jessie dropped the hot pan onto a cutting board and closed the oven door, turning to her with a spatula in her hand. She surveyed Joanna with a wry expression.

"I see you forgot what day it is. Welcome to River Haven Day, according to our ambitious Main Street association. Remember?"

Joanna took a sip of scalding coffee, blinking, and groaned. "You're right. I did forget. I wish I could go on forgetting."

Welcome Day was the brainstorm of this year's

chairperson of the merchants' society. The second week of every month was now given over to promoting Main Street businesses. Each business had a special sale, and they all took turns hosting refreshments. Today was their turn for snacks.

"Ach, I'm sorry." She was letting her business and her aunt down. "I'll hurry and get dressed and come help you."

Aunt Jessie's expression softened. "I'm just teasing you. Go rest a little longer. I have it under control, and you look like you didn't sleep well."

If she looked like she felt, that would be pretty sad. "I'll go dress," she repeated.

To say she'd slept well wouldn't be true, but she didn't want her aunt worrying about her. Taking the coffee with her, she hurried into the bathroom.

A splash of water on the face gave her the courage to look in the mirror. Goodness, no wonder her aunt had noticed it. Apparently, a night filled with bad dreams had left its mark.

She scrubbed her face with vigor and found that helped, making her eyes brighter and bringing pink to her cheeks. Too bad she couldn't erase the memory of her dreams as easily. It was strange, in a way. She'd been thinking about Noah before she went to sleep, remembering that moment when he'd come close to kissing her. She might have dreamed about that. Instead, she'd had just one dream, over and over. Meredith, trapped in a dark place, afraid.

Joanna tried to shake it off. Merry, she reminded herself of the nickname Owen had used. Did that reflect her normal attitude? The nickname projected an image of a laughing young girl, ready for life, with no lines on her face from concern or worry.

Meredith's face was still unlined, younger than she'd thought in her first glimpse of the girl on the stairs. But in the dream, Meredith had been frightened, her pretty face distorted by fear—the fear of something coming toward her in the dark. She'd been calling out to Joanna, trusting her to help. Joanna felt again the desperate need she'd experienced in the night. The need to reach her—to save her.

Joanna slapped her face with cold water again. It had been just a dream, and besides, she would do everything she could to help her...what, cousin? Relative anyway.

She hurried about her dressing and putting her hair up in its usual knot, over which she adjusted a fresh, snowy kapp. There, she looked better, didn't she?

Apparently not, to judge by the look Aunt Jessie gave her when she returned to the kitchen. She slapped a plate down on the table. "Eat first. Then you can get busy. And remember—the best cure for worry is to keep busy and trust the good Lord."

Abashed, she nodded. "I'll try."

Once she'd finished eating, Joanna hurried outside to feed her mare. The fall sunshine was back again, but she didn't like the look of those clouds on the western horizon. Well, a little rain wouldn't discourage the regular shoppers. They came out as much for the refreshments and the chatter, she suspected, as for the sales.

Feeding and watering Princess took little time.

She'd come back later and put the mare in the paddock. She hurried out of the stable and nearly ran into Noah, who was going in.

Keeping her expression peaceful took a little effort, but she managed it. Fortunately, because, as he greeted her, Noah gave every impression that those moments between them yesterday had never been. He moved back as she came forward, clearly keeping space between them.

"I hope you got a little more sleep last night." She thought again of her realization that he'd been spending nights on the second floor of the hardware store, listening for anything that might go wrong.

He shrugged, not meeting her gaze. "Not bad. Isaac stayed over and took turns with me. I don't know what he thought, but at least he didn't ask questions. Just as well he did, because it looks like it will be a busy day again today."

"I'd forgotten it was Welcome Day until Aunt Jessie reminded me." She gave him a teasing smile. "So your business is picking up, is it?"

He was expressionless for a moment before his face relaxed. "You want me to admit I was wrong to be so pessimistic, don't you?"

"Well, weren't you?"

He nodded. "Guess I haven't done as gut a job as I thought getting over thinking people were waiting for me to make a mistake. I'm trying."

"As my aunt would say, try harder."

She kept her voice light. If he wanted to pretend there was nothing between them, that the moment of recognition yesterday had never happened, she could do that, as well.

He gave a nod and started on into the stable. She thought he wasn't going to reply, but as he passed her, he muttered one word. "Bossy."

Irrationally pleased by that, she headed back to get on with what promised to be a busy day.

The cookie baking and sales display signs took much of the time until they opened. Since most people were waiting for the afternoon sale to come in, it was quiet enough to allow them to set up the area for refreshments. Aunt Jessie also insisted on setting containers of wet wipes in several places, along with signs reminding customers to use them before touching fabrics.

"Don't you think people might be offended by the sign?" Joanna knew it was no use, but she couldn't help herself.

"Then they can go elsewhere," Aunt Jessie retorted. "I'm not having folks touching bolts of new fabric with sticky fingers."

"More likely they'll appreciate the reminder."

Joanna spun around at the voice and hugged her friend Rachel. "Rachel, I'm wonderful glad you're here. It seems like ages since I've seen you."

"Just since worship," Rachel pointed out.

"A few days can seem like ages." And these days had been crowded with incidents, that was certain. "Anyway, I'm happy to see you. Can I help you find something?"

"That's not why I'm here." Rachel took off her

bonnet. "I had to come to town anyway, so I thought I could help for a bit."

"We won't say no." The thought of a few minutes of talk with Rachel was irresistible. She so seldom got away from her demanding father. "Komm to the back room and hang up your bonnet and sweater."

With a glance at the clock to be sure they had a few minutes before the sale officially started, she led her to the back room.

"Now, then," she said once they were alone. "How did you get away today?"

"It's not that bad." Rachel always defended her father and her siblings, no matter how much they took her for granted. "And I did have some shopping to do. Might as well come on sales day, ain't so?"

"For sure." She waited while Rachel hung up her bonnet and smoothed her hair back, not that it was ever out of place.

"There now." Rachel turned back to her. "Has something more happened? You look as if you've been fretting."

"I wish everybody would stop telling me that." Joanna suspected she even sounded fretful. "I'm all right. It's just been busy with the shop and trying to visit the hospital every day."

"Ach, I'm sure it has been." Her sweet face filled with sympathy. "Have you found out yet why that poor girl came to your door?"

"Not really." She hesitated, but it was useless to try to hide things from one of her oldest friends. Rachel knew her too well. "It turns out that I might be related to her. It's…upsetting."

Rachel considered for a moment. "I don't see why. You've always known you were adopted. Your birth parents had to be somebody. What does it matter if they were Englischers? You're still you."

"Yah, that's true."

And she was glad of it. But that didn't ease her worry about her parents. If it got out that they might have broken the law by not reporting that they'd found her, what might happen? She didn't think they could be charged with anything after all this time, but it would hurt them so in the community. Daad would probably have to resign as bishop, and that would be about the worst thing that could happen to him. He'd made a vow to serve for life. How could he break that? It would destroy them.

She hoped she hadn't been silent too long. The easiest way out was to agree with Rachel.

"You're right as always. Komm." She opened the door. "Let's get to work."

The sale started with the slight rush that Joanna had expected, and then settled down to a steady pace as their normal customers came, shopped, snacked and chatted. Along with Aunt Jessie and Rachel, she moved from customer to customer, chatting about projects, helping them decide on fabrics and trying hard for endless patience when one old customer had nearly every bolt in the store out for comparison before finally deciding.

Aunt Jessie stopped by while Joanna was cutting

the various pieces. "So, Lovina, it looks like you're making a new quilt. Having trouble deciding?"

Lovina Fisher chuckled. "No more than usual. I must say Joanna has a good eye for matching patterns. She's a lot more patient with me than you would be. And she's got a lot on her mind with that Englischer and all."

It was said kindly, and Joanna tried hard not to take offense. She couldn't help being frustrated by the endless curiosity of everyone from the eldest Amish widow to the youngest bride. It made her feel that wherever she went and whatever she said, eyes were on her.

She handed Lovina her package and smiled. "The patient is doing much better now, and we're wonderful glad. It's a terrible thing to have someone injured on your property, ain't so?"

Lovina patted her hand. "It wasn't your fault, that's certain sure. You'll be happy when she's gone off home and forgotten River Haven."

Would she? She absently watched the door closing behind Lovina and then opening again as someone else came in. If she could be sure Meredith was going to be safe, she supposed she would, but it would haunt her to never know the answers to the questions that plagued her.

Aunt Jessie nudged her. "Is that the woman you told me about? The cousin, or whatever she is?"

Sure enough, Emily Graham stood looking at a display of quilted place mats, fingering them.

"Yah, it is. I wonder what brings her to the shop."

"She's sure not from around here." Joanna looked at her aunt in time to see a mix of emotions cross her face in quick succession. "I don't suppose she's making a quilt. You'd best find out what she wants."

Nodding, Joanna came reluctantly from behind the counter. With that attitude, she certain sure couldn't let Aunt Jessie wait on her. If indeed she'd come to shop, which she doubted. Well, if Emily was here to ask questions, she'd just politely refer her to Chief Jamison.

Managing to look unconcerned, Joanna approached her, dodging a small child whose mother was in close pursuit. She came up beside Emily, convinced the woman had seen her approaching but, for whatever reason, was pretending she hadn't.

"Mrs. Graham. It's nice to see you in our shop."

Emily Graham reacted with well-simulated surprise. "Is this shop yours? That's right, someone did tell me that, but I'd forgotten. It's so sweet. And busy." Emily glanced around at the seven or eight customers who were currently in the shop.

"For us it's busy, but this afternoon is a special event. All the businesses on Main Street have special sales, and we're serving refreshments. I hope you'll help yourself to a homemade cookie and some lemonade."

Aunt Jessie had insisted on lemonade rather than coffee as being less messy to set up and not so dangerous if spilled. Sticky, though. Joanna had already decided she'd have to point that out. Thank goodness it wouldn't be their turn again until spring.

"That's so sweet." Emily shifted to a rack of table runners, most of which they handled on consignment. "We're staying at that nice hotel down on the square, and I thought I'd take a look around town before we go up to visit Merry. She is doing much better, isn't she?"

She seemed genuinely concerned, and Joanna's heart warmed to her. "Definitely. She's improved so much in the past few days. I pray she'll be back to normal soon."

But Emily didn't seem to hear the answer, her attention distracted by a display of wall hangings.

"I intended to spend all day with Merry, but Owen said if I didn't stop fussing over her, I'd drive her crazy. I don't see why anyone would feel that way when I'm just showing I care, do you? But these young people think they know everything. She'd certainly rather see me than Landon Bristow. I never met anyone who was such a stuffed shirt. Now, he *would* drive a person crazy. Do you know him?"

Emily stopped, probably for breath, so Joanna was able to answer the question. "I met him when he came to identify Meredith. Is he here now?"

"He arrived this morning. And tried to take over right away, of course." She sniffed. "I don't know why he's making such a fuss over Merry. He's never been close to her. He's just taking too much on himself, that's all."

Emily seemed to have taken offense at Meredith's other cousin. Or maybe she'd always felt that way. Remembering her own reaction to the man, Joanna could hardly blame her.

"I'm sorry he's upset you. What is it that he wants to do?" she asked.

"He thinks he should make all the arrangements about taking Merry home on his schedule, and he even wants to put her in some nursing home he knows about. She doesn't need a nursing home, and I told him that. Told that policeman, too. What do you think?"

"I wouldn't think so, either, as long as she takes it easy. But the doctor…"

"Right. That's so silly, Landon butting in, when Owen and I had already come and made the plans ourselves. I know Meredith will be much better off in her own home. She'll remember more easily there than in another strange place. Don't you think so?"

Appealed to, Joanna tried to find the right answer. She agreed that Meredith would probably do better at home, but would it be safe? And what would Chief Jamison say?

Perhaps Aunt Jessie saw from her expression that she'd welcome an interruption just then. She came over to them, and Joanna grabbed a reason to change the subject.

"Mrs. Graham, I'd like to introduce you to my aunt Jessie. She's my partner in the business."

Emily seemed a little intimidated by Jessie's stern face. She wasn't the first person to react that way, and Joanna had to hide a smile.

"Aunt Jessie, this is Mrs. Emily Graham. She's Meredith's cousin, come all the way from Philadelphia to see her."

"Wilkom." Aunt Jessie nodded gravely. "She is doing better, ain't so?"

"Oh, yes, that's what we were just talking about. I think it's time she was in her own home, and I'd be happy to stay with her and take care of her." A hint of her annoyance with Landon Bristow showed in her voice. "I'm sure you'd agree that a woman can handle that much better than a man."

"No doubt about that. Can we help you with something?" Aunt Jessie's words were an obvious hint.

Reminded, Emily hastily pulled a wall hanging from its rack. "I'll take this one, please."

Joanna turned her attention to the sale, relieved at seeing Emily on her way. She accepted the bills the woman held out.

"Oh, and I did want to ask Joanna if we could take her out to supper tonight. We would so like to visit with you, and I'm sure you know the best places to eat here. We'd drive you, of course. And bring you home." She glanced at a slim gold watch on her wrist. "Goodness, I should go if I'm going to see Merry this afternoon. May I pick you up here for supper, then?"

Joanna glanced at her aunt, wondering if accepting the invitation would be wise.

But Jessie nodded. "As long as they bring you home right afterward, it's fine, ain't so? Anna Miller has been asking me to come by for supper, so I'll do that."

She couldn't think of a reason to refuse. "Denke. Thank you. I will go up to see Meredith after we finish here, so maybe we could meet there."

"Fine." Emily took the bag Joanna held out to her. "We'll pick you up at the front of the hospital at six. Is that all right?"

Joanna nodded. It seemed she was going out to supper with them. Well, she couldn't seriously believe that Emily meant any harm to her, and they'd be in a public place. But she'd better tell Chief Jamison about it anyway.

JOANNA WALKED INTO Meredith's room after a busy day at the shop, and the smile froze on her face. The room was empty. Fear gripped her. Where was Meredith?

Before Joanna could panic, Meredith came in with Mary Ellen holding her arm in a secure grasp.

"You're just in time, Joanna. Look how well our patient is doing—she'll be walking right out of the hospital before you know it."

"Wonderful gut." She couldn't help beaming. "That's amazing, Meredith."

"I'd be proud of myself if it weren't that my legs feel like overcooked noodles," Meredith said. "I'm about as strong as a baby." But her smile showed how pleased she was.

"You've had more than enough physical therapy for one day." Mary Ellen steered her firmly toward the padded chair, and then hesitated. "Chair or bed?"

"Chair, please." Meredith looked tired, but she spoke firmly. "I've had enough of lying around."

"That's what we like to hear." Mary Ellen was probably used to being professionally cheerful, but this sounded real. "Have a chat with Joanna, and I'll bring you some juice."

Mary Ellen disappeared on her errand, and Meredith gave Joanna a wry smile. "She says that as if it were a real treat."

"Maybe it is when it comes to hospitals." Joanna pulled up a straight chair. "As well as you're doing today, they will be kicking you out soon."

"It's about time." Meredith said the words strongly, but she had let her head fall back against the cushion, and her hands lay limp on her lap.

A spasm of concern, maybe fear, ran through Joanna. Brave words. Meredith didn't lack for spirit, but she was still so terribly weak. If she left here, how could she possibly defend herself?

"Talk to me," Meredith prodded. "Tell me about your day."

"Busy. We…the town merchants…always have sales one week of the month, except during the winter, when it's awfully quiet here. This time it was our turn to have refreshments. You should hear my aunt on the idea of letting folks have food around fabric and quilts."

Meredith's forehead wrinkled. "Somebody said you had a quilt shop. Does your aunt help you?"

"We're partners." It seemed to her that Meredith was trying to orient herself to a strange place, so probably anything she said about it would help. "Our shop is right down on Main Street." She gestured toward the one window of the room. "When you look out that window, you can see Main Street going away from you, with shops on either side. Our is on the left, about halfway down."

Meredith nodded slowly. "I'll look out later. Maybe I'll see the sign." She fell silent, seeming to expect Joanna to pick up the conversation.

"Your cousin Emily came into the shop today. She bought a wall hanging." She smiled. "Or rather, Aunt Jessie sold her a wall hanging."

"Good." She was surprised at the firmness in Meredith's voice. "The Bristow family ought to be repaying you for your kindness."

Joanna shook her head at that. "That's not necessary. I didn't see Owen, though. Did you remember him yet?"

Meredith got what she could only call a mischievous look. "I did, but I pretended I didn't this afternoon for a bit. Owen's ego could stand being taken down a peg."

"That's how I feel about my little brothers sometimes. But what about your other cousin? I heard he was coming today."

"Landon?" She made a face. "He was here, complete with lawyer, planning to arrange my life to suit himself. He wanted to shove me into a nursing home, of all things. I told him I could arrange my life by myself."

Compelled to try to see the best in him, probably because she'd taken such an instant dislike to the man, Joanna sought for an excuse for him.

"I suppose he feels as if you depend on him, that he's responsible for you. At least he wants to help."

Meredith shook her head. "Not him. He's been try-ing to take control ever since my grandfather died, not that I would let him. Grandfather wouldn't have." She stopped suddenly, looking startled.

"What is it?"

Meredith shook her head slightly. "Funny. I just realized I remembered that while I was saying it."

"That's a good sign, isn't it? I wish I could un-derstand what it must feel like. I'd like to be able to help you."

"Maybe you can." Her fingers moved on the arm of the chair as if searching for something. "Mary Ellen told me that you were the one who found me when I was hurt, but I don't remember anything about it. Tell me about it. Was I shopping at your store?"

"I...I'm not sure the doctor would want—"

"It's *my* memory."

Joanna had to smile. The expression, the words, the tone—all said that she was used to people listen-ing when she spoke. Maybe that was part of having been born with money. Or maybe it was a reminder that she wasn't far removed from her teen years. She'd probably been rebellious.

"I'll tell you, but if it starts to upset you, that's it. Agreed?"

Meredith wrinkled her nose, looking very young for a moment. "Okay. Agreed."

"You weren't exactly at the store." She tried to think how to explain it. "It was past closing. You see, access to the store is from the street, but we have an apartment upstairs. The steps to it go up the back of the building. That's where you were."

"Had I been visiting you? Did we know each other?"

Joanna shook her head. "I'd never seen you before, and I wasn't expecting anyone. I'd been out, and when I came home, it was after dark. So I started up the stairs, not bothering with a flashlight, and almost fell on you."

Meredith seemed to ponder that for a long moment. "What was I doing there?" The question seemed addressed to herself. "Why?" Her fingers knotted on the chair arm.

Concerned that she was getting upset, Joanna tried to find a way to get Meredith off the subject, or at least to allay her frustration.

"You'll remember eventually," she soothed. "Probably faster if you don't push, don't you think so?"

That earned her a contemptuous look. "I have to know, don't you see? I had some reason for coming to River Haven and to your home. I don't do things without a reason."

"I thought maybe your relatives would know, but they don't have any idea. They didn't know where you were." The more she thought about it, the odder it seemed. "Emily gives the impression that she's very close to you, but..."

"But she's making things up." Meredith's voice was tart. "I don't mean she's lying, but she always wants to play an important role in whatever's going on. I can just see her talking about how much she cares about me." Her fingers moved rapidly on the chair arm.

Joanna subdued the giggle she felt coming when she remembered Emily's fussing over her poor little cousin. "I know what you mean. It's human nature, I guess. Some people are like that."

"I guess. She probably means well, but a little bit of Cousin Emily goes a long way."

That seemed to describe it very well. "Are there other people…friends, maybe…who might know more about why you came here?"

"I don't know. Maybe." She rubbed her forehead. "I can't seem to think straight."

"Then you should stop trying." Joanna leaned forward to take Meredith's hand in hers, holding it gently until the restless moving stopped. "I'm sure it will come. Isn't that what the doctor advised you to do?"

Meredith strained against her for a long moment, but then she let out a breath and relaxed a little. "Just about, but it's so hard. It's like…"

"Maybe you ought to wait…"

She shook her head. "I need to say it. It's like I'm pushing against a fog. Every once in a while, some little piece comes clear, or maybe there's just a hint, and I feel that if I can only grab it, I'll understand everything. But it always slips away from me."

"Now you're making me feel that way, too." She tried to keep her voice light, but Meredith couldn't seem to accept the release she was offering.

Meredith shot a sharp look at her. "Why? I mean,

you can remember it all. There's no need for you to feel lost."

"But there are things I don't understand. I think I wonder just as much as you do about what brought you to my door that night. If only I hadn't been away. If I'd been there, when you came, if I'd talked to you, what would things be like now?"

Meredith nodded, and they sat there holding hands for a moment. Then Meredith smiled and released her hand. "It's funny. I keep feeling if I had one solid thing to hold on to, it would all come back to me."

Something solid…like a tiny gold heart? That was something solid that had a story for Joanna, if not for Meredith. Would it help if Meredith saw it? Maybe it would mean something to her.

The words trembled on her lips, but a second thought made her clamp them closed. It was too dangerous for her to take on the responsibility of telling her. Meredith didn't know about the DNA test yet.

The chief had been careful not to fuss when she'd told him the story of the necklace. But was he doing something about it without telling her? He might feel he had to. For a moment she regretted saying anything to him. How could she do anything that might hurt her parents?

Too many secrets were being kept—even if it was for good reasons. Secrets that strangled anything she might say or do. Whichever way she went, she could end up hurting someone.

No, she couldn't say anything now. She'd have to think about it long and hard, and before she could say a word to Meredith, she'd have to talk to Chief Jamison, wouldn't she?

It all came back to her parents. Why should they be hurt when all they'd done was take her in and love her? Any resentment she'd felt over the fact that they hadn't told her the truth had long since been swept away by love.

CHAPTER SIXTEEN

BY THE TIME Joanna left the hospital room, she was dreading the thought of having supper with Emily and her son, but there seemed no polite way of getting out of it. She couldn't excuse herself by saying that she didn't trust any of them, even though that was the truth. Still, what could they do to her at a public restaurant? And Aunt Jessie knew she was with them, and so did Chief Jamison.

It was possible that she could use this meal together as a chance to find out more from them about Meredith and the family. She must have been about the same age as Meredith's father. Would she have known his sister, the one who'd apparently disappeared? It was possible that she was Joanna's mother—the girl her mother had seen, who'd looked so lost.

Like Meredith. Her heart twisted at the thought of Meredith, groping her way through the fog, trying to remember whatever it was that seemed so important to her. She longed to protect her, and she felt as if she walked on thin ice whenever she was around any of Meredith's relatives.

Were they her relatives, as well? Trying to think her way through the possible connections only left her more confused than she had been before. It didn't matter anyway. It didn't affect her lack of trust in them, whether they were related or not. She'd still have to be careful around them.

Joanna stepped out the front door, glancing around for her ride. Almost immediately a car pulled up to the curb, and Emily opened the car door, waving, and got out.

"You sit up front with Owen, and then you can give him directions to a nice place to eat. I'll sit in the back."

There was no good reason why she couldn't give directions from the backseat, but Joanna obediently got in where she was directed. Owen rolled his eyes at his mother and nodded to Joanna.

"You'd better take us somewhere that has Amish food, or Mom's going to be disappointed. She has her heart set on it."

"We don't want to disappoint her, ain't so? Just go out of the driveway and turn right. I thought we'd go to Harvest Acres restaurant. It's very pleasant and people love the food. You want to go straight about three miles. I'll tell you when to turn."

He nodded, pulling out, and Emily leaned forward to ask a question. "Is it really Amish cooking? I can't go home without tasting the real thing."

"We usually call it Pennsylvania Dutch cooking. The Amish, the Mennonites and most of the longtime residents have a lot of recipes in common. This place is owned by a Mennonite family, and a lot of the teenage Amish and Mennonite girls get jobs there during the busy season."

Joanna could only hope she was making sense. It was hard to focus on trivial things when her mind kept darting around like a hummingbird, looking for answers.

She leaned forward, pointing. "You can turn left at the next corner, and then pull into the parking lot that's on your left. That's the restaurant."

There weren't many cars in the lot, about what she'd expect midweek in the fall. Most of the tourists were confined to the weekends now that summer holidays were over.

Owen parked near the entrance, and Joanna led the way inside, and exchanged a few words with the hostess, who took them to a table near a window. She hoped the other occupied tables near them might discourage Emily from too much talk about Meredith. There'd been enough interest locally in their mystery woman that probably everyone in the dining room knew who they were and thought they knew even more. Naturally, folks would be curious about why she was with them, but wasn't it understandable that they would want to take her out to supper to thank her?

"This is charming." Emily looked around with what seemed genuine pleasure. "We're not all that far from Lancaster County Amish, of course, but that area is much too busy with tourists." She gave a lady-like shudder. "I just don't enjoy that sort of thing."

There didn't seem much to say to that, so Joanna didn't speak, but Owen made a disgusted sound.

"Really, Mom. For all you know, Joanna might have relatives there."

Emily's eyes widened. "I didn't mean anything. I wouldn't..."

Joanna spoke quickly, annoyed with Owen for embarrassing his mother. "That's all right. I do have relatives there, and they don't care for all the tourists, either, except for the ones who are in businesses that deal with tourists."

Owen should know better than to speak to his mother in that tone of voice. Their forced togetherness seemed to be getting on his nerves. But she could imagine Daad's reaction if any of her brothers ever spoke to Mammi in that tone. They'd go straight to the woodshed.

"I like the hex signs," Emily said, looking at the painted emblems arranged above the windows all the way round the dining room. "So bright and colorful."

"They are, aren't they? We don't use them on our barns, but some people do."

And when they did, they'd be quick to point out that it was "just for pretty" and not for protection. No one would want to be thought superstitious in that way.

With a little pushing on her part, they became engrossed in the menu, and she could sit back and try to relax, glancing at them now and then. It was impossible to believe that either of these normal people could have been involved in the attack on Meredith.

Certainly, Emily couldn't have. The person she'd struggled with in the hospital room had been a man.

Owen? It was possible, she supposed, but all he seemed interested in at the moment was getting back home to enjoy whatever was left of his fall vacation from school. Of course, it would be possible for any of them to have hired someone.

The very idea seemed outlandish to her, but she knew it happened. Just not here.

Chief Jamison seemed convinced that money was behind everything that had happened. No doubt he'd been investigating the question of who benefited if Meredith died.

Usually family members waited until after a person died to argue about who should benefit… That was what made for family feuds. Everyone in the community knew about the two elderly Fisher sisters who hadn't spoken to each other in twenty years because they each thought they should have inherited their mother's quilting frame. It was silly and sad at the same time.

Soup and salad came promptly once they'd ordered, along with a large basket of fragrant, freshly baked bread and rolls. A little food seemed to put Owen into a better frame of mind, and when his mother said again how important it was that they take Meredith home, he even agreed with her.

"You could go and stay with her for as long as she needs you," he said. "I'll be back in school next week, so you don't have to worry about me."

"What are you studying in college?" Joanna paused to make room for the chicken potpie that she'd ordered, smiling her thanks to the server. It wouldn't be as good as her mother's, of course, but the restaurant was known for it.

"I haven't quite settled on what I want to do," Owen said. "I'm just taking general courses and seeing what best suits my talents." He waved his fork airily. "I know one thing for sure. It won't be business. I wouldn't be in Merry's shoes for anything. I'd go crazy if I had to run that whole company."

"That's silly," Emily said, almost sharply for her. "If her grandfather had been smart enough to leave it to you, you'd have been brilliant at it. Far better than Merry could be."

Joanna had to blink at the expression of fierce maternal pride in Emily's face. She looked ready to take on tigers for her young. This new side of someone she'd considered a rather silly woman startled her, making her see Emily in a new light. What might Emily be willing to do if she could persuade herself it was for her son?

Emily's comment made her uncomfortable, although she didn't think the others noticed. Joanna focused on the food, keeping her comments to brief ones about how the different dishes were made. She hadn't given up hoping for some insight into the Bristow family, but she didn't know how to bring up the subject.

"At least the doctor says that if Merry continues to do well, she can go home by the weekend. Or maybe before." Emily looked satisfied that things were going her way. "I'm sure she'll want us to take her, rather than Landon. She knows what a good driver Owen is."

Owen indulged in a roll of the eyes, but he sounded polite enough. "You know I'm glad to take her, Mom. But I can't hang around here much longer. I can't afford to miss a day of classes."

And she still hadn't learned anything useful about the family. Maybe the only thing was to plunge right in. "It seems a shame that Meredith doesn't have more family. Does she have any brothers or sisters?"

"It is sad, isn't it? Our family just gets smaller and smaller." Emily didn't look especially sad, but she was used to it, Joanna supposed.

Obviously, she'd have to push a little more. "Owen said her mother had remarried. He didn't tell me anything more."

"I'm afraid my cousin…her father, that is…died in an accident."

"Tell the rest of it, Mom," Owen said impatiently. "He loved anything fast—especially fast cars. He was going way over the limit when he just missed a school bus and crashed into a bridge abutment. It was his own fault."

"You shouldn't talk that way about him," Emily said. "It was still sad. He was spoiled, that's what he was. He was his father's pride and joy, and whatever he wanted, he got. We were afraid he'd made the same mistake with Meredith, but he seemed to have done better."

"I'm so sorry. Meredith must have been fairly small then. What about her mother?"

Emily's face set in disapproving lines. "A year later she married again. The man had a business in

California, and she insisted on moving out there. Naturally, Gregory didn't want to lose his only grandchild, and in the end, she left Meredith with him and off she went." She reached across the table to grasp her son's hand. "I can't imagine a mother doing that. I wouldn't leave my son for anything."

Owen eased his hand away, flushing. "I know, Mom. Hey, look at the time. Do you want any dessert?"

Of course his mother did, and the talk turned to whether she should get pie or bread pudding. By the time they'd finished dessert, Joanna was relieved that the evening was nearly over.

Her bruises were beginning to complain, and she no longer knew what she thought about any of Meredith's relatives, except that she shouldn't confide in any of them.

The drive back to the shop was taken up with Emily's description of how pleasant her house was and how perfect it would be if Meredith agreed to move in with her. Owen, catching Joanna's eye, raised his eyebrows and shook his head slightly.

Owen slowed as he approached the shop, flipping on the turn signal. "Do you want us to drop you off at the front of the shop?"

"That's fine. It looks as if my aunt isn't back yet, but she'll be here soon. Thank you again for supper."

"It's our pleasure, Joanna." Emily reached forward to pat her shoulder. "We'll have to be sure not to lose touch with you once we're all back home. We do appreciate your care for our Merry."

Joanna nodded, feeling as if Emily wanted to remind her that Meredith was part of their world, not hers.

That was true, of course. And if she believed Meredith could leave and have a safe, happy life, she'd leave it at that, even if she never had any answers. But she couldn't.

With final goodbyes, Joanna slid out of the car and stood watching as they drove away. Relieved, she turned to walk around to the back door, fumbling for her keys. There was no sense in going in through the store. Aunt Jessie would have closed up, assuming she'd come through the back.

The light Noah had installed allowed her to unlock the new dead bolt without resorting to a flashlight, and she quickened her pace as she went up the stairs. Looking at the tiny necklace wouldn't give her any answers, but she felt a need to hold it in her hand. She'd have to decide, and soon, whether to show it to Meredith or to keep silent. Once Meredith left River Haven, it would be too late.

Joanna paused on the top step as she unlocked the door. Meredith must have been about here when she'd fallen. A shadow of foreboding slipped through her as she pictured it. Had Meredith knocked, and, hearing no answer, turned away and fallen? Or had someone else been there—someone who slipped up the steps behind her, someone who wanted Meredith out of the way?

Trying to shake off the grim thoughts, Joanna stepped into the hall, reaching for the battery lamp they kept on the small table by the door. Her fingers found nothing but empty air. Leaning to the side, she reached farther.

Something…a creaking floorboard, the brush of a sleeve against the wall…warned her. She turned. A blow brushed the back of her head, striking her shoulder, and shooting pain down her arm to her hand. She cried out, reaching for something, anything, to hold on to, and fell into darkness.

NOAH HAD PERSUADED his brother to go home, but he'd lingered in the storeroom, checking supplies while keeping an eye out for Joanna and wishing she hadn't gone to supper with those people. Even if they weren't a danger to her, they could draw her closer to the Englisch world and away from him.

The back lights went on, and he reached the window in time to see Joanna disappear into her entrance and the door shut behind her. She was home safely, then. He could relax.

But he couldn't. He stood where he was. When it was this quiet, he could imagine the faint echo of her footsteps going up, sense the momentary pause when she unlocked the upper door.

And then came a sound he wasn't imagining—a cut-off cry and a dull thud.

He moved before his brain caught up with reaction. Joanna. His heart stuttered and began thumping so loud that he felt it would fly out of his chest as he grabbed the key from its hook, flew out the door and raced toward Joanna's apartment. Thank the Lord Joanna had suggested he keep a copy of the key in case of an emergency. He had the door open in a moment and plunged into the dark stairwell, transported back to the night Joanna had found Meredith. He shouted Joanna's name, thundering up the stairs.

But this time it wasn't a stranger who lay sprawled, head down, at the top of the stairs. Joanna lay there, with the faint light from the upstairs windows letting him see her face. He dropped to his knees and gathered her into his arms.

"Joanna, say something. Are you all right?"

She moved, turning her face to his chest. "All right," she murmured.

Relief flooded through him, but when she fell silent again, the fear crept back. "Don't try to move," he murmured. "You're safe now."

He could feel her breathing and thanked the Lord for it. She shifted her head a little, and he realized she was looking up at him. He touched her face gently and she turned her cheek into his palm.

"You're here," she whispered. "I knew you'd come."

She moved, or maybe he did, and it was the most natural thing in the world to kiss her, murmuring the words of love that he'd been longing to say.

He forced himself to draw back. Joanna needed care, and the man who'd hurt her... Rage against the person who'd done this started to build, taking control of him. Anger was poison. He tried to control it. He'd seen what it did to his father. What if it did that to him?

He lifted Joanna carefully so that she could lean against the wall. He had to get away before he succumbed to his feelings.

"Will you be all right there for a minute? I'll come right back."

Waiting only for her nod, he plunged through the kitchen and to the stairs that led down to the shop.

The door stood open—Joanna's attacker must have gone out this way. Noah bolted down and through the shop to the front entrance. It stood ajar, moving a little as if someone had just gone through, but by the time he reached the sidewalk there was no one in sight.

If he ran, Noah might spot him, but which way? Realizing the futility of dashing off in the wrong direction, he slammed his clenched fist into the door frame. Even that didn't dispel his anger, but the pain distracted him enough to make him step back inside.

Joanna called out from upstairs. He started up and realized he should call for help first.

"I'll be right there. Let me call the police first."

"No!" Her voice was loud enough, frightened enough, to send him running back to her, his heart racing.

"What is it?" He knelt beside her. "Do you need an ambulance? Tell me."

She shook her head slightly. "Just help me to the sofa and get the lights on." She reached out for him to help her up.

Afraid to argue, he slipped his arms around her and lifted her. "I can walk…" she murmured, her face against the curve of his neck.

"You're not going to." He carried her carefully into the sitting room and put her down on the sofa before going to the lamp on the table. "We have to call the police. Please don't argue."

"I won't argue, but you have to wait a minute." She caught his hand and drew him onto the sofa next to her.

With the light on, he could study her face. There was a slight red mark on her temple, and she held herself as if favoring her left arm.

"You're hurt. If your arm is broken…"

"It's not. It's my shoulder." She frowned as if trying to see what happened clearly. "He…whoever… must have tried to hit the back of my head. I think I moved, and the blow landed on my shoulder." She explored lightly with her right hand and winced a little.

"A doctor—"

"An ice pack," she said firmly, and he knew he was beaten.

"All right, I'll get you an ice pack. But I must call the police. He's getting away." Even as he said it, he knew a few minutes wouldn't make a difference. The man was long gone.

"Yah, I know, but don't call the station. Jamison's number is by the phone. Call him. Tell him to come in quietly by the back. The last thing either of us needs is a lot of flashing lights and sirens in front of our businesses again."

She leaned her head against the back of the sofa, looking as if she'd said all she could at the moment.

Noah had to admit she was right. This had to be

part and parcel of what had gone on since Meredith had come into their lives. The less they gave the neighbors to talk about, the better.

"All right." And if he mentally added the word *bossy*, she didn't have to know. Any more than she could know that it was part of what he loved about her.

Detouring through the kitchen, he found a blue ice pack in the freezer, wrapped a towel around it and brought it back to her, resisting the temptation to put it on her shoulder himself. Then he went downstairs to make the call.

With Chief Jamison promising to be there in five minutes, he went back to Joanna. To keep himself from feeling—or, worse, saying—his love, he focused on the investigation. How was the break-in tonight involved with everything else that had happened? He couldn't guess what the man had been after, unless he was looking for the little necklace. But what good was that to him? They already knew where it had come from.

He stood for a moment, studying Joanna, recognizing the vulnerability as well as the strength in her face. "This can't go on," he said abruptly. "He must have been after the baby necklace, but why?"

"If I had any idea what to do to resolve this, I would. But I don't."

"Have you shown the necklace to Meredith yet? She surely knows something about it, or why would it be so important?"

Her face set stubbornly. "I haven't. I couldn't take the chance of it upsetting her."

"I would think that she'd want to see it. If it means something to her, we might be further along. What else could have brought that man here tonight? He couldn't have known when you'd be back or if Jessie would come first. He must have been searching for something. What could it be but the necklace?"

She frowned at him, but then the defiance seeped slowly from her face. "I know. I'd already thought Meredith should see it, but I didn't know if it was the right thing or not."

"Let Jamison decide…" he began when he realized that Joanna looked suddenly horrified. "What?"

"You said he was looking for it… What if he already has it? What if he found it tonight?"

"You're not wearing it?"

"I was afraid someone might see it if it slipped out."

She moved, wincing as she tried to stand. As he helped her up, he heard the car pulling into the yard in back.

"You look and see. I'll go down and let Jamison in."

When he was halfway down, he realized that he'd left the door open when he'd rushed in, so Jamison was already entering.

"Is she all right?" he said, coming up the stairs at a trot.

"A bruised shoulder, that's all she'll admit to." He led the way back to the sitting room. Joanna greeted Jamison and then met Noah's gaze, holding up a small tissue-wrapped object.

"It's still safe."

He nodded, not sure whether to be glad or sorry.

Once Joanna had told her story, and Noah had added his unsuccessful pursuit of the man, Jamison growled, sounding like an angry bear.

"Three times, and he's gotten away clean each time. It's like he's invisible. And it has to be an outsider. Meredith doesn't even know anyone here."

"It can't be Emily or Owen," Joanna said. "They had insisted on taking me to supper, and the man must have already been in the apartment when they dropped me off."

"Doesn't clear them," Jamison muttered. "They could have been keeping you out of here to give the guy access."

Frowning, Noah shook his head. "They wouldn't have known Jessie was out. Where is she anyway?"

"She went to supper with Anna Miller. Once they start talking, they forget what time it is. But Emily knew that. She was standing right there when Aunt Jessie said it."

"We can't clear anyone, so let's get at this another way. Why did he come anyway? What did he want here? What haven't you told me?" Jamison leveled a frown at Joanna as he shot the questions.

"There's nothing, except for the necklace, and I already told you about that. But I can't think why it's that important."

"Right," Jamison said. "I've gone over it myself. Maybe he was looking for something else that he's afraid you might have. Like something Meredith gave you."

"But she didn't give me anything. You know that."

Jamison leaned forward, his gaze intent on her. "Are you sure you can't tell me who your birth mother was?"

"I can't." Joanna sounded on the verge of tears, but she seemed to force them back. "I don't know who she was, and neither do my parents. She turned me over to them and asked them to take good care of me. Which they have," she added.

"Well, we all know that." Jamison sounded embarrassed. "We keep coming back to the necklace. You haven't shown it to Meredith yet, have you?"

"No." She hesitated. "I've wondered if I should. Maybe it would mean something to her. But I was afraid of upsetting her."

Jamison considered. "It seems to me we'll have to take that risk and show it to her. If she doesn't remember, well, there's nothing lost, but we have to know. I'll pick you up in the morning."

"I think I should warn my parents about it first." Joanna's face set in the stubborn expression he knew so well. "My mother kept it for me when it probably was tempting to get rid of it."

Apparently, Jamison recognized that she couldn't be moved. He nodded. "There's no time to waste."

Noah cut in. "I'll take Joanna out to the farm first thing in the morning, and then we'll meet you at the hospital."

He waited for objections to his inserting himself

into the investigation, but none came. Joanna, looking tired, nodded.

So he would take Joanna in the morning. And
maybe he should tell her why, despite the feelings
he'd clearly shown, he couldn't possibly marry her,
because if he didn't tell her soon, he could lose his
nerve and let them both in for sorrow.

AFTER A RESTLESS NIGHT, including the task of explaining what happened to Aunt Jessie when she came in,
Joanna had to struggle to get moving early the next
morning. She straightened the dress Aunt Jessie had
had to help her slip on over her painful shoulder. Then
she picked up the first of the straight pins that secured
it in the front. Long practice had made it easy to put
them in place without letting them show, giving her
time to try to stop her stomach from churning at the
thought of seeing Noah this morning.

Who wouldn't be upset? He had held her as if he'd
never let her go. He comforted her and kissed her.
And then he'd drawn back and she'd seen the fear and
regret in his face.

If Noah really regretted those kisses, she would
hide her feelings and put on a brave front. But she
didn't—couldn't—believe it. He loved her. She wasn't
imagining it, but that didn't mean he'd overcome his
feeling that this wasn't right.

For an instant she was in his arms again, feeling
his lips warm and urgent on hers. She'd been so sure
that his heart was in that kiss, that it meant forever.
What if it couldn't be?

Even so, she couldn't forget. She could live with it, but she'd never forget. And Noah wouldn't know how she longed for the future that for a moment had seemed so sure.

Patting her hair to be sure her kapp was in place, Joanna went to the kitchen, planning to wait until she heard the sound of the buggy before she went down.

"You'll have some toast, at least," Aunt Jessie said, her tone as gentle as Joanna had ever heard it.

"Not now," she said, knowing she'd never choke it down. "I'll just get some juice."

"I'll get it. You sit." Her aunt put a glass of apple juice in front of her. "How is your shoulder?"

"Not too bad," she lied.

Jessie's expression made it all too clear that she didn't believe her. She touched Joanna lightly on the cheek. "Don't worry so much about your mamm. She'll understand why you have to do this." She hesitated. "Just remember that she's your mother. Your real mother."

"I know. I don't want to hurt them." That was the one thing she was sure of in the midst of confusion.

The sound of the buggy gave her a good reason not to say anything else. She drained the juice and went out, moving carefully so as not to jar her shoulder.

Noah had pulled the buggy up next to the stoop, making it easier for Joanna to climb in. She did it quickly, knowing it was going to hurt but not wanting him to come and help her. She settled down, finding she could stop holding her breath.

Noah nodded, not speaking, and clicked to the

horse. Good, that made it easier for her not to talk. Instead, she could stare, unseeing, at the street as they moved through traffic. By the time they'd reached the edge of town, she tried to relax, easing her bruised shoulder against the inevitable jolts. She didn't want to talk, not unless Noah could say the words she longed for. But Noah didn't seem to feel that way. "Joanna."

"Yah?" She carefully didn't look at him, afraid of what he might see in her eyes.

"There's something I must say, even if you don't want to talk." His voice was low but firm, and she could hear in his tone just what she'd feared. And she didn't want him to say it, not when she had such a precarious grip on her feelings.

"You don't need to say anything." He wouldn't say what she wanted to hear—she knew that now. So silence was better.

"I have to," he said doggedly. "I told you once what it was like to grow up with a father who drank. I didn't tell you everything. I didn't talk about my daad's temper, or the anger he turned on everyone when he was drinking. Or how he'd strike out physically at anyone who was in his way."

Her breath caught. She'd suspected, looking beneath what he'd said, but that wasn't like being sure.

"I'm sorry," she murmured, but he didn't seem to hear.

Noah stared at the road ahead. Whether he saw it or not, she couldn't tell.

"I could take it for myself. But not when he hit my mother." He shot a glance at her. "You understand?

He hit her. He hurt her. I saw the love in her eyes turn to fear. How can anyone stand to fear the person they love most?"

Pain for him, for the child he'd been, ricocheted through her. "I'm sorry, Noah. So sorry. But it's over now. It doesn't mean you can never be happy." Or love, she added silently.

"You don't understand." He bit out the words. "That anger—that wanting to hit out—that's in me, too. I've felt it there. I felt it last night, when I chased the man who'd assaulted you. It made me afraid of what I might have done if I'd caught him."

"Noah…feeling it doesn't mean that you'd have done it. Still less that you'd have turned that anger on someone innocent."

"I can't risk it."

He said it with a frightening finality. He really did believe that about himself.

"I can try to live at peace with all, but I can't risk hurting you. Once this is over, I'll do my best to stay away from you. That's all I can do." His lips twisted as he struggled for control. "I'm sorry."

Joanna felt as if she were about to burst with all the things she wanted to say—all the words that would convince him that he was wrong, that he was foolish to think he had to be like his father.

But they were already turning into the lane to the farmhouse. She'd have to save it all up, but she'd have her say, even if she couldn't convince him. She felt as if she were two different people—one struggling to keep from hurting her parents while the other struggled to convince Noah that he'd never hurt her. How did anyone cope with that?

CHAPTER SEVENTEEN

WHEN NOAH PULLED to a stop at the back porch, Joanna got down quickly, disregarding the pain it cost her. It wasn't that she was eager to get into the conversation with her parents, but for probably the first time, she really needed to get away from Noah. She didn't know what to say to him just now, and anything she did say might be something she'd regret.

Daad was already coming from the barn, no doubt having heard them pull in. He nodded to Noah, and then came to put his hand lightly on Joanna's good shoulder. With a sudden need for more contact, she hugged him, holding on for a moment, her throat tight.

Then she let go and looked up into his face, wondering how many of the lines in it she was to blame for. "I need to talk to you and Mammi for a minute."

"Komm," he said. "There's coffee hot and shoofly pie ready." He glanced back toward Noah. "Will you come in, Noah?"

"Not just now," Noah said, relieving her of the responsibility of saying anything. "Maybe later."

The words had probably been a warning to Daad that something serious was coming. But he wouldn't expect anything else, she guessed, given the tangle they'd all been enmeshed in since Meredith had appeared on her stairs.

Was the end in sight? She hoped desperately that she was doing right in revealing secrets that had been kept so long, but she couldn't see any other way forward.

She moved into the kitchen, her hand in Daad's, and Mammi turned from the stove to greet her, coffeepot in hand. They'd talk here, she knew. The kitchen table had always been the right place for serious as well as lighthearted conversations.

"Joanna." Mammi said her name, seemed to try to say something more and then just hugged her. Joanna held her, praying to find the way to keep from hurting her.

"Komm, sit. You have something to tell us, ain't so?"

Joanna nodded in answer but ushered her mother to a chair first and then poured the coffee. She suspected she'd need it, even if they didn't.

She automatically sat in the chair that had been hers ever since her first brother was born. She'd been moved from the seat next to Mammi to the seat next to Daad, and whichever one was the baby was put in the seat next to Mammi. From this vantage point she'd watched her brothers grow and change, and it had been from this seat that she'd first broached the idea of going into business with Aunt Jessie.

She'd thought that would be difficult. It had been nothing compared with what she had to bring up now.

A sip of the hot, strong brew seemed to ease the constriction in her throat, and she managed a smile.

"I wanted to be sure you knew this as soon as possible. I... Since the DNA tests confirmed that I'm related to Meredith, Chief Jamison knows it." She saw Daad's hand tighten on the table, and she hurried on. "He's not interested in how it came to be, honestly. I don't think we need to worry about that with him."

"What, then? There's something more, yah?"

"Yah." She knew that Daad always seemed to be a step ahead. "Someone is out to harm Meredith, and Jamison feels that it's connected to the money she was left by her grandfather."

There was no need to say they were rich, not to Daad and Mammi. They all agreed that money, no matter how much, wasn't an excuse for doing bad things.

"Does she..." Daad hesitated as if not sure how to refer to Meredith. "Wouldn't she have some idea if her relatives were that sort?"

It was a reasonable question, but she didn't think Meredith and her relatives were all that close. Anyway, it didn't matter as things stood.

"She might, but she still doesn't remember everything, although she's doing better every day." And the very fact that she was starting to remember might put her in worse danger. "Anyway, Chief Jamison wants to show her that little gold necklace and see if that prompts her to remember. Just knowing why she came here might help."

"She wouldn't have come unless she knew about you." The words startled her because they came from

Mammi. She was convinced of that herself but had imagined Mammi might want to deny it.

"Yah." Daad sounded as if they'd discussed this and tried to prepare for it. He exchanged looks with Mammi. "We understand it all has to come out now."

"Your daad was right all along." Mamm reached out tentatively to her, and Joanna clasped her hand, her heart aching. "We should have told you by the time you were grown, but we didn't because I was afraid. That was wrong. But you...you must do what's right, no matter..."

She let that trail off, and Joanna wondered what the end of that sentence was going to be. Did Mammi fear it would send Joanna away? Or did she fear what the law might do? Somehow, she had to reassure them as best she could.

"As far as the law is concerned..." She hesitated, wishing she knew more. "I really don't think Chief Jamison will do anything. And surely my birth mother had the right to ask you to raise me if she thought that best for me."

"We have always told ourselves that," Daad said. His face softened as he looked at Mammi. "And we tried our best to bring you up as loved as if you were our own by birth."

"I know that, Daadi." She managed to get the words out, but it was a struggle when her throat was tight with tears. She put her hand in his, and they sat linked as she tried to foresee what the future would bring.

But that was impossible. So she said what was certain in her heart. "We're family, yah? Any trouble that comes, we'll face it together."

Love seemed to flow through their clasped hands, and she felt it wash away all the doubts. Whatever happened, they would be together.

NOAH WAITED PATIENTLY with the buggy, knowing this was the sort of difficult conversation that was best done alone. Much as he wanted to make it easier for Joanna, that was impossible, even if he'd had the right to interfere. Which he didn't, and never would.

He hated to see her so stressed and worried. Some people would have avoided this encounter, but Joanna was too honest for that course. She couldn't do anything else but what she was doing, but it was hurting her as much as she feared it would hurt her parents.

The door began to open, and he swung himself back into the buggy, ready to help Joanna up but suspecting she wouldn't welcome it. Sure enough, she ignored his outstretched hand and pulled herself up to the seat beside him. Her face was averted, but he had a quick glimpse of tears shimmering in her eyes.

When Joanna didn't speak, Noah picked up the lines and clicked to the horse. They started back along the farm lane to the county road, and he could feel Joanna's parents watching them from the window.

The distant trees were ablaze with color after the cold night, but neither of them was in a mood to appreciate it. As far as Joanna was concerned, she probably saw it through a sad gray cloud of misery.

Once they were on the road toward the hospital,

he ventured another look at her. She could probably stand to talk to somebody about now. He'd given up any right to her confidence, but that didn't mean he wasn't a friend.

Finally, he cleared his throat, hoping to find the right words. "If you want to talk about it…"

She shook her head vigorously before he could finish, and he fell silent. So much for that idea. He wasn't going to be allowed to help her.

But a moment later she raised her head. After a fleeting glance at him, Joanna stared straight ahead between the horse's ears.

"They're putting on a brave front." Her voice was husky with suppressed tears. "But they're hurting, and I'm the one who's hurting them."

He couldn't let that pass without comment. "They must have known all along that the truth of your parentage would come out someday." He was about to say more but feared it might sound critical of her parents. That certainly wouldn't help her just now.

"I'm sure Daadi realized it, but he took the risk for Mammi's sake." Her voice had eased a little as if saying something had helped. "If I'd found out in some other way, if I weren't involved with Meredith already… Well, wishful thinking can't help now." She rubbed the center of her forehead with her fingertips, maybe trying to release the tension that had built up moment by moment.

"They're afraid of losing you." He spoke gently, saying the thing she couldn't lose track of in all this. What had come over him, that he was defending the bishop, of all people? Seemed that this situation had changed him, almost without his noticing.

"I've already told them that this doesn't make a difference in the way I see them." She flashed a defiant look at him.

"You may be sure of that, but I'd guess they can't quite believe it, no matter how much they want to."

Did she even believe it herself? She'd already changed since the night she found Meredith on her stairs, although she probably didn't realize it. She was more confident, and certainly more daring about the need to find out about her past and to protect Meredith.

"No, you're right." She spoke after a long moment during which that momentary flare-up ebbed away. "They're afraid of losing me. I'm afraid of hurting them. And you're afraid of hurting me, but not, I guess, of losing me."

For an instant he felt as if someone had jammed a pitchfork into his chest. He struggled to breathe. Finally, he said the only thing he could.

"It's not the same."

"No, it's not." The anger threaded through her words. "Because in your case, it's not necessary. You aren't your father. You aren't in the least like him. You're not an alcoholic."

"I've never had alcohol, not even when everyone else in my rumspringa group was hiding beer cans under the hay bales. I didn't dare, because I'd seen the costs and I knew the seeds of it were in me. Just like I know my father's temper is alive in me."

"That's ferhoodled," she snapped. "I've never even seen you angry."

If she could look into him, she'd see the anger stirring, even now rousing because she couldn't accept what he knew. "You haven't seen it because I clamp down on it. You could have last night, when I chased after the man who hurt you. If I'd caught him, I'd have taken it out on him. As I didn't, I slammed my fist into the door frame instead."

He held out his bruised knuckles for her to see. Her quick, indrawn breath was audible. There, maybe that had done it. He almost congratulated himself when she was silent.

But not quite. How could a man be congratulated when he'd just hurt someone he loved? Still, it was better to be brutally honest. Better a little hurt now than a terrible life. He could never bear to see her turn into someone like his mother used to be—terrorized, loving and fearing at the same time. That was no way to live.

Joanna didn't speak the rest of the way to the hospital. He longed to know what she was thinking, but for once he couldn't begin to read her expression, except to know that she was fighting pain.

It probably would be best for both of them if he'd been able to drop her at the hospital entrance and keep on going, but of course he couldn't. Jamison would expect him to stay close to her until he'd delivered her safely to him, if not longer. So he tied the horse to the posts that had been provided for Amish patients and visitors, and hurried after her.

Jamison waited for them just inside the door, and

he nodded as they came in. "Good timing. I got here a few minutes ago. Landon Bristow was already talking to the doctor, his attorney in tow, I guess to force us locals to get out of his way."

"You're not going to let him take Meredith away, are you?" Joanna sounded appalled at the prospect.

"Not if I can help it." Jamison didn't look very happy about any of this. "I want you two with me. You can agree that she doesn't want him telling her what to do."

Noah's mind spun. Could he say that? He knew it from what Joanna had told him, but he didn't think Meredith had said anything the times he was there.

But Jamison didn't give him time to come up with an argument. He ushered them down the hallway. "They're in the lounge with the doctor. He'll be the one to decide where Meredith goes, and Bristow is putting up a convincing argument."

They entered the lounge to see the two sides lined up—Bristow and his attorney confronting the young doctor who looked at bay against the two of them and Emily Graham and her son on the other side.

Bristow seemed to have reached the crux of his argument as they came in. "…best if I'm responsible for Meredith until she's well, if she ever is. I'm the only other Bristow, and as a close relative, it's the only reasonable solution. As a businessman, I'm capable of taking care of the business interests for my cousin, which Emily Graham clearly isn't."

It sounded impressive to Noah, even though he knew that Joanna had taken a dislike to the man. Still, as he was apparently single, how was he going to take care of a young woman?

The Graham woman struck immediately at that point. "And how would you take care of Merry? That's the important thing while she's recovering. I would be happy to have her stay with me, or if she wants to be in her own home, I'll stay with her there. What could you do?"

Bristow looked like a thundercloud. "I'm sure the doctor will agree with me that my young cousin needs more care than you could provide. A business acquaintance has an interest in a private nursing home that could provide her with the physical therapy and emotional support she needs. Isn't that the best choice, Doctor?"

Appealed to directly, the young man wavered. "Well, I suppose—"

Joanna, with her newfound confidence, stepped forward. "I think you're missing an important point."

Bristow looked at her as if a piece of furniture had spoken. "This isn't your concern, Miss…."

"Kohler," the attorney supplied, with an apologetic look at Joanna.

"Ms. Kohler has been with Meredith since her accident. I'm sure the doctor wants to hear what she has to say." Jamison was more official than Noah had ever heard him.

The doctor seized upon that point. "Yes, Ms. Kohler?"

If Joanna was embarrassed, she didn't show it. "Meredith has recovered much more in just the past day. She's perfectly capable of deciding what she wants to do herself. Don't you think so, Doctor?"

He nodded, looking relieved. "I'm inclined to think you're right about that. She should make the decision, with medical advice, of course."

Bristow elbowed the attorney. "Why aren't you saying anything? You're supposed to be representing me."

Watson looked at him coolly. "I represent the family interests. That includes Meredith. If she's competent to decide in the doctor's opinion, that's where my duty lies."

"Right," Jamison said quickly. "I have a few questions to ask her myself right now, so I'll have to insist that the rest of you wait. I'll have questions for you, as well." He glanced at Joanna. "I'll want you with me, and I'll have you driven home afterward." He looked at Noah. "If you'll keep an eye on things at Joanna's place…"

Noah nodded, trying to avoid catching Joanna's gaze. She was in safe hands with Jamison, and it was time for him to fade out of the picture. In fact, the sooner, the better. Moving quickly, he headed for the parking lot.

JOANNA TRIED NOT to watch as Noah walked away, but her mind's eye followed him out of sight. Despite the distraction provided by Meredith's relatives and the difficult challenge of keeping her safe, Joanna knew that underlying everything else was the pain in her heart that would strike without warning.

If she wasn't so sad, she'd be furious. How could

he do that to both of them? How could he sentence them both to a lifetime of loneliness for a foolish scruple? She knew Noah, maybe better than he knew himself. Whatever his father's failings, they didn't apply to him.

Determination welled up in her. If he thought this situation was resolved, he'd better think again. She wasn't giving up without a fight.

"Joanna?"

She came back to the present with a start, finding Chief Jamison looking at her with concern. "Are you okay?"

She nodded, trying to arrange a normal smile on her face. "Fine. Are we going to see Meredith now?"

"That's the idea." He hung back for another moment to let the others clear the room and then guided Joanna to the elevator.

Once they were inside the elevator with the door closed, he turned to Joanna. "What did you think of them?"

She refocused her thoughts. "Mostly, I thought they all wanted their own way. Well, except for the lawyer. He seemed embarrassed at the whole thing, but I suppose if he's employed by Bristow, he has to do what the boss says. Still, he seems clear that Meredith is his client, too. I don't think he'd do anything against her interests."

"I agree with you. The question is, is it safe to let Meredith go off with any of them?" The elevator reached the floor, and he kept his finger on the button that held the door closed. "If Meredith remembers anything, it could clear up this whole muddle. That's why your relationship to her is so important. It could unlock those memories."

"Could," she repeated, emphasizing the word. "We can't be sure. Did you find out any more about the financial arrangements?"

He nodded. "Meredith's a wealthy woman since her grandfather's death, but the other family members benefited, as well. The Philadelphia cops have been trying to find out who benefits if she dies, but they haven't been able to shake that loose from anyone yet."

"If she remembers, she will tell us." Joanna tried to look on the bright side, if that was how it could be described.

"Right." The door had started an irritating buzzing, so the chief let go of the button. The door opened, and they stepped out. "That's the key to everything."

Joanna took a deep breath and tried to calm herself. But how could she be calm when it seemed everything relied on her?

That's foolish, she told herself sharply. She would do what she could, but if Meredith didn't respond to what she had to say or to the baby necklace, it wouldn't be her fault.

She was tempted to blame Chief Jamison for putting so much pressure on her, but that probably wasn't fair, either. He was a good man, and he was trying so hard to keep Meredith safe. He probably knew that all she could do was try. The rest was in the hands of the Lord.

When they walked into the room, the first thing Joanna saw was the flow of dark auburn hair. Meredith stood…yah, stood…at the dresser, brushing her hair while looking in the mirror. She caught sight of them and turned, smiling.

"I'm glad the doctors didn't have to cut off any of my hair."

"I am, too." Smiling with pleasure at the sight of her obvious improvement, Joanna moved toward her. "Do you usually wear it down?"

"Yes, but if I don't…" She stopped, then laughed. "I remembered that. When you asked the question, it popped right into my head. That keeps happening. I wear it down unless I'm doing something like weeding the flower beds. Too hot and messy doing that."

"Do you have a lot of flowers?" Joanna sat down on the bed, watching her.

"Elaborate gardens at my grandfather's house, but a service takes care of them. But at my town house, I have a nice little backyard with lots of mums this time of the year. What about you?"

Joanna shook her head. "There's no space at the shop or the apartment, but Mamm makes up for it by putting me to work in the garden whenever I'm at the farm." She said a silent prayer that Chief Jamison wouldn't plunge into questioning too quickly and cut off this flow of memories.

"Speaking of home, my flowers are probably dying from lack of water." She looked at Jamison inquiringly. "What about it, Chief? Can I go home?"

"You sure that's a good idea, being home alone?"

Jamison asked. "You might need some help until you've got your strength back."

Meredith plopped down on the bed next to Joanna and grimaced. "That's what good old Cousin Landon says. He wants to pop me in a nursing home, of all places. Those are for eighty-year-olds with broken hips. Not for me."

Joanna couldn't help but smile at that description. "No, you're certain sure not that. But what if you did too much and felt faint? You might want someone around."

"I could get one of my girlfriends to stay. Or Cousin Emily would. She's always eager to move in."

"And your cousin Owen?"

"No, not for a minute. Not that Owen would want to. He's busy living it up at college these days. A nice kid, but so immature." She wrinkled up her nose.

Jamison cleared his throat and shifted his weight from one foot to the other. Clearly, he wanted her to get on with it, but Joanna was having trouble thinking of a way to switch to a different subject. Especially the subject of who would benefit if she died—how could anyone bring that up in casual conversation?

But Jamison didn't wait for her. "Do you remember what brought you to River Haven?"

She frowned. "Well, I…I probably drove, didn't I? I usually do, unless it's someplace where I have to fly."

"What about the trip to the hospital?" he asked, maybe deciding hopping from one subject to another was less leading.

"I…" she began, but then stopped and shook her

head. "I don't. The doctor said I'd had a fall and I'd hurt my head."

"Yah, we know." She shook her head at Jamison, afraid his questions would do more harm than good. "It's natural there are things you can't remember right away. That will all come back to you as you heal, I'm sure."

But Jamison wasn't ready to quit yet. He frowned at Joanna before turning back to Meredith. "Joanna has something to show you. We hoped it might help you remember."

Joanna reached hesitantly to take out the necklace, not really convinced this was a good idea. But time was running out. They wouldn't be able to keep Meredith here and safe much longer.

She unwrapped the tiny necklace from its tissue paper and held it out to Meredith. "Have you ever seen this before? Or one like it?"

Meredith glanced at it, at first not seeming to know what she was looking at. Then her gaze sharpened, and she reached out to take it.

"It…it's a baby necklace, isn't it?" She moved her fingers over it as if memorizing the curves. She frowned, seeming to try to remember something. "Where did you get it? The Amish don't wear jewelry, do they?"

"No, we don't." Joanna kept her voice even with an effort. "I was adopted, you see. My birth mother left this with me for my parents. Does it… Is it familiar to you?"

Meredith looked up from the necklace, and quite

suddenly her eyes filled with tears. "I have one just like it. My grandfather said it was a tradition in my grandmother's family. My father wore it for his baptism, but then it was put away because Grandpa didn't think a boy should wear a necklace. And then it came to me." She paused. "I don't understand. Why would you have one just like it?"

There was the question, and Joanna wasn't sure she should or could answer it. "I guess it could be a coincidence…" she began.

Jamison looked about to blurt out something, but Meredith spoke first. "Not a coincidence. See this tiny letter engraved on the heart? It's a *P*, for *Prentice*. That was my grandmother's maiden name. She insisted on it. For both of them."

"Both?" Jamison looked gratified and surprised, as well.

Meredith nodded. She looked at Joanna. "It belonged to my aunt Katherine, my father's sister. I never knew her. She'd run away before I was born, but my grandmother told me she had a heart, too. Was it this one?"

"I think it must have been." Now Joanna teared up. "You see, the chief had DNA tests done to help identify you. He had the idea of having me tested as well, since we didn't know who my mother was."

She came to a stop, trying to assess how Meredith was taking it. She might not be pleased at having an unknown relative thrust on her.

But Meredith's expression was like the sun coming out on a dark day. "We are related, aren't we? I knew it, even before you said so. I felt it." She reached out to clasp Joanna's hands in both of hers. "If Aunt Katherine was your mother, then we're first cousins."

"I guess we are." Joanna blinked away the tears and managed a tremulous smile.

So that, at least, was explained. She knew there was more to come, but that could wait, as far as she was concerned. There'd be time for more explanations, even more questions, but it was enough for now.

CHAPTER EIGHTEEN

FOR A FEW minutes they just sat, smiling at each other. Meredith seemed to feel the way she did. Questions and explanations could wait.

Meredith closed her eyes briefly, and Joanna was stricken with guilt. She'd been afraid this would be too much for Meredith. After all, she was barely on her feet again.

"Why don't you scoot back on the bed and rest against the pillows for a bit? This has been a lot to take in." She stood, moving to help her if needed.

Meredith let Joanna help her, smiling as Joanna lifted her feet onto the bed. "It's funny to have a big cousin worrying about me. But nice," she added quickly. She reached out for Joanna's hand again, and Joanna pulled the chair up close enough to the bed to make that possible.

"Nice," Meredith said again. "But I suppose you have a lot of girl cousins, don't you?"

"A few," Joanna admitted. "But none like you."

"I'm glad." She leaned back against the pillows, seeming content to enjoy this new relationship.

Naturally, Jamison wasn't at all content. Grasping

the back of Joanna's chair, he leaned forward, intent on Meredith's face.

"Now, the important thing is this—you say you already felt you and Joanna were related. Are you sure you didn't already know it, even before you came here?"

She blinked, clearly surprised. "I... How would I know that? What makes you think so?"

"You're here," he said simply. "What would you be doing in River Haven, even more at Joanna's door, if you didn't have some suspicion?"

"I don't know." Meredith's smooth forehead wrinkled, her eyebrows drawing down. She was clearly trying to remember something. After several moments of tense silence, she shook her head.

"I really don't know. It makes sense, I guess, but all I can see when I think about coming here is a blank."

"Try harder." Jamison ground out the words. Joanna could feel the tension in him, so taut he was like a string about to snap. "You must remember—"

Joanna grasped his arm and shook it slightly. "Don't. That's not going to help. She won't remember just because you try to force it to happen. Leave it alone, and maybe it will come back."

He glared at her and then let out a long, exasperated breath. "Yeah, all right. Let's try something else."

Joanna looked at him with apprehension, even while knowing she couldn't stop him.

"Tell me this, if you can." He seemed to be trying for a softer approach. "Do you know who would benefit if something happened to you?"

Meredith seemed blank at that, and she glanced helplessly at Joanna.

"He means, have you made out a will?" She sent a warning glance toward Jamison, but she had a feeling he'd ignore it.

"Oh, I see. Well, yes, my grandfather's attorney insisted on it. It seemed like a lot of nonsense to me, but I did it."

Joanna could see that Jamison didn't consider making a will nonsense, but he pushed on.

"And who would benefit under your will if…for instance…your accident had been fatal?"

"The Red Cross," she said promptly. "And I left a few mementos to different friends. But anyway, it doesn't amount to much."

"Not much?" Jamison didn't bother to hide his disbelief. "According to the Philadelphia police who looked into it, you're a wealthy young woman."

"But that's the company." She said it as if they should understand. "Grandfather controlled all that. I was provided for when I was growing up, and then I have a trust, so I guess you'd say the money comes to me on my next birthday. I never really consider it mine. If I die without children, the rest is tied up in various trusts and in the company."

"So you mean you can't dispose of it by willing it to someone else?"

"That's right." Meredith didn't sound as if she cared, one way or the other. Maybe that was a sensible reaction, not to worry about what she might or might not have.

Joanna didn't particularly care. She was just glad that Meredith was provided for.

"If something happened to you, who would gain control of everything?" Jamison was still hanging on to his patience.

Meredith shook her head, looking increasingly tired. "I don't think I remember. Does it matter?"

Jamison looked ready to explode, but he seemed to make a huge effort to calm himself. "There's been at least two, maybe more, attempts to kill you since you came to River Haven. So yes, I'd say it matters."

Meredith paled. "Tried to... You mean, when I fell it wasn't an accident?"

"Chief Jamison..." Joanna murmured, cautioning. She hadn't realized that Meredith didn't know or apparently understand the suspicions that everyone else had. She patted Meredith's hand, wishing she knew how to help her cope with this unwelcome news.

The chief took a couple of minutes to breathe deeply, letting the maroon color of his face fade to a brick red. Maybe he was regretting having pushed for answers. She hoped so.

"It looks as if it wasn't an accident." His voice was gentle when he spoke again. "But you don't need to worry," he added quickly. "We have an officer on your door all the time to keep you safe."

Meredith didn't look all that reassured, and her grip on Joanna's hand tightened. "I don't understand. Why would anyone want to hurt me?"

"We don't know, either," Joanna said gently.

"That's why the chief hoped you would remember and maybe come up with a reason why."

"I can't. I don't." Her voice rose, and she yanked her hand away from Joanna as if she was responsible. "Why are you telling me this? What's—"

"What's all this excitement?" The door swung open, and Mary Ellen appeared, looking straight at Chief Jamison as if convinced he was responsible.

Without waiting for an answer, she went to Meredith and eased her back against the pillows, putting her fingers on Meredith's wrist. "Now, let's get that pulse down a bit. There's no need to get excited—it's not good for you."

"He said—" Meredith began, but Mary Ellen cut her off by putting a thermometer in her mouth.

"Sounds like he hasn't been a very good visitor. I think he'd better leave now."

Jamison glared at her, but Mary Ellen, secure in her professional ability, met his look with a steely composure Joanna hadn't seen in her before.

"Out," she said.

The chief gave in, recognizing he'd gone too far. "Sorry," he muttered to Mary Ellen. Then he turned to Meredith. "Don't you worry now. We're going to keep you safe."

He headed for the door. Joanna paused long enough to pat Meredith's hand, sure she needed some time alone just now. "It'll be all right."

Meredith managed to smile around the thermometer, and she squeezed Joanna's hand. Reassured, Joanna followed Jamison out of the room.

As FAR AS Noah was concerned, Thursday had been dragging on forever. It had turned cloudy in the afternoon, and now it was constantly threatening but only spitting rain intermittently. They'd been reasonably busy, but it wasn't doing the job of distracting him.

He was grateful once again for Caleb. The boy was doing a fine job, and he stayed cheerful no matter how cranky a customer might be.

He'd been relieved, he told himself, to leave Joanna in safe hands with Jamison at the hospital. True, that batch of relatives was there, but they couldn't do any harm with Jamison around. He still didn't like the way the chief had involved Joanna, but she had been in the midst of it from the beginning. Once she'd learned that Meredith was related to her, there had been no stopping her.

Not that he blamed her. Family was family, even one like his. And Joanna couldn't help being the person she was…conscientious and caring, and easily hurt by causing pain to someone else, no matter what the cause.

That reminded him of Joanna's assessment of their situation, but there was no point in going back over it. He'd never forget what he felt for her, but he'd made his decision and he'd stick to it.

He'd seen Joanna return to the quilt shop an hour or so after he'd gotten in. He'd studied her face as she walked to the shop but hadn't been able to make much from her expression. The temptation to ask her what had happened with Meredith was strong, but he'd managed to push it down. He shouldn't be seeking out reasons to talk with her, not now.

The bell over the front door jangled. Noah glanced that way and put down the box of nails he'd been sorting. Had he thought about cranky customers? Well, here was one for sure.

Bernie Crawford had stuck with him despite the temptation of the chain hardware store out on the highway; he had to give him that, at least. But Noah guessed it was more a matter of not wanting to drive out there, wasting gas, when he could walk down Main Street easily.

He went forward, arranging a smile on his face. Bernie wasn't one to look around for himself. He expected to be waited on.

"Mr. Crawford. Nice to see you. Can I help you find something?"

"I need a couple of three-inch screws. And none of those cheap things that fall apart when you try to install them, either."

Noah had no idea if the man had been this cross for all of his seventy-nine years, but he certainly had been since Noah had known him. A small man to begin with, he'd been getting smaller as he aged, and now he peered malevolently up at anyone who tried to help him.

"Just right over here." Noah put down the box of nails and gestured to the next set of shelves.

Crawford grunted. "Let's have a look."

Noah led the way, glancing back at the front window automatically when he heard the sound of the door opening next door. That wasn't Joanna going out again, was it? He caught a glimpse of someone in Amish dress and craned to see while handing Crawford a package of screws. No, it wasn't Joanna, it was someone short and plump.

"What are you trying to pull on me?" Crawford shoved the pack back at him. "Three-inch screws. Can't you hear? And I don't want anyone telling me I have to buy a whole package when I only need two."

Noah nearly snapped back that he could take his business elsewhere but managed to control himself just in time. Caleb, apparently sensing trouble from afar, slipped in next to him and sorted out the right package.

"Here you are, sir. Are these the ones you want?"

Crawford sniffed and examined them. "Good enough, but open that dang package. I don't want more than I need."

"Sure thing." With the flicker of an amused look at his brother, Caleb slit the package open and extracted two of the screws, handing them over for Crawford's inspection.

"Those'll do, all right. See that you wrap them up so they don't get lost on my way home."

"Come right over to the counter and I'll take care of that for you."

To Noah's relief, he followed Caleb to the counter, giving him a string of instructions as to how the screws should be wrapped. Noah stayed where he was, transferring the remaining ones to a box used to store unpackaged screws. He heard Caleb jollying the man along while he rang up the purchase, relieved when the door finally closed behind Crawford.

Caleb, grinning, came over to him. "I'm not sure it's worth it to listen to Mr. Crawford for the sake of twenty-nine cents each," he said.

"Any sale is worth it, I guess." He clapped Caleb on the shoulder. "Thanks for taking over. I'm afraid I was distracted."

"It's okay." The boy's face sobered. "No wonder, as little sleep as you've been getting. I can stay tonight, if you want. I don't mind missing a little sleep."

Noah shook his head. "That's okay. I can manage. But thanks again. You're doing a gut job, you know. How did you get to be so responsible?"

Caleb flushed with pleasure at the compliment, making him feel guilty he hadn't said that to his brother earlier.

"I like it. Anyway, I figured out a long time ago that I couldn't count on Daad to show me how to act. So I decided you were the opposite, and I should be like you."

Seeming embarrassed again by expressing such thoughts, he wandered off self-consciously, leaving Noah standing there, dumbfounded.

If he'd considered how Daad affected the younger ones, he'd assumed that he was the only one who really knew what was going on. He and Mamm had certain sure done everything they could to hide things from the two youngest boys, at least. It looked as if they hadn't succeeded.

He felt another flicker of guilt that he hadn't realized how much they might know and how they might feel. He and Aaron had done their best to take care of them since Daad died, but if he'd considered what they thought of him, he'd have said they probably thought him too strict and bossy.

And for Caleb to say something like that just melted his heart. Caleb was actually modeling himself on his big brother. It made him feel even more responsible, in a way, but it was a good feeling.

The thought struck him suddenly—Caleb believed in him. He didn't think Noah was like his father, any more than Joanna did. It was about the most humbling thing that had happened to him in a long time.

As she and Aunt Jessie prepared to close for the day, Joanna found herself wondering if Noah had begun his vow to stay away from her already. She'd more than expected him to look for an update on what had happened at the hospital after he left. After all, he'd said he wouldn't back off until the current situation was resolved.

Shaking her head in annoyance, she began reorganizing the bolts of print fabrics that customers had left in complete disarray. This had to be the work of Betty O'Donnell. When she was starting a new project, they could count on at least three visits that left chaos behind before she settled on what she wanted.

Catching Aunt Jessie's eye, she gave her a questioning look. "Was Betty here while I was out?"

"Can't you tell? This time she's torn between doing a crib quilt for a niece or a double bed quilt for her son's wife because they're redecorating." Her lips twitched. "She still hadn't decided when she left. We'd better look for several more visits."

Giving Noah a push out of her surface mind, she tried to respond properly. "Doesn't it depend on which comes first, the baby or the redecorating? Maybe we can nudge her into a decision that way."

Aunt Jessie gave her a wry smile. "I wouldn't count on it." Her face sobered. "How did it go with your mamm and daad this morning?"

She blinked back the tears that came too readily when she thought of them. "As well as it could, I guess. I tried to reassure them that Chief Jamison had no interest in pursuing how I came to be part of the family."

"It might not be up to him." Aunt Jessie's face hardened. "What then?"

"I'll tell you what I told them. We're family. We stand together against whatever comes."

Her aunt gave her the rare smile that was as good as a hug from anyone else. "That's what they needed to hear. What we all need to hear." She hesitated before going on. "Don't worry too much. You already know how strong your daad is. As for your mamm… I think she can handle anything as long as she doesn't lose you."

"She won't." Joanna hesitated, not sure how much to say. But she could trust Aunt Jessie to keep confidences. She always had, from Joanna's secret childhood fears to her foolish teenage crushes. "I did wonder if the fact that my Englisch blood made me different…more independent and questioning than most Amish girls my age. But Noah said…" She let that trail off.

"What did Noah say?" Aunt Jessie didn't seem surprised that Joanna talked to him about it.

"He said that I was Amish by raising and by choice, and who my birth parents were didn't affect that."

She gave an approving nod. "Noah has a gut head on his shoulders. But it could be he's too stubborn for his own good."

Joanna was inclined to agree, but she decided not to respond. Right on the heels of that decision, she heard a knock on the locked front door. It was Noah.

Aunt Jessie was closer than she was, and she unlocked the door, let Noah in and then relocked it. "No need for any more customers today." She glanced from Noah to Joanna. "I'll go up and get supper started. Stay if you want, Noah. It's nothing fancy."

Without a look back, she marched upstairs, rather obvious about leaving them alone together.

Joanna pushed bolts of fabric into place, trying to think of something to say, but she couldn't come up with anything. After the emotional talk they'd had earlier, whatever she said would sound awkward.

Noah cleared his throat as if he had as much difficulty as she did. He came a little closer, watching the movement of her hands instead of looking into her face.

Just when she'd begun to think he'd leave without a word being spoken, he cleared his throat again.

"Don't mean to interrupt you when you're working.

But I thought I should know if anything's changed. About Meredith, I mean," he added hurriedly, most likely afraid she'd think he meant their personal problems.

She patted the last bolt as if it was urgent that it be in exact alignment with the other bolts.

"Well, I don't know what the chief would say to that, but I did show her the necklace." She paused, remembering that moment. "She recognized it."

Noah exclaimed in surprise, and she realized he'd thought it a dead end. "How? Why?"

"She said she has one just like it. Her grandmother had gotten one for each of her children. So hers came from her father to her."

"And the other one?" His impassive face didn't give anything away now that the momentary surprise was past.

"That was given to her father's sister. Meredith couldn't have known her, because she left home several years before Meredith was born. I don't know why, exactly, but I'd guess she didn't get along with her father. From the things Owen let drop and what Meredith said, he sounded like a man who wanted things his own way."

Noah frowned, considering. "Still, it doesn't necessarily follow that she was your birth mother. Other people might have bought similar necklaces."

She shook her head. "I suggested that, but Meredith could identify it, because it had a tiny initial worked into the design. It's not likely anyone else would have an identical one." She shrugged, wondering why he was putting up an argument against what seemed so obvious. "And there's the matter of the DNA test. Cousins, most likely, according to the results."

"Does she think that you're her cousin?"

"Yah, she does." Joanna couldn't help but smile, remembering her face when she'd realized. "She was happy, but I'm not sure it's all sunk in yet."

"Or for you, either, I'd guess."

"That's about right. It's answered one big question, but it's left a lot of others yet to be answered. Why did she leave? Why did she give me away? What happened to her? I'm not sure I'll ever really understand."

Compassion broke through the rigid expression he'd taken to using with her. His eyes darkened as if he shared her pain. "I'm sorry. And you may never know."

She nodded. "I suppose somebody from the family must know a little. Like whether they looked for her or not. I can't imagine a family that wouldn't want to know what had happened to her."

"They are different from us, ain't so? Meredith... she'd tell you, if she could, I think. Did she talk about it at all?"

"No. I'm not sure how much she's able to remember, and I couldn't push her. She talked about some things very naturally, but others... Well, it's hard to tell. And she got tired so easily. Jamison kept pushing."

She felt a surge of fresh irritation at the chief. Maybe he was trying to do his job, but badgering Meredith wouldn't help him.

"He was trying to find out who would benefit if she had died. But it just seemed to confuse her."

He nodded, understanding. "Jamison's plenty frustrated at not getting this situation cleared up. Maybe he should talk to that lawyer instead. He must know things like that. And it still doesn't explain why someone would try to harm you."

The worry in his face over her safety twisted her heart. It was so obvious that he cared about her. Why couldn't he just accept the love she offered? It wasn't what she had expected for her life, either. If she could risk the independence she prized so highly, why couldn't he take a risk, as well?

"Being run off the road doesn't seem as important to me as it did when it happened. If that driver had really wanted to put me out of action for some reason, he didn't do a very good job of it. And when he broke in, he probably had no desire to run into me."

Noah's jaw hardened. "That doesn't mean he wouldn't finish the job another time. And the next time he might want to be sure you couldn't interfere again ever."

He sounded angry, maybe at her for being involved, or maybe at the culprit. It roused her own spirit, and she'd rather feel anger than pain right at the moment.

"You needn't raise your voice at me. I didn't do anything."

He looked at her, seeming baffled as well as angry for a moment. "If you don't care about your own safety, other people will have to," he snapped.

"At least promise me you won't budge an inch out of here tonight."

"I don't intend to go anyplace." She softened in the face of his obvious worry. "Let's not argue. I'll stay home with Aunt Jessie. Nobody's going to take on both of us, remember? And you try to get some sleep."

He gave a short nod, obviously not entirely satisfied.

She glanced upstairs. "Will you stay for supper with us? Aunt Jessie has a beef stew cooking."

"No." As if aware of how curt that sounded, he added. "Thank your aunt Jessie for me. And if anything happens, anything at all, even if it doesn't seem like a threat, call me. Or call the police. Or both of us. Throw something at the wall, if you have to."

With a last frown, he spun toward the door and went out, standing there until she'd flipped the locks.

Once he was gone, Joanna stayed where she was for a few minutes. She should be getting used to his insistence on getting away from her, but it hurt fresh each time it happened. How could he try so hard to avoid temptation and yet not see that he was strong enough not to be what his father had been?

She had better get herself under control before she was subjected to her aunt's sharp gaze. Aunt Jessie already suspected too much.

Too stubborn for his own good. Aunt Jessie was right about that. But maybe Noah didn't know just how stubborn she could be when she had to.

A small voice in the back of her mind wouldn't be

silenced. *What if stubbornness isn't enough? What if this time you can't succeed?*

All those years when she'd been convinced that this independence was the life she wanted now seemed hopelessly naive. Even if she hadn't fallen so resoundingly in love, the experiences and shocks of the past weeks had shown her that independence was a mirage. As long as you loved anyone, you were not truly independent, and what would life be without love?

CHAPTER NINETEEN

BY THE TIME supper was over and the dishes were washed, Joanna began to feel she'd regained her balance. With nothing to be said or done about either Meredith or Noah at the moment, she followed Aunt Jessie's example and settled down with some hand sewing.

To anyone else it would look like a boring evening, she supposed, with Aunt Jessie in her usual rocking chair, her head bent over the creation of an intricate floral block for the quilt she was making.

There was never a time when she didn't have sewing to do in an evening, like most Amish women, but while Mamm was probably repairing a rip in one of the boys' shirts and clucking over how hard they were on clothes, Aunt Jessie would be working on the quilts that were her passion.

Joanna studied her intent face. Much as she loved the quilt shop and the work they did, she would never, if she worked on it from now until she was ninety, achieve her aunt's level of expertise.

But they made for a good partnership that way. Her aunt knew all there was to know about quilts, and she'd turned out to be pretty good at running a business. Probably Noah could use a partner that way, and it sounded as if Caleb was shaping up to be that person for him.

Spreading out the dress she was making for Cathy's wedding, she took out the thread she'd matched so carefully on the trip to the big fabric store. That had been the day that Meredith came into her life.

Funny that her visit to the store seemed only yesterday, and yet she felt that Meredith had been part of her life forever. Time was a strange thing, depending so much on what happened in a person's life.

A moment's reflection told her that Meredith always had been, in a way, part of her life, even though they couldn't have dreamed of each other's existence. What kind of relationship had there been between Meredith's father and her mother? Were they close as children? So many questions occurred to her, but probably not even Meredith would know the answers to some of them.

Her hands fell idle while she thought of Meredith, safe in her hospital room, and remembered her impatience to be gone. She could understand it when she tried to imagine how she'd feel in a similar situation. She'd be impatient herself, eager to get back to her life. But for the moment Meredith was surely safer where she was. The problem would be to convince her of that.

"That's a nice shade of blue," Aunt Jessie commented, nodding at the nearly completed dress. "Blue is not the best color for you, but this shade will be fine."

Joanna smiled. "Exactly. That's why I picked it out. With three women as different in coloring as Cathy, Rachel and I am, we could have spent months arguing about the right shade. Not that Rachel is likely to argue. Sometimes I wish she would."

"Yah." Aunt Jessie shook her head. "That poor child. If she'd stand up to that selfish father of hers more often, she'd be better off."

"For sure. That's what Cathy and I are always telling her, but Rachel doesn't see it that way. She's been hearing that it's her duty to take care of her father and her siblings for so long that she doesn't see when they take advantage of her."

"It's not gut for them, either." Aunt Jessie was tart. "They ought to be standing on their own at their ages."

Joanna agreed with her, and she wondered if that was something she should point out to Rachel.

"At least she's out tonight," she said. "She and Cathy were getting together to work on the dresses. Somebody has to be there to keep Cathy focused on the job—she can handle a classroom full of kinder but is completely ferhoodled at getting ready for her wedding."

Aunt Jessie chuckled. "You and Rachel are fine side-sitters for her, yah? You'll see her safely married no matter what." She paused, studying Joanna's face. "You're wishing you were with them tonight instead of sitting here with me, ain't so?"

"I don't know about that. I would like to be in on every moment of getting Cathy married, but I couldn't very well ask Chief Jamison to arrange for someone to drive me back and forth. He's got enough to do with trying to find out who's causing all this trouble. Besides, it's pleasant to have a quiet evening with you."

"Ach, well, you're doing something useful while you're stuck at home." Jessie nodded toward the dress. "Are you doing a new white cape and apron, as well?"

"I think so. It seems only right to have everything new for a wedding. We wouldn't want to embarrass Cathy."

"True enough. But still, it wouldn't be a wedding if something didn't go wrong. I remember the time the groom's friends decided to put his buggy on top of the shed at his bride's house. A funny joke, they thought it, until they realized that no one had stayed to bring him to the wedding."

"I don't remember that one. What did the groom do? Who was it anyway?"

"Elijah Schmidt. You'd never think it to look at him now, but he set out to run the five miles to the wedding. His buddies did catch him and drive him the rest of the way. Their faces were red, that's for sure."

"I imagine." She was diverted at the thought of staid, portly Elijah running along the road in his new black suit.

"Weddings always bring their share of trials, it seems to me. Sometimes I've thought it better when the bride is a bit older, like you and your friends."

"Maybe so." She kept her voice noncommittal, hoping Aunt Jessie wasn't going to bring up Noah.

Her aunt seemed to be lost in thought for a moment, and then she looked at Joanna. "You've always been one to push ahead. To go after whatever you want as hard as you can."

"Isn't that a good thing?"

"Sometimes," her aunt allowed. "But sometimes getting to what's best takes more patience than anything else. Sometimes people can't be rushed."

"I know." She did know, even though it made her want to tear down barriers with her own hands. "That's a lot harder."

Jessie nodded in agreement. "Maybe the prize is all the sweeter if you have to wait for it." A roll of thunder seemed to punctuate her words.

"I hope so." They both knew they were talking about Noah, though neither of them would mention his name.

Thunder rumbled again, closer this time, warning of a storm coming. "I thought this storm was going to miss us since it took so long to get here." Aunt Jessie started to lay aside her work. "I'd best check the windows. I don't think anything's open, but better safe than sorry."

Joanna was already on her feet. "You stay there. I'll do it." She glanced at her aunt's needle, memory making her smile. "Remember when Grossmammi wouldn't let us sew when there was a storm, because lightning might strike the needle and hit us?"

Aunt Jessie's rare smile seemed to go with her on her round of the windows.

There was no point in going down to the shop, since she was quite sure everything there had been closed and latched. She headed into the kitchen, where, sure enough, the window next to the range had been left open an inch. Rain was already spattering the windowsill.

After tending to that, she moved through the rest of the rooms. A flash of lightning hurried her steps, but nothing else was open. In her bedroom, overlooking the street, she paused to look out the window.

The rain pounded against the windows now and swept sideways down Main Street. Streetlights made pale circles on the streets, glistening with water. Normally, there wouldn't be very many people out at this hour on a Thursday night, and tonight the streets were completely deserted. It was so dark that the lights across the street were just blurry images.

Suddenly, she caught something—some slight movement—at the corner of the building. She craned to see, not sure she wasn't imagining things. Nothing there now, but the impression unsettled her.

Nothing to worry about, she assured herself. If anyone had gone toward the back entrance, the motion lights would come on. Even as she thought it, the back lights lit up, visible when she glanced from the doorway to the kitchen.

Hurrying now, she raced toward the window that would allow her to see the back step and anyone who was near it.

"Joanna, what's wrong?" Jessie was on her feet in an instant, following her.

"I thought I saw someone outside. If I open the back window, I'll be able to see—"

Jessie caught her arm. "Don't. We should call the police, yah?"

"Just wait." She freed herself. "It might be nothing, and then wouldn't we feel foolish?"

The back window overlooked the area between the house and the stable, but she'd have to open it to look straight down. Fortunately, the rain came from the other direction. Joanna pushed it open and leaned out.

Someone was there, just approaching the back door. In another second the face lifted. Incredibly, it was Meredith.

"Just wait," she called, interrupted by a clap of thunder. "I'll be right down."

"Who is it?" Aunt Jessie caught her arm. "Don't go down."

"I have to. It's Meredith—all by herself out there in the wet." She tossed the words over her shoulder as she opened the door and hurried down.

After a muffled exclamation, Aunt Jessie came hurrying behind her, talking as she went. "That poor child. She must be soaked and she'll probably get pneumonia. Whatever were they doing, letting her out in this?"

Joanna grabbed the dead bolt, twisting it and then turning the knob. Meredith all but fell into the stairway, wet and shivering, saying something she couldn't understand.

"Hush, hush now." Aunt Jessie grasped her with strong arms, pulling her close. "You're all right. You're here with us. Just come upstairs, and we'll get you dry and warm."

It was the voice she'd always used with any of the little ones when she or her brothers had fallen or otherwise injured themselves. Somehow, it still worked. Meredith responded to her embrace and docilely started up the stairs, stumbling a bit, water dripping to the floor.

Joanna quickly took a look around, but no one else was visible. She locked the door again, hurrying up the steps in the wake of the others.

Jessie took Meredith straight to the kitchen with the instinct that said here was the most comforting place. Helping her sit, she stroked the tangle of copper-colored hair. "Just catch your breath. It's all right."

She looked over Meredith's head at Joanna. "Towels and a blanket. Hurry."

Biting back the questions that ricocheted through her mind, Joanna rushed to do as she was told. Aunt Jessie knew best. Even a glance had told her that Meredith was dazed, hardly able to speak for shivering.

When she rushed back into the kitchen, Aunt Jessie had already put the kettle on the stove. They helped Meredith out of the soaking jacket, wrapping a blanket around her while toweling her hair.

She looked up at Joanna, her face dead white, her eyes huge. "I…I came to you."

"I know." She kept her voice soft as if she was speaking to a hurt child. "I'm glad. But why did they let you out of the hospital?"

The ghost of a smile crossed Meredith's strained face. "They didn't."

A spoon rattled against a mug as Jessie looked up from stirring a liberal amount of sugar into the tea she was making. "However did you do that?"

"And why?" Joanna added, her mind whirling with all the things that should be done. *Call Jamison, call the hospital...*

"Someone was trying to get into my room." A shiver ran through her, making her whole body shake.

"Here." Aunt Jessie held the mug against her lips. "Sip a little of this hot tea. It will help warm you up."

Calm, above all, she had to remain calm, Joanna told herself as her mind began racing, clamoring for answers. Joanna patted Meredith's back, wordlessly reassuring her. "What made you think that? Did you call someone?"

"I...I rang, but no one came. So I peeked out the door, but there was no one except the man sitting beside the door. He was asleep. I shook him, but he didn't wake, and I was afraid to speak." It all came out in a rush of words that seemed to exhaust her.

"You're safe now," she said. But was she? She and Aunt Jessie exchanged glances.

"I'll call," Jessie murmured, and slipped away to the stairs that led to the shop.

"You got dressed," Joanna said, hoping to help Meredith along in telling what happened.

Meredith nodded, seeming to struggle to keep her eyes open. "I thought... I heard something happen down at the other end of the hall. Around the corner. Things falling, footsteps going that way. I thought someone was trying to get to me."

A flash of lightning was accompanied by a clap of thunder that seemed to shake the house. Meredith gave a little cry, and Joanna put her arms around her. "It's all right. It will move off now."

Meredith clutched her. "I knew you'd help me." Her frightened eyes held something close to panic. "But what if he saw me? What if I brought him here?"

"You're with us. We'll keep you safe." But could they? If someone had been watching Meredith, waiting to catch her alone, he might well have seen her sneaking out of the hospital.

Aunt Jessie emerged from the hallway. A glance at her face, and Joanna knew she hadn't gotten through. "The phone is out."

"The storm?" Joanna hoped.

Her aunt shrugged slightly. In the momentary silence that followed, Joanna thought she heard something brushing against the plate-glass windows in the shop, and her heart jolted.

If someone tried to get in, if he was willing to risk breaking a window—who would hear in the storm? He must think he was running out of time to be so bold. What could they do?

There were three of them. Surely, they could deal with one man. But just the thought of a struggle turned her stomach. Meredith was weak still, and Aunt Jessie was getting older, though she wouldn't admit it. Could they hold off a desperate man?

"I will go out the front," Aunt Jessie said suddenly. "He won't bother me—he can see I'm not Meredith."

She dragged on her black coat as she talked. "I'll get help."

"No, you can't." Joanna felt paralyzed, trying to think of a way to save everyone. "It's too dangerous."

"He doesn't want me." Aunt Jessie emphasized the words by picking up the huge black umbrella that would keep a whole family dry. "But he'll be distracted. You can take Meredith out the back. Best put something dry on her. As soon as either of us reaches someone, she'll be safe."

Before Joanna could marshal an argument, her aunt had headed back for the shop. A tinkle of glass downstairs decided for her. She yanked her short coat from the peg and hustled Meredith into it, grabbing a thick sweater for herself.

"Komm."

Putting her arm around Meredith, she urged her toward the back stairs. Meredith came along like a sleepwalker, apparently too shattered to object. This would work, she told herself. It had to.

The instant she heard the front door of the shop open downstairs, she hurried Meredith down toward the back. She just had to get them both out. She could scream then and run toward Noah's door. It was only a few steps. Once they were out, they'd be safe.

As soon as they'd cleared the door, Joanna knew she was wrong. He hadn't been distracted by Aunt Jessie, and already heavy footsteps sounded along the side of the building, audible even over the pounding rain.

Joanna hesitated for a moment, torn between possibilities, knowing she had to do something right now. Reaching up, she pressed the switch Noah had shown her, turning the lights off and plunging this side of the area into darkness. The footsteps stumbled, slowed.

Her arm around Meredith, Joanna pulled her quietly toward the stable, praying he didn't hear them. All they needed was a few minutes in hiding. The stable would shield them, and by then someone would have come. Jessie would get help, or Noah would see that the lights were off and come.

The man was still coming, but more slowly, probably feeling his way along the wall. Single-minded. He'd given up all pretense now, no longer trying to hide. He would silence them, and they'd never even know why.

Shaking off the dread, she propelled Meredith into the stable. The horses, already stirred up by the thunder and lightning, stamped restlessly in their stalls, hooves thudding on the wide wooden planks. Princess whickered softly in recognition. Joanna patted her, praying for silence and darkness to hide them.

She hurried Meredith past the buggy, feeling her way. Even as her eyes adjusted to the dark, she couldn't make out anything in the depths of the stable. Good—the darkness would hide them. Another step, and her foot bumped a bale of straw.

"Almost there," she whispered, and felt Meredith nod. Good, she was hanging on.

Swishing ahead of herself with her left hand, still holding Meredith with her right, she found the bales, stacked four high in the rear of the stable. She felt her

way to the end of the row and crept into the space behind them, pulling Meredith with her. The wall was
behind them, the straw barrier in front. They were as
safe as Joanna could make them.

Meredith shivered, her whole body shaking. Joanna pulled her close, wrapping her arms around Meredith. She whispered softly, hushing her even as the
trembling began again.

"Shh. Be still. Help will come." Noah would come.
At his name, warmth touched her. Noah loved her. He
would sense she was in danger. He'd come.

And if he didn't? Second thoughts flooded over her
in the enforced stillness. Should she have screamed
as soon as they reached the door? But if she had, the
pursuer could have been on them before anyone could
come to help.

The softest whimper came from Meredith. She
stroked her young cousin's back, filled with love.
Meredith was too young to be fighting for her life.
She'd hardly begun to live, and they'd hardly begun
to know each other. It was as if she held one of her
young brothers in her arms.

How long? How long before help came? It felt as if
they'd been huddled behind the straw for hours, but
it could only have been a minute or two.

She listened, trying to hear any foreign sound
beyond the rattle of rain on the metal roof and the
restless movement of the horses. Nothing. Was he
gone? Or was he lurking, waiting for them to give
away their hiding place by moving?

He couldn't have known where they'd gone. He

might even now be looking down the alley, thinking they'd run that way.

Should she risk moving? Risk calling for help? Slowly, very slowly, she rose enough to peer over the top of the bales. There was the square opening of the stable, a paler darkness against the black of the stable interior.

The pressure built in her, compelling her to move, to speak, to do anything but huddle in silence. Then, even as it became irresistible, there was a whisper of movement and in the next instant a man-shaped shadow filled the doorway.

For a terrible second Joanna froze. Holding her breath, she slid silently down and out of sight. She put her finger to Meredith's lips and felt her nod in response. Thank the gut Lord Meredith was still with her. She wouldn't be surprised if the girl had passed out from sheer exhaustion after what she'd been through. But she was here, ready to…to what? Fight?

That was what it came down to. Already her mind, with the stable contents as familiar as her bedroom's, reviewed anything that could be used in defense.

The manure shovel. It was propped against the post at this end of the stalls. But could she get to it in time? And if she did, could she strike another human being?

Turn the other cheek. Care for the widow and the orphan. Didn't caring include protecting from evil? If the man got to Meredith, he'd kill her. There were no doubts in her mind about it. But could she hit, possibly kill, him even to save Meredith's life?

A sound penetrated the dark silence—distant but

coming closer. A siren, and nearer at hand, confused shouts. Help was coming. He'd run away, wouldn't he? They'd stay silent in the dark—

Light pierced the stable, a small circle of brightness from a penlight. Instead of running, he was risking everything, probably in panic, with little chance of getting away. Even now he was moving toward them. In another moment he'd be there, shining the light behind the bales.

There was no more time. Desperate to protect Meredith, she dove from cover, heading toward the shovel that was the only possible defense. The noise brought the light swiveling around to her, and she prayed Meredith had the sense to slip out against the far wall. If she could keep him distracted, even for a couple of minutes, Meredith would be safe.

Hands grabbed her as she cleared the last of the bales. She swung around, struggling against the iron grip. Another foot and she could catch hold of the shovel...

But he had her. The light shot crazily to the loft, to the stables and then crashed to the floor, but he had both hands on her throat, tightening, cutting off her breath.

She heard him grunt and realized someone had barreled into him. His grip loosened, and then he was struggling with Meredith. With one hand he threw Joanna away from them. She collided with the post, seeing stars. He'd choke Meredith—he would—she'd never get there in time—

Her hand brushed metal, and she knew what it was.

The shovel. Grasping the wooden handle, she pulled it free of its hook and swung it toward the dark figure bending over Meredith.

It connected with a resounding clang. He collapsed slowly, falling like a tower of blocks to the floor.

"Meredith—are you okay?" She groped for her. "Say something."

Suddenly, a lantern threw the inside of the stable into bright relief, showing Meredith, trying to struggle clear of the man, who still grasped at her throat. Joanna raised the shovel again, but in that instant Meredith kicked her way free and a voice called her name.

"Joanna." Noah's voice. Noah's hands, taking the shovel away and holding her tight.

More lights, noise, voices. The stable was full of people. Aunt Jessie wrapped Meredith in a comforting hug. Chief Jamison and another officer shoved the man flat on his face and pulled his hands behind his back. Handcuffs glinted in the light.

"Now." Jamison sounded angered and satisfied all at once. "Let's see who we have here."

He grabbed the man's shoulder and rolled him over roughly. Joanna gasped. The light picked out the usually pleasant features of Tom Watson, the Bristow family's attorney.

Confused questions bounced through her mind, but then she and Meredith were being led away. Noah had her, and it was over.

CHAPTER TWENTY

JOANNA AWOKE TO the mingled aromas of coffee and baking. She didn't attempt to move but lay watching the sunlight dapple the ceiling. Mammi's walnut streusel coffee cake—that was what she smelled. Her mind slid to early mornings on the farm, with Mammi busy in the kitchen and Daad coming back from the barn, stamping his feet on the mat.

Her brain started to percolate, and she was back in the present, in her own bed over the shop. Scrambled memories from the previous night flashed in her mind, memories of hiding, of fear, of confused voices talking all at once, and of Noah holding her. She seemed to hear Meredith flatly refusing to go back to the hospital and being tucked up in Aunt Jessie's bed, while she was propelled firmly to her own. Had all that really happened?

She sat up abruptly, shaking off the lassitude that had kept her lying there inert. Anxious about Meredith, she hurried barefoot to the door, opening it a crack. At the sound of male voices in the kitchen, she closed it again. It seemed a meeting was taking place in the kitchen.

Hurrying through her dressing, she spotted the

blue dress for Cathy's wedding hanging on the wall, the needle she'd been using tucked neatly through the hem. Even in the midst of crisis, Aunt Jessie didn't forget anything. Or maybe it had been Mamm. She vaguely registered that it had been her mother who'd helped her undress and tucked her into bed.

Finally ready, she went out to the kitchen to find it nearly full, with Mammi, Daad, Aunt Jessie and Noah sitting around the table. They all looked up at her entrance, and Mamm hurried to hug her and lead her to a chair.

"Did we wake you? You should have slept longer, but…"

"The chief wanted us all here. He's going to come in to bring us up-to-date and tell us what we need to do." Noah took on explaining, maybe feeling his presence needed accounting for.

At the mention of Jamison, a hundred questions sprang to her lips, but Aunt Jessie met her eyes.

"No point in going all over it and then having to do it again when he comes," she said. "Sit down and eat. Everybody could do with it." She took another coffee cake from the oven and started beating eggs with considerable vigor.

Joanna accepted a mug of coffee, very aware of Noah sitting next to her. She slanted a look at him, but he was staring straight ahead. If he felt her gaze, he didn't give any indication.

She dragged her thoughts away from him. "What about Meredith? Is she still sleeping? Is she all right?"

"She's fine," Aunt Jessie said. "Bright as a bird this morning. She'll be out as soon as she's dressed."

"She must spring back faster than I do." Joanna took a sip of the coffee, hoping it might stop her head from spinning. "Of course, she's younger."

As the scrambled eggs sizzled into the pan, the bedroom door opened. Meredith came out and then stopped, seeming taken aback at all the people in the kitchen. Joanna hurried to her, hugging her. "You're sure you're all right?"

"Definitely." Meredith smiled, seeming to have thrown off last night's terror easily. "I think you'd better introduce me."

"Yah, for sure. Aunt Jessie you remember from last night. And Noah. And this is my mother and father."

Daadi stood, nodding gravely as if not sure what to say. Mammi didn't seem to have any doubts. She came straight to Meredith, holding her at arm's length to study her face.

"You are our Joanna's cousin, yah? So that makes you our niece." She drew Meredith into her arms for a hug. Meredith froze for an instant, and then she wrapped her arms around Mamm. Joanna saw tears glisten in Meredith's eyes, and her own heart warmed.

"Komm. Sit." Daad pulled out a chair for Meredith. "You must be hungry."

"Famished," she said, sitting down and smiling up at him.

"The more you eat, the happier you'll make Aunt Jessie and Mammi," Joanna said, some of her tension evaporating at how easily that had gone. Maybe having two families wouldn't be a struggle, after all.

Footsteps on the stairs announced the arrival of Chief Jamison. He stopped in the doorway, looking around the table.

"Good, you're all here." He glanced from Joanna to Meredith. "How are you ladies doing after your exciting night?"

"I'm fine," Joanna said quickly, ignoring the bruise in her ribs from when she'd hit the barn post, to say nothing of her sore shoulder.

Meredith nodded with a quick smile for the chief. "I feel great. See, I told you I didn't need to go back to the hospital."

"Guess not," he said grudgingly. He took the chair that Daad brought in for him. "Ms. Bristow, your relatives want to see you, but I managed to hold them off for the moment. I said they could come by sometime after noon. Okay?"

Meredith nodded, looking relieved.

"So like I said, we'll need to go over everything..."

"Never mind that," Joanna interrupted, causing her mother to give her a chiding look. "Tell me I didn't dream it. It really was the lawyer, Tom Watson, wasn't it?"

"It was."

"Did he admit it?" Noah asked, his voice sharp.

Jamison snorted. "Small chance you'd ever catch a lawyer admitting to anything. All he'll say is that he wants to see his own lawyer—some guy who has to come from Philadelphia."

"But why did he do it?" Joanna couldn't help asking. Of all the people who might have a reason to wish Meredith out of the way, he was the last she'd have pitched on.

"Wish I knew," Jamison grumbled. "Without a motive, it's going to be tough to pin anything on him. He could even say he followed someone suspicious into the stable and in the dark, grabbed the wrong person."

"That's ridiculous. He certainly knew what he was doing." It was beyond belief to Joanna that the man might get away with what he'd done.

"I know, but without knowing why he did it—"

"I know why."

They all turned to look at Meredith, who seemed as surprised as they were. "The missing bit fell back into my mind. It was the trust."

"You said your grandfather put his fortune into a trust for you." Jamison clearly didn't understand.

"Not that one." She seemed to collect her thoughts. "About a month before he died, my grandfather wanted to talk to me. He said he'd been worrying about his daughter, that would have been my aunt, and he wanted to do something to show he'd forgiven her. He'd tried to find her, but he couldn't. So he was leaving money in a trust for her, just in case she showed up someday. He didn't want it known, because he was afraid of people falsely claiming to be her or her child." She glanced at Joanna and smiled. "He said Tom Watson had drawn it up, and no one was to know."

Joanna frowned, trying to wrap her mind around

it. "But I don't understand. Why would Watson care who inherited?"

"I imagine because there was nothing left in that trust. Somebody will have to look into that, but I'd guess Watson figured no one would ever turn up and helped himself. Is that your idea, Ms. Bristow?" Jamison's face had lit with understanding.

Meredith nodded. "I think so, too. It makes sense. I didn't say anything to Watson about the trust until recently, and when I did, he seemed...well, shocked that I knew about it. He explained that by saying my grandfather told him he didn't want anyone else to know."

Jamison nodded, but Joanna spoke before he could. "What made you bring it up? Had you found something out?"

Meredith seemed pleased at all she was remembering. "The investigator Grandfather had hired had been in touch with me. He'd unexpectedly come across some information. So I told Watson I thought there was a good chance we'd find some trace of her."

"How did he react to that?" Jamison was intent, scribbling notes on a pad in front of him, while the rest of them could only listen, trying to understand.

"He acted like that was a great idea. In fact, he wanted me to let him take charge of it, saying it was a lawyer's job. But by then..." She suddenly looked very young. "Well, I felt like it was *my* duty to carry out what Grandfather wanted."

Daad nodded approvingly. "That's right."

"Did you find her?" The question spilled out before Joanna could stop it. "My...my birth mother?"

Meredith reached across the table to clasp Joanna's hand, and she knew by Meredith's expression what the answer was.

"I'm sorry. The investigator found out that she'd died sometime ago. It must have been not long after you were born. I'm sorry," she said again.

Joanna nodded, trying to assess how she felt and feeling Mammi's sorrowing gaze on her. To her surprise, the grief she felt was that for any young woman dying too soon, but not really personal.

"Denke." She struggled to express what she felt. "I never knew her. Somehow, she always seemed unreal to me." She squeezed Meredith's hand. "I guess I never even thought of what it would be like to meet her."

It was sad to say that about the woman who had given birth to her, but it was the truth. She had given birth, and she'd also given Joanna a good life with people who loved her, and Joanna would always be grateful.

Jamison cleared his throat, breaking through the emotion. "So I'll pass this on to the Philadelphia police. They'll be able to find out about the truth quicker than we ever could." He glanced at Joanna. "Pity if the money was all gone, Joanna. Sounds like you could have been rich."

Joanna shuddered, not even wanting to think of taking money from someone she'd never known. "I couldn't have taken it anyway, so it doesn't matter."

Noah moved slightly. "It mattered enough to Watson to make him want to kill."

"He hit me, you know." Meredith looked surprised at herself. "I remember now. When I got the information that led to Joanna, I wanted to come alone, but Watson insisted that as attorney for the estate, he had to be there. He drove me here." She frowned. "I don't remember all of it, but he was behind me on the stairs. I felt him move, and then something struck my head." She nodded to Chief Jamison. "He did it. I'll swear to it."

Jamison, looking satisfied, made another quick note. "Okay, that's enough to start building a case. Maybe we'd better stop there for now before we wear you out. Do me a favor and don't talk about this to anyone."

Meredith nodded, shivering suddenly. "Why would I want to? Just think of him smiling and being helpful and all the time planning to get rid of me."

Jamison rose. "I'll be moving on this and talking to the district attorney, and he'll want you to make a formal statement."

"Whenever you want."

Jamison disappeared down the stairs, looking eager to get on with his job. For a moment the rest of them just sat in silence. Joanna didn't know about everyone else, but it was all she could do to absorb what had happened. Her head was still reeling.

Aunt Jessie was the first to breathe the silence. "Looks like we could all use a fresh cup. And I'll cut another coffee cake."

With that, the strange quality of the past half hour suddenly dissolved into normal. What could be more normal than an Amish woman meeting every crisis by feeding someone? Smiling, she got up to help.

"I'll get the coffee, Aunt Jessie."

"Wait." Meredith rose, her gaze fixed on Joanna. "It's not fair if all your money is gone when there's plenty for me. I'll split with you."

Joanna's heart warmed at her young cousin's quick reaction. "Ach, that's wonderful kind, but I don't want it. I couldn't take anything from someone I never even knew."

"Not even to show you forgive him?" Meredith must have seen the impact of her words, because she smiled. "I'll tell you what. When it's all settled, we'll get together and figure out how to give it away— maybe something to help children. I'll come for a visit, and we'll talk." She stopped suddenly, seeming uncertain. "I mean, if you want me to come."

Joanna couldn't get to her fast enough. "Of course we want you." She wrapped her in a hug, followed immediately by Mamm and Aunt Jessie.

But through the tears and the chatter, she found herself looking for Noah, wanting to share this moment with him. But Noah wasn't there. He was going down the back stairs. Her heart plunged. Although no word had been spoken, she'd believed things had changed between them after last night. Was she wrong?

Noah paused as if he'd felt her gaze, and his eyes met hers.

"I'll go and see to the horses."

She couldn't actually hear the words over the tumult around her, but she knew what he was saying. And what he meant.

NOAH REACHED THE outside and took a deep breath. He didn't think he could have stayed there any longer, feeling on the fringes of the group of people who loved Joanna and had the right to express that love. He had to talk to her, but not there, with everyone around.

He glanced up at the windows of the apartment and then started slowly toward the stable. The tape that had surrounded it earlier was gone now, once he'd pointed out that the horses had to be tended, whether it was a crime scene or not. He'd go in, check the horses and hope Joanna might understand what he'd been trying to convey.

And if not, he'd keep trying until he got her alone, no matter how long it took.

It only took about five minutes—just long enough for her to detach herself from the family. He heard her light step, and she appeared in the doorway, blinking a little at the switch from the bright sunlight to the peaceful dimness of the stable. Then she moved forward until she was standing only an arm's length away from him, a look of determination on her face.

Before he could say a word, she'd plunged into speech. "Noah Troyer, will you marry me? It's very un-Amish for me to ask, but if I wait for you to say it, it's never going to happen. It's ridiculous for us to sacrifice our happiness and the lives of the kinder we might have for a silly scruple. And furthermore—"

Noah stopped her the only way he could...with a kiss. And not a hurried, regretful kiss like the last time, but a slow, sweet kiss that held all the promises any two people could make to each other.

When he finally drew back, still holding her, a soft smile curved her lips. Her eyes were filled with so much love he felt humbled that she could care for him so. He nearly had to kiss her again, but there were things that must be said.

"I take it you've changed your mind," she murmured, a hint of laughter in her eyes.

"Yah, I've changed my mind. Or maybe just recognized that you had been changing it for me every day of the past weeks." He grew more serious. "But you have to know that marrying me is a risk. I swear I'll never touch alcohol, but what if the taste for it comes out in our kinder? How could you bear that?" The torment brought by the idea swept through him, clawing at his heart.

"Hush." She reached up to put her finger lightly on his lips. "If it happens, we'll be ready for it, and we can bear anything if we face it together. Don't you feel that way?" For a moment his bright, determined Joanna looked anxious.

"Yah," he said, knowing it was true. "We can take anything together."

The words were so lovely that he had to draw her close again. Together they leaned against the stall, arms around each other. Curious, Princess nuzzled at them. Then, deciding they weren't going to feed her, lost interest.

"When did you know?" Joanna said at last.

"That I loved you? Always, I think. That we really could do this—I guess a lot of things came together. Working with you to help Meredith helped, and knowing you were in danger nearly pushed me into marrying you at once so I could protect you. Even Caleb had a part in it, reminding me that I was the opposite of my father. Everything."

She let out a long, satisfied breath. "When shall we be married?"

He chuckled. "Won't you leave anything to me? Let's see if your father will agree to a wedding in November. That should give you enough time for all the things brides do, ain't so? But aren't you forgetting something?"

"What?"

"I didn't answer you yet," he said, and laughed again at her expression.

"Well, do I have to ask you again?" she demanded, sure of him again.

"No, once is enough. And yah, I will marry you, Joanna Kohler. I love you, and I'll do anything to protect you and be with you forever." He paused, and the smile she loved came again. "I suspect that's the only way to deal with a strong-minded woman like you."

She leaned her head against his shoulder, and when she spoke, her voice seemed to resound with love. "Aunt Jessie always did say I'd never marry until I found a man as strong as I am." She looked into his face, smiling. "Now I've found him."

Noah held her close, feeling the steady beat of her heart against his chest, and knew just how much they were blessed to have found each other. After the loneliness, the danger and the darkness, they had come through it into the sunshine of a new day.

* * * * *

Ready for more love and mystery in River Haven?

Don't miss Amish Secrets, *the next book in
Marta Perry's River Haven series.*

Rachel Hurst sacrificed the life and marriage
she wanted to care for her father and siblings
after her mother's death. But now that her father
has decided to remarry, there's no room for Rachel. Desperate to find a job rather than become
a lonely old maid, she accepts a housekeeping
position with a wealthy elderly English woman
whose isolated mansion had been the setting
for Rachel's childhood nightmares. But Rachel
finds more to worry her at the Withers house
than bad dreams...

Jacob Beiler, the man she'd almost married,
is doing carpentry work at the house, and he
hasn't gotten over her rejection. When strange
accidents begin happening to her employer, she
finds herself plunged into danger, with only the
hope of a new beginning with an old love to
rescue her.

Available soon from HQN Books.

SPECIAL EXCERPT FROM

LOVE INSPIRED SUSPENSE
INSPIRATIONAL ROMANCE

Someone is trying to force her off her land, and her only hope lies in the secret father of her child, who has come back home to sell his property.

Read on for a sneak preview of
Dangerous Amish Inheritance *by Debby Giusti, available April 2020 from Love Inspired Suspense.*

Ruthie Eicher awoke with a start. She blinked in the darkness and touched the opposite side of the double bed, where her husband had slept. Two months since the tragic accident and she was not yet used to his absence.

Finding the far side of the bed empty and the sheets cold, she dropped her feet to the floor and hurried into the children's room. Even without lighting the oil lamp, she knew from the steady draw of their breaths that nine-year-old Simon and six-year-old Andrew were sound asleep.

Movement near the outbuildings caught her eye. She held her breath and stared for a long moment.

Narrowing her gaze, she leaned forward, and her heart raced as a flame licked the air.

She shook Simon. "The woodpile. On fire. I need help."

He rubbed his eyes.

"Hurry, Simon."

Leaving him to crawl from bed, she raced downstairs, almost tripping, her heart pounding as she knew all too well how quickly the fire could spread. She ran through the kitchen, grabbed the back doorknob and groaned as her fingers struggled with the lock.

"No!" she moaned, and coaxed her fumbling hands to work. The lock disengaged. She threw open the door and ran across the porch and down the steps.

A noise sounded behind her. She glanced over her shoulder, expecting Simon. Instead she saw a large, darkly dressed figure. Something struck the side of her head. She gasped with pain, dropped the bucket and stumbled toward the house.

He grabbed her shoulder and threw her to the ground. She cried out, struggled to her knees and started to crawl away. He kicked her side. She groaned and tried to stand. He tangled his fingers through her hair and pulled her to her feet.

The man's lips touched her ear. "Didn't you read my notes? You don't belong here." His rancid breath soured the air. "Leave before something happens to you and your children."

Don't miss
Dangerous Amish Inheritance *by Debby Giusti,*
available April 2020 wherever
Love Inspired Suspense books and ebooks are sold.

LoveInspired.com

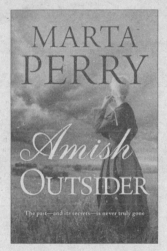

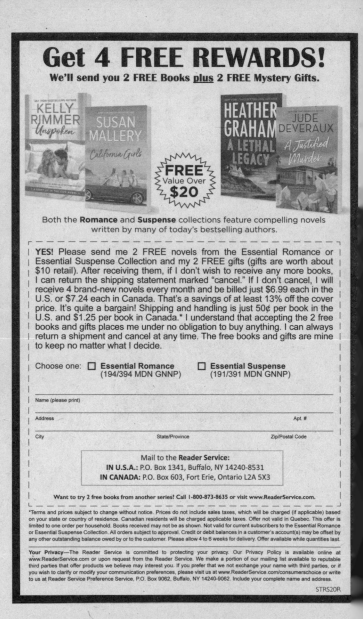